One Winter's Night

One Winter's Night

Kiley Dunbar

hera

First published in the United Kingdom in 2020 by Hera Books

Hera Books
28b Cricketfield Road
London, E5 8NS
United Kingdom

A CIP catalogue record for this book is available from the British Library.

Print ISBN 978 1 78863 985 9
Ebook ISBN 978 1 912973 44 6

Printed and bound in Great Britain by Clays Ltd, Elcograf S.p.A.

This one's for Liz, with love and gratitude, x
'I can no other answer make but thanks, and thanks'
(Shakespeare, Twelfth Night)

A Letter from the Author

Hello! It's me, Kiley Dunbar.

Welcome to beautiful, historic Stratford-upon-Avon. If you've read *One Summer's Night* (2019) you'll already be familiar with Kelsey Anderson and her new life in this pretty English theatre town on the banks of the River Avon, but don't worry if this is your first visit. You don't need to know much, really. Here's a little taste of what happened in *One Summer's Night*. Feel free to skip it, you can enjoy *One Winter's Night* as a stand-alone novel without letting any of this stuff bother you.

Kelsey Anderson had played it safe all her life, having seen her mum, Mari, lose the love of her life months after Kelsey's little brother was born, and the three of them had to pull together and get by. Kelsey grew up as a homebody, stuck in a rut while her mates got on with adulting.

All that changed last summer, when Kelsey took a risk.

Finding herself out of work, and unsure of her staid boyfriend Fran, she packed her suitcase with her well-thumbed copy of Shakespeare's *Sonnets* and her vintage camera (both gifts from her much missed dad), left Scotland, and took a job working for the indomitable Norma Arden at her tour-guiding agency in faraway Stratford-upon-Avon.

The move started a chain of events she could never have predicted – which included the not exactly supportive Fran rapidly becoming her ex-boyfriend (*hurray*), and Kelsey becoming entangled in a messy, passionate attraction to an American stage actor in Stratford only for the summer season (*sigh*). She thought Jonathan Hathaway was loved up with his co-star, the stunningly beautiful Peony, but time untangled that knot – it was all just a midsummer misunderstanding – and his heart was Kelsey's all along.

But as summer came to an end and handsome, talented Mr Hathaway hopped on a flight to Canada and an autumn of work commitments on the other side of the world, Kelsey was left alone and in a long-distance relationship. That's where we find her, working hard to set up her own photography studio in town.

You should know that Kelsey's a modern girl with retro tastes. She's more likely to queue up for a matinee at the Royal Shakespeare Theatre than she is to binge on a Netflix boxset; she's a fan of writing snail mail over WhatsApping; and instead of Instagramming camera phone selfies, she'd far rather pop 35mm film spools in the post and wait for real, old-school glossy prints to come back from the developer's lab.

This is the story of what happened after Norma Arden shut up her tour guide agency for good and the summer tourists went back home to their busy lives. This story is about what Kelsey did next, and follows Mirren, Kelsey's best friend since forever, who at last broke up with poor old Preston after letting him down one too many times. We're going to get to the bottom of her love story too.

Happy reading.

Love, Kiley x

Chapter One

'The seasons alter: hoary-headed frosts
Fall in the fresh lap of the crimson rose'
(*A Midsummer Night's Dream*)

The autumn came in quickly this year. Even in early October the leaves of the rowan trees in Kelsey's shared gardens at St. Ninian's Close are tinged golden brown. Gritty breezes gust down Henley Street, whipping past the house where, once upon a time, William Shakespeare was born. Chill morning dews make the grassy banks of the River Avon sparkle, and dawn mists settle over the subtle valley that the town nestles inside. Above its tangle of medieval streets, church spires, theatre turrets and flying flags, up on the gentle rises of the Welcombe hills the brambles have swollen fat and blushing on thorny boughs and the blackbirds sing out that summer is over.

Having worked as a tour guide, pounding the streets of Stratford all summer long and getting to know its most beautiful treasures and best-kept secrets, Kelsey thought she had discovered everything there was to know about her new home, but as she observed autumn creeping in, she came to the realisation that fall in Warwickshire was even finer than the summer months.

Fall. That's what Jonathan calls this time of year. But he isn't here to see it with her. He's been wowing the crowds at an Ontario Shakespeare festival with his *Hamlet* and after Christmas he'll be heading to California to take up his drama teaching residency for the winter. But he writes, and he video calls…

'Don't wake up, I'm just taking my stage make-up off before bed and calling to say goodnight. I love you, Kelsey.'

'Don't go, I'm awake. Wow, you look good.'

Jonathan held the phone closer to his face, letting Kelsey see the subtle black eyeliner that deepened his ice-blue eyes and his messy brown hair lightened a little with dye for playing the Prince of Denmark.

'I was gonna say the same thing about you. Is it after six in Stratford?'

'Uh-huh, but old habits die hard, I've been up for a while. There was a blackbird going crazy under the oak tree at six, so I'm already on my first coffee, just listening to him sing. How's the run going?' Kelsey gathered her duvet around her for warmth. Her little garret room at the top of the building which had been so warm in the summer was growing chillier by the day.

'Pretty good. Full houses, excited crowds. They're a lot more vocal than the Stratford audiences. I forgot about the spontaneous applause and the interaction. You don't get that with English theatre. Tonight the first row were whooping and hollering when I kissed Ophelia, kinda threw us both.'

'I can see how that would be distracting. How is Peony? Did she get the postcard I sent her?' Kelsey asked. The confusion of the summer months when she'd been convinced Jonathan and his co-star and childhood sweetheart were still an item, had been left far behind.

'She did, and she's good too, sends her love. She's kinda pissed I'm leaving the company after our Stratford run of *Love's Labour's Lost* in the spring but she gets that I'm ready for a new beginning. Anyways, I'm counting down the days 'til I fly home to you for the holidays.'

Kelsey had never heard Jonathan call Stratford 'home' before, and although it sent a thrill through her, she worried he was counting his work-visa chickens before they hatched. He was allowed to stay in England for the spring run but after that, nobody could know what would happen.

'What's today? Ninth of October?' he added. 'That's only... seventy-five days.'

'*Only?*'

'I'll be home soon and we'll get to spend a few days of the holidays together. Until then I'll just have to make sure I catch every English sunrise with you.'

Kelsey smiled, listening to his breathing and enjoying the flex of his dimpled jaw when he grinned. For a while they let the silence speak between them. They could do this, she had found; just say nothing and be together, feeling somewhere close to contented, three and a half thousand miles apart.

'I've been thinking about you a lot,' Jonathan said eventually, his deep Oklahoma drawl crackling.

'You have?'

She saw the light blazing in Jonathan's eyes as he carried the phone over to his hotel room door, turning the lock. '*Uh-huh.*'

'What have you been thinking?'

Jonathan made a low laugh which was followed by a moment of hesitation before he settled on his bed, holding the phone at arm's length so Kelsey could see his loose black stage shirt open at the neck and offering a glimpse of the broad, honed torso she missed touching so much. 'I'll tell you... if you lie down with me.'

Kelsey cast a quick glance at the pillows behind her, her face flushing pink and her pupils dilating in the way that made Jonathan's heart pound.

'All right then,' she said, as she settled back, blushing and grinning at the same time.

'First of all...' His voice was low as he looked confidently into the lens. 'I miss being able to kiss you whenever I want...'

Kelsey fought to catch her breath, narrowing her eyes, intently watching as Jonathan slowly tugged the shirt over his head, letting it muss his hair.

Jonathan talked with increasingly shallow breaths and Kelsey listened, losing her inhibition as the bubble formed around them. They forgot the miles between them; their separate time zones realigned and whole continents moved to bring them closer together. Yes, this felt somewhere close to contentment, and for now that would have to be enough for both of them.

Chapter Two

'The web of our life is of a mingled yarn, good and ill
together'
(*All's Well That Ends Well*)

'Long-distance relationships have their perks,' said Mirren, with
an air of authority, holding her phone in one hand, scarlet
lipstick in the other, reapplying it in a confident sweep as she
only half-looked in the mirror of the ladies' room down in the
basement of the *Edinburgh Broadsheet* newspaper offices.

'But you've never been in a long-distance relationship, have
you, Mirr?' Kelsey said, rummaging in her satchel for a lip balm
and failing to find one, her other hand clasping the phone to
her ear as she walked purposefully into Stratford town centre,
still smiling over that morning's call with Jonathan.

Mirren searched her memory, making exaggerated contem-
plative *umm*ing sounds. 'Well, no... But you could say I'm
having one with you. When are you nipping back home for
the weekend? I'm missing you, Kelse. You haven't been home
since you packed your bags back in June.'

Giving up the search, Kelsey's hand fell upon the keys
to her studio as she reached its steps, unlocked the outer
door and punched in the security code. Fifteen sixty-four, the
year Shakespeare was born. Familiar digits to Kelsey after her
summer spinning yarns about the Bard for tourists around the
town's heritage spots.

'I've got a million things to do here, Mirr, otherwise I'd be up those train tracks like a shot.'

Kelsey climbed up past the accountancy office and the landscape artist's design place to the second floor landing and her own studio door. *And I've got a million things to do and supplies I need to buy if I'm ever going to get this place up and running properly,* she thought, but the weight of those worries didn't dampen the thrill of pride and excitement that she felt every time she turned the key and stepped inside her new business premises. It had been five weeks since Norma had handed over the keys and the novelty most definitely wasn't wearing off.

'I do have a favour to ask though, Mirr. Will you pop in and see how my mum's doing? You could tell her I've asked you to dig out some photography stuff from under my bed, or something like that?'

'It's OK, I don't need a reason,' Mirren replied. 'I'll call in. I'll take some muffins or something. It'll be nice to see her. I take it you're missing her?'

'Am a bit.' *There's an understatement.* 'Just give her a hug from me. Do you mind picking up a bag of Edinburgh rock for Grandad? You know it's his favourite and he must miss the bags I'd bring him on Fridays.'

'Consider it done. You know, if you're lonely I can come visit one weekend? Help out with the studio, maybe? If I can clear my backlog at work, that is. There's always so much admin to do and I always seem to be the one lumbered with it.'

'Thanks, Mirr. I'm fine, honestly, and you're so busy. I'll see you when things settle down here, OK?' *Or if I ever earn enough money to afford the rail fare to Scotland.* 'I've got so much to do here, I've barely had time to think about being lonely. It is a bit strange without Jonathan, though. I keep seeing him around town, and I have to do a double-take before I realise it's just some other brown-haired tall drink of water.' Kelsey curtailed a sigh with a shrug, her renewed positivity kicking in. 'I suppose this is what happens when you meet the love of your life in June and spend all summer faffing around him only *finally* getting together at the end of August, a few days before he has to leave town for six months.'

'Excepting Christmas,' said Mirren.

'Yes, excepting Christmas. And maybe Valentine's weekend.'

'There you go, that's not so bad, is it? He'll be back soon, just hang on in there, Kelse. Listen, I'd better get back to work. I'm in a long-distance relationship with my own desk at the moment. The only women's loos in this building are down three flights of stairs in the bowels of the earth. Ridiculous! I'll call you soon, OK? Cheerio.'

Kelsey blew a kiss, hung up her phone, and placed it on the desk. Once belonging to Norma Arden, her old boss, the desk had until recently been cluttered with staff tour-guiding rotas and payslips and a huge diary from which Norma ruled her heritage industry empire.

Kelsey could still feel her here in the room and not just because she was grinning down at her from the framed shot of her wedding day with the entire Norma Arden Tours gang giving her a group hug. She was just an unforgettable kind of woman: tenacious, oh so very loud, an odd combination of posh and brassy, and with a huge, welcoming heart and a penchant for bringing together the town's artistic waifs and strays, as well as dabbling in a bit of matchmaking among them. She may well have left the country to spend her retirement in newly wedded bliss on the Amalfi coast with Gianfranco, but she'd left a feeling of emptiness in the town, a great void that could only be filled with her whirlwind energy and ten to the dozen speech. Kelsey missed her every day and often thought about the great debt of gratitude she owed her.

Norma must have had some kind of sixth sense in order to pick Kelsey out.

How had she foreseen that the insecure Scottish homebody, who she hadn't known from Eve, would become a great tour guide and a valued member of the agency team? Had Norma recognised the fact that a working holiday in her favourite place on the planet was just what Kelsey needed to bring some sunshine back into her overcast life? And just in the nick of time too: Norma had read her – slightly desperate – job application in the spring when Kelsey was losing faith in her dour, hard-working boyfriend Fran and unexpectedly unemployed from what was supposed to be a stop-gap job at a dusty old camera shop back home. Norma's job offer had changed her life.

Kelsey often wondered how much Norma had been responsible for engineering her meetings with Jonathan too. It was Norma, after all, who put together the rotas that had thrown them together in the planning of the theatrical gala evening back in August, forcing them into closer acquaintance, giving them time to get to know each other better. And when had Norma realised Kelsey was the ideal candidate to take over the let on her office?

Norma signed it over at a tiny peppercorn of a rent, set for six months, 'until you get your business off the ground,' she'd said, while flashing her lipstick-stained teeth beneath her signature purple specs and shocking, severe red bob.

'What business?' Kelsey had asked.

Kelsey smiled at the memory of that moment, only a few weeks ago, when she had been so green.

'Your photography studio, of course,' Norma had replied, and within minutes the rental agreement was signed and Kelsey, always a little unsure of herself and what she would do with her life, suddenly had a career mapped out for her.

Looking back, Kelsey reflected, Norma had probably never once seen her without a camera around her neck, and even though she had loved working for Norma at the agency, it was plain to see that Kelsey wasn't dreaming of a life of tour-guiding, instead she had her heart set on a life she didn't dare waste any daydreams on. Deep down, Kelsey was only really *truly* happy behind the lens of her dad's lovely old camera. Norma had known instantly this fact that Kelsey was only dimly becoming aware of.

Taking the feather duster from the cupboard under her desk, the autumn light spilling in through the bare studio windows, Kelsey ran it around the sparse room, carefully going over her camera on its new tripod facing the blank whiteness of the smoothly plastered wall where she planned to shoot passport and ID photographs. She hadn't had the opportunity to do an actual, proper portrait shoot yet either, which wasn't great when, technically, she'd been in business for almost two weeks.

The place had needed a full makeover and it had taken time to source and set up the (new to Kelsey) second-hand reflectors and modern studio backdrops she'd found she needed. She'd had a sign installed over the studio door – 'Kelsey Anderson Photography' in delicate purple calligraphy – and she'd had to master the new photo-editing software on her tablet. Yet, she had managed all of that, working methodically and efficiently, trying to avoid the temptation to splurge on pretty soft furnishings and extras she didn't need. Now the studio was complete, and it was her pride and joy.

She knew there was nothing left to do but prepare to open her studio properly to paying customers, if she could find any.

She carried on whipping the still-settling post-decorating dust off the shelves she'd mounted all by herself on the wall behind her desk, now neatly stocked with boxes of 35mm film, before finally coming to a stop and sitting down in front of her new diary, spread open at today's date. A glance confirmed what she already knew: nothing booked in for this morning. *Maybe it wasn't my best idea launching a new business in Stratford's off season? Maybe Fran was right after all when he said photography studios have had their day? No, come on, Kelse. Positive thinking. The phone might ring any second now.*

Expectantly, she watched her mobile for a few moments, before checking that the ringer volume was definitely turned up.

With a sigh, she conceded it was time. If she was ever going to establish some regular trade she'd have to make the phone call she'd been putting off in the hope that somehow word of mouth would be enough to signal her presence in town, but that hadn't happened. She was going to have to part with some serious cash. She reached for her phone and dialled.

'Is this the right number for placing adverts in your newspaper, please?'

'Hold on,' replied the brusque, harried man's voice.

Kelsey listened to the sounds at the other end of the line, papers being shifted, rummaging and cursing, and a sudden triumphant, 'Got it. You'd think you could find a pen in a newspaper office, wouldn't you? Right, what do you want?'

'Well, I need an eye-catching advertisement for my new business, please? But... I don't have much money.'

'They never do,' the nasal voice said, cutting her off. 'It's fifty pence a word.'

'Oh, OK.' That didn't sound too bad. 'How about, *Kelsey Anderson Photography, wedding and family portraits, school visits, passports and ID shots, theatrical headshots. Pets and kids photographed in your home or in studio.*'

'Address?'

'What?'

'Won't your customers want to know where you are?'

'I was just getting to that. It's Second Floor, Corner Buildings, off Henley Street, Stratford. You'd better give my number as well.'

'You think so?'

Kelsey stiffened her neck in response. *Doesn't this newspaper want my custom?* There were other rival papers in the town, perhaps a little more respectable, with smart offices overlooking the town square or the river, but she had already called them both and their ads started at fifty quid for a black and white box somewhere in the middle pages beside the pets for sale and the lonely hearts, and she simply didn't have money for ads people might not take note of.

It really should be a big announcement, a 'new business in town' sort of thing. The *Stratford Examiner* was one of many freebie papers delivered to most residents whether they wanted it or not, and a pile was always dumped at the train and bus station every Friday, so Kelsey hoped it would reach just as many potential clients as the smarter papers. Still, this guy wasn't doing much to reassure her of the paper's professionalism.

Kelsey told the man her mobile number, crossing her fingers in the hope that sharing it with the world wouldn't result in a barrage of cold calls about double glazing and PPI claims. The studio no longer had a landline connected; she had worried she couldn't afford the bills, and Norma Arden's clunky nineties phone was now wound up in its beige cables in the desk drawer.

'Logo?' the man barked.

'Sorry?'

'Do you have a business logo you want to include?'

'*Ahh*, no, not really.' *Dammit, another thing I've failed to sort out.* She didn't even want to think about how much hiring a logo designer might cost her.

'That it?' the man asked, sourly, and Kelsey heard the sounds of additions taking place under his breath accompanied by a nib moving scratchily across paper. 'Seventeen fifty for a front pager. Will you take it?'

Kelsey gulped. 'Yes, please. For eight weeks.' It was an essential expense, and the other papers only had inside pages to offer, so this was an improvement, right?

'One hundred and forty pounds. How do you want to pay?'

And with that, Kelsey parted with her money, using the business bank account she'd set up only the month before.

'Processed. First ad will appear next Friday.' And with that, the man hung up.

Kelsey was still shaking her head and looking at her phone in her hand when it rang.

'Hold on, you're a photographer?' the same voice asked. 'I might have some work for you. Cheap, are you?'

A moment of stunned silence passed before Kelsey stammered, 'Competitively priced.'

'If that means cheap, call in at the office. Today.' She could tell he was about to hang up again and managed to quickly enquire who she should ask for when she arrived.

'Ask for Mr Ferdinand, lead editor.' And he was gone.

Chapter Three

'Come, bring me unto my chance'
(*The Merchant of Venice*)

Kelsey climbed the stairs following the sign indicating that the editor of the *Stratford Examiner's* office was at the top of the building. So far, nobody had stopped her to enquire why she was there. The reception desk at the foot of the stairwell was unmanned and seemed to be little more than a storage area for cycling helmets and coats. There had been no reply when she buzzed at the outer door and, finding it was off the latch, she had pushed her way inside.

As she climbed, the steps became increasingly cluttered with piled books, folders, and old editions of the newspaper. Thinking of the steely-faced fire officer who had visited her studio last week to make sure it was workplace compliant (no filing cabinets in front of fire doors, no smoke alarms with the batteries taken out for use in a telly remote control, that sort of thing) Kelsey wondered how on earth this place could have passed an inspection any time recently.

At the top of the second flight of stairs, Kelsey passed a man coming down and was struck by his model-handsome features and wild black hair sticking up in what, in front of his mirror this morning, might have looked like artfully crafted peaks.

He said nothing as they passed on the landing, only smiling politely, if a little bemused, before turning back regretfully and calling to her up the stairs, 'Do you know where you're going?'

'Mr Ferdinand?' Kelsey asked awkwardly.

She witnessed his look of horrified amusement and heard the suppressed snorting laugh, before he replied, 'God, no. He's up there.' This was accompanied by a sharp jab of his finger towards the top landing. 'I thought we were done for the day. Are you here about a story?' He looked begrudgingly beyond Kelsey and up the stairs as though nothing could induce him to follow her and do more work, not when the weekend was within reach.

'Not a story, no. He's expecting me. Something about a job? Photography?'

'Ah! OK.' His eyes flickered as if a thought had struck him, before he added in a low voice, 'You sure you want this gig?'

Kelsey had no idea whether she wanted it; she didn't know anything about it, and now there was this guy's dubious expression putting her off before she'd even investigated it. She simply shrugged.

'Just be sure he pays in advance.' He cast a furtive glance to the unseen boss above them before turning again and rushing down the stairs with the air of a schoolboy let loose from class.

Kelsey wasn't fazed; far from it. She'd been in town nearly five months now and had long ago grown used to Stratford's more eccentric residents. The place was chock full of them; from the arty, elderly, and oftentimes wealthy, locals raised on theatre and poetry – drama running through them like silver seams through rock; to the younger population – lively, creative and often totally skint but full of ideas and enjoying the benefits of the local networks and organisations designed to support their arty inclinations. Then there were the others: the barflies; the international students in town to study Shakespeare on dreamy year-long courses; the holiday-makers who had visited once and never left; the new arrivals in town hoping for an audition, serving coffee in the theatre bars while they waited for their big break.

Back on the hot summer afternoon when she'd first run into Jonathan in the little café with the pink stripy awnings by the marina, Kelsey had remarked to him how Stratford seemed to attract people from across the world, arty nomads looking for self-discovery, and he had looked at her in her tour guide uniform with her dad's old camera around her neck and seen in an instant that she was one of them. 'It looks to me as though you're actually a photographer,' he'd said. Kelsey smiled at the memory now. He'd seen straight to her core, recognised her dreams and ambitions, and he'd engaged her services there and then to shoot his new theatrical headshots. Now here she was with her very own photography studio and about to negotiate another commission if she played her cards right.

With Jonathan's belief in her abilities in mind she felt ready for anything as she came to a stop at the closed door with its smoky glass and a yellowing piece of paper taped across it bearing the words, 'C. Ferdinand, Editor'.

Kelsey had visited Mirren in her newsroom once, and she'd seen them on TV dramas, and, generally, they all looked alike: rows of monitors alive with the day's copy, coffee cups beside every keyboard, pictures being edited, phones ringing, facts being checked, experts being consulted, interviews and advertising deals being secured, doors swinging, Ubers being hailed, and everywhere the rush and bustle of news-gathering.

But this place was as still and soundless as the grave.

Kelsey's knock was answered with stony silence and the door creaking open a few inches. Instinctively, she peeked her head around the frame, sure it would confirm her suspicions that everyone had gone home for the weekend.

Glancing inside the room, the first thing that hit her was the smell of hot dust emanating from the ancient computer on the desk, mingling with the unmistakable smell of cigarettes smoked furtively by an open window with an arm waving away each exhalation, fooling precisely no one.

Instead of the modern, sleek, grey and white office Kelsey had expected, everything was a dull and dusty manila. Folders and documents were piled high on every surface, and what must have, once upon a time, been a leafy pot plant by the window was now reduced to crunchy brown rot slumped in its pot. There in the middle of it all, well-nigh camouflaged among the clutter, his thinly combed-over head lolling on the cracked brown leather of the headrest, a curling cheese sandwich on its torn cardboard package on the desk before him, was Mr Ferdinand himself, his eyes closed and mouth agape, as beige and uninspiring as the office he inhabited.

Horrified, Kelsey pulled her head back out of the office and closed the door quietly. Was he dead? He was deathly pale. There was nothing for it but to bang loudly on the glass and, if there was no answer, ring the paramedics.

Fortunately, her determined knock was greeted with a loud snort, a few moments' rustling, the sound of the stale sandwich hitting the bottom of a metal wastepaper basket, and a terse, discomfited, 'Come in!'

'Mr Ferdinand? I'm Kelsey Anderson, the photographer,' she said, half entering the room again. She loved the sound of the words as they made their way through the stuffy air. A part of her still expected them to be greeted with a '*Pfft*! No you're not!' from everyone she met, but Kelsey was learning that people accepted her just as she presented herself, no questions asked, actually. The only person she had trouble convincing of her new professional status was herself.

Mr Ferdinand, still blinking in the early afternoon light, was indicating she should come in and sit down, so she moved the pile of newspapers from the only other chair onto the desk and lowered herself into it, her nose prickling from the dust in the air.

'Looking for a job then, are you?' He scratched thin fingers over his forehead and narrowed his eyes as he spoke.

'*Um*, well, if you remember, you invited me here?'

The silence that descended was so uncomfortable and Mr Ferdinand's eyes so penetrating, Kelsey mentally gave the situation twenty seconds to improve before she excused herself and raced out of this weirdo's office.

At last he spoke. 'What makes you think you would be a good replacement for our old staff photographer?'

'Is that what you're after?' Kelsey's mind raced, trying to catch up. If this was to be a regular thing, she could certainly use the money, no matter how brusque her boss would be. 'I *could* do some freelance work for you, yes. No problem. How many jobs a week would it be?'

'Depends. Sometimes one, sometimes none. I re-run old pictures from our archives where I can.'

'Oh, OK.'

'Today I need someone to take some pictures for an interview with a retired actress. It's for a feature we're running in the lead-up to the sixtieth anniversary of the town's main theatre company.'

'I can do that.'

'Today?'

'Is this actress expecting a photographer to turn up?'

'Does that matter?'

'*Um*, well, yes. I expect she'd like to know I'm coming.'

'I'll ring her now, tell her you're on your way.'

'Oh!' She hadn't even confirmed she was free this afternoon, and he hadn't actually offered her any money yet. This guy was something else. 'Should we talk about payment first?'

Kelsey had learned her lesson on this score, arriving in town early that summer, having already signed a contract with Norma Arden for her guiding services and never thinking to ask about the hourly rate until she was sitting in Norma's office. Kelsey inwardly groaned at how green she had been only a few short months ago.

'Eight pounds an hour. You can do this in an hour, I expect. She's local.'

Eight quid? *That would buy bread, milk and tea for a week. Come on Kelsey*, she told herself, *screw your courage to the sticking place.* 'My hourly rate is thirty-five pounds for jobs within the town boundary.' Instantly, she felt her cheeks flush. She hadn't been required to provide an hourly rate since setting up her fledgling business and had plucked this figure out of thin air.

He was staring her down. 'Sixteen and you've got a deal. If you get the pictures to me by five.'

Hold on, she thought. *He needs these pictures by five, and he doesn't exactly have a queue of photographers lining up to take them, so short of doing it himself, I can afford to stick to my guns.* Kelsey rose to leave. 'My rate is thirty-five pounds, but if you can find someone else...' Her voice was just beginning to waver when he interrupted.

'Fine. But go now. Here's her address, and my email address. Send the pictures straight away.' Mr Ferdinand handed her a Post-it note.

That was like something off The Apprentice, Kelsey congratulated herself. *Who knew I was so good at wheeling and dealing? Wait 'til I tell Jonathan about this!*

'Get some shots of her with some old theatre memorabilia or something, some old costume or a prop?'

The nasal whine of his speech woke her from her self-congratulatory state, and she recalled the young man's words as they passed on the stairs, sharpening her thinking. She'd better ensure she got paid first. She drew a slim notebook from her satchel, wrote her new bank account details in it and tore the page free.

'I'll invoice you properly later today, but this is my account. You can transfer the money direct.' Her heart swelled with the feeling of triumph, and even better than that, of competence. She really was prepared for anything her new career brought her way. She had even asked a member of the legal team at Mirren's newspaper – who did a bit of freelance work of her own – to draw up a copyright agreement for exactly this kind of situation, and she'd send it to Mr Ferdinand to sign along with her invoice for payment.

Her smile of self-assurance faded, however, as Mr Ferdinand snatched the paper and skewered it through an upturned nail on a wooden block upon his desk which was, she noticed, rather ominously pierced with at least a hundred other notes.

'Unusual in-tray you've got there,' she said with an awkward nod towards the rusty spike, but Mr Ferdinand simply blinked with a little scowl of annoyance. 'I'll be off then.'

'Deadline's five p.m., Miss…'

'Anderson?' *Has he forgotten already, or does he simply not care?* 'Kelsey Anderson.'

Harrumphing, he showed her the door with a weak swing of his bony hand.

And that was it. Kelsey had a new freelance commission and, potentially, a long term client. She clutched the paper to her chest as she made her way downstairs and out into the October afternoon light.

She wasn't a stranger to sudden turns of fate, so this new development felt comfortingly familiar. Hadn't she signed a contract with Norma knowing next to nothing about her new boss, or indeed, about her new town? And now here she was, the newest recruit to a newspaper's staff in that very town, and why not? Recently, life seemed to want to take Kelsey in all manner of new directions and she intended to go with it.

She checked the time on her phone: two thirty. Turning the paper in her hand, she peered down at the address, hoping this actress lived not only nearby but in an area of town she was familiar with. She gasped in delighted recognition at the words.

Blythe Goode. Ground Floor, Flat A, St. Ninian's Close.

Her new commission, it seemed, would take her back to her own doorstep. At last, she was going to meet one of her mysteriously quiet and unobtrusive neighbours.

Chapter Four

'Tis best to weigh the enemy more mighty than he seems'
(*Henry V*)

There was a buzz in the *Edinburgh Broadsheet* office, not because it was almost the weekend – most of the junior staff would end up working over the weekend so it was no kind of break really – but because Friday was bacon roll day and they were due to arrive in half an hour, all floury bread and smoky, salty, ketchupy deliciousness, to be devoured greedily over today's copy.

Reporters, Mirren had learned long ago, lived for this kind of pick-me-up in their busy working lives. Mr Angus, the paper's Editor in Chief, and Mirren's boss, would eat his later at his desk, as he signed off the upcoming feature allocations before leaving early for a weekend on the golf course at St Andrews. Mirren could tell this was on his mind as he tried to hurry along the Friday meeting, shuffling the agenda papers in his hand.

'Any other business? Oh yes. Rae's off on leave, so I've got a double-pager for one of you. Who wants it?' He surveyed the assembled reporters around the table.

'A feature? *I'll* take it.' Mirren said, having forced her mouthful of coffee down in the race to beat Jamesey, her nemesis in the news pool, to the claim.

Both Jamesey and Mr Angus responded with pointedly blank stares at her audacity.

'No need to bite my hand off, Mirren. Do you think you're up to feature-writing? Aren't you better off sticking with your magistrates' court reports?' said the boss.

'I'm sure I'm up to it, and you've promised me a crack at writing a feature more times than I can count. So, *umm*, what's it about?' She was struck with a sudden panic that in her haste she'd pushed herself forwards to write her first ever feature on one of Jamesey's specialist subjects. He was the go-to staffer for motoring stories, technology, and consumer rights stuff.

Mr Angus exhaled through flaring nostrils, not with anger but with something that looked like impatience. 'I want the low-down on the theatre season across the country for the first November weekend supplement women's pages. Theatre mini-breaks, where to see the stars of the stage this winter, who's wheeling out their Widow Twankey for the twentieth year running, that sort of thing. But remember to…'

'*Put a kilt on it,*' pre-empted everyone around the table in an obedient chorus, Jamesey's voice booming louder than the others.

This was well rehearsed. Every Friday pitch meeting saw this scene repeated at least once. *Put a kilt on it*: the newsroom's mantra. It meant making sure there was a Scottish slant to every piece.

Mirren tried not to wriggle in her seat. The conversation that would take place over the next few minutes felt suddenly vital to her future here at the newspaper. She'd never had the chance at feature-writing before, though in every appraisal meeting she'd ever had she'd explained her ambitions of moving out of courtroom reporting to writing weekend features.

She gripped the arms of the chair and gulped down her nerves. Could she get a by-line over a weekend feature, or would she lose out to Jamesey again, a humiliating, maddening occurrence she was well used to by now?

Mirren glanced at Jamesey across the overly large oval desk which had the kind of frustratingly outsized proportions that meant if the meeting's pastries were placed at its centre, which they usually were, no one could actually reach for one. Mirren had sat through many a meeting as her stomach growled audibly, prompting Jamesey to throw her a smirk over the vast wasteland of mahogany and leather.

It was all right for him. She'd heard him boasting proudly that his wife made him porridge with maple syrup every morning and sent him off to work with a packed lunch every day. God knows how, but he'd managed to convince some poor, confused woman into catering to his every whim. Mirren shuddered at the thought. It sharpened her mind and her focus returned.

'Pitch me, then,' said Mr Angus.

Mirren jumped in first, even though she could hear Jamesey's, 'Well, actually...' from across the table.

'I'd look at festive staycations across the UK, places where you can combine a stay in a nice B&B or a boutique hotel with a Christmassy evening show, or a matinee.' A little flash of inspiration hit her. 'Like Stratford-upon-Avon, for instance, where you can mix Christmas shopping with a bit of culture and a champagne cream tea. Our readers will like that.'

Mr Angus turned his head to Jamesey, eyebrows raised in expectation.

'You were saying, Jamesey?'

Mirren watched as the disgruntled flash of anger that had seconds before lit her colleague's face was hastily wiped away under their boss's gaze.

'*Hmm*, I like your thinking, Maureen,' Jamesey began, and no one round the table, including Mirren, dared to point out he'd got her name wrong, again. He was still talking anyway. 'But I'm not sure about the overall *thrust* of the piece. Who's got money for expensive Christmas trips in the current climate?' A smiling shake of his head accompanied this final, fatal blow as Mirren's idea was dismissed. Jamesey turned to Mr Angus. 'No, I'd give you the low-down on all the *local* shows happening across Scotland, low budget stuff, as well as listing what the big regional theatres are offering.'

Mr Angus was already nodding his approval, so Jamesey carried on, eyes glinting now.

'I'll interview a few local heroes, the blokes who make am-dram productions happen in venues all across the country every year without fail. I might go in search of an island community's Crimbo production, Orkney or some backwater, get pictures of the rehearsals, mad artsy types in the bottom half of a donkey costume, that kind of thing.'

A ripple of laughter went round the table, and Mirren found herself forcing a smile. She'd learned long ago not to court the disapproval of Mr Angus, who inexplicably seemed to like Jamesey Wallace. Actually, it wasn't that inexplicable, Mirren reminded herself. They'd both gone to the same school, albeit two decades apart, and they were in the same golf club, so they had a lot in common, a priceless connection that she couldn't ever hope to replicate.

She looked around the table at the other women present, all graduates from different universities across the globe. What united them? Right at this second, a combined adoration for Jamesey Wallace seemed to unite them, judging by the tipped heads and smiles as they listened. *These are smart women,* Mirren raged internally. *They ought to know better than lust after the vile slime that is Jamesey Wallace.* Then again, she'd seen no evidence that Jamesey was in direct competition with any of *them,* in fact, he was as affable to them as he was with everyone else. Jamesey reserved his vitriol for only one person: Mirren.

Mirren and Jamesey's dislike for one another had been born at their very first meeting when they were both applying for the same job as the paper's magistrate court reporter, five years ago now.

He'd initiated the whispered conversation as they'd sat outside Mr Angus's office door, gripping CVs and notepads, and rehearsing answers to common interview questions in their heads. Mirren had them all planned. 'What would you say is your greatest weakness at work?' 'Oh well, let's see' – pause for effect – 'I'd have to say it's not being better at saying no, so I end up taking on too many jobs and working extra hard to get them done, and I *do* get them done.' *That's always a good one*, Mirren was thinking, as the man in the blue suit leaned closer and she was treated to a whiff of his overpowering, expensive aftershave.

'James Wallace, pleased to meet you.'

'Mirren Imrie. Hello.'

'Feeling hopeful?'

Mirren had sniffed a dismissive laugh. No, she didn't feel hopeful but she didn't want to voice her self-doubt moments before walking in to face an interview panel. 'Quietly confident,' she'd said, hoping it didn't sound too cocky.

'Oh. Well, good for you! So are you a reporter?'

'Uh-huh, I'm a news-gatherer for my local weekly.'

'Big circulation?'

'Not bad.' There was something in his tone that seemed hopeful for a low number, something she wasn't prepared to give him, because it was indeed low. Nothing compared to the huge reach of the *Edinburgh Broadsheet*. 'You?' she deflected.

'I'm at the *Chronic*. Lead reporter.'

Mirren nodded, smiling in recognition at the *East Coast Chronicle*'s nickname amongst its reporters, and possibly many of its readers. But it was a big paper, as big as the *Broadsheet*.

'Why do you want to leave there, if you're lead reporter?'

James Wallace shrugged casually. 'A change is as good as a rest.' He looked around the corridor, suddenly unwilling to meet Mirren's eyes.

She'd been told many times that her thoughts showed themselves on her face, and she remembered this unwelcome trait in that moment. He no doubt saw her mind working, wondering what had happened to make him want to apply for an inferior position at a very slightly inferior paper.

'It's all right for you girls, you have the upper hand in these situations,' he said, with a sniff, pulling his suit trousers up at the knees and slouching in the chair. Mirren in contrast was sitting bolt upright, knees together in her black pencil skirt, anticipating the door to the interview room being flung open at any minute.

'*Huh*?' She turned her head sharply to her new acquaintance who scanned the bare wall opposite as he spoke.

'Well, for a start *you* can wear make-up and that gives you an advantage, doesn't it?'

'In interviews? *You think*?' Mirren's neck stiffened.

'Obviously. Think about it. *I* can't very well slap on loads of lipstick and eyeshadow and swan into an interview looking a million dollars, but all you girls can. And who are they going to hire, me looking… just ordinary, or the woman?'

Mirren suppressed an eye-roll but her tongue was already drawing back ready to unleash its sharp reply. 'You genuinely believe that?'

He nodded once, still looking away, cautious now they could hear chairs being scraped across the floor and low rumblings of discussion from Mr Angus's office. The interview panel must almost be ready to begin.

Mirren kept her voice low. 'Well, first of all, men are more likely than women to exaggerate their skills and experience on job applications so they're walking into the interview with an automatic advantage. And secondly, I've literally *never* been interviewed by a woman, not when they're the boss or in charge of the decision. Sure, there have been women in the room, but they were usually from HR. And I have to overcome that every time. You don't.'

'Overcome what? Bosses fancying you and wanting to give you a job? Oh, poor you.'

'No, that's not what I'm saying. I have to contend with the fact that men tend to hire men, so even if I'm one of five candidates and the other four are blokes, I have to outshine all of them.'

'By wearing make-up and making yourself look as good as possible. My point exactly. You really painted yourself into a corner there, Maureen.'

'Mirren.'

'What?'

'It's Mirren.'

'What did I say?' But he didn't pause for an answer. 'And it's *some* men.'

'What?'

'Some men tend only to hire men, not all men.'

'All right,' Mirren conceded.

'You should try for a job at the *Chronic*. Editor's a woman there, isn't she? And she hires women all the time. Place is overrun with them.'

The little sneer, barely suppressed, on his thin white lips, said it all. Mirren didn't need to ask why he was looking for another job; some run-in with the lady-boss or one of his female colleagues most likely had him desperate for work in the industry, any work. *Has he been booted out or is he pre-emptively searching for work in a more male dominated environment? Wonder what it was*, she thought. Could she put out some feelers? She knew people who worked at the *Chronicle*, getting the goss would be easy enough. If there was one thing reporters were good at, it was spreading word fast. Jamesey interrupted her thoughts.

'You're more likely to get this job than I am, so don't worry about it.'

Mirren knew this wasn't coming from a place of consolation or encouragement. It was competitiveness and grievance, and she couldn't understand it. They'd only just met. Why the animosity?

The door opened. 'Ms Imrie? Mr Angus is ready for you,' said the woman from HR. Mirren, not entirely sure why, quickly wiped her red lipstick off with a tissue before stepping inside, smiling, hopeful that she'd at least have the upper hand over this bitter hack from the *Chronical* with a sudden shady departure from the newsroom to explain away. That wasn't likely to go down well at the stoic, strait-laced and (dare she admit it?) dour, *Broadsheet*. Its reputation was as solid and impressive as the great grey building it inhabited on Princes Street with Edinburgh Castle looming over its hunched grey shoulders. The paper's reputation was timeworn and weathered, having survived for a century in increasingly competitive markets, but it was trusted and true, a Scottish institution. They weren't likely to hire some dodgy bloke (possibly) fresh from a workplace scandal, were they?

–

'Wonderful, we'll look forward to seeing you back here first thing on Monday morning.'

Mr Angus was pumping James Wallace's hand warmly as he showed him from his office, and James had been sure to flash a quick smile at Mirren sitting on the chair by the door as he'd said, 'Please, Mr Angus, call me Jamesey.'

They'd asked Mirren to stick around after her interview, which hadn't gone quite as well as she'd hoped. All her answers had been greeted by cool silence and the thrust-out chin of a frowning Mr Angus. In the years since, she'd come to learn this was his 'thinking face' but in the interview it had been utterly disconcerting and she'd found herself rambling on, piling on evidence of her skills and experience at the local rag, hoping to get at least one nod of approval from any of the grey-haired men around the table. Only the nice HR woman, Mandy, had smiled enthusiastically as she'd taken her notes, and Mirren increasingly found herself addressing her answers to her, hoping she might have a say in the hiring after all.

Mr Angus was showing Jamesey towards the newsroom. *A private tour for the new hiring? Great!* Mirren wanted to slump in the chair in defeat, but Mandy smiled from the door and invited her inside the room again.

Mirren followed her and took the hot seat once more. A dry, tweedy smell now hung in the air with Jamesey's aftershave, and… were those whisky glasses on the table?

Mirren looked down at her hands clasped on her lap over the closed notebook. Well, they weren't going to offer *her* a dram, but at least she might get some feedback about why she hadn't been hired and what she could improve on for next time. Every cloud.

'Mr Wallace has accepted the role of principal court reporter,' Mandy said gently, before adding, 'but Mr McManus wanted to have a word with you.'

So much for Jamesey Wallace's cosmetics theory, Mirren thought, but she looked up at the deputy editor, suddenly hopeful.

Mr McManus had been quiet throughout the interview, but now his eyes crinkled into a smile, and Mirren wondered why he hadn't shown this kindness earlier when she'd been struggling in the face of the four fusty journos.

'We'd like to offer you a junior position, supporting Mr Wallace. You'll go to the courts when there are parallel magistrates sitting; you'll cover the minor cases. Would that be of interest?'

After years at her local paper and dreaming of writing for a bigger one she wasn't about to turn the offer down. But as she accepted and shook hands over the table, she couldn't get Jamesey Wallace's triumphant smile out of her mind.

Mirren tried to block the infuriating memory now as she looked across the pitch meeting table at Jamesey, smiling that same old smile, the cat that always got the cream.

'Hmm, let's see,' Mr Angus was mumbling, his chin thrust out a little more than usual, meaning he really was weighing up the two ideas; Jamesey's and Mirren's. Mirren sat bolt upright in her chair. This really could be her chance. 'Another impressive pitch, thank you, Mr Wallace. But, you've got the "Techy Christmas Gifts for the Discerning Man in Your Life" feature to research for the mid-November women's pages. And, don't forget we've got the autumn tournament at the club next weekend.'

Mirren felt her heartrate pick up and her cheeks redden as Mr Angus turned to her. 'You take the feature. Show us what you're made of. Two thousand words, mind? Centre spread. In my inbox by next Friday. And don't let it interfere with your court duties, you hear?'

'I won't. Thank you, Mr Angus.' No matter how demeaning his mode of delivery, basking in the light of her boss's preferment felt wonderful.

Mr Angus's eyes lit up at the sight of the delivery woman from the deli down the road arriving with the rolls, and he quickly called the meeting to a close and shuffled out the door of the glass meeting room.

Mirren didn't look at him as she gathered her belongings ready to leave, but she could feel the burning glare of Jamesey Wallace as he smouldered in defeat across the table. She hid her smiles until she was out of his sight.

Chapter Five

'Be blithe again, and bury all thy fear in my devices'
(*Titus Andronicus*)

Kelsey knew the downstairs flats in her towering Victorian redbrick were accessed by doors leading off from the cool and spacious tiled hallway with its scent of lavender and beeswax emanating from the polished oak balustrade and the carved wooden owl who, from his perch at the foot of the stairs, had witnessed every visitor passing through Number One, St Ninian's Close for the last century. What she hadn't known was who lived in the flats, and it had intrigued her for so long now.

Not once had she seen anyone arrive at or leave the other flats in her building: no Ocado deliveries, no visiting relatives, no one stretching in the tarmacked drive before a morning run, nothing. She *had* seen mail filed neatly in the rack by the door, and its disappearance every day meant someone was collecting it. The only flats which never received any mail whatsoever were those on her own floor up at the top of the building which she believed to be entirely unoccupied. Maybe the rent and their tiny proportions put people off. She really ought to look for another flat, something slightly cheaper and larger than her own little shoe box, flat 2B, but she loved its compact, pristine white simplicity and the fact that she had access to the building's roof terrace with its wonderful views across Stratford and the wide Avon valley.

She'd pressed the doorbell of Blythe's flat twice and had no answer when she noticed the faded note taped beside the little peephole.

Come to side door through garden.

The existence of a side door was news to Kelsey, so with an enhanced sense of curiosity, she made her way outside and around the back of the building, passing under the branches of the spreading oak tree in the centre of the communal lawn, her camera cases with their long straps slung across her body, bumping at her hips.

At the back of the building there was a dense shrubbery of fading purple buddleia choked with teasels and bindweed. She'd seen it before but hadn't noticed the path worn through the weeds. Following it, she found it led to a rickety gate, half off its hinges and framed with a tumble of rambling roses, the blooms now turned to swollen red hips.

Lowering her head to squeeze through the gap in the greenery and getting her hair caught on a thorn, she passed into a small courtyard with lichen-speckled Victorian flagstones interspersed with colourful, cracked patterned tiles underfoot. There were wind chimes and birdfeeders hanging from the branches of densely packed small trees, and a chair and table by the door to a wood-framed glass lean-to which looked as old as the building itself. Its peeling mint-green paint contrasted wonderfully with the late sprigs of Cotswold lavender growing in great round clumps under an unkempt hedge bordering this little wild Eden.

Kelsey was just becoming aware of a sweet scent in the air; not a natural, floral, garden scent, but a strange, not-unpleasant, chemical tang.

Early autumn leaves made scratching sounds on the flags as they blew around her feet and, as she looked down at them, she realised they were joined by a black cat which had clearly come to suss her out. It was parading haughtily in front of her, its tail tensed bolt upright.

'Hello, kitty.' Kelsey crouched to pet it, but it fluffed its tail and gave her an outraged glare, a mixture of angry and afraid. It was just opening its jaws to hiss a warning to stay back when there was a loud bang from inside the house followed by the sound of shattering glass and a cry of 'Bugger, bastard and blast!' The cat scarpered up a tree, sending a startled blackbird squawking from under the hedge.

'What on earth...?' Kelsey made her way to the glass door, propped open with a pile of rain-damaged paperbacks, and as she went she became increasingly aware of the same hot, acrid smell in the air, now mixed with a slight odour of something singed.

'Hell's bells! Not again,' came the voice from inside; an elderly woman's voice, shaky and thin.

'Hello!' Kelsey called as she put her head inside the glass lean-to, which was full of faded books and red geraniums in pots, the scent of their leaves mixing with the burning smell and the white vaporous clouds now emanating from the gap between thick purple velvet drapes which separated the inner space from the green world outside.

'Is everything all right? Do you need help?' she called.

'Bloody, bloody, bloody bastard and blast!' This was muttered under the breath of the person behind the curtain and accompanied by the sounds of shards of glass being swept up.

Kelsey was about to cry out again and was reaching for her phone – in case she had to alert the authorities to a chemical spill or a gas leak on an epic scale – when the purple drapes twitched and a head poked out.

Kelsey took a step backwards at the sight of the woman, easily seventy years old, with long, thin white hair splaying messily around her face, and piercing, suspicious violet eyes peering through skew-whiff plastic goggles.

'I thought I heard somebody snooping about. What do you want? I've told your lot already it's perfectly safe and you should keep your sticky beaks out of an old lady's private goings on.'

'*Umm*, are you Blythe Goode?' Kelsey managed, taken aback. The woman was surveying her from head to toe, the curtain still clasped shut beneath her neck so only her head showed.

'You don't look like you're from Environmental Health.'

'What? I'm not, no, I'm from the *Examiner*. I've come to take your picture to accompany the interview you did recently? Didn't Mr Ferdinand ring a few minutes ago to let you know I was coming?'

'He didn't, no. Hardly surprising; man's a buffoon. Makes a mockery of that paper. Clement Dickens would be spinning in his grave if he could see what's become of that place. Fine man, he was, Clement.'

Kelsey could do nothing but shrug. 'I'm afraid I don't know anything about that, this is my first job for the paper.'

'*Hmm*, well, make sure he pays you.'

'You're the second person to tell me that. Doesn't exactly inspire me with confidence.'

'Mind out the way.' Blythe had released her grip on the curtain and was attempting to bustle past Kelsey, holding before her a dustpan containing what looked like lumps of congealed burnt sugar, still smoking slightly. 'Marlowe! Where is that cat? Very sensitive, he is, always disappearing.'

'He ran off under that tree,' Kelsey said, distractedly, trying to peer between the curtains. 'Look, has there been an accident? Are you all right?'

Blythe shuffled by, one hand moving a walking frame in front of her, the other shakily grasping the dustpan. 'Open the bin, then.'

'Oh, sorry.' Kelsey dashed to the silver trash can tucked around the corner of the glass house, lifted the lid and watched as Blythe walked painfully slowly towards it and tipped the acrid contents in.

'Just a small explosion. Nothing to worry about. Come inside, but mind your feet, there's glass everywhere.'

She waited for Blythe to walk her way back through the curtains then followed her in. The smell was much stronger inside the cluttered kitchen. Kelsey looked around in amazement. 'What's all this?' she asked.

Around the walls and from the pulley on the ceiling hung drying herbs and flowers, and there were two great pots with what smelled like fruit jam bubbling on an old stove. On the shelves lining the room stood many hundreds of books, all decidedly dusty-looking. What must have once upon a time been a fine oak kitchen table was piled high with glass beakers raised on frames, bell jars, strange metal coils and pipes, and in the centre, a tall copper rocket-shaped pot with some kind of pressure gauge, its needle fluctuating wildly from black to red – whatever that signified – on its cylindrical belly. Copper tubes led off from the device to what appeared to be an eccentric copper kettle. The whole kitchen gave the impression of a cross between Dr Jekyll's laboratory and a *Downton Abbey* scullery.

'Don't gape. It isn't polite,' Blythe said as she turned the knobs on the stove. The gas flames died away but there were still alarming gurgling and banging sounds coming from the great copper device on the table. 'It's a still. Have you never seen one before?' she said, a hint of terseness in her voice which, now Blythe was recovering from the blast, Kelsey registered as surprisingly commanding and theatrical.

'*Umm*, no. What on earth is it for?' she said.

'Gin, of course. Would you care for a glass? I've had greater success with my other batches.'

'Perhaps we should clear away the broken glass first?'

Blythe simply handed Kelsey the dustpan and a long-handled brush and shuffled out of the room.

It took ten minutes for Kelsey to sweep up the shards and wipe down the surfaces, and all the while she could hear Blythe singing, 'the rain it raineth every day,' in the next room.

'Aren't you done yet?' Blythe called out just as Kelsey finished washing her hands and was on her way into the sitting room. 'Oh, you're not going to start gawping around the walls again, are you?'

Blythe was installed centre stage on a faded dusky pink velvet armchair surrounded on all sides by cabinets stuffed full of curious objects.

Kelsey could make out a pair of delicate lace gloves posed on elegant display hands reminiscent of a nineteen forties' fashion house in a Hollywood movie, a white handkerchief embroidered with strawberries, a fan painted with an Arcadian scene and a strange white mask that gave her the creeps. All of these were enclosed behind glass and arranged with a thousand other dainty objects, each more intriguing than the next.

'Sit, down, Miss...'

'Anderson. Kelsey Anderson. I'm your neighbour, actually. I live upstairs in 2B,' she replied as she sat on a plump green upholstered stool with gold fringing. Blythe had arranged a silver tray on the low table between them and on it sat a dish of sliced Madeira cake and two small glasses with short stems filled to the brim with clear liquid. Kelsey could have sworn there were vapours rising from the drinks.

'This is my finest. Heavy on the juniper. Try it.' Blythe's violet eyes sparkled. She had removed the mad scientist goggles and arranged her hair neatly in silky white curtains pinned back behind one ear with a large pink paper rose. Seeing Kelsey's eyes pass over the bloom, Blythe said, 'One should make an effort for cocktail hour, don't you think?' before reaching for her glass, raising it to her delicately painted pink lips, and muttering a quick, 'Good health.' She tipped her white head back, swallowing the whole measure in one gulp, like a student downing happy hour shots at the union bar. Her glass clicking back down on the silver tray sounded like a challenge to Kelsey to do the same, so as Blythe nibbled a slice of cake, a linen napkin spread daintily over her lap, Kelsey lifted her glass and tried a sip.

'*Hough*!' The words she was trying to say burned up in her throat as the spirit headed straight for her bloodstream, stopping to remove at least one layer of skin on the way.

Blythe chuckled and dabbed at the corners of her mouth with the napkin. 'Delicious, isn't it?'

'It's certainly strong. No tonic?'

'Too much faff goes into serving gin these days. If you so much as put a slice of lime or a head of lavender anywhere near my gin, you'd send me prematurely to my grave.'

'You're a purist?' Kelsey grinned.

'I don't go to the trouble of distilling my own liquor for it to be namby-pambied up with a lot of unnecessary nonsense.' Blythe's sharp nod told Kelsey this was her last word on the subject.

'So,' Kelsey cleared her throat. 'Mr Ferdinand said you were an actress?'

'That's right, ten years without a break on stage at the Old Vic and Stratford… and other bits and bobs here and there. Interested in the theatre, are you?'

'Very much.' Kelsey couldn't help her beaming smile.

'Well, I made my debut in a leading role in nineteen sixty-three, just a child I was then, but I'd been *discovered* and I was going to be one of the youngest Ophelias ever to set foot on an English stage. Her Majesty the Queen was in the royal box on opening night.'

'*Wow*!'

'Exactly that. Now, where do you want me?'

'*Mmm*?'

'You're here to take my picture, aren't you?'

'Oh, of course. Just there in your chair is fine. Mr Ferdinand asked me to photograph you with an old theatre prop. Is that OK?'

'Darling, I *am* an old theatre prop.' Blythe cast her eyes over the cabinets. 'Pass me the veil.'

Kelsey followed Blythe's gaze to a corner cabinet housing a dummy head in a long brown wig with a dramatic black lace headdress over it; half the dummy's face was obscured with delicate black filigree.

'Careful with that, it must be over fifty years old. I wore this as the Duchess of Malfi, you know?'

As Kelsey lifted it out of the cabinet, she spotted a picture in its frame of a young woman wearing the very same veil with a long black gown in a medieval Italian style, a swollen stomach accentuated by the folds of the dress.

'Is this you?' she said as she handed the veil over as though she were cradling a delicate new-born thing in her hands.

'That's me. Nineteen sixty-seven. I caused a stir because I was with child at the time. Handy, because the Duchess herself is pregnant for part of the play. The critics went wild. It was the Summer of Love, the height of the permissive society, supposedly. That's what some people called it, anyway. You see, I wasn't married, and there I was, barely nineteen, up in the spotlights, big-bellied and not a bit ashamed.' Blythe's eyes flashed. 'I was magnificent. But, that's when my career began to falter. The permissive society was only really for the boys. Shame nobody told me. I didn't have many starring roles again after that. A lot of long memories in this town. It doesn't do to rock the boat.'

As Blythe spoke, she arranged the veil over her hair, artfully folding the material without the aid of a mirror so that it framed her face without covering it.

Kelsey looked again at the picture. 'You were beautiful.'

This was greeted with a loud tut. 'You young ones assume that's a compliment for an old bird like me. You *were* beautiful! I am *still* beautiful, if only people would take the time to see it.'

'I'm sorry, I didn't mean to offend you.'

'*Tsk, tsk,* little matter.' Blythe waved the moment away with a studied flourish of her wrinkled hand.

'May I open the shutters a little more, please?' Kelsey asked, switching to professional mode, the place where she felt safest.

Her camera was already in her hands, its lens cap unscrewed. She pushed the white wooden shutters apart and the afternoon light dappled by the trees surrounding St. Ninian's Close seeped in, bathing Blythe in soft pink warmth.

'Can I take a few warm-up shots with this one first?' Kelsey held up her old camera. 'I'll give you copies to keep?'

Blythe simply shrugged her agreement and rearranged herself for the shot, saying, 'Haven't seen a camera like that in a quarter of a century.'

'It was my dad's. He left it to me when he died, and it was old even then.' Kelsey mounted the square flash unit to the old camera, sliding it onto the hot shoe plate above the viewfinder and flicking its switch, sending the bulb within into a high-pitched frenzy as it charged up ready for the first shot. 'I love this camera more than I could say.'

Blythe smiled, her lips pressed together. It wasn't the kind of smile Kelsey was used to when she told people about her father. She usually got the lowered eyes, the awkwardness and the sympathetic thin lips. Instead, Blythe's eyes sparkled. A look that said *I know exactly how you feel, and it's all right*. Kelsey felt strangely comforted by it.

Raising the camera to her eye, she positioned herself in front of Blythe in a low crouch and let her breathing settle. Turning the focusing ring brought Blythe's features into greater and greater clarity. Kelsey always found she could see people most clearly through a lens.

Blythe was right; she *was* beautiful. Beautiful right now; not just as some relic of a golden age of her beauty, but a truly beautiful woman. Her skin was thin and her flesh pale and plump. The lines around her eyes were lightly tanned from the summer and had the look of sunrays beaming out from her violet eyes which were soft-lidded and vibrant. Her hair was purest white and her nose long and Roman. Kelsey held her breath and pressed the shutter button, activating the bright flash of light, forcing open the aperture window inside the lens and closing it again in an instant, the light, and Blythe's image, now impressed on the film.

The romance of old-school photography never failed to speak to Kelsey of better times, and she could tell from the look on Blythe's face that she too had been caught up in it.

The actress turned her face to the window and tilted her jaw downwards, letting the natural light catch in her irises. This was a woman who, once upon a time, had been used to having her photograph taken.

Kelsey knew, even though she couldn't see it there and then, even though she'd have to wait a few days for the film to be processed, that she'd caught a perfect shot. And she also knew she'd have to switch to her digital camera soon if Mr Ferdinand wanted his pictures emailed to him by five o'clock, but she still had time, and there was something in Blythe's distant, dreamy expression that told Kelsey she needed to hear the sound of the flashbulb charging and the shutter snapping again, so she raised the camera to her eye once more and Blythe posed, no longer a septuagenarian surrounded by dusty memories and remnants of a bygone era, but a woman bathed in flash light sinking back into the days when she was a sixties stage siren, the hottest new talent, a darling of the golden age of English theatre. Blythe Goode: beautiful, talented, fierce and fearless, the leading lady of the Old Vic and the Royal Shakespeare Theatre.

–

The phone rang to voicemail, and Kelsey pressed it close to her ear so she could revel in the deep drawl of Jonathan's voice. 'Leave a message,' he said with his optimistic upwards inflection. 'And if that's you, Kelsey, I love you.'

This never failed to make her smile, but she didn't leave much of a message, other than an echo of his 'I love you'. She'd call him again later. She wanted to tell him all about her meeting with her wonderful, eccentric neighbour, about the second and third glasses of gin that Blythe had pressed upon her, and how the two of them had sat chatting until nearly five o'clock, Blythe telling her increasingly risqué back stage gossip, all fifty years out of date, but still surprisingly shocking.

'And Larry! Wonderful stage presence and so photogenic, but Kelsey, an absolute rogue and a terrible kisser,' Blythe confided.

'Larry?' Kelsey had asked, squinting now, possibly very squiffy from the gin.

'*Olivier*, darling. Like kissing a tailor's dummy.'

'You acted with Laurence Olivier?' Kelsey had gasped.

Blythe cackled wickedly. 'I didn't say I'd *acted* with him.'

Kelsey knew Jonathan would love her neighbour's stories, even if they were, as she suspected, peppered with exaggeration. She also knew he'd be proud of her scoring freelance work with the newspaper. She'd emailed him the digital images at the same time as she'd sent them to Mr Ferdinand at exactly five to five – it wouldn't do to miss the deadline on her first commission. They were beautifully quirky and characterful portraits of Blythe in all her dramatic lacy head-dress glory.

Kelsey had been pleased with the pictures for the newspaper but she knew the images she'd taken on her new digital SLR wouldn't be a patch on the deeply saturated glossy depth of the pictures hidden away in her dad's old manual Canon AE1.

Tossing her phone onto her bed, she reached for the heavy retro camera, so very comfortingly solid and metallic, and she wound the spool back into its metal case before flipping open the camera's back. If she made a dash for the high street she could get the film in the last post of the day to the specialist developer she'd used since moving to England, and in a week or so she'd be sent the traditional silver gelatin prints all the way from the lab in Cheshire, one of the last of its kind in the country. Kelsey grabbed the film, stuffed it in an envelope and ran for the door.

Chapter Six

'Though those that are betray'd do feel the treason sharply,
yet the traitor stands in worse case of woe'
(*Cymbeline*)

Mirren was a proponent of the 'in car scream'. She'd told Kelsey
about its therapeutic benefits many times, but not having a car,
the advice had never helped Kelsey.

In the past, Mirren had used the technique to scream out her
frustration or to ward off tears and disappointment as she drove
home from work of an evening, and she'd found the release of
energy helped her switch from miserable work mode to a new
frame of mind; her 'heading home to eat ice cream from the
tub and drink wine' frame of mind.

Tonight, as she drove through late afternoon twilight along
the coast heading out of Edinburgh to the harbour town where
she lived, Mirren had drawn a deep breath and screamed
her loudest celebratory scream, her lungs fit to burst with
exhilaration and triumphant joy.

This was what success felt like, something Mirren had little
experience of at the *Broadsheet*. Hard work, graft, slogging her
guts out and being passed up time and again for promotions,
she knew what *those* felt like, but actually reaping the rewards
and being recognised for her dedication? Never. At least, not
until today.

She gripped the steering wheel, bouncing her shoulders off
the backrest as she let her voice soar. Nobody could hear her, or

see her, and no one thought she was crazy; that was the beauty of the in-car scream.

She was going to write the best feature Mr Angus had ever read. She'd research her topic in forensic detail, she'd conduct her interviews like a reporter uncovering a world-changing scoop, and she'd write up her copy with the linguistic flare of Robert Burns, Maya Angelou and Christina Rossetti combined. To be clear, she was going to prove herself and at last get the promotion she deserved.

Anybody could write up the court stories – the brilliant interns could do it in their sleep, instead of spending their days restocking the stationery cupboard, making coffee for other people and, on rare occasions, collecting senior reporters' kids from school and taking them to McDonald's until their dads were done for the day. Anybody with even a vague famil-iarity with the English language could write the stories she wrote. Only this morning she'd filed a sixty-word report about a woman charged with stealing twelve pairs of scissors. The accused hadn't turned up for her court appearance and was bound over to stop nicking things for twelve months in her absence. Nothing to it. But writing a feature required a whole other skill set, and Mirren was more than ready to prove she had what it takes to wow the readers of the women's pages in the weekend editions.

What with the joyful vocalisations and all of her daydreaming as she navigated the congested traffic that choked up her little quayside town, she didn't realise exactly what she had done until it was too late. Not until she had found a parking space, pulled on the handbrake and unclicked her seatbelt did it occur to her where she was.

She wasn't at her mum's house where she now lived. She'd found her way back to the grey stone flat she and Preston had shared until only a few weeks ago. The softest unconscious parts of her brain had led her there, and deep down Mirren knew why.

She'd wanted to tell Preston all about her day. He had been the first person she'd thought of when Mr Angus accepted her pitch. As her heart had swelled with pride it had nudged the little muscle of long habit that told her to get home quick and tell Preston. He'd want to celebrate, probably insist on going out to buy some bubbly and having a chippy tea on the harbour wall, watching the late boats come in, like they used to. But that subconscious reflex that forever linked feelings of home, safety and celebration with Preston was a faulty one. She didn't live here anymore, and neither did Preston. But it was too late. Here she was.

Mirren looked up at the windows of their flat on the second floor. The new occupants had gone for green curtains over the blinds Preston had fitted all by himself when they'd moved in together way back at the end of high school. Everyone had said they were too young, none more vociferously than Mirren's mum, but they'd been so happy, at first, and they had shared every aspect of their lives from the ages of sixteen to twenty-eight – everything except Mirren's cheating.

The blue light from a screen flickered in the window. Someone would notice her soon if she didn't get away and Mirren couldn't bear to look at the flat any longer. *Regret is a terrible, clever thing,* she reflected. *It mingles with all of your guilt and comes creeping up on you when you're not expecting it, and baam! It hits you.* Her chest heaved and a hard sigh forced its way out of her mouth. Then the tears welled. She'd hurt him so badly.

She could remember it all so clearly. The first of September; the day she'd arrived home from Stratford after visiting Kelsey, resolved that she'd cheated on Preston for the last time, determined to make things right and leave him in peace. She'd had no idea how he would take it. He'd always been so docile, so gentle, accepting of people's failings and frailties. He'd been fun too, quick to laugh and make light of difficult situations. Then there were his talents: for music (he could make his Gibson guitar sing like Springsteen); for making friends, and keeping them; for caring for people – he'd visited Kelsey's grandfather for tea and chats when everyone else was at work or just plain busy, and nobody had ever thought to thank him properly. Poor, loving, overlooked Preston. She'd trampled on his feelings and everything he'd believed in.

She hadn't just told him about her fling with Will Greville – the guy with the posh accent and auburn hair and condoms in his wallet at the theatrical gala in Stratford – she'd told him about the others too, dredging up memories from years ago of men whose faces she couldn't even remember. It had been a great unburdening, a full confession.

Looking back now, she saw how cruel that had been; handing him the guilt that had troubled her for years, passing it on to him to convert into pain and shock. Some things are better left unsaid. Mirren had come to learn that the hard way.

Yet, a deep part of her had resolved to go all in. That's how self-sabotage works. She'd told herself that if she didn't stand there, look Preston in the eyes, and reveal to him the full depth of her infidelity, there was a chance he'd simply forgive her for making a one-off mistake, no matter how much he'd suffer in silence afterwards. The thought of what that forgiveness would feel like sickened her. He'd promise never to mention it again and he'd stick to his word, and every kind thing he did for her from then on would drag Mirren down into the mire of her guilt.

Preston had been her safe space since they were kids when the three of them, Kelsey included, were firm after-school theatre club friends. He deserved better than a patched-up relationship riddled with lies, faithfully residing with someone unable to admit to another living soul the terrible, secret thing she'd done five years ago that kick started all the self-destruction. She would barely allow herself to acknowledge it, and she hadn't told Preston either, not even during her great confession.

No, he deserved better than her, always had. She'd had to bring about the absolute implosion of her relationship, making sure Preston couldn't ever forgive her.

It had crushed her heart to see it work so perfectly.

He'd sat in silence, tears running down his face, distraught. He hadn't believed her at first, then he simply hadn't wanted to believe her. Then he'd asked her to stop talking. He had gathered up his books, a bundle of jeans and t-shirts, his laptop and his wallet, slung his guitar cases over his shoulders and walked out the door, leaving his key behind. And she hadn't seen him since. Their friendship of fifteen long years was severed.

She'd sat in the flat for days, letting it all sink in, thinking of the pain she'd burdened him with in order to set him free, as she replayed over and over again images of what she'd done in Stratford.

It had been such a beautiful evening at the theatrical gala, the last day of what had been a dazzling and beautiful August. Mirren had felt like a knockout in her red, sequined dress. She and Kelsey had been roped in to taking part in a *tableau vivant* by Kelsey's pushy, brilliant boss, Norma Arden.

The thrill of being on stage that night, striking a frozen pose under the spotlights as they created the wonderfully artistic living picture in front of a cooing audience, along with the heady buzz from the complimentary drinks all evening had somehow made it seem acceptable to Mirren to take Will's hand and let him lead her through the garden.

It had seemed enchanted and full of music and magic that late summer's night, as she'd followed him up the steps into the old tree house and let him kiss her in the half light.

She remembered his velvet Elizabethan costume, and his English accent, classy and crisp, saying, 'You really are some-thing else,' as he'd slipped his hands inside her dress, and for a moment she'd let her mind go blank and her senses take over.

He'd been passionate and gentle enough, but he hadn't noticed her breathing stilling as her excitement faded and as she opened her eyes to watch the dust motes sparkling in the dying light from the stained glass of the tree house's antique windows. She'd let her head roll loosely against his shoulder as his breathing and his movements sharpened, and she'd thought the same two familiar words that she'd thought on other occasions with other devilishly handsome, smart-talking men: '*This again?*'

Mirren had known then she'd have to go home and tell Preston it really was over this time. And so she'd watched his car pull away from the home they'd shared for years and the relationship they'd settled into since high school, knowing that the little flame of love that Preston had always carried for her, when no one else in the world – excepting Kelsey – adored her, was snuffed out by her own hand.

She didn't know how long she cried for, sitting in her car outside the old flat, but it had grown cool and dark when she lifted her head from her hands and reached for the ignition. She drove home to her mum's house in the silence of the autumn evening.

She'd only lasted a fortnight alone in that flat. It was impossible keeping up the rent on her own, so she'd moved to her mum's, trying not to acknowledge that both of them knew it was absolutely her last resort.

—

'I'm back,' Mirren called, placing her keys in the bowl by the door.

The little kitchen was spotlessly clean. The strip light buzzed above her. She tiptoed over the vinyl tiles and onto the landing at the foot of the stairs. The television was on in the otherwise dark living room and through the glass door Mirren could make out the broad Scottish accents of the gritty detective serial her mum was currently addicted to. *Should I go in and tell her about getting the feature?* Mirren wondered. *Will she be pleased?*

'You didn't come straight home then?' her mum called from the living room and at the slurred sound of the greeting Mirren dismissed all thoughts of sharing her good news. She pushed the door open and popped her head round the frame. Jeanie Imrie didn't look round from her armchair where she sat with her legs curled beneath her.

'I had a wander down Princes Street to see the sales. Didn't get anything though.' A little white lie was needed, Mirren knew. She couldn't tell her mum what had happened; how her full heart had turned back into a broken one after her autopilot journey towards Preston. She was about to pull her head back out of the room and climb the stairs to bed when her mum spoke again.

'You missed him.'

'Who?' Mirren made her way into the living room now, but stood behind her mum's chair. She couldn't mean her father, could she? Not when he hadn't shown his face once in almost a decade?

Jeanie, eyes fixed on the screen, nodded towards the pile of clothes neatly folded over the arm of the sofa, exactly at the moment Mirren spotted them.

'Some of your things were mixed up with his when he packed his bags. So he brought them round.'

Mirren looked towards the door she'd just come through. 'Preston? How long ago was that?' Her mind raced. Could she catch him up? Was he still walking to his car? She hadn't seen it out on the street as she'd pulled around the back of their row of houses and into the garage.

'An hour since.'

'Oh.' Mirren tried to shrug off the sudden hope and the disappointment. Before she could ask how he'd seemed or where he'd been going, Jeanie was on her feet and walking over to the TV, switching it off with the button at the side.

'You didn't deserve a nice laddie like that.' Jeanie Imrie sailed past her daughter towards the door, and as she passed by Mirren caught the familiar sickly smell of whisky and cola. She hadn't needed to look for the glass by the side of the armchair, but she did see the unsteadiness in her mother's steps and the dark glaze over her eyes that she'd known since her childhood.

It had been a few weeks since she'd seen her like this – not drunk, not by any means, but what her dad, long ago when he still lived with them, called 'topped up'. But she knew the pattern, the steady daily drinking, a few whiskies every night, gradually building up into a whole bottle at the weekend, and her mother never being entirely sober for weeks at a time. When had she started again? Mirren couldn't be sure. But she knew it meant she was going to hear her mum's opinions on Preston tonight and there was very little she could do to avoid it.

'OK, well I'm going to bed now. Night night,' Mirren said weakly.

'He asked after you. Don't you want to know how the poor laddie's doing?' Jeanie didn't meet her daughter's eye, not once, as she bustled around the living room, rearranging the ornaments and the box of tissues with fumbling fingers, repositioning a vase of tall gladioli on its crocheted mat.

Mirren said nothing, mentally calculating how long it would take her mum to run through her routine – there was still the compulsive bedtime wipe-down of the kitchen surfaces with neat bleach to go – and she could quietly take herself off to her childhood bedroom upstairs.

'You just couldn't look after him though, could you? Couldn't control yourself. He was a perfectly nice boy, but did you want him? No, not you, not Mirren. She always wants what she can't have, and look where that's got you,' said Jeanie, a slur slowing her speech, and all the while she was tidying the magazines in the rack by the side of the sofa.

'All right, well, I'm tired, I'm going to get to bed.' Mirren knew not to challenge her mum, it was easier just to listen and try to deflect the worst bits, try not to let it sink in. But, as she also knew from long experience, some things stick in your mind, especially when it's your own mother saying them.

At last, Jeanie was on the move into the kitchen, and Mirren followed her through the door and turned for the stairs, but she knew there would be a parting shot.

'If you were meeting another of your dates tonight, you ken exactly what I think of that. Don't even *think* about bringing one of your men friends here. You treat this place like a hotel as it is, don't be turning it into a brothel too.'

Mirren paused halfway up the stairs, but didn't turn round. Her mum was gone anyway. She heard the sound of the cupboard under the sink being opened and the hollow thud of the bleach bottle being placed on the draining board. Her mum was busy, cloth in hand.

By the time Jeanie had scrubbed the already gleaming kitchen taps, Mirren had her teeth brushed and was changed into her pyjamas. She slid under the covers in the dark and listened for her mum making her way to her own room, accompanied by the chink of a glass against a whisky bottle at every step.

She lay in bed thinking over every word that had been slung at her. All true. She couldn't just be happy with her lot, she always selfishly wanted something, or someone else.

She hadn't needed to ask her mum how Preston was, she already knew. She'd seen his band's Instagram and Facebook pages; they were in the middle of a tour of clubs and bars across Scotland. In the pictures Preston was smiling, or looking cool and moody, his Gibson low on its strap across his body. He'd been waiting for this moment all his life, when the local gigs, demos and studio time began paying off. Before she'd set off for that fateful weekend in Stratford in August she'd known there was an indie label showing interest in them. Preston must be having the time of his life. She hoped with a sad pang that the broken heart she'd handed him wasn't tainting the newfound success he'd worked so hard for.

She'd seen the pictures, posted by women, tagging him. Blurry, dark nightclub scenes, tables cluttered with glasses. Beautiful young women and the boys from the band, cheek-kisses and heads close together, white-teeth grins. It stung to be reminded how much she missed being that close to him, but she wouldn't let herself regret setting him free. The band had a following of fans already. He'd soon be on tour in England too, and then... anywhere. The world was at his feet, now she'd let him go. He'd taken to being single as though it hadn't just been Mirren waiting for their life to begin.

It was too late to call Kelsey, and she was crying too hard to make sense anyway, so she reached for her phone, as she always did late at night now she was installed back at her mum's house. Opening the app, she started scrolling, swiping left, looking for a stranger to talk to.

Chapter Seven

'All days are nights to see till I see thee,
And nights bright days when dreams do show thee me'
(*Sonnet 43*)

Autumn always brought with it a 'back to school' feeling of renewal that Kelsey never failed to get caught up in. *This* was the start of the new year as far as she was concerned. A time when, if she was lucky, she treated herself to new boots to see her through the cold months; a time when, inspired by the changing colours around her, she'd feel inclined to experiment with her make-up palette, not something that interested her much at other times of the year, and she started reaching for her berry lipsticks instead of her pink nudes.

She'd bemoaned her situation to Mirren over the phone, telling her, 'Jonathan's missing the three weeks of the year where I look ace,' and she just knew Mirren was rolling her eyes and readying herself for an emphatic speech about how Kelsey looked great every day of the year so she'd better stop putting herself down like that.

But Kelsey, like all autumn-born babies with an affinity for this magical time of year, knew what she was talking about, and it was the weather that did it. October's dry days were perfect for her Celtic hair, prone to bedraggling in summer heat and winter damp. These few weeks between seasons were the Goldilocks time for her golden-brown locks, and she made the most of it.

Her autumn bloom always coincided with her birthday, and Kelsey had turned twenty-nine only days ago. Mirren had phoned to wish her well and, noticing her friend was down, Kelsey tried her best to draw out the reason why, but Mirren wouldn't say a word other than her usual breezy, 'You know me, Kelse, I'm always fine, just busy.' So Kelsey had dropped it and thanked Mirren for the big bags of Percy Pigs chewy sweets – which hadn't lasted long at all – and the Netflix gift card which Kelsey had immediately splurged on a Keanu Reeves marathon.

Her mum, little brother Calum and grandad, all living together back home in Scotland, had posted a big package of things they knew she'd love to her little bedsit.

There was a new jar of moisturiser, and a book about photography her mum had doubtless found in a charity shop and which was perfect inspiration as Kelsey settled into her new job. There was a new jumper too, big, baggy and super soft in sapphire blue, a departure for Kelsey from her reliance on autumnal browns and oranges all year round. Best of all, there had been a gift card for a hair salon in the town centre.

Kelsey had walked past its doors many times that summer as she'd beaten the streets leading her tour groups from ancient building to hidden garden, but she'd never set foot inside. The salon always looked intimidatingly trendy to Kelsey, but she had delightedly pushed through the doors to make her appointment.

Only this morning she'd left through those doors, an eighty-quid gift token and ten inches of wild, tawny-blonde hair lighter.

'Like it?' she said, peering at Jonathan's grinning face on her tablet now she was home again, swishing her hair and enjoying the novelty of the neat ends skimming her shoulders.

'Beautiful. You look beautiful.'

'Like someone who owns their own business? You'd trust this woman with your wedding photos, right?'

'I'd trust you with anything, my heart included.'

They smiled at their screens, Jonathan's straight white teeth flashing beneath curling lips in the American smile that had kick-started Kelsey's slow-burn attraction to him the day she had, literally, bumped into him at the café with the pink awnings by the marina; the slow burn that had soon turned into a loved-up inferno no distance or time apart could extinguish.

After a moment she turned her phone, angling it to the table and vase in the corner of her tiny white bedsit, showing Jonathan the lavish flowers he'd sent her for her birthday. 'They've opened up even more. Aren't they lovely? I wish you were here to smell their perfume.'

He'd taken care to contact the florist in the town's smart shopping arcade that she had admired so often, and he'd listed every flower he'd ever seen mentioned in a Shakespeare play or poem for the florist to choose from. When the delivery arrived at St. Ninian's there was a note attached in Jonathan's handwriting listing each flower in turn. The whole thing must have taken days to orchestrate.

> For Kelsey, my love and my leading lady, on your
> birthday. Here's flowering rosemary for remem-
> brance (Hamlet), sweet musk-roses and eglantine
> (A Midsummer Night's Dream), lady-smocks all
> silver-white (Love's Labour's Lost), and carnations
> and streak'd gillyflowers (The Winter's Tale). I
> hope you like them. They're sent with all my love,
> J, x

The whole spray was bold and bright and a little untidy with a hint of wild nature about it, much like Jonathan himself. He really couldn't have sent a more appropriate gift.

'I'm wishing the days away until Christmas and you flying in, but I wish I could freeze this bouquet in time and have it last forever,' said Kelsey, letting him see her face once more.

Jonathan smiled fondly, his eyes shining. 'I'll just have to send you more when those ones fade.'

'Does acting pay that much?' she laughed.

'Ah, well, let's not talk about that.' He flashed his smile again, his cheeks making his eyes close in crescents and showing Kelsey that dimple on his chin, the one that should have been illegal it was so appealing.

'I wish you were here,' she said in a quiet voice. Not for the first time she felt the miles between them. So often as she walked through town she'd see their old haunts and be struck with the knowledge of how depleted her everyday life was without the possibility of running into him there, so closely was he linked to her sense of the place, and yet she'd forced herself to carry on and discover new sides to Stratford, and herself, and to keep testing out her independence all the more. Still, she was allowed to sulk sometimes and this was one of them.

'I wish I was there too,' said Jonathan. 'But I'm with you all the time, and I'm not going anywhere. Just hold on. You keep working on the studio, and I'll keep dying on stage every night as Hamlet.' He mimed his body recoiling from the sword-stabbing action of his fist towards his chest and pulled a face at his own joke. Kelsey couldn't help but smile at his goofiness. 'It'll be December twenty-third before we know it, 'kay?'

'All right.'

'Talk to you tomorrow?'

'Sunrise?'

'Sunrise. I love you.'

His image disappeared from her phone screen and she sat back on her bed with a sigh. This waiting was proving harder than she thought. Last month she'd been convinced that the morning he left had been the hardest part, but this was a whole new kind of longing.

She thought back to the last time they'd been in touching distance, trying to bring back the feel of his hands and the scent of his skin. That night, their last together until midwinter when Jonathan would return for the briefest of Christmas vacations, had proved to be the most intense of their short relationship.

It was September the fourth. His flight was at five a.m., so he'd be setting off from Stratford in a cab in the pre-dawn light. Neither of them intended to sleep that night.

It had been only the fourth night they'd spent together after a long summer of getting to know each other. Four nights since they'd shared those first ardent 'I love you's and fallen into Kelsey's bed.

On their last night, they'd spent the evening drinking champagne at the Yorick pub with the rest of Norma's tour guide staff, all out of work and wondering what the autumn ahead held for them, but they'd left before everyone else, keen to make the most of their last precious hours together.

Still light enough in the evenings for the room to glow with the orange and pink of a watery summer's end sunset, they'd begun peeling away each other's clothes, letting their eyes take in each new inch of skin as it was exposed, standing over Kelsey's single bed in her pristine white bedsit at the top of the Victorian building under the terracotta tiles and the sloping eves where the summer heat still lingered.

Kelsey remembered how Jonathan's breath caught and grew increasingly shaky as she traced her fingertips across his broad collar bones and down his chest, while both of them tried to forget his suitcase by the door, ready for his departure.

'I can't believe you're going and I won't be able to do this to you whenever I want,' she said, stretching up on her arches to press a kiss into the thick sinewed warmth of his neck.

For a moment, Jonathan wordlessly relished her lips skimming his skin, rolling his head back and closing his eyes drowsily before bringing Kelsey's face before his, steadying her with his hands cupping her jaw, his fingertips reaching the nape of her neck.

'It'll pass and I'll come back to you, for Christmas.' His eyes narrowed as his gaze fell to her lips again.

'I love you, Kelsey. Now I've found you, I won't ever let you go,' he said as he trailed his mouth from her lips to her neck and slowly down over her stomach to between her thighs where he'd lingered, making her inner muscles tense and soften as he listened to her moans, letting her responses guide his tongue and soft lips.

She'd told him she loved him too, the words getting lost in gasps as she scrunched his dark brown waves in her fingers, loving the softness of his hair against her skin. There wasn't a thing about this beautiful man she didn't love.

No, they'd had no intention of sleeping that last night. She'd had time enough to make sure he understood exactly how she felt before three a.m. and the cabby's knock.

He'd left, Kelsey calculated, staring at the blank phone screen in her hands with a heavy sigh, six weeks, four hours, forty-three minutes and twenty-two seconds ago.

Jonathan wasn't the only one faithfully counting the days.

Chapter Eight

'Thou art thy mother's glass, and she in thee
Calls back the lovely April of her prime'
(*Sonnet 3*)

'Mirren! What a nice surprise, come in.'

Mari Anderson, Kelsey's mum, knew how to make people feel welcome. She'd opened her home up years ago to her hair-dressing clients, many of whom outstayed their appointment times to drink tea and chat. The house was often full of Calum's friends too.

Kelsey's little brother was known amongst his group of cosplaying, sci-fi obsessed pals as the host of his nerdy friendship circle. Moments before Mirren arrived, a four and a half foot tall Boba Fett and a surprisingly well made-up Queen Amidala had run inside and were now scoffing popcorn and energy drinks in Calum's room. Mari never seemed to mind the stream of kookily dressed kids who appeared at her door, and she had always made Mirren feel welcome too whenever she'd called round. That was just the kind of woman she was.

Kelsey's grandfather, who had recently moved in with the family, was reclined open-mouthed and dreaming in front of the TV. He'd been sleeping in Kelsey's old room and benefitting from Mari's home cooking and the lightening of the burden that looking after his old marital home had become since the death of his wife many years ago now. Mirren slipped the big bundle of Edinburgh rock she'd brought for him onto the kitchen worktop.

'I'm sorry to intrude. Are you busy?' Mirren asked.

'Don't be daft. I was just away to put the kettle on and you'll save me eating this coffee cake all by myself.'

Mirren's shoulders dropped with the relief. This was exactly the kind of welcome she knew she would receive, having been all but adopted by the Anderson family since her school days, and yet, having been raised in a volatile home, a small part of her still expected that one day the calm, friendly Andersons might not be pleased to see her and she might be turned away. Such is the never-ending insecurity that accompanies the adult child of parents who swing between extremes of kindness and cruelty.

'Kelsey told me you might drop round actually, and I was hoping you would,' Mari said with an easy smile.

After a little while chatting, brewing tea and arranging the plates and forks, the pair settled in front of the old range in the kitchen of Mari's little grey stone terrace overlooking the steely waves of the Firth of Forth beyond the concrete sea wall.

'So how are things back at your mum's?' Mari asked, diplomatically avoiding eye contact by pouring the milk.

'It's… well it's…' Mirren struggled for the words. She didn't like to criticise her mother and would more often than not avoid the topic altogether, but Mari was familiar with the cycles of drinking followed by long periods of sobriety and renewed fervour for life that Jeanie Imrie suffered through. Mari knew all about the hospital admissions too and that one summer Jeanie spent in a private rehab facility which had prompted Mirren to move in with Preston's family and the sixteen-year-old had started eating healthily, sleeping well, and for the first time in a long time she lost her gauntness and had the look of teenage bloom about her. Recently, Mirren had let herself wonder if she and Preston would have begun the search for a flat of their own at eighteen if it wasn't for her precarious home life, but she packed the thoughts away now.

'It's strange after living with Preston for so long,' Mirren said in a rush. 'I'm looking for my own place, just haven't found anything yet,' she said with a shrug as though it was only a small worry.

'Oh well, it's not for too long then, is it? You'll soon find somewhere nice,' Mari said generously, but seeing through Mirren's bluff.

A loud snore from the living room caused them both to turn their heads in Kelsey's grandad's direction. Mari's eye caught Mirren's, conveying so much without any words. She would have offered her daughter's best friend a bed if she'd had the room, but with her elderly dad's new living arrangements it wasn't possible. Mirren returned the look with a crinkle of her eyes in an understanding, grateful smile.

'I quite fancy doing what Kelsey did, just getting away, a complete change of scene, you know?'

Mari nodded. 'She's certainly found her place.' Unmistakable pride and warmth accompanied the words. 'I was worried she'd never spread her wings.'

'I know. I see how happy she is. I'm tied to work, though. I can't exactly leave the country.'

'*Hmm.*' Mari trod carefully. 'How did your promotion go?'

'Oh, it didn't. They gave it to… someone else.' The utter smugness mixed with faux modesty on Jamesey Wallace's face as Mr Angus awarded the promotion at the team-building away day last month flashed in Mirren's memory. She'd been sure that this time she had it in the bag. Losing to Jamesey made being passed over yet again smart all the more.

'Next time, eh?' Mari said, handing Mirren the larger of two slices of cake.

'Yeah, next time. They are letting me write a feature though on Christmas theatre excursions.'

'They are? And we're sitting here drinking tea?' Mari was already on the move, reaching for the fridge door and the prosecco inside. 'We're celebrating that!'

Soon they were sipping bubbly and Mirren was asking how things were going without Kelsey around.

'Aye, great,' Mari answered. 'We're busy. Dad's nurse visits every few days. Calum spends most of his time with his friends in other galaxies, and I'm working a lot. People will always need their hair cut, right?'

Mirren leaned in a little, cocking her head at Mari's expression, wondering if she didn't look a little sad. '*But?*' Mirren coaxed.

Mari swiped a hand and smiled, dismissing the little niggle she'd betrayed.

'You can't kid a kidder,' Mirren added.

'Well… oh, God, don't tell Kelsey, she'll only worry.' Mari huffed out a sharp breath, meeting Mirren's eyes. 'It's just one of my clients, a friend actually, *umm…*'

'Go on.'

'She set me up with a friend of hers, a guy, and I can't say it went well. We met in the Bonnie Prince Charlie for a drink last week but it was all a bit stilted. I haven't been out on a Friday night since Lewis passed, let alone going out on a date, and even though it felt like it might be the right time, it definitely wasn't the right person. I haven't slept very well since, thinking about it all, you know? I feel a bit unsettled, a bit… lonely.'

Mirren had to tell herself not to let her excitement show too much. This was exactly what Kelsey had hoped would happen and she'd often told Mirren her dream that one day her mum would feel ready to meet someone new.

It had been fourteen long years since Kelsey's dad passed away in a tragic, horrible motorway accident that had stolen a devoted dad from baby Calum and teenage Kelsey, and left Mari mourning the love of her life and her childhood sweetheart.

This was the first time Mari had ever shown any signs of being ready to take the first tentative steps into dating and Mirren knew if she let the excitement fizzing within her show she could easily spook Mari and put her off dating for the rest of her life.

After a measured breath, Mirren reached for her phone. 'You could try one of my dating apps. I use them sometimes.' *All the time*, she thought. 'And I've met some really nice men on them.' She tried to remember exactly which of the men she'd have classed as *really nice*. Fair enough, some of them were friendly but some were plain dull, and then there were the guys with their wedding rings hidden in their wallets, the no-shows, the liars and fantasists, and the one whose profile picture featured a muscled underwear model from Italy when in reality he was a paunchy chip shop owner from Kilmarnock.

Mirren thought it best not to mention these small misgivings to Mari who was peering with some interest at Mirren's phone as she scrolled through the apps.

It took half an hour and only a little cajoling to convince a blushing, flustered Mari to set up her profile picture. She had a fortnight's free trial on a site for women over forty seeking dates with single professionals.

Mirren snapped a picture of her by the window in the soft autumn light and attached it to her profile. It was a good picture. Even Mari liked it. Mari had always been proud of her long hair, once dark, now beautifully sparkling with a few silvery strands. Kelsey got her light brown Celtic waves from Lewis's side of the family, who were firmly in the freckled, sandy-haired-leaning-towards-ginger part of the genome, but Mari was dark, tall and curvy, more like Mirren than her daughter Kelsey.

They clicked the 'Go Live' button on Mari's dating profile, and refilled their glasses, clinking them in celebration before reopening the app and scrolling through the profiles, placing a love-heart 'bookmark' on some of the sweeter-looking men.

Mari's reactions showed she definitely still had a type; quiet-looking strawberry blonds with glasses and soft smiles, men like Lewis. They'd married straight out of school and Kelsey had come along after a few years of domestic bliss. Though no one could ever come close to replicating his kindness and gentle nature, Mari Anderson, for the very first time, and at the age of fifty-six, was ready to meet someone new, and Mirren grinned at the sight of Mari blushing and trying not to get too swept up in the excitement as she pored over the profiles.

Mirren couldn't help thinking of how Mari was intent on changing her life, just like her daughter had recently with her move to England. If they could do it, she thought, could her own mum, who she loved so much in spite of everything, turn things around in her sixties and begin a happier, healthier life again? Would she ever be able to talk unguardedly with Jeanie the way she did with Kelsey's mum? Her heart sank in answer to the questions so she drained her glass and fixed her eyes on Mari's scrolling profiles once more.

Chapter Nine

'I count myself in nothing else so happy
As in a soul remembering my good friends'
(*Richard II*)

'OK, that's definitely a bit of blue sky. If I don't try now, the rainclouds will be back.'

Kelsey grabbed her camera case and the box of business cards her mum had sent her as a gift weeks ago and headed out of the studio and down the stairs. She'd spent the first two hours of her working day sitting at her desk waiting for the phone to ring, hoping even just one of the local schools would respond to her hastily sent on-spec emails and invite her to do the new term photographs, but nobody had. Mr Ferdinand hadn't given her another commission yet either, and nor had he paid her. She glanced at the date on her phone. It was Friday the sixteenth of October and her business *still* wasn't off the ground.

'Sitting here isn't working; this is just wasting time,' she scolded herself, so she took to the street, all the while repeating the mantra, 'Make Success Happen'.

This was something she'd heard her ex-boyfriend, Fran, say many times. It had worked for him; he was well on his way to becoming a young headmaster at his posh grey-walled school back in Scotland, his dream job and life's ambition.

A light autumn breeze blew down Henley Street, making the leaves swirl. The cafés were still busy, mainly with locals and their dogs stopping mid-walk for a cream tea in spite of the morning's rain bursts.

'Desperate times, and all that,' Kelsey muttered as she made her way towards the house where Shakespeare was born, now a major tourist attraction and one of Kelsey's favourite spots in all the world. She had visited with her dad years ago on their last ever family holiday and he'd handed her his camera for the first time, letting her snap pictures of the pretty, old cottage. She couldn't walk past the spot now without imagining her younger self there and her gentle dad by her side, coaching her on how to turn the camera's focusing ring and get the light metering right. That holiday, and in particular that one moment, had influenced her future path so much that the spirit of Lewis Anderson was inextricably entangled in her love of the town, of Shakespeare, and photography; loves that had only grown as she aged.

Stopping across the wide street from the heritage spot where the Shakespeare family crest flapped wildly at the end of the flagpole in the cottage garden, she scanned left to right. Now the weather was improving the tourists would hit the streets again on the hunt for selfies and souvenirs, and she'd be there to meet them.

Having worked as a tour guide that summer she'd found her voice and lost the self-consciousness that seemed bred into working-class Scottish girls back home, so she knew she'd be fine approaching the bus-loads of tourists as they made their way from beauty spot to historic wonder.

'Hello, I'm Kelsey Anderson of Kelsey Anderson Photography. Would you like me to take your picture? I'll print them within the hour, ready for you to collect at my studio. Eight pounds for a ten by twelve...'

She lost count of how many times she ran through her spiel, almost never getting to the end of it before being met by a silent, polite bow, a clipped 'no thank you', a full body swerve, or worst of all, the blank disinterest of someone intent on ignoring her as though she weren't even there.

'Excuse me, *emm*, excuse me, sorry. One hour portraits in front of Shakespeare's birthplace? Only five pounds, yours to treasure... OK, never mind.'

Dropping her prices wasn't working either. Yet another couple waved their hands in awkward dismissal. She could see herself from their point of view and it made her cringe. They had no reason to believe that she wasn't some kind of fraudster, out to trick unwary tourists into parting with the unfamiliar sterling in their wallets.

An hour passed and she hadn't taken a single shot, let alone raced along the street to the chemist's where the photo-printing machine she'd planned on using waited idly.

'You don't have examples of your work? How am I supposed to know what these shots will turn out like? And what guarantee do I have that you'll even be here in an hour?' asked a bluff American in a red baseball cap pushed down over sandy hair. 'You could be anybody.'

'I know, but I'm not. That's my studio just over there, and here's my business card with my mobile number, you can ring it now if you like, so you'll know for sure...'

But he was already walking away, re-joining his family as they queued for tickets for Shakespeare's house. He'd made a good point. She needed a board of some kind with pictures on and a price list, something that made her look more legit. Was she even allowed to do that? Unsure if taking commercial street shots was even lawful, she felt convinced some local statute or other would prevent her setting up an actual stall or putting out a board without a permit.

The bells of Holy Trinity on the riverside tolled one o'clock as she called it an unsuccessful day – besides, the clouds were closing in again and the air was growing damp.

'Well that was a total failure. I should have planned this properly,' she chided herself, zipping her camera away in its case ready to trudge back to the studio for a long afternoon hitting 'refresh' on the inbox.

'*Kelsey?*' someone called from a distance behind her.

It was a voice she knew well; a loud, Texan drawl like Jerry Hall. She spun round to be greeted by its owner pacing down Henley Street towards her, her arms outstretched.

'Myrtle! I *knew* that was you.'

'Honey, are you tour-guiding again? What about your photography studio? Is everything OK?'

'Oh, no, things are fine, brilliant in fact, but I could use a little more trade at the studio... and I thought...' Kelsey's words faltered. She'd worked closely with Myrtle, one of the agency's best and longest-serving tour guides, all summer. Myrtle had been able to see through Kelsey's hidden attraction to Jonathan and she could see through this false jollity too.

'You look like you need a break. You got time?' Myrtle was already looping an arm into Kelsey's and walking her through the clusters of tourists making peace signs into their selfie sticks towards the little café by the newsagent's. The foody aromas in the air reminded Kelsey she hadn't eaten yet.

That was one of the best things about Stratford, Kelsey had found; you're never more than ten feet away from the nearest freshly baked scone, but today she hesitated, thinking of the dwindling cash in her bank account. She'd managed to save a tiny proportion of her tour guiding wages and all of her tips, but now that money was running out. Even the money from the joint bank account that Fran, her ex back home, had split between them, was almost gone, spent on her rents – the bedsit and Norma's old office – paid for until February, thank goodness. The rest was spent on getting the studio up to scratch. 'Oh, I don't know, I...' she flustered.

'My treat.' Myrtle patted her hand. 'Have you been hiding away at the studio? We haven't seen you in weeks.'

'I've been so busy, but I don't feel like I've achieved much yet— Hold up a sec!' Kelsey's eyes fell upon the newspaper stand between the newsagent and the café's doors. '*Look!*' There on the rack amongst the garish, alarmist tabloid headlines was

Blythe Goode, a vision in pastel pink and black lace, raising her gin glass with a bold stare down Kelsey's lens. 'I took those pictures.'

Myrtle was by her side and reaching for her own copy of the *Examiner* as Kelsey showed it to anyone walking by who would listen. 'Front cover shots! I took these!'

'That's my girl, Kelsey. Come on, let's buy a bundle and then we're getting the *prosecco* cream tea! Come on.'

They pushed inside the café, all knowingly on-trend chintz and so welcome after the autumn chill on Henley Street. They found a table in a quiet corner and devoured the cover page. Blythe really did look wonderful, a true star.

'I had some experience of this paper before,' Kelsey said after a few moments. 'Do you remember that hack-job they wrote about Jonathan and his co-star, Peony, in the summer, saying they were as good as engaged? It was all made up but I fell for it completely.' The resentment still stung. If she'd had her wits about her she'd have questioned what she read, spoken to Jonathan, clarified everything, and then maybe they'd have got together sooner. Kelsey pouted, thinking of all the kisses she'd missed and how the *Examiner* had been her only option for placing cheap business ads.

'I'd take most of the stuff printed in this rag with a big pinch of salt,' said Myrtle. 'They're notoriously slapdash. It's kinda sad. Years ago, when I first moved to town it was famous as a theatre paper, covering all the arts news, but it's gone downhill. Ninety per cent of it is advertising now... though it's clearly improved drastically since they got you on board.' Myrtle winked and bowed her closely pixie-cropped white head to read again.

Kelsey spotted the advertisement she'd shelled out for on the front page, smaller than she'd expected but a nice bold purple and there all the same.

Her mouth turned down as she scanned the article accompanying her pictures. '*Hmm*. That's weird, this story's pretty good. It's so complimentary about Blythe, *and* it's well researched. I didn't think Mr Ferdinand had it in him, to be honest. He was so strange when I met him, half asleep and kind of disinterested in his paper. But look, the by-line says Clive Ferdinand wrote this.'

Myrtle read aloud, her accent drawling wonderfully.

'During Stratford's theatrical heyday Blythe Goode (72) drew crowds from across the country to see her starring roles as Shakespeare's Ophelia, Juliet and Beatrice, as well as her ground-breaking and controversial Duchess of Malfi.

'Goode's career came abruptly to an end in nineteen sixty-eight following her double billing as Cleopatra and Queen Margaret in Stratford. She retired from the stage after a mysterious illness that winter, leaving British theatre sadly depleted in her absence.

'Her modest Stratford-upon-Avon home is a treasure trove of theatre memorabilia. Goode is pictured wearing the black lace headdress she wore onstage as Webster's Duchess of Malfi in nineteen sixty-seven, hailed as a landmark performance in the history of experimental British theatre, in spite of the production's ill-fated cast. Local legend, actor John Wagstaff, playing the Duchess' steward and lover Antonio, as well as Antony to her Cleopatra that same season, famously fell from the stage, breaking both legs...'

'Woah, no way! I must ask her about that. She's my neighbour you know? Lives in my building,' interrupted Kelsey.

'A celebrity neighbour, huh? You'd better take her a copy of this.'

'I will. She'll be thrilled… I think.' Kelsey thought for a moment about smart, fierce, fabulous Blythe Goode rattling around her kitchen conducting her explosive gin experiments. 'She must be lonely, hidden away from the world in that downstairs flat, especially after years in the spotlight. I didn't even know she existed until last week. She clearly doesn't get out much. I've never seen her leaving our building anyway.'

'Well, now she has you. Lucky Blythe. You can talk Shakespeare together to your hearts' content.'

'True. I'm glad I got the commission from the *Examiner* or I may never have met her. So it wasn't a complete disaster.' A frown formed as Kelsey spoke. 'But I'd hoped Mr Ferdinand would have paid me by now. I sent my invoice for this job straight away. I could do with the money.'

'Oh honey, that's how things are these days. You could wait weeks to see that money.'

'Mirren said the same thing when I talked to her last week.' Kelsey registered with some alarm that she hadn't heard from Mirren in days, not since her friend had got the good news about her weekend women's pages feature and she was planning on visiting Mari to let her know. She set a mental reminder to ring her soon for a proper catch-up.

A waiter brought over a tray piled high with scones, little pots of strawberry jam and two dishes of clotted cream. As the women prepared to dive in, he reappeared with two tall stemmed glasses.

'Well, here's to your success, Kelsey. See, there *is* life outside of tour-guiding,' said Myrtle. 'Cheers.' They both sipped the prosecco.

'Well, this is an unexpected treat, thank you,' Kelsey said, letting herself relax. 'So, what have you been up to since the agency closed? And how's Valeria? I haven't even asked yet, sorry.'

Valeria was Myrtle's partner, another ex-tour guide. It had taken the unobservant Kelsey the whole summer to figure out they were together and she'd been embarrassed to hear they'd shared a life in their little terraced cottage in the old town for seven years by that point. She really had been very green and more than a little self-absorbed as she'd tried to figure out her new life over the summer months.

'We're good,' Myrtle was nodding. 'In fact it was Valeria who helped us out of our fix. You know it was kinda tough both of us being out of work after so long guiding for Norma.'

Kelsey slathered jam then cream on the split scone, still warm from the oven, occasionally looking up into Myrtle's eyes. 'Got you out of the fix? How?'

'Valeria heard that the main theatres were having a costume sale and we used some of our savings to buy up as much stuff as we could. Five chests full. And not just costumes; there were stage swords, wigs, shoes, everything. We're setting up a costume rental shop by the riverside; you know, fancy dress hire as well as theatrical rentals? I already sent out flyers to all the am-dram companies in the county. We'll be opening our doors for the first time a week on Saturday.'

'Wow, you've got it all figured out. Good for you two.'

'I know, right? Let's hope it pays off. We sank what was left of our money into the business rates for the year.'

'Can I come visit?'

'You better. Come to the grand opening, OK? We're right between the Yorick pub and the Willow Studio Theatre. You know the little door nobody ever seems to use?'

Kelsey couldn't picture it. Had she ever noticed a door there? She'd always been so focused on the Willow theatre and wondering if Jonathan was in there whenever she'd passed by that summer. He'd wowed the crowds there all season long as Oberon in *A Midsummer Night's Dream*.

'Another secret little place I've yet to discover in town.' Kelsey shrugged happily. 'Doesn't surprise me; this place is full of magical nooks and crannies the tourists don't see unless they're really paying attention. I can close the studio for an hour and come along to the opening next Saturday. It's not like I have many bookings.' *Or any bookings.* Kelsey gulped at her drink.

'It'll pick up. Just you wait.' Myrtle was always reassuring. She was smart and steady and believed in Kelsey too; it showed in her face.

Kelsey wished she had Myrtle's confidence in her. She had all the equipment, the perfect studio, and as of today she had her advert going out to every house in the *Examiner*'s circulation. The only thing she lacked was the clients and their money.

'And look, there's your name on the front page of the paper,' Myrtle was pointing to the wording under the largest picture of Blythe, '*Photographs by Kelly Anderson.* Oh!'

'*Kelly*? Ugh, that Mr Ferdinand! That's exactly what I'd expect of him. Can't even get my name right.'

'There'll be other opportunities. You can set him straight for next time,' Myrtle reached a hand over and tapped Kelsey's forearm. 'So… I can't hold out any longer, tell me about you and Jonathan. Things going OK?'

The prosecco and the sudden shift to her favourite topic of conversation brought heat to Kelsey's cheeks. 'He's lovely, thanks.'

Myrtle gave a satisfied chuckle and took a big bite of scone, leaving Kelsey to fill the silence.

'He's so busy with his run of *Hamlet*. I read some reviews online; the Canadian critics are loving him. One of them said he was the greatest Hamlet of his generation.'

She couldn't stop her mind flitting to the now indelible image of Jonathan, hot from the evening's spotlights and curtain calls, reclining on his hotel bed in his black Hamlet garb, his phone held aloft, his shirt strings loosened, as he unbuckled his belt, smiling slyly, biting his lower lip, his kohl-lined eyes narrowed with wicked intent.

'*Gawd*, Kelsey. If he's responsible for making you blush like that, I can tell things are going well.'

'Yeah, things are definitely good.'

Kelsey suppressed a self-conscious grin and set to work on the cream tea again, enjoying the unexpected reminder that Stratford was still the wonderful place she'd fallen in love with and that, even though some of her favourite residents had left along with the summer crowds, there were still precious friends in town. All she had to do was make more effort to see them.

'I'm happy you're happy,' Myrtle was saying, holding her glass out. 'We've got this. We're entrepreneurs. We got the knowhow, we got the guts. Let's show these Stratfordians how it's done! *Cheers.*'

By four thirty, as Myrtle kissed Kelsey goodbye, making her promise again to come to the costume shop's grand opening, the sky had darkened with heavy-looking clouds. Her mobile hadn't rung all afternoon, so Kelsey forced herself to sit at her desk for another still and silent half hour repeatedly checking the empty email inbox for signs of life before locking up the studio and making her way home to St. Ninian's Close before the rain came on and soaked her bundle of newspapers.

Chapter Ten

'Is this the generation of love? Hot blood, hot thoughts and
    hot deeds?
Why, they are vipers. Is love a generation of vipers?'
(*Troilus & Cressida*)

'You're looking fancy,' Jamesey said, oiling over to Mirren now
it was past five on Friday afternoon. The newsroom had cleared
for the day and Mirren was alone by the photocopier. She pulled
the papers in her hand close to her chest – her copy for her
theatre feature. She'd worked on it in stolen moments between
courts reporting all week and was almost ready to send it to Mr
Angus.

It was at times like these that Jamesey liked to strike, always
timing his chats for the moments the bosses were out of earshot
and no one who mattered was looking. Yet he didn't seem
to mind the cleaning staff hearing him as he performed his
chummy familiarity with Mirren, they probably weren't important enough for him to worry about. In fact, she thought, he
enjoyed it most when he had an audience of subordinates.

'I look *fancy*?' echoed Mirren, looking down at her knee-
length black dress and long leather boots. She'd put on her
silver pendant and hoop earrings that morning too. 'Hardly.'
What does 'fancy' even mean? she worried. *It's unlikely to be a
compliment and is nowhere near the same as saying I look nice. 'Fancy',
coming from his lips means overdressed, try-hard, and ridiculous.* The

little flicker of rage Jamesey always managed to ignite within her started to burn in her chest.

'Got a date, have you?' he leered.

Mirren flinched, shuffling the sheets, warm from the photo-copier and hers to keep until the real article appeared in the November women's pages. She'd wanted to end her working week quietly re-reading her carefully researched piece at her desk but here was Jamesey bothering her once more. And she did have a date, as it happened, someone she'd met online, but she wasn't telling Jamesey anything about it. She wasn't just going to hand over ammo like that so he could smile and smack his lips at her as he enjoyed speculating on what kind of loser would use dating apps.

'No, I'm meeting friends for cocktails, actually.' *A small lie won't matter.*

He often asked her to join him and his laddish mates for a drink after work but she always declined, and she knew he wouldn't offer to join her out on the town tonight if he thought she was meeting up with friends and not workmates.

He was always uncomfortable – and markedly silent – in new company until he had figured out the hierarchies and power dynamics, fearful of making a gaffe in front of someone who might be useful to his career or his ego – or he'd fall back on making jolly, amiable remarks, the kind that had new acquaintances wondering at the charming young man and his lovely manners and witty talk.

He saved his worst behaviour only for Mirren, so nobody would ever believe he was this way, not that she'd ever tried to tell anyone about it. Mr Angus prided himself on running a tight ship with a loyal staff and Mirren couldn't be sure how he and the other bosses would react to complaints about Jamesey talking down to her all the time.

The arch of Jamesey's eyebrow suggested he didn't believe her lie. 'What happened to that one you lived with? Peter something-or-other? Did you give him the elbow, then?'

This was said with a smile that didn't reach his eyes which, Mirren noticed, not for the first time, were glassy and small like a pig's. It's funny how the more you disliked someone, the more their face, their very being, took on the shape and resonance of grotesque things, Mirren reflected. Right now, she hated the way his flesh clung to his jaw, pale and mottled pink at the same time, somehow speaking of the gristly sinew beneath.

'His name's Preston, and we're separated, yes. Amicably.' This too was a lie, bigger than the first. Much bigger. Jamesey Wallace didn't deserve even to hear Preston's name spoken aloud, let alone to mock and jeer about their fractured, dismantled, never-to-recover love.

'What happened there, then? Were you giving him the run around? Poor bastard.'

'It's nothing to do with you, is it?' She tried not to snap but couldn't help the terseness. 'Right, I'm going, it's gone five.'

As Mirren grabbed her bag from under her desk and carefully shoved her papers inside it, she knew he wasn't done yet. His footsteps were behind her.

'Walk you out.' He wasn't asking. He already had his coat and stalked behind her at a too-close fixed distance like a car being towed. Mirren increased her pace as she headed for the stairs.

'Not using the lift?' Jamesey had stopped in front of its doors and was calling her back. How did she say, *no thanks, I'd rather be carried across the Sahara in a metal coffin than ride in a lift with you*? That would be crazy, wouldn't it? And rude.

Like many women, she'd been trained from her earliest childhood not to be rude to men, to appease them always, to bear the burden of any social discomfort herself, especially when it was the bloke causing the discomfort in the first place.

She'd look irrational if she kept walking towards the six flights of lethally slippery stairs that led down in a spiral to the far side of the building – out of her way if she wanted to head for the Edinburgh bars. Of course she had to relent and get in the lift. He knew it, and she knew it.

A thin-lipped smile spread on his face as he saw her give up and turn back to stand by the lift door.

Please let there be someone in there when it comes, she prayed, but of course there wasn't.

'Going down?' Jamesey said in an oil-slick faux-American accent as he pressed the button, making the doors close upon them.

Mirren felt the air in her lungs constrict as they were sealed in the box together. Why was her heart thumping so erratically? Her cheeks were suddenly hot. Were they red? Could he see the effect he had on her? *Of course he can,* she thought. *He loves it.*

Jamesey took a step closer towards her so he occupied the very centre of their descending cage, and she retreated an inch further into the back corner, hitting her elbow on the hand rail.

'If I were Preston I'd be gutted, letting go of a stunner like you. He must be kicking himself. What was it? Roving eye, eh? You fancied a bit on the side over the summer? Can't blame you.' This fired out his mouth along with a too-loud laugh.

Mercifully, the door pinged open and Mirren inhaled the cool autumn air tainted with petrol fumes. The lift opened directly onto the little carpark behind the newspaper offices. She could just glimpse the trams gliding by on Princes Street through the gaps between buildings. There was no one else there but them. She stepped out briskly, tightening her grip on the bag over her shoulder. How could he talk to her like that? How could he *still* be talking?

Jamesey fixed her with a steady stare as he delivered his parting words, quick and sneaky. 'You know, you women are all the same. You pretend like you want the nice guy who cooks for you and picks you up when it's raining and all that, but deep down...' he leaned in closer, making her draw her neck back avoiding his breath on her face '... all you really want is a good fucking.' With that, he turned sharply and walked away.

Angry white heat seared within her as she heard him laughing, amused with himself. Her voice had activated before her brain had time to catch up and her feet carried her in his wake. 'That is *it*!' she yelled. 'You *cannot* speak to me like that. What is wrong with you? I'm your colleague.'

Jamesey turned his head back briefly, still smiling wolfishly. Mirren had thought she'd be able to go on, that she'd give him a piece of her mind fed by the outrage burning in her chest, but instead, she was horrified to realise, she was going to cry, and that, she knew, would be fatal. He'd have made a silly woman cry at work. He'd have won. And he wasn't done yet.

He shouted over his shoulder, 'Oh, don't be like that, you daft prude. It's only banter, isn't it?' He was almost at his car now. 'I'll see you Monday. Hope you get lucky tonight, might cheer you up a bit. Maybe give your Preston a booty call?' He punctuated this with a double press of the key fob in his trouser pocket and she heard the cheeping sound of a door unlocking.

'Why don't you fuck off, Jamesey.'

He laughed once more as he lowered himself into his car seat. He'd made her swear. He'd seen her angry tears welling. He'd won.

She watched him go, still frozen to the spot in the shadow of the building, her eyes burning into the side of his face as he started the ignition and pulled away.

When the carpark barrier lowered again and she had lost sight of him she clutched her hands to her eyes and let angry tears fall, still aware of the fading sounds of Jamesey over-revving his souped-up engine as he sped home to terrorise his poor wife.

She wished her lie had been true and that she really was meeting friends, but Preston was gone and Kelsey was in England, and instead she had a date. After fixing her mascara she wandered out onto Princes Street and joined the after-work crowds.

The first glass of wine was very welcome, the second harder to swallow, it was so bitter and Mirren's stomach was empty. She'd allotted her date half an hour to make an impression, telling him in advance that she had to catch a train home at six, but it was ten past now, and she was still at the bar.

Andrew seemed nice enough at first. He was some business type or other, she couldn't quite recall what he'd said he did, even though he'd only just told her, something to do with security in South Africa. He looked reasonably OK, predictably greyer of face and thinner of hair than in the grinning, suntanned profile picture she'd swiped right on. He hadn't yet smiled on this date, and she was having a hard time remembering why she'd picked him out.

He was talking about his team of workers and their reverence for him – in fact he'd been talking solidly about himself for the past fifteen minutes, only stopping to throw back his wine, a quarter of a glass with each glug. He was on his second too. Mirren didn't mind. She wasn't listening. She was thinking about Jamesey and how he'd spoken to her in the carpark.

Why had he singled her out from their very first meeting to treat her like that and not any of the other women in the office? She wasn't the youngest woman in the newsroom, or the greenest, so she wasn't obviously an easy target. She was competent and capable, so it wasn't that she was weaker or less skilled. Maybe he didn't like her smart mouth and the fact she was popular with the team in ways he just wasn't. But he had the bosses for that. He had his weekends at the golf club with Mr Angus to feel included and valued. Mirren wouldn't swap her water cooler whispered gossip and her catch-ups over coffee and homemade cakes with the interns for that. Could that be why he bristled whenever she spoke, or pitched an idea at meetings, or got praise of any kind? She supposed he could be nursing some residual jealousy over the New Journalist of the Year nomination which she'd got after the interns, her junior colleagues and all the guys in the print shop and tech department put her name forward for a freelance piece on Brexit she'd submitted to the *Scottish Student Magazine*, but that was almost a year and a half ago now and she hadn't won.

Even so, the article was still doing well online, and it had been shared tens of thousands of times before the nomination. After she was shortlisted, her words had briefly gone viral too. It had gotten her a round of applause at the Friday meeting from everyone except Jamesey, who'd sat smirking, arms folded, beady pig-eyes glancing round the room, incredulous. Mr Angus had clapped along but had seemed confused about the significance of a piece of writing only shared online – he was a man utterly convinced of the pre-eminence of print journalism over all other forms of writing. The *Broadsheet* didn't have to worry about innovating since it still had a huge, loyal readership who would pick it up from newsagents' every morning or have it delivered to their doorsteps all across Scotland. So Mirren's greatest writing success had failed to make much of an impact on her standing in the newsroom.

Jamesey, meanwhile, had his promotions, two so far, and now he was a press agency liaison and often got cushy investigative trips and freebies where Mirren got none, so he obviously didn't envy her position, but perhaps his deep-seated, stewing anger came from a resentment of her way of simply being herself and the popularity it won her among the junior staff. *For all the good it's done me with Mr Angus,* she thought bitterly. *God, how can this Andrew bloke still be talking?*

'We cleared six mil net last quarter, got a sweet ride with the bonus. Do you like the new three series? I got the sport in sapphire black,' he was braying.

She nodded, eyebrows raised in patently faked interest. These blokes could never tell when a woman was just not listening. His voice droned on, and in between self-aggrandising tales of his corporate successes he swigged another glass of red wine. His nose and cheeks were turning an unhealthy red. *Maybe if he stopped for breath once in a while he'd be less beetrooty.*

Mirren was gathering her things, ready to excuse herself. If she was quick she could get home before the chippy on the high street closed, maybe pick something up for her mum too and they could attempt a civil supper together in front of the telly. Andrew watched her getting ready to leave, at first affronted, but then, after a moment's boozy deliberation, a delighted smile revealed his wine-stained teeth.

'Leaving, are we?'

Mirren flicked her long black hair over her shoulder and settled the strap of her bag there. 'Yep,' she said, not making eye contact.

'I've got a room at the Radisson,' he said, low and shifty, so at first Mirren wasn't sure she'd heard correctly.

'Good for you,' she replied, and as she was about to stand up and say 'Cheerio, then,' it happened, too quickly for her to be able to do anything to prevent, but also somehow in slow motion so she knew exactly what was coming.

His hand slipped from his lap and down onto Mirren's knee before reed-like, cold fingers slithered along her thigh, under her hem. She caught his wrist and held it fast, pulling his hand away and shifting herself off the barstool in one movement. '*What the*—?'

'I thought we were getting on?' he said, insulted.

'You always do, your lot, don't you?' Mirren said as she threw his wrist back and attempted a dignified walk from the bar.

Just as she was straightening her jacket and looking around, hoping no one had seen, she heard him say it. The word was thrown towards her, hissed between teeth and fat wet tongue. '*Slut.*'

She let the door swing closed behind her and walked mechanically towards the station wondering when these encounters would cease to shock and unsettle her. After all, it had happened so often, and to most of her mates too, in one form or another since she was a young teen, except when she was with Preston. Nothing like that ever happened when she was with him.

All the way home from her encounters with Jamesey and Andrew, she'd let their behaviour sink in and her indignation rose.

That night, as she sat up in bed, she drafted a message in the *Edinburgh Broadsheet*'s staff email app on her phone, leaving it unsent until Saturday morning to be sure it was worded correctly and giving herself time to change her mind. *Always best to sleep on these things; nothing worse than sending an off-the-cuff flame-mail and instantly regretting it,* she cautioned herself.

When she opened her eyes the next morning, she reached for her phone and read it all through once again, just to be sure.

> Look James, I don't know what it is I've done to you to become the target of your secret little hate campaign, but I'm telling you this: if you tell me I look like I need a good fucking one more time I'm reporting you to HR and Mr Angus. Stay away from me, you creepy arsehole. We're not friends.

She hit the send button before she could crumble and chicken out.

Moments later her phone flashed into life again. A new email – but she was surprised to see it was from Mr Angus. Why would he be contacting her at – she looked at the time – eight fifteen on a Saturday morning?

> Did you mean to send that to me? Come to my office first thing on Monday.

Her thoughts raced. Could Mr Angus be talking about the theatre feature she'd sent in yesterday? He'd been expecting that though. She looked again at the email she'd sent and there it was. Mr Angus's name in the CC line. Somehow, stupidly, she'd copied in her boss to the warning meant for Jamesey.

She hurriedly re-read her words, checking exactly what it was he had just seen. The wave of nausea nearly knocked her onto her back. Heat was spreading from her stomach up her spine and to her face; red, horrified, zinging heat, making her nerves prickle and scream. It was followed by cold, creeping white despair as the blood drained away again, seemingly sinking down into her legs, making them leaden and leaving her dizzy. Now she'd *really* rocked the boat in the newsroom, and the horrible, humiliating matter she'd hoped to sort out by herself at long last had, thanks to her blundering, ended up escalated right to the top of her organisation.

Mirren switched her phone off and slid under the covers with a groan.

Chapter Eleven

'I could a tale unfold whose lightest word
Would harrow up thy soul, freeze thy young blood'
(*Hamlet*)

'You've already got a copy of the paper?' Kelsey said after Blythe let her in, and shuffled ahead of her, leading her through the purple velvet drapes and into the sitting room, which Blythe referred to with lavish French pronunciation as her *salon*. She'd hoped to surprise Blythe with a Saturday afternoon visit to look at the pictures in the paper but someone had beaten her to it.

'My young man brought it round. Roses, too.' Blythe indicated the blushing blooms in the vase by her side as she settled on her pink chaise once more.

Unsure how to respond to the idea of Blythe having a young man, Kelsey steered a safe course. 'Did you, *umm*, did you like the pictures?'

'Not bad at all considering I was rusty. Paid you, has he?'

'Not yet, no.'

'*Hmm*.' Blythe raised an arch – browless from decades of over-plucking – and reached for the gin bottle on the silver tray beside her, arranging two glasses. 'Ice is in the freezer, my dear.'

Within moments they were sipping another lethally strong batch of Blythe's gin and Kelsey had settled on the velvet stool by Blythe's stockinged feet which looked tiny and doll-like, and cold too.

'Do you want me to fetch you a blanket, Blythe?' she asked.

'Hand me my *mantoncillo*.'

'Your *uh*, what now?' Kelsey followed the line of Blythe's elegantly extended hand to the back of the door.

'My Spanish shawl, dear. I wore it for a revival of Spanish golden age drama in the early seventies. It was supposed to be my comeback. I played some kind of prostitute if I remember rightly. Didn't have any lines. I was out of favour by then. I liberated the shawl from the costume department at the end of the run.'

Blythe chuckled drolly as Kelsey spread the wonderful, deep-purple, fringed silk shawl embroidered with red and yellow flowers across Blythe's lap.

'What happened? It said in the paper you retired.' Kelsey didn't want to mention the 'after a mysterious illness' bit. 'And it called your last season on stage "ill-fated", what's all that about?'

Blythe was silent for a moment as she took a swig of gin, placed her glass down on the table and closed her eyes, raising her face to the ceiling. She inhaled dramatically.

'I'm sorry, you don't have to talk about it if you don't want to.'

One violet eye opened and peered at Kelsey.

'I was preparing my monologue,' Blythe said curtly.

Kelsey muttered an apology before clamping her lips together, chastened. Blythe took another deep breath and closed her eyes again like a medium reaching out to the other side.

At that moment Blythe's black cat prowled into the room, disappearing under her chair before slinking out between the draped folds of the Spanish shawl as though it were making a dramatic entrance at a burlesque show. Even the old lady's moggy seemed steeped in the life of the stage.

When Blythe's eyes snapped open she fixed them upon the glow from the standard lamp in the corner of the room. This was a woman who could always find her light, Kelsey thought, but she dared not speak again.

'It was nineteen sixty-six when I met him. Oh, he was a handsome devil, tall and dark, matador's waist, hips I died for, hair deep black like the winter night's sky. We were cast together in Ben Jonson's *Volpone*. I took the role of Celia; he was in the title role. Whirlwind, our romance was. We were wonderful together, on stage and off. For a little while the press were hailing us as the leading figures of the sixties' theatrical renaissance, you know?

'By the next season I was under the lights as the Duchess of Malfi, big-bellied and bold. The managers, and Daddy, told him to marry me, but I didn't feel he needed to. It wasn't the *eighteen* sixties, after all, and I was the Duchess of Malfi, for crying out loud! She's a wonderful character to play, braver than any solider. She took on the ruling powers and the church all by herself, and *she* wasn't afraid.'

The glaze over Blythe's eyes told Kelsey the actress was getting lost in memories of the role. Blythe began reciting the Duchess' lines to the lamp in the corner as though she were addressing an opening night audience.

'... *As men in some great battles by apprehending danger have achieved almost impossible actions (I have heard soldiers say so) so I through frights and threatenings will assay this dangerous venture.*'

Blythe sighed wearily as the Duchess' strength left her. 'Oh, the scandal! You couldn't imagine it. It was dangerous to speak your mind and refuse to be ashamed in those days. The theatre managers wanted to bring in my understudy when my condition got too obvious, but I bit back, told them they couldn't control *me*. I was lucky. I had a little status and a little money. Some of my girlfriends weren't so fortunate. I'd seen the laundry girls and the seamstresses who'd fallen pregnant disappear one by one. Some of them came back after a few months away, without their babies, left at some nunnery or hospital or other, taken from their hands they were, to avoid the shame, you see? The ones that fought for their babies never came back and we never heard of them again. It was as though they fell through a crack in the pavement and stopped existing. Well, I wouldn't go into one of those homes for the "ruined" to wait for my baby's birth, not on your nelly, and anyway *I* was of age. I stayed in town, I got up on that stage every night, and I wouldn't be budged.

'I answered every question the newspapermen asked me at the press calls. "Will we hear the sound of wedding bells soon, Miss Goode?" they asked. "Not bloody likely," I said, bold as brass, waving my cigarette around. Oh, I was magnificent. I was a *tour de force*, even if I did cry behind the scenes every now and then.

'I was reprimanded for my unseemly conduct and for bringing the company into disrepute but my lover didn't hear a word of it, of course. The men always got off scot-free, just like the sneaky thief Volpone himself. I didn't mind. I loved him.

'I bore the brunt of the anger and the gossip and I bore his child. I'd signed a contract by then for the next season and what with Daddy being a QC, the managers didn't dare try to oust me. My son was born right there in the dressing room; just me, my lover and the company seamstresses. I was back onstage a week after. The show must go on, no matter what, my dear, but...' Blythe's voice thickened with an ominous, weary tone. 'My body had different ideas. I fell ill. No one was sure what it was; it started as a simple case of measles, the doctors thought, but I ended up quarantined for weeks, drifting in and out of fevered states. I don't remember any of it. They told Mummy and Daddy to prepare for the worst, but I surprised everyone *as is my way*,' she smiled indulgently, 'and I got back on my feet. Well, almost.' Blythe tapped her hip. 'Whatever it was, it damaged my joints, ate away at my pelvis. I struggled through my Cleopatra and Queen Margaret roles the following winter, but the pain was something sinister. I was so thin with it. I hope you never come to learn how pain steals away your appetite.

'Then Wagstaff fell off the stage on *Cleopatra*'s opening night, straight into the orchestra pit, almost crushing that poor bassoonist! Wagstaff was in the role of Antony, blind drunk on stage, thinking he was Oliver Reed. The damned philanderer broke both his legs and that was that. We struggled on with the understudies but no one could command a stage like Wagstaff, and he was devilish handsome, everyone adored him, if only he'd been sober for long enough to grasp the fact, and so the audiences dwindled. The press called the season "ill-fated", and it certainly was for me. The managers saw my illness as their opportunity to get rid of me at last. They never fired me but they stopped giving me lead roles, in fact, they stopped giving me *lines*! Apart from a few bit-parts in the years afterwards I didn't act again, not properly. Not as a star.'

A moment of silence fell for Blythe's bright career and Kelsey made sure to observe it. Eventually, Blythe blinked as though waking from a dream and sipped her drink.

'What, *umm*, what happened to your baby?' Kelsey asked, softening her voice.

'Ah, he's in Granada in Spain. He didn't take to the acting life. You *could* say he had his fill of drama in his early years and he went looking for something less… bohemian. He lives a steady life there, sends postcards every now and then.' The sadness showed in her eyes before a stoic smile chased its shadows. 'But I've no regrets, not a one.'

'And his father abandoned you both? That's terrible.'

'*Abandoned* is too hard a word. What passed between us was all our own. I wouldn't change a moment of it. In any other era we'd have lived a whole life together and the world wouldn't have batted an eyelid.' Blythe drained her gin glass in one quick swig while Kelsey was struck by the impression that the old woman was suddenly smaller and frailer than she had been as she was telling her tale. 'Anyway, what's done is done,' Blythe added. 'The whirligig of time brings in its revenges and all that. Goodness, is that the time, darling?'

Kelsey turned to the clock on the wall between the framed black and white photos of glamorous actors she couldn't put names to. 'It's after six. Are you getting tired? I should go. I've intruded, I'm sorry.'

'Don't be silly, my dear. It's almost cocktail hour. I'm expecting company.'

Kelsey didn't say anything about Blythe's cocktail hours seeming to fall at all kinds of irregular times. 'Is it your, *erm*, your young man? The one who brought you the roses?'

'That's right. He's a sweet thing.' Blythe smiled thinly, her eyes heavy.

'Oh, right. I'll be going then... let you get ready.' But as Kelsey rose to leave, Blythe simply stretched herself in her chair and tucked the shawl around her knees, showing no sign she intended to move from her spot. The room was growing dull as the autumn light from the windows faded. Kelsey felt increasingly convinced Blythe's young man was a figment of her vivid imagination.

'Is there anything you need before I go?' she asked.

'Nothing, my dear,' Blythe said sleepily. 'Pull the door so it locks, won't you?'

After she climbed the stairs to her own flat, Kelsey opened the window at the head of her bed, crouched on her pillow and watched for the visitor Blythe had spoken of, but no one came – or at least they didn't let themselves in at the side of the building down Blythe's overgrown garden path.

Soon the cold air had filled the room and made Kelsey shiver. Pulling the window closed she thought of the dozing Blythe all alone downstairs, surrounded by memories of her theatrical glory days, and the way she'd been written off for nothing more than falling in love with a stage scoundrel. Was her seducer her co-star; the drunken, stagediving John Wagstaff that she'd spoken of? There was no way of knowing without prying, and did it really matter? What mattered was that life had thrown Blythe and Kelsey together and even though Blythe seemed self-sufficient and happy enough with all her memories around her, Kelsey hoped they could become friends. As well as being fabulous company, Blythe clearly knew a thing or two about love and longing, and so would be the perfect person to spend time with while she waited for her own leading man to come back to her.

Chapter Twelve

'My unsoiled name, the austereness of my life, my vouch
          against you,
and my place in the state, will so your accusation overweigh,
that you shall stifle in your own report and smell of calumny'
(*Measure for Measure*)

Monday morning in Edinburgh brought the first dewy frost
where breath turns to swirling vapour in the chilly air and the
pavements shine with the silver sparkle of autumn. The last of
the summer begonias in the municipal flowerbeds along Princes
Street gardens had been touched by the sudden change and the
edges of their fading petals were dark and shrivelled.

Mirren had awoken early, showered, and taken care over
dressing, choosing her best black suit with the flippy skirt. For
the first time in months she put on her glasses, leaving her
contact lenses in their case. Her eyes were tired and dry after a
restless night worrying over what her meeting with Mr Angus
would hold.

She couldn't face any breakfast even though her stomach
ached with hunger, and the toothbrush made her gag, but
Mirren smiled to see that her mum had made her a packed
lunch of cheese and pickle sandwiches and left them in the
fridge before she'd gone to bed the night before. Jeanie often did
this on her better days and it gave Mirren a moment's comfort
and hope that calmer times were ahead for them, at least for a
short while.

As usual she switched her phone on before heading out for the bus, and logged in to the *Broadsheet*'s staff email app. As her inbox loaded onscreen she told herself to breathe deeply. *In for five, out for seven. And again.* But the counter-current of anxiety was too strong to resist, and as one unread email revealed itself, a vicious rip curl and the twisting waters receding under it hit her, impossible to swim against. Reading Jamesey Wallace's words felt like drowning.

> Thank you for your email. I'm sorry if you got upset. I thought we were having a friendly, informal chat and suddenly you got very emotional. I've been thinking about all the things we discussed, and I can't fathom what prompted your reaction. I hope you feel better now, but if you took something from our conversation that was offensive to you then that is a shame.
>
> All the best, Jamesey.

Mr Angus was busy when Mirren arrived at his door, knocking once and walking in as was the custom. He stopped her and sent her back out to wait. She chose the same chair in the same spot where she'd waited for her job interview five years before, when she'd been so full of hope and excitement and ambition. She was glad she'd already submitted her feature on festive theatre breaks on Friday, anything to win her brownie points with her boss and make him more inclined to excuse her emailing faux pas.

She was surprised to find Mr Angus was the one to open the door after a few minutes' wait during which her heart fluttered in her chest.

'Come in, Mirren. You don't mind if Mandy from HR sits in with us, do you?'

'No, that's great.' In fact it was a relief to see Mandy there. She was a true ally, having once warned Mirren that Mr Angus was known to get 'a wee bit handsy' after a few whiskies on a work weekend away.

That was how the news spread in organisations like this, Mirren had learned. Similarly, she had heard on the grapevine (via Selina, one of the PAs) that Mr Leonard, the sub-editor had a propensity for making jovial remarks about the hem lengths of the women in the office and so it was best not to wear heels around him because that only encouraged him.

As Mirren sat down, Mandy threw her a quick smile and that helped settle her nerves even more. Perhaps Mandy's presence meant they'd taken Jamesey's behaviour seriously? Maybe he'd been suspended, or fired even, and this was her chance to state exactly what happened and how long he's been treating her this way. Mirren sat a little straighter in her chair and took a deep breath.

Mr Angus clasped his hands on the desktop. 'Miss Imrie, I don't appreciate staff sending inappropriately worded emails, especially over the weekend.'

'*Umm*, OK, that's fair. I was angry. I could have worded it more appropriately,' Mirren murmured. 'But I'm glad you mention that, Mr Angus. You see, I had my phone switched off all weekend and when I put it on this morning, this is what appeared.' Mirren handed over her phone with Jamesey's email open on the screen.

It took Mr Angus a few moments to read it. He seemed to be having trouble with his spectacles and held the phone at varying distances until he settled on an oddly close scrutiny of Jamesey's message.

'Ah, I see,' he said blandly.

Mirren interlaced her fingers and let her hands settle over her crossed knees. Any minute now it'd be over, she'd be sent out the room, perhaps having been praised for her courage in bringing this matter to her boss's attention and she'd be able to function at work normally without the creeping spectre of Jamesey Wallace haunting her. He'd been released from his previous employer for some kind of dubious behaviour – although Mirren had never heard that confirmed – and now he'd struck again and was about to be sent off into the world, unemployed and chastened once more. Good riddance, Jamesey Wallace!

'I'm pleased to see Mr Wallace has had time to rethink his unfortunate phrasing and has offered an olive branch.' Mr Angus clicked his gold pen shut and slipped it into his jacket pocket, signifying the meeting was over. 'It would be seemly of you to accept it.'

Mirren's eyes bulged. 'Seemly? An olive branch? Mr Angus, will you please read it again. You'll see that's not *actually* an apology. It's him blaming me for taking his friendly banter the wrong way, like I'm some irrational, over-emotional harpy who insists on being offended by perfectly innocent behaviour...'

Mr Angus took off his glasses, and squeezed a finger and thumb across his screwed-tight eyelids, as though utterly fed up with this nonsense. Mandy looked down at her court shoes.

'Miss Imrie—' he began, with a weary tone.

Mirren pressed on regardless. 'I hope now you can see how awkward this makes things...'

'Miss *Imrie*.' This was delivered sharp and loud, cutting Mirren off. Mr Angus raised his hand in the space between himself and Mirren, spreading his fingers wide like a police officer stopping traffic. 'James Wallace is harmless.'

'*Uhh*... What?'

'He's *harmless*.'

She felt an invisible punch at her breastbone and the air forced from her lungs. No words would come out. Her mind churned and the feelings circulated: disbelief, indignation, anger, all rising up, followed by something worse, and far more dangerous; the buried-deep childhood feeling of having been disciplined for bad behaviour, for overreacting, and the accom-

96

panying feelings of guilt and shame and humiliation. They settled in the pit of her stomach, heavy and nauseating.

'Miss Imrie, you've been a good magistrates' reporter, but it doesn't do to be over-sensitive in this business. We're dealing with the cut and thrust of a busy newsroom here; tempers will fray, words spoken in jest will be taken the wrong way, and, Mirren, if you cannot cope with these realities, you need to ask yourself if you're really cut out for a career in journalism.'

Mirren blinked, her neck stiffening as her boss's voice rose. Was *she* being disciplined? 'That's not entirely fair, Mr An—'

'Mirren. Let me speak plainly. You need to be robust to get along in this business, and you must assume a certain level of professionalism, which right now I'm wondering if you have let slip?'

Mirren's mouth worked, gaping and gasping. What was she supposed to say in response to this? Mr Angus wasn't done yet. He was smiling a little now as though giving fatherly advice.

'I feel it's my place to warn you that although I don't know *precisely* what's passed between you and Mr Wallace, if you're allowing your overactive love life to spill over into the work-place, perhaps it is you who needs to modify their behaviour.' With that, Mr Angus nodded once, set his mouth into a firm, straight line and watched her from behind folded arms, waiting for her to leave.

That's when it happened.

She hadn't meant to but it all came rushing in a great tsunami of sadness: every single unwanted hand resting on the small of her back and her bottom; every whistle in the street as she walked by in school uniform; every boozy, whispered '*slut*'; every unseen grope on every dancefloor; every pair of eyes running their way over her body as she rode on crowded trains, or ate lunch hunched on a bench in the town's gardens, or read on the bus; every single person who had ever silenced her, chosen not to believe her, or taken the wrong side. They all came flooding back and She Was Livid.

Mirren returned her boss's stare, surveying the dandruffy, grey man in the rumpled suit who prided himself on running his news empire like the tightest ship, whose paper espoused its belief in justice and freedom and peace at every given opportunity. The hypocrite.

She let him have it, and this time, even though she was shaking from the top of her head to her toes in her boots and her heart was trying to punch its way out of her chest, she wasn't going to cry. She was going to deliver the resignation speech of the millennium and do it with weapons-grade self-righteousness, the kind that comes when you know you've lost and there's nothing more to lose but there's still hope of gaining just one ounce of dignity and pride.

Mandy saw the great intake of breath Mirren took, her eyes widening into astonished circles as she reached for the Human Resources tablet on the table and swiped off the dictation function which would have recorded every word Mirren was about to say. Mandy nodded sharply at her colleague, silently willing her to sock him one for her as well.

Mirren flattened her palms on the desk and spoke loud and clear.

'With all due respect, Mr Angus – which in this instance is zero respect – you're wrong, and you know it. But you'd rather not see it because it would be too awkward for you to discipline your golden boy, your golf caddy, your drinking buddy.

'You're worried what would happen if he took a dressing-down from you and the other managers, aren't you? What if it hurt his pride, or his career, or his reputation, if you were seen to be taking the word of the daft wee woman who's causing trouble in the newsroom?

'And you're worried reprimanding him will set off all the other trouble-makers, and soon we'll all be complaining about the whole pack of you, and then where would you be?

'I'll tell you where. You'd be shitting yourselves and running for cover, trying to pass off that arse-grab, or that knee-fondle, or that filthy comment at the Christmas party as locker-room banter, and saying *after all lads will be lads, won't they* and *can't you say anything to your female colleagues nowadays without them accusing you of harassment*?

'Or maybe you're thinking back to how long it's actually been going on for, and how soon you'll all be preparing statements about how you don't remember it happening, and even if it *did* happen it was years ago when you were all so much younger, before you knew any better. *Hmm*? Is that what you're thinking, Mr Angus?

'Or maybe you're hoping it'll be enough to say, *well, if they didn't complain at the time, why bring it up now? What kind of grudges have these mad bitches got against us? Can't we go to work and ogle girls and belittle them and undermine them and refuse to promote them without them kicking off and dredging up things we'd rather forget? Things we don't want our wives and our daughters to hear about?* Aye! I know you're worried about *all* of that.

'And that's why you want to sweep me under the carpet and pretend it didn't happen, and I have to be a good wee girl and keep my mouth shut so you can all carry on like before.

'Well, I tell you what, Mr Angus, I am *done* being quiet. And you needn't worry about me any longer, because I've had enough of this rotten place. You can shove your boys' club up your tweedy, hypocritical arses. Put a kilt on *that*, Mr Angus.'

If she'd had a mic she would have dropped it.

The breath she needed to get her standing straight and heading for the door was immense. As her lungs filled she felt herself expanding to great proportions, her shoulders and back straightening in a way she hadn't stood up tall and proud for years, not since she first encountered Jamesey and the rest of them; since she'd learned to make herself as small as possible, to compact herself into the least offensive, most sweetly packaged shape she could fit into; since before she'd practised both lowering her voice in meetings so she couldn't be called shrill and raising her voice at events so she wouldn't be ignored.

She felt her spine clicking into place, one vertebra after another and she towered over Mr Angus who seemed to be cowering at his ridiculously oversized desk. Flicking her hair back, she walked out the room, down the corridor and into the lift, where she finally exhaled and cried her heart out, shaking and screaming her way down in the lift to street level.

When the doors opened to the chilly October air and she slipped her sunglasses on, nobody who saw her would be able to tell what had just happened in the offices of the *Edinburgh Broadsheet* or suspect that she was utterly drained and listless; they just saw a pale, elegant woman with a thin, fixed smile walking tall and stately into the afternoon crowds on Princes Street.

Chapter Thirteen

'If we do meet again, we'll smile indeed'
(*Julius Caesar*)

As Kelsey walked into town the next Saturday morning the sky was blue and cloudless and the leaves blew around her boots as she strolled, travel mug of hot tea in hand, enjoying the smell of burning coal and logs from the chimneys in the old town.

It was a day for boots, jeans and a jumper. Kelsey was grateful that her mum had kindly packed up and sent down some of her winter clothes. The approach of autumn had made Kelsey suddenly realise she hadn't packed any warm clothes when she had moved down to Stratford back in June, not expecting to stay beyond the summer. Luckily Mari had sent her favourite tan leather jacket and scarf and she was glad of them today. She was warm and cosy and looking forward to seeing her friends, if she could locate their new business premises.

There it was, just as Myrtle had said; a narrow wooden door Kelsey had never noticed before secreted away in the shadow of the Willow Studio Theatre with its imposing glass façade.

The little door was propped open with a sign above it in the shape of a rainbow which read 'Theatrical Costume Hire and Fancy Dress'. Curled leaves blew in sweeping circles at the entrance and some rustled inside and onto the bare floorboards beyond the threshold.

Kelsey smiled to hear Myrtle's loud Texan twang from within instructing Valeria to man the doors, but before she passed inside she cast an eye along the street towards the main theatre, grand and glamorous in the low sunlight.

There by its steps was the spot where she had stood only a few weeks ago surrounded by her very last tour group of the summer. They had applauded at the end of her – by then well practised – spiel and she had bowed, sad and proud all at once. Today on that very spot stood a woman with her phone pressed to her ear. She was kicking and scuffing her black biker boots against the pavement, drawing Kelsey's eye all the more. There was something so familiar about her. She could have sworn it was… it couldn't be? '*Mirren?*'

The woman's head snapped round. 'Oh my God, *Kelsey!* I was just trying to phone you.'

They made a beeline for each other, Mirren already holding her arms out for the hug that was coming. As she walked, Kelsey felt at her pockets before realising her phone was switched off. 'What are you doing in Stratford?' she asked as Mirren crushed her and planted a kiss on her cheek.

Kelsey squeezed back, eyeing the black suitcase her friend had trundled behind her. Something was definitely up. Mirren wasn't even wearing lipstick, and her usually beautifully thick, sleek black hair hung in limp curtains with flyaway ends. *No product? Whatever's wrong, it must be serious.* 'What's going on? Are you all right?'

Mirren let go. 'I'll tell you, but I've only got the energy for the short version.'

'Oh no, what?'

'I quit the newspaper…'

Kelsey mouthed a silent 'Oh'.

'… and I needed a break from Mum's place, and I thought to myself, what better time to visit you in Stratford, so I hopped on a train at Waverley Station at some ungodly hour and – *ta-dah!* – here I am.'

'Aww, Mirr, come here.' Kelsey pulled her back into a hug. 'I'm so happy to see you, just shocked that's all. But your job? I—'

'Let's not get into it right now. I know what you're thinking, but it's done now, and I'm here to stay for a wee while, if that's OK with you?'

Kelsey was thinking of all the years Mirren had given to that place, all the success she'd had and all the hassle she'd faced with Jamesey. She'd be willing to bet he'd had something to do with this impromptu resignation and sudden Warwickshire escape, but the look on Mirren's face, so weary and so unlike her, told Kelsey that now wasn't the time to press for details.

'Well, I hope you're planning on staying at mine, we can top and tail.'

Mirren looked relieved and ready for a change of topic. 'Thanks Kelse, I knew you wouldn't mind. So what are you doing out and about? I called at the studio but it was locked up, and I was going to make my way to your flat but… here you are.'

'I was just about to go in there,' Kelsey indicated the door and started walking Mirren towards it. 'Remember Valeria and Myrtle?'

'Your guide friends? I never met them, but they sounded nice when you talked about them…'

Suddenly, a musically accented voice rang out from the little doorway. 'Kelsey! You made it. Come in, come in.' It didn't take long for Valeria to bustle the two women inside the long, narrow, windowless store room with the slight whiff of damp and thrift store about it.

While Kelsey made the introductions, Myrtle joined the little party and Valeria, petite and pretty with her long hair swishing, dished out Spanish kisses on both cheeks. Long ago, Valeria had swapped her little tourist trap hometown in the foothills of the Pyrenees where France meets Spain for Stratford-upon-Avon. What was supposed to be a gap year's tour guiding had turned into a permanent stay when she was swept off her feet by Myrtle and the prospect of a shared life in her little cottage.

'You're the first ones here,' Myrtle smiled, handing them both a glass of something sparkling. 'And there's cupcakes too, check them out.'

Valeria lifted the lid on the bakery box, showing off the thickly frosted cakes with their edible toppers in the shape of comedy and tragedy masks. Mirren and Kelsey didn't need to be asked twice and they unpeeled wrappers and took messy bites while surveying the low room stuffed with theatrical treasures.

'Wow, I love this place, you two,' admired Kelsey through a mouthful, taking in the wonderful cache of Elizabethan-style dresses, bodkins, jerkins, codpieces, bum rolls and hose hanging along the walls. Two shelves of antique-style shoes in various colours of velvet and shot silk drew her eye like jewels, and from the ceiling hung swords, fans, string purses, and bodices thick with embroidery and pearls. Kelsey couldn't help but gape, hand covering her mouth.

'Wow,' Mirren echoed, already rummaging through piles of garments set out like a jumble sale on a long bench. 'This is very me,' she said, holding an armour breast plate attached to a chain mail shirt against her body, grinning.

'And I could see myself in this at the retail park on a weekend,' said Kelsey, now under the wide brim and drooping feather of an Edwardian lady's hat.

'All our stock is available to rent but this table is for sale pieces. That hat could be yours for only eighteen pounds, Kelsey.'

'A princely sum,' Mirren mugged, now wrapped dramatically in a deep purple velvet and faux ermine cloak, waggling her eyebrows for effect. Myrtle laughed loudly while Valeria added a rope of fake pearls to Mirren's get-up.

'You know, Kelsey, you ought to bring Jonathan and his director to meet us when they fly in this Christmas,' Myrtle said in hushed tones even though the store was empty but for them. 'Maybe we can talk them into hiring their stage costumes for the Stratford run of *Love's Labour's Lost* from us?'

'Ah, I think they already have their costumes. In fact, I'm sure of it, but I'll definitely point them in your direction anyway.'

'If I still had an income I'd definitely be getting this,' Mirren butted in from further along the rummage table where she was now resplendent in a gold crown. 'What time do you open officially?' she added, and everyone looked at her.

'We *are* open,' said Valeria, ominously. 'We opened half an hour ago.'

'I knew we should have invited the mayor to cut a ribbon or something,' Myrtle said. 'Created more of a buzz.'

'I'm sure it'll pick up, it's still early,' Kelsey soothed.

'The guy from the newspaper isn't here either,' said Valeria. 'He promised he'd be here for ten. It's your friend from the *Examiner*, Kelsey.'

'Not Mr Ferdinand? That doesn't surprise me. He doesn't pay and now he doesn't even turn up. He's ignored my emails chasing my money and there's been no new commissions. He really is the most useless...'

'Morning!'

Everyone turned to face the door where the voice had come from.

Against the glare from the street stood a man, silhouetted in the frame, tall and smart in black trousers and a black high-necked sweater. As he stepped into the artificial light of the shop Kelsey felt a spark of recognition, but she couldn't place him.

'Adrian Armadale, from the *Examiner*. Sorry I'm late. I *uh*, wasn't aware I had a job this morning, not until I got a call half an hour ago from the boss. I was on my way to a day out with my brother and his family and I... well, I'm here now. So, what's the story?' He drew out a notebook and pen.

Myrtle welcomed him in and whisked him into a corner at the back of the room. Valeria followed, wielding the cupcakes.

'Aren't you going to say anything?' Kelsey asked, turning to Mirren.

'About what?'

'About him.'

'Who? The reporter? Why would I?'

'Well, because he's gorgeous and you never let a hot guy pass within a two-mile radius without rating him or...'

'*Shush*, he'll hear you.' Mirren's stern hissing was rendered comical by the fact that she was wearing a droopy moustache and curly red wig.

'What do you look like? But, seriously, you saw him, right?'

'I thought you only had eyes for Jonathan?'

'Obviously, but... Mirren, are you feeling all right? He's a clear ten and I thought you'd be wrestling him to the ground for his phone number by now.'

'That's not very nice.'

'Did I lie though?'

'Maybe I've changed. Maybe I couldn't give a toss about blokes anymore, no matter how good-looking they are.'

Kelsey blinked. 'Is this one of those out of character things you're supposed to say when you're being held hostage to let your mates know something's up? Are the kidnappers watching us now? Blink once for yes.'

'People can change, Kelsey.' Mirren cast her eyes towards the reporter who was beset by the shop owners loudly repeating the details of their new venture so he didn't miss anything. 'Adrian, or whatever his name is, could be a millionaire K-pop idol, heroically working for Médecins Sans Frontières on the weekend, with a Beverly Hills mansion full of puppy dogs and chocolate bars and I'd *still* not give him a second look.'

'*Umm*, okaay.' Kelsey pulled a face.

'Come on, seems like they're busy, let's go for a walk and nip back later?' Mirren suggested.

'I've met him before,' Kelsey said as they stepped out into the cool breeze.

'Who?'

'That guy. He was at the *Examiner* offices when I was going to meet Mr Ferdinand. He was the first person to warn me I might not get paid and he *works* for the guy. I really should have listened.'

'*I'm* in town now, I could help you try to get your cash.'

Kelsey's eyes widened. 'Really?'

'Oh, didn't you know? I'm Mirren Imrie, slayer of badly behaved journos. Come on, I've a lot to fill you in on.'

–

'Two tickets, please,' Kelsey asked the woman at the cash register.

'A butterfly house? Really?' Mirren glanced around the souvenir shop.

'Why not? You're on holiday, aren't you?'

'OK, but I'm paying,' Mirren insisted.

After a long argument in increasingly broad Scottish accents with lots of purse slapping and *no, I'll pays*, Mirren inevitably won, paid for the tickets and the friends passed through the plastic curtain into the lush warmth of the big heated greenhouse.

'*Ahh*, it's like summer all over again,' said Mirren, while forcing her purse back into the little zip on her suitcase.

Struggling out of their coats, they took in their new surroundings. The humid air was heavy with the zesty scent of tropical vegetation and alive with fluttering wings of every colour. Great blousy blooms neither of them could name adorned every green thing and great palm fronds reached up to the glass roof.

A pale blue butterfly settled on Kelsey's sapphire jumper and she froze to the spot smiling down at it. 'What do I do now?'

'Just stay put,' Mirren said, instantly lifting her phone and snapping a picture.

'You could have warned me, Mirr.'

'It's beautiful, look.' Mirren turned the screen.

Kelsey grimaced even though the picture was nice. 'The thing about being a photographer is people stop taking your picture. I'm not used to it anymore. Do you mind sending it to me?' She'd forward it to Jonathan later. He'd like that. 'Not that I'm taking *any* pictures of anyone at the moment,' she added glumly.

'Let's sit.' Mirren perched on a wrought-iron bench and slipped on glamorous dark sunglasses, looking as though she were in a beachside bar in Saint Tropez and not a centrally heated greenhouse in Warwickshire, beautiful though it was. Kelsey joined her, bringing her butterfly friend along for the ride.

Mirren had filled Kelsey in on her mic-drop resignation on their walk across the old bridge over the Avon towards the butterfly house. Kelsey didn't want to complain too much about her own work problems in light of her friend's joblessness, so she said brightly, 'So, it's been, what? Six days? Have you looked into finding something new?'

'I've already messaged my friends at other papers. I'm sure they'll have some leads, but it's best to let the dust settle first, get out of Edinburgh for a while. I'll keep using my contacts. I'll find something… with any luck.' Mirren fell quiet.

It was hard for Kelsey to see what was going on behind the dark shades but she knew when her friend was acting bluff and bold but feeling small. She reached for her hand and gave it a squeeze, being careful not to disturb the butterfly which was slowly flexing its blue wings open and closed on her chest.

'Do some of these contacts include the women you know at the *Chronical*?'

'That's right. There's Lucy in the advertising team and Aurora in editorial, they said they'd keep an ear to the ground and let me know.'

'There you are then. Do they know what happened?'

'They'd heard about it before I even rang them,' Mirren said with a wry laugh. 'If a job ever does come up there it would give me the perfect excuse to ask them about Jamesey and why he had to leave the *Chronic* five years ago. Not that the details would help exactly but it would be good to know if there was anyone else on the receiving end of his sleaze so we could at least compare notes and commiserate.' Mirren seemed to think for a moment and they both watched the delicate insects flitting to and fro in the heat haze. 'I *did* make quite a sweary exit, so I guess word's got round all the newsrooms in Scotland by now. I might not be the *best* prospect on the market… but I can always try freelancing?'

Kelsey was determined to rally her spirits. 'Think of your Brexit piece. That went viral *and* you got shortlisted for an award. That means you're basically famous for your writing, and now you're famous for taking a stand. It's admirable.'

Mirren squirmed. If only she could have maintained the dignity and swagger she'd felt as she let Mr Angus feel her wits-end wrath. All she felt now was the same recoiling shame and burning resentment she'd experienced time and again as a child when she'd tried to stand up for herself at home and been met with laughter or dismissal in return for her bravery.

Mirren's expression was all defeat, and even briefly thinking of home and her childhood had her reaching for her habitual, knee-jerk response of trying to re-spin unhappy memories into something more upbeat; an old survival strategy that she'd comforted herself with as a child and which was second nature to her now. 'I suppose I'll always have a bed at Mum's, so I can't really complain, can I? That's more of a safety net than most folk have.'

Kelsey turned to her friend. 'You've got me and my place, always, OK?'

'OK.' This time it was Mirren who squeezed Kelsey's hand. She wasn't one to wallow, and especially not when she had the distraction of her best friend right there in the room with her for a change. 'So, tell me about the studio, how's it going, really?'

'Well… *umm*,' she faltered. Kelsey wasn't used to voicing her concerns about her fledgling business, even to Jonathan or her mum. She'd done a good job of putting on a brave face until now, but the words were queueing up, ready to spill out. 'Don't people *need* photographers anymore?' she blurted. 'Is everyone masterfully snapping selfies on their phones and editing and cropping, filtering and sharing them like a pro?'

Mirren only frowned, still listening.

'I've done everything I can think of. I approached local schools about portraits, I'm advertising in the local press, I even tried shoots with tourists on the street, but I'm getting nothing coming in. My portfolio's growing all the time because I'm taking so many lovely pictures out and about, and I just added these gorgeous portraits of my neighbour Blythe, which is good, but nobody can actually see them, apart from on the studio's website. I don't know where to go next.' Kelsey winced as she said the words. 'I had a proper business plan and everything, but the money's all going in one direction at the moment. I mean, is the idea of going to a studio to have portraits shot positively Victorian? Something even your granny would hesitate to do these days? Maybe opening a studio isn't exactly a healthy business model for a young start-up in the twenty-twenties? Maybe I missed the boat on a photography career?'

Mirren's mind was working, Kelsey could see it on her face. She wasn't going to let her friend wallow. 'Do you have any industry contacts you can call upon to help you out? With the studio, I mean.'

Kelsey thought for a moment. 'Contacts? I only know a bunch of actors and ex tour guides, and most of them left town at the end of summer.'

'OK, so what you're saying is you're a photographer with lots of links to the theatre, entertainment and heritage industries?'

'I wouldn't put it quite like that.' Kelsey talked Mirren through the people she knew from her summer job. There had been Norma Arden and Gianfranco – off enjoying married life in Italy now. Norma had already done so much for Kelsey, leasing her the studio for pennies until she was properly established. Fellow guide Lukas was teaching foreign languages in his hometown of Novosibirsk. Will Greville, the one Mirren had her midsummer night's fling with – though she wouldn't dream of mentioning him to Mirren right this second – was off in Ontario preparing to take over from Jonathan as the lead actor in the Oklahoma Renaissance Players next summer when Jonathan would leave the company after the run of *Love's Labour's Lost* to try his luck for a life on the English stage. Will's devoted parents owned the Osprey hotel in town and they kept him in cash year round, funding his ambitions and auditions, and it had paid off at last, now that he was under-studying Jonathan's roles preparing to take over from him. He'd be a perfect addition to the troupe and he was, according to Jonathan, still tentatively and respectfully wooing Peony, the company's leading lady – his devotion to her representing a real departure from his flirty, bad-boy behaviour back in England. Maybe Will *could* have used his connections to introduce Kelsey to important people in town, but how was that possible now? He didn't even live here anymore. And that was it. Apart from Valeria and Myrtle with their costume hire place, she didn't really know anyone, and neither Mr Ferdinand nor the director of the summer theatrical gala – who'd commissioned her first ever paid job back in August and been delighted with her work at the time – had engaged her services again.

Kelsey forced a sigh and her butterfly took flight. She watched it flutter its way to a purple buddleia flower which overhung the Aztec water feature in the pond where fat orange carp circulated.

'I need to make money and quick,' Kelsey said quietly, lost in thought.

'Think of your skills and your contacts and join up the dots,' Mirren said sagely, watching her friend. 'You've got friends with a hotel, a costume hire place and you're a photographer, so…'

'*So*…?'

Mirren waited for Kelsey to catch up.

'So, I could… get hold of some of Valeria and Myrtle's costumes?'

'Uh-huh, *and*…?'

'… and, I could take photos of people wearing them?'

'And where might you do that?'

'In my studio?' Kelsey looked doubtful.

'Close, but no coconut.'

'God, you're infuriating, just tell me your brilliant business idea, Lord Sugar.'

'OK. You ask Will if they're doing Christmas party nights at his hotel; the Osprey, right?'

Kelsey's eyes lit up. 'I offer fancy dress photo packages at the hotel's Christmas do?'

'That's right. You're set up to do that kind of thing, aren't you?'

'Actually, I am. Do you think Will Greville will put in a good word with his parents for me?'

'Only one way to find out.'

'It's half seven in the morning where Jonathan is now, he might not be awake, but I can leave a message and he might mention it to Will.' It crossed her mind that Will may not want to hear from her. They'd had a fun, flirty friendship over the summer and had come very close to spending the night together on one occasion back in July. At the time, Kelsey had been convinced Jonathan wasn't interested in her and Will's relentless flirting and a lot of bubbly at Norma's engagement party had worn down her defences so he'd suddenly looked very kissable indeed. She had come to her senses and he had seemed to take the rejection with equanimity, so she thought there shouldn't be any hard feelings, but she still felt a little unsure.

Kelsey suppressed a shudder at the memory, refusing to meet Mirren's eyes as the full extent of the tangled, awkward mess they'd all got themselves into that summer hit home. She was on her feet and scrolling for Jonathan's number in seconds.

Mirren watched as her friend absentmindedly wandered off along the little path between the hibiscus bushes and onto the ornamental bridge over the carp pool. She saw the sudden smile light up Kelsey's face when Jonathan answered her call and although she couldn't make out the words, she heard her friend's laughter and the happiness in her voice as she spoke with the man she loved all the way across the wild Atlantic and the rugged Rocky Mountains.

Mirren smiled for her friend. She deserved her happiness with Jonathan. A wistfulness settled in her chest, followed by the visceral pang she was growing used to by now. The pang of loneliness and the feeling of being very, *very* single.

Yet this, she told herself, was her chance to take a break from her messy life and to spend time with Kelsey, helping her out with her new business. She could email job applications and CVs from anywhere in the country so she may as well do it somewhere she was welcome.

Mirren kept her eyes on Kelsey who was pink of cheek and still talking, her hands held close around her phone, smiling down at her boots as she scuffed them in the dreamy, distracted way of the newly in love.

Just then, an alert sounded on Mirren's phone. Pulling the screen into focus, she read the notification.

Four eligible singles meeting your criteria within a ten-mile radius.

Mirren, absorbed, began to scroll.

Chapter Fourteen

'Lay aside life-harming heaviness,
And entertain a cheerful disposition'
(*Richard II*)

It was a true English autumnal downpour and neither of them
had umbrellas. There was nothing for it but to link arms and
run, made all the trickier by Mirren's wheelie suitcase refusing
to go in a straight line and frequently overturning as she hauled
it up and down the kerbs on their hurried way to St. Ninian's
Close – that and the fact they'd both glugged three (or was it
four?) glasses of business-launch bubbly back at the costume
hire shop.

They'd returned from the butterfly house to find Valeria
and Myrtle were finished with their interview with Adrian
Armadale. By then the shop was busier with a slow stream
of curious locals dropping by to investigate the new venture.
The cupcakes were all gone as were a scarlet velvet bodice and
matching Regency-style silk heeled boots.

Myrtle smiled proudly as she slipped the money into the cash
register and finished filling in the sales ledger. 'Not too shabby;
fifty quid,' she said as she wrote, her accent making heavy work
of the English slang.

'Your first sale?' Kelsey asked.

'Uh-huh.'

'Well I might have another for you,' she replied, smiling
mysteriously. 'Not a sale, as such, but a bulk rental.'

Kelsey had set out her idea, reading aloud William Greville's text message which had popped up on her phone only half an hour after she ended her call with Jonathan.

> **Well, well, Kelsey Anderson! Jonathan told me your idea and I got straight on to Dad. The Osprey has fully booked corporate and office party packages every Friday and Saturday in December, ending on Saturday 19th. You can run your dress-up photo stall by the bar in the main ballroom, 8pm–1am. No charge, you can keep all your profits. From one friend to another, good luck. You can do it! Give Myrtle and Valeria a squeeze from me when you see them. By the way, you have GOT to talk some sense into Jonathan when you see him at Christmas. He's making the company nervous with all his smiling and singing and mooning over some knockout Scottish girl he met this summer. Whoever she is, poor old boy's whipped for her. Be good, love Will, x**

Valeria and Myrtle had enthusiastically talked Kelsey through their entire stock of costumes fitted with Velcro fastenings at the back, perfect for a quick-change photo booth at a boozy Christmas party. They'd selected various floppy hats, wigs, swords and helmets, all ideal for drunk work colleagues to pile on and pose for daft pictures of events they'd barely remember.

Costings had been drawn up, mates' rates agreed and hastily noted down onto Kelsey's phone, and they'd shaken hands and hugged and toasted each other's success with another glass of bubbly.

That's when Kelsey spotted the box stuffed with gaudy colours under the sale table. 'What's that?' she asked.

'That's the seasonal stuff, I'm going to do a proper display by the door,' Valeria told her while pulling out Mrs Claus costumes, snowmen suits and pumpkins in various sizes.

Kelsey ran her hands over the smallest of the pumpkin outfits, little stiff felt globes with a hole for the head to pop through. 'Are these for kids?'

'Sure are, they were from a production of *Cinderella* years ago,' drawled Myrtle.

'The Tinkerbell ballet group took part in the curtain-raiser, did a little dance. Gawd, they were so cute.'

'I know them,' said Kelsey. 'They took part in the *tableau vivant* with us, remember the little fairy kids, Mirren?'

Mirren squirmed; she didn't like to think of that night, least of all when she had Kelsey's friends watching her blushing. 'Yeah, adorable,' she muttered.

'Can I have these too?' Kelsey asked, her eyes bright, still gripping the littlest pumpkin.

'For the Osprey Christmas parties?' Valeria was confused.

'No... for kids' pumpkin patch portraits. If I can pick up a few pumpkins from the supermarket and decorate the studio a little, I could offer cute Halloween shoots from now until the end of the month! The parents around here will really go for those, I bet! There's still time to advertise it, right?'

'I can hand out flyers on the street if that'll help?' Mirren offered.

'Well that's settled then. I'll add on the three kids' pumpkin costumes,' Myrtle grinned.

'With green leaf hats,' added Valeria, balancing the tiny felt headpiece with its curling tendrils on her head.

'*With hats,*' Myrtle echoed, and Kelsey clapped excitedly. With this sudden turnaround, thanks to her friends, the studio might well survive the winter. All she had to do was make it work.

As they were preparing to leave, Valeria was still chattering about all the other possibilities for costumed-photo rentals.

'Think of all the wedding receptions and high school proms and college balls! Hen dos and birthday parties too. We could make a brochure together, Kelsey, advertising our dress-up photo packages. We'll drum up lots of trade, I'm sure of it.'

With Valeria's only half joking cry of '*We'll be rich!*' ringing in their ears, Kelsey and Mirren made their way into the spitting rain that had after only a few minutes' walk turned into a downpour. They were making their way back to what would be their shared home, at least for a while.

–

'Remember this?' Kelsey said, as they clambered up to flat 2B, dragging the bag of pumpkin costumes and Mirren's case with them.

'I don't recall there being quite so many stairs,' huffed Mirren.

Once inside her little bed-sitting room at the top of the building, Kelsey pulled the key from the lock and let Mirren take in her surroundings, familiar after her summer visits. The significance of what Mirren had done slowly sank in for both of them.

'I forgot it was a single bed,' Mirren said, a little guiltily.

'You'd never fit a double in this space,' Kelsey shrugged, nowhere near as bothered as Mirren. 'We'll be fine.'

Mirren stepped forward and opened the Perspex shower door at the foot of Kelsey's little white bed and listened to the knock it made as it met the bedframe, leaving a gap of only eight or so inches for bodies to squeeze through. 'I'd forgotten about the weird shower situation as well.' She forced a smile, telling herself it was only temporary and Kelsey was being generous, but the compact quarters of her friend's tiny apartment brought it home to her that she really couldn't impose on Kelsey for longer than a few days.

'Mind out the way,' Kelsey said as she opened the fridge door behind Mirren's knees and put away the bottle of prosecco, the bag of salad, coleslaw and the rotisserie chicken they'd bought from the deli on the way home. Mirren had insisted on paying in spite of Kelsey's best efforts and they'd agreed that from now on they'd split everything they shared fifty-fifty.

Mirren pressed herself against the closed door that led to the cramped toilet cubicle, looking down at the draining board, microwave and small portable hob on the kitchen work surface. 'I'd forgotten cooking wasn't much of an option.'

'Hence the rotisserie chicken,' Kelsey said with a laugh. She was used to living a cosy, contained life here and was secretly enjoying Mirren's efforts to suppress the dawning horror that was clearly showing on her face.

'Oh well,' Mirren pressed on breezily, 'I'll still be able to rustle you up some scrambled eggs and toast in the mornings.'

Kelsey laughed again. 'I'll look forward to it.'

But Mirren didn't join in. She slumped on the bed and clasped her hands. 'Aren't you going to ask how long I'm staying for?'

'Nope. Stay as long as you want.'

Mirren looked at the head of the bed and Kelsey's white pillow, everything in the room was, by necessity, neat, compact and orderly. 'I arrived thinking I'd hide away here for a while, but...'

'I know. It's scary. Believe me, I know.' Kelsey was thinking of her first nights spent alone in this room so far from home with all its comforts and routines. 'You'll find your feet if you stick around. You have to give new places time.'

'You make it sound like I'm moving to Stratford permanently.'

Kelsey threw Mirren a knowing smile that she didn't catch. 'This town has a way of keeping people here.'

Mirren didn't answer; she was lost in trying to remember exactly how much money was in her bank account and how long a stay she could actually afford. Could she meet the expense of a room in a cheap B&B for a few weeks and get out of Kelsey's hair as soon as possible? Could she find work here, temporarily, to help pay her way? Maybe she could write articles on spec for online magazines and try sending them off in the hope one or two would be picked up? Or should she bid for freelancing work online like some of her writer friends did to make extra money outside their more regular employment? The idea of scouring through ever-changing lists of writing jobs all day, every day and then competing with other interested journalists to see whose bid would be chosen didn't appeal to her all that much. She'd heard how this new trend in acquiring writers had driven down rates and some of her friends were providing daily copy for bestselling magazines or multinational corporations' websites for far less than they'd earn in a Saturday job at the supermarket. But if she was staying in England she'd have to get money fast. She'd have to pay her way even if she was only hiding out for a few weeks.

Kelsey joined Mirren on the bed, slipping her hand into her friend's and grasping it tightly. 'You've gone a funny colour, Mirr. Don't panic yet. This is a holiday, OK? You should enjoy it. You need a rest.'

'I don't think resting's very likely, but thanks. What's that?' Mirren nodded to the bundle of envelopes in Kelsey's free hand. She'd emptied her little compartment in the mail rack downstairs when they got in.

'Dunno, let's see,' Kelsey replied, sorting the mail on her lap. 'Water bill.' Now it was Kelsey's turn to look worried but she soon forgot it. 'A postcard from Jonathan.' She held up the image of a beautiful Ontario park looked over by a statue of Shakespeare. The back was marked only with her address and the words, '*I'll be home soon. Hang on in there. J, x*'. They both smiled at that, and Kelsey paused over it for a moment before remembering she had company. 'And there's this… from Italy, *oh,* it must be from Norma.'

Mirren released Kelsey's hand, allowing her to tear into the white envelope. She read aloud in a shrill English accent which made Mirren – who had met Norma twice and would never forget her – smile at the likeness.

> Kelsey, dear,
>
> I hope you're not wasting away longing for that American of yours, not when there's work to be done and pictures to take.
>
> Thank you for the email with the lovely images of the studio, you've made it your own and I'm simply **thrilled** for you. Gianfranco wants me to tell you he's delighted for you too! We've just returned from **quite** the honeymoon on the Veneto and we're settled into Gianfranco's mother's Amalfi pension. Well, it is **a dream**, dearie, and I'll expect you to come and visit once you've given Diane Arbus a run for her money and made your fortune. Until then, do you remember I mentioned the barge?

'Oh no.' Kelsey's comedy accent faltered. She *did* remember Norma saying something about letting her rent out what had been the tour agency's ticket sales boat on the marina but she hadn't thought of it again, not when she had the studio to manage and everything that came with starting a new business to attend to. She read on quickly and in quieter tones now.

> I've instructed my solicitors to prepare the papers and hand over the keys. They'll be with you in a few days. You'll need a second premises, something more accessible and in amongst the tourist biz – as I expect you're already learning? Same agreement as the studio: peppercorn rent for six months starting

this week until you're established. Let me know when the grand opening is, we'll pop over and smash some Bolly on her hull.

I'd say good luck, but as my mother told me when I was your age, luck is nothing compared to grit, and I know a gritty woman when I see one. That doesn't sound quite as encouraging now I see it written down.

Must go, Gianfranco's loading up the yacht for a sail to Capri, and I've cocktails to mix before we haul anchor,

Pip pip, Norma, x

'She's still absolutely barking then?' said Mirren, reaching for the fridge door and the prosecco inside while Kelsey gaped in shock at Norma's astounding generosity and her world-leading meddling skills. And just *what* was Norma expecting her to do with a barge?

The cork popping brought her focus back and the two friends set about finding glasses and preparing their meal which they ate cross-legged on what was now their shared bed, shaking their heads and marvelling at the strange twists and turns their lives seemed to be taking.

Chapter Fifteen

'I am as constant as the Northern Star'
(*Julius Caesar*)

Sunday morning dawned misty and cool. Kelsey and Mirren, both in shades to help with their prosecco hangovers, strolled into town wrapped in coats and scarves on the hunt for early morning espressos and intending to take a look at the barge Kelsey was somehow now in possession of.

Holding her head as still as she could while walking along gingerly, each footstep resounded like gunshots in Kelsey's head. 'I'm done with prosecco, Mirr.'

'Me too.'

'New life, new rules.'

They made slow fist bumps at their resolve just as Mirren's phone sounded a loud pinging notification that made them wince. Mirren squinted at her phone before turning it towards Kelsey so she could read the one-word message she'd been sent.

'*Pics?*' read Kelsey, confused.

'It's some random geezer on this dating app. I get lots of these,' Mirren said dryly, just as another message appeared from the same guy, who if you believed his profile picture was a dead ringer for Ryan Reynolds.

'*Knockers!*' the message read.

Mirren let Kelsey read it while saying, 'Who says romance is dead, eh?'

'I think you should send him what he wants.'

'Eh? Not likely.'

Kelsey had stopped outside the front of the rambling Tudor house where the theatrical gala had been held in the summer. With her lips quirking wickedly, she took the phone from Mirren, snapping a close-up image of the pendulous brass knockers on the property's ornate front door. She'd clicked 'send' before Mirren had time to register what was going on. '*Aaand* block,' Kelsey said with a nod of finality and still grinning before handing Mirren's phone back. The pair fell into as raucous a fit of laughter as their headaches would allow before strolling off down towards the theatre gardens on the riverside.

One of the coffee chains was open and they were soon making short work of their take-away pastries and double shots. As they approached the marina with its colourful narrowboats moored beside the little bridges and locks in the lush, dewy green public gardens, flanked on one side by the main road into the town centre and on the other by the grand cluster of theatres, Kelsey kept an eye on Mirren, waiting for her friend's reaction to the beauty of the town at this time of day.

The river Avon, wide and smooth, swollen with yesterday's rain and dotted here and there with elegant swans, glittered in the misty morning light. Only locals got to see the town like this; dog walkers and joggers, up with the chirruping robins and hungry cygnets.

Kelsey always woke up early, even on Sunday mornings, and even after a night's laughter and drinking with her best friend. She was glad to see the look of awe spreading across Mirren's face as she took in the view from left to right from the shuttered canal boats inside the lock gates all the way downriver past the theatres to the mists hugging the spire of Holy Trinity church in the distance. They only briefly let their exclamations about how pretty it was interrupt Mirren's tales of her recent encounters with dating apps back home in Scotland.

'I should have known when this one guy suggested we meet at the petrol station at four in the afternoon that it wasn't going to be a dream date,' Mirren was saying between sinking her coffee and twirling between her fingers a rusty-orange leaf she'd lifted from the grass. 'The first thing I noticed, after the car door opened, was his Crocs. I mean, who wears Crocs on a date? With socks? Then there were the sweatpants, the mullet, and the bag for life.'

Kelsey grimaced.

'His dating profile said he was thirty-six but I swear, Kelse, he was sixty-six if he was a day. He said, "I'm just nipping inside for a pint of milk", and I was left standing by the sacks of barbecue charcoal feeling like a right plum. When he came out again he looked at me, all wide-eyed and disbelieving and said, "You're still here? Usually, my dates have left at this point." *That* was when I left.'

'Oh, Mirr! What are these blokes thinking?'

'Then there was the farmer. Out of all of them, he'd sounded the most promising. I went all the way to Fife to meet him. Arranging to meet in a nightclub is never ideal though, is it? I mean it's all right for *meeting* someone for the first time, if you know what I mean, before maybe possibly leaving with them, but it's not an environment conducive to an actual date, especially when the nightclub in question is above an Argos on the high street and half the people in there are just knocking off from their shift in the warehouse downstairs and are still wearing their work tabards.

'The first thing he said was, "You can buy your own drinks, if you don't mind." So I told him of course I didn't mind, but I realised when the barman came over that this guy didn't have a drink and he wasn't reaching for his wallet either, so I ended up offering to get him one, like an idiot.

'We only got as far as one drink though. He started quizzing me on what I do for a living. He kept saying, "So you've got money of your own?" because, apparently, he was fed up with the local women thinking he was a millionaire just because he was a farmer with two thousand acres, a vintage Lotus Elise, six luxury holiday lets and an award-winning farm shop on site.'

'Right, so he *was* a millionaire then?' said Kelsey.

'Aye, and with zero personality and a complex about gold-digging women, or any women really. I was out of there by half nine, just as the S Club 7 medley was starting. He said he'd walk me down to the street only I'd probably expect him to spring for a cab, so I left him sitting by the bar. I heard him ordering himself a beer as I walked away.'

'Charming.'

'Right? But that wasn't even the worst one this month.'

'You've been on three dates this month? It's only the twenty-sixth today.'

'Two evenings, one lunch. Oh, and there was another one in a bar, didn't go well either.' Mirren tried not to think about Andrew and his grabbing hands and red face. 'What of it? Anyway, I never really got the chance to date, what with meeting Preston at school, so I've tried making up for it.'

Kelsey assumed a blank expression.

'Anyway, me and this army recruiter guy were supposed to meet at the pub for a ploughman's and we'd had a really nice chat setting it up, see?' Mirren flashed her phone screen at Kelsey long enough for her to glimpse an alternating sequence of coloured boxes indicating a long conversation, but not long enough to catch any specifics. 'But he never showed up. I'd been there long enough to order and eat my food – I wasn't going to pass up a ploughman's – when he messaged, just as I was getting ready to leave, saying he'd been delayed at work and could he come now, but I didn't reply. You either show up for our date as planned, or you don't. No second chances.'

'Wow, Mirr, that's tough.'

'If that's his attitude to a first date what would he be like in an actual relationship? Naw, hard pass for me. But it's a shame, I was imagining him as the nicest looking one of the bunch.'

'Hotter than Crocs man?'

'Hah, Funny. No, look at his profile.' Mirren enlarged the picture and passed her phone to Kelsey.

She squinted. 'OK, promising.'

'I had high hopes based on that jawline and that army buzzcut.'

'Sounds like you liked this one. Maybe you should give him another chance?'

'Nope. I am as constant as the North Star. Once I've made up my mind, it's made up.'

They came to a stop in front of a fountain with a silver swan at its centre. Mirren stepped up onto its little raised platform so she towered over Kelsey. 'In fact, Kelse, that's what I want to tell you. I thought about it all the way down on the train and I am now completely, utterly, decided. Drum roll please.'

Kelsey obliged, tapping out a rhythm on her empty espresso cup.

'Thank you.' Mirren stretched her spine and proclaimed dramatically to the sky, 'I've come to a resolution. Henceforth, Mirren Imrie is swearing off men. I'm clearly no good at picking them and no good at keeping them either, and frankly, I'm sick of the weirdos and the perverts and the liars and the Flash Harrys and...'

'I get the picture,' said Kelsey.

'Right, good. I'm done with the lot of 'em.' Mirren nodded her head sharply only to wince at the hangover pain, but they both still laughed and sat down on the edge of the fountain.

Kelsey watched as her friend's curling smile slowly faded. A dullness sneaked across her previously animated face. Kelsey knew exactly what Mirren was thinking. 'Preston?' That was all she had to say.

Mirren nodded, shrinking a little. 'I did the right thing there, but still, regret is a horrible feeling.'

'You regret breaking up with him?'

'No, it's not that. I just regret not being better with him, kinder, more... committed.'

Looks passed between them; Kelsey's sympathetic, Mirren's self-recriminating and pained.

'You tried, for a long time you tried. All the romance was gone, you said it yourself, and you found yourself wanting to see other guys, to "play the field," you said. Remember? You couldn't stay together feeling like that.'

Mirren winced again, scrunching up the paper bag her pastry had come in.

'No. Stop beating yourself up. There's nothing wrong with liking men and enjoying their… *erm,* company?' Kelsey said, trying to coax Mirren's smile back.

Mirren merely shrugged. She loved Kelsey for many things, and the way she never judged her was topping the list right this second. She was right; loving the thrill of meeting new guys and enjoying hooking up with them wasn't wrong, not at all, and it wouldn't have been a problem if Mirren had really, actually enjoyed her encounters with them, but every one had been laced with something other than pleasure and empowerment. It wasn't guilt exactly and it wasn't shame either – in spite of years spent absorbing her mum's unkind comments about her personal life. It had been instead a kind of sadness, sadness that even after breaking up with Preston she hadn't come close to getting what she actually wanted.

It was only becoming clear to her now that she was in England and seeing her old habits as through a rear-view mirror, receding away and less worryingly close, that Mirren fully realised what that was. What she wanted was the kind of love and security that Preston had given her since her mid-teens, combined with the deep attraction and excitement she'd felt with other guys in more elicit circumstances. Why couldn't she have both combined? The best dating app designers in the world couldn't find that guy, it seemed. That guy didn't exist.

Mirren's shoulders heaved then relaxed as she exhaled. 'I can't change what's happened, and I wouldn't, not really, but I can take better control of what's to come. So, I want you to witness this, Kelsey…' Mirren hovered her index finger over the 'delete profile' button on the app and let Kelsey watch as her online dating life disappeared. 'While I'm in town with you, I am single, I'm not dating, and I'm concentrating on *me*.'

'Nice one, Mirren,' Kelsey grinned. 'You've had a big break-up and it makes sense to take some time for yourself.'

'Thanks,' Mirren sniffed. 'If I'm really being honest, it's not so much about not wanting to *date* anyone, it's about not wanting to *feel* anything at all. I just want some peace, to be alone with myself and not to always be swinging between extremes of excitement, then disappointment, and guilt or embarrassment. If I only have myself to focus on I can control my life better, actually be in the driving seat for once. That's the idea anyway. I'm just... so *tired*, Kelsey.'

'I know. I'm here for this, with whatever you need, OK?' Kelsey was a little alarmed to see Mirren's smile slipping again and her bottom lip wobbling. Mirren never cried in front of her. She was always the brave one, the one with all the answers, the confidence, and the smart comebacks. How had the tables turned so much? Kelsey pulled her friend close and for a few minutes they held their heads together while Mirren sniffed away tears.

'Come on, let's walk along the riverside and see if we can find this mooring,' Kelsey said, at last, clutching Norma's letter with its pencil sketch on the back showing the old ticket barge's new position down river. Even if she didn't yet have the key they could look the boat over.

'OK,' agreed Mirren, and the pair set off, Mirren looping her arm in Kelsey's. 'I only hope your mum has better luck with dating than I ever did.'

'Me too. Wait, *what*?'

'Ah, yeah, about that. I *might* have encouraged your mum to sign up for a dating app. Just the one, Kilted Cupids, and uh... I didn't know if she'd mentioned it to you yet, so...'

'She hadn't, no. When I called home on Friday night Calum said she was out and...' Kelsey's eyes widened with the realisation. 'Do you think she was on *a date*?'

'I hope so.' Mirren had found her smile again.

'I'll have to ring home, get the details.' Kelsey's eyes flickered with wonder as she adjusted to the idea.

'Ask her to send the guy's profile picture over,' Mirren grinned. '*What*? Just because I've sworn off men forever doesn't mean I can't be excited for your mum.'

'I know. I just don't want *her* to get her hopes up only to be disappointed. The way you describe these apps makes choosing a partner sound like a blood sport.'

'Oh honey, it can be, but your mum knows what she's doing, and… Kelsey, are you all right?'

Kelsey's grasp increased in pressure on Mirren's forearm. They had stopped in front of a wide, high-roofed barge painted in burgundy, green and gold. Kelsey's breath seemed to have stilled. 'This is it.'

'You're sure?' Mirren replied.

'Yes, look, there's Norma's old A-frame sign with the tour prices and times on.' Kelsey pointed at one of the low windows.

'It's bigger than I remember,' Mirren said, watching Kelsey swallowing a nervous lump and still gripping her arm tightly.

Kelsey wasn't speaking, but her lips moved silently as her mind worked. Mirren would have to reassure her and fast.

'You can do this, Kelse. You renovated the studio, right? You can make this… nice too. Oh look, a nest!'

Sure enough, there on its roof was a mess of sticks and feathers topped with a sleeping mallard.

'A barge, Mirren? What exactly am I supposed to do with a forty-foot riverboat with peeling paint and ducks with squatters' rights? It's been hard enough trying to make money at the studio! Add to that a second premises – and one I have to keep afloat, literally – how am I going to manage?'

'We'll think of something,' Mirren said. 'And you've got your pumpkin shoots idea, and the Christmas parties. Come on, you've got this!'

Kelsey swung her head to peer at her friend, not at all convinced.

Swans, hopeful of some bread, appeared from every direction, gliding slowly across the water's surface casting widening ripples as they sailed, honking loudly for their breakfast, blissfully oblivious to Kelsey's spiralling panic.

Chapter Sixteen

'I had rather hear my dog bark at a crow than a man swear
he loves me'
(*Much Ado About Nothing*)

Mirren Imrie, Stratford's newest resident, settled in to a quieter
kind of life. The days were growing shorter and the window of
time she spent out of pyjamas and in the fresh air was decreasing
with each day. At first she'd been full of energy, sending out
speculative CVs and queries to magazines and papers across the
country with ideas for articles, and she'd subsisted on the hope
and excitement that at any moment her cell might ring.

She'd helped Kelsey as much as she could too, handing out
the hastily designed and printed leaflets for pumpkin patch
photo shoots on Stratford's chilly, windy high street for two
whole days and there had been a brief flurry of bookings that
was now keeping Kelsey occupied at the studio.

Somewhere in between refreshing her emails in the bedsit
and watching her phone, Mirren realised no work was coming
her way and out of sheer embarrassment at finding herself idle
after years of non-stop striving, Mirren let herself morph into
a kind of proxy housekeeper to Kelsey, having nothing else to
contribute.

She took over launderette duties and learned how to cook up
one-pot hob recipes so at least Kelsey had something delicious
waiting for her when she came home in the dark afternoons,
and at night they drank wine and streamed box sets on Mirren's

laptop, trying not to look at the evening's sauce-streaked dishes in the sink only two feet away from the little bed which Mirren suspected was somehow shrinking a little more each night.

By the time the rather lacklustre Halloween afternoon rolled around, and after a series of little imperceptible shifts, of niggling inconveniences piling up, of never having enough space to store anything or to spread out and really work on her writing – especially now that the rooftop terrace at St. Ninian's was cold and slippery and out of bounds – Mirren was feeling the strain of bedsit-sharing.

Kelsey had come home, buzzing with excitement after a busy day.

'Sorry I'm late, is it ruined?' she said.

Mirren stirred the pot of congealed goulash on the hob. 'Well, it was definitely more appetising an hour ago.'

'Sorry, I just had such a good day, I was fully booked all morning and all of the customers wanted real prints as well as the digital file emailed to them, so I had to run to the chemist's three times! There were twins in today, only nine months old. Their parents had dressed them in little Halloween onesies. Oh my God they were so cute, wobbling all over the place. One of them fell asleep and we had to prop him up against one of the pumpkins. Here, I've got the pictures on my tablet.'

Mirren served up the meal and took a few cursory glances at the pictures. 'Adorable,' she agreed, reaching for the wine in the fridge and knocking Kelsey's knee with the door. 'Sorry.' She threw her hands up and Kelsey saw how exaggerated the movement was.

'I'll get out your way.' Kelsey held her coat and satchel up in the air attempting to squeeze between the bed and Mirren bustling at the little kitchen work surface. As she made her way through the door to the little loo to wash her hands, Kelsey knocked Mirren's dresses that were hanging over the doorframe, and they all fell off their hangers, again.

They both spent a few moments silently rehanging them. 'We've got to find somewhere else to put these,' Kelsey said gently.

'But where? There's no wardrobe.'

'I know, this place is daft.' Kelsey attempted a laugh, but noticed the area under Mirren's eyes was a burning red and she was close to tears. 'I never really minded just keeping my stuff folded in my open suitcase under the bed. We could go to IKEA one day and buy loads of storage bits?'

Mirren turned back to serving dinner. 'That reminds me, I put away all your jumpers, but some of your tops are still damp, they're hanging inside the shower cubicle.'

Kelsey glanced at the limp laundry inside the Perspex box. 'Right, great. Thank you.'

'Something wrong?' Mirren's voice was pitchy.

'Nope. Why would there be?' Kelsey said with a shrug, hoping to defuse whatever this was. They never fought and she didn't want to start now. She made a show of dumping her satchel and coat on the floor at the end of the bed to show how easy she was with all the clutter, and for a moment they both looked down at their feet and the piles of CVs and envelopes neatly stacked on the white carpet.

'They'll be gone tomorrow, I promise,' Mirren said in a small voice.

Kelsey only smiled. 'Let's eat. I'm starving.'

And so another little moment of tension passed. There was no point talking it through. The bedsit was just too small but there was no other solution, right at that moment. Not until Mirren found a job and she could go wherever her new employer was. Kelsey settled on the bed with her food, saying twice how delicious it was, and tried not to think uncharitable thoughts. Not when Mirren had no one else to turn to.

The wine helped and Kelsey chatted breezily about how with a bit of luck she could buy herself a decent photo printer of her own, maybe after Christmas, if the Osprey parties paid off. She certainly wouldn't miss bolting down the high street to the big chemist's to use their expensive, clunking machines.

–

After dinner, neither of them were willing to be the one to decide what they watched and the tension was rising again when Kelsey's phone rang. She took her mobile outside the bedsit door, feeling every inch like that one undergraduate in halls who was always on the phone to her boyfriend but glad of the respite from the stuffy humidity of the room.

'Trick or treat?' Jonathan's voice was a dopamine hit and Kelsey felt the tension in her shoulders melt a little.

'I'll take the treat please,' she said wistfully. 'Shouldn't you be at the matinee?'

'No show 'til tonight, for a change, so I thought I'd try to catch you before you hit the town and go wild with Mirren.'

Kelsey laughed. 'Some chance. What with neither of us having any spare cash and Mirren's new life as a nun to consider, it's just another night of streaming movies and crisps for us.'

'You OK?'

'Yeah, I'm fine, just… a bit cooped up. There's not a lot of room for guests and the weather's taken a turn for the worse.'

'Tell me about it; it snowed here at the weekend.'

'Oh, I meant we had some drizzle but sure, October snow in Canada means winter's on its way.'

'Not long now and I'll be there with you. Fifty-three days.'

'You're still counting?'

'Aren't you?'

'Course I am. Did you book your flights?'

'Uh-huh. I'll arrive early December twenty-third so we can step right into Christmas, OK?'

Kelsey let out a long breath. 'That sounds perfect.'

'Don't get down about it. It's not forever.'

'I know, I just… sometimes it feels like it might be, and having Mirren here is amazing and everything but we seem to have gone from being best friends to being an old married couple in the course of a week and a bit. If she were busier, or if we had better incomes maybe it wouldn't feel so…'

'Claustrophobic?'

Kelsey nodded guiltily and Jonathan understood the silence. 'It's not your friendship; it's the bedsit. It's too tiny for you guys, and you've grown used to living alone so sharing was always gonna be tough, even if you were in a bigger place. But I admit, I'm kinda jealous.'

'You are?'

Jonathan sniffed a laugh. 'Wishing it was me getting under your feet.' Again, he understood the silence down the line and the new shift in feeling. 'I wish I could turn around and always find you there, close to me.'

They listened to each other's breathing.

'Me too,' Kelsey said at last.

'So what are you gonna do?'

'Wait it out? Hope Mirren gets a job soon? I don't like to say it but she's been getting sadder since she arrived, and this was *supposed* to be her big escape. She's lonely and… her stuff is everywhere.' Kelsey blurted this last part and Jonathan laughed again. 'I mean seriously, it's *everywhere*! Cotton wool pads around the sink in the mornings and her vitamin bottles, and the clothes! She's not messy, it's just the flat's definitely designed for one.'

'How will you manage when I fly in?'

A new kind of silence fell, betraying Kelsey's panic.

'I'm hoping she'll have got herself sorted by then.'

'And if she hasn't? Sounds like she really needs a friend right now. I can look around for some place to stay if—'

'There is one solution,' she interrupted, not liking where this was going.

'Already with the solutions. That sounds like my Kelsey Anderson.'

'You know the barge I'm renting from Norma? Well, I got the key this week and its huge inside, I mean, relatively speaking. After the squeeze here at the bedsit anything where you can stretch your arms out and stand up straight feels big. Not that *you'd* be able to stand up straight, you'd definitely bump your head.' For an instant Kelsey's brain ran its show reel of Jonathan's tall, lean body and the image of him with his arms outstretched lying on his back on her bed with his head tilted back and his lips parted. For a moment she struggled to think of anything else. 'Yeah, you're so tall... tall and...' Her voice tailed off.

'Ontario to Stratford? Is Kelsey there?' Jonathan laughed, but there was heat in it.

Kelsey jumped at a sound behind her, cutting her off.

Mirren, on tiptoe and making a show of quietly sneaking past, handed Kelsey her keys, shrugging on her black leather jacket. 'I'm heading out for a walk,' she mouthed. 'Back in a few hours.' Her face was stiff. Had she overheard?

'Oh, all right,' Kelsey replied. 'It's dark, will you be OK?'

'Course I will. Try to have a nice quiet evening, get some rest. Don't watch any scary movies.' She kissed Kelsey's cheek and headed downstairs, turning as she descended to call back, 'Oh, and give Jonathan my love.'

Now Mirren was out of sight, Kelsey's smile faded into a worried frown. She made her way back into the bedsit. All the dishes had been washed and put away and the bed covers were straightened. The dresses over the bathroom door were gone.

'Did you hear that? Mirren hasn't gone out on her own since she arrived. Do you think she knows I'm suffocating?'

'You've been best friends since you were kids, there can't be much she doesn't know about you, and she must be feeling it too.'

Kelsey sighed and sat on the bed, ruefully eyeing Mirren's little black suitcase zipped up and stowed neatly under the bedside table.

'Go easy on yourself. OK?' He waited for her reply, but didn't get one. 'So, what were you going to say?' Jonathan's words reached her through the sinking feelings of being a horrible friend.

'Oh, I was going to say, there's a bed on the barge.'

'There is?'

'A double one. The whole boat's nice really, if a little dated. There's a big step down into an open area – that's where the big window hatch is and the ticket sales used to happen; then there's a door through to a galley kitchen and a little foldaway table – that's where we'd all sit on lunch breaks, sharing our guiding stories from that day and counting out our tips – and beyond that there's a bedroom with little painted cupboards and shelves all around the walls.'

'Sounds idyllic.'

'It's not as fancy as all that, but Norma had it all professionally cleaned so it's spotless inside, even if the outside is in need of some TLC.'

'So what were you thinking?'

'That maybe when you come back to Stratford in April to do your run of *Love's Labour's Lost* we could live in it together? We could try it out when you're here for Christmas and when you visit for Valentine's Day...'

'Uh...'

'What is it?'

'Kelsey, I can't live on the water.'

'You can't?'

'I get seasick, real bad. I mean it. I couldn't even ride Bricktown water taxis back home without throwing up.'

'Oh. I didn't know that about you.'

'Hardly surprising, we didn't have all that long to get to know each other over the summer, did we?'

A flutter of anxiety troubled Kelsey's chest. What else didn't she know about the man she hoped to spend her life with once this long wait was over?

'Are people even allowed to live in it? Didn't Norma say you should use the boat as business premises?'

'*Mmm.*' Kelsey was still distracted thinking of the sea sickness bombshell.

'Well then… can you make it a second business premises?' he pressed, but she wasn't hearing him properly.

'Jonathan I…' Her words failed. 'How will we… I mean, where…' The words were all there, lining up, wanting to spill out, but she gulped them back. *Where will we live? How will we live? Where will our money come from? Can I even say 'our' money? Is it too early to even think about combining our lives like that? And how exactly do two people who don't know each other very well, but really, really love each other, merge their separate lives and make it work when everything's so new and they've never done anything like it before?*

She didn't say any of it. Instead, she let her unsettled feelings swell and get mixed up with her guilt and irritation about living in such close quarters with Mirren, which really had proven that the bedsit wasn't fit for two people to cohabit comfortably – even if Kelsey *could* lay upon Jonathan's chest and they could squeeze into the shower together and be closer in a thousand ways that she and Mirren couldn't.

'I just don't know how we'll manage,' she said weakly.

'We'll manage somehow.'

'That's not a plan, Jonathan. Do you even have your work visa?'

'I'm covered for the Stratford run of *Love's Labour's Lost* from April to June next year. That's a start, right?'

'But it's not a promise that we can stay together, and it's not a home we can share, and if I'd known you get seasick I might not have spent the past few days imagining us living on the barge together and…'

'Kelsey, it's OK. Just breathe it out. We'll find our way. Just like we found each other. And all this waiting and insecurity? It's temporary. We *will* find our way.' He said each word slowly and calmly and Kelsey pressed the phone closer to her ear, waiting for her anxiety to subside.

Chapter Seventeen

'Tis one thing to be tempted [...] another thing to fall'
(*Measure for Measure*)

Down at the Yorick pub on the riverside, Mirren – who had made her way into town along back street pavements dotted with giggling vampires and tiny spectres all clutching pumpkin buckets brimming with sweets – was ordering herself a double shot of Jack Daniels and wondering if she had enough money left in her bank account to pay for it.

She'd been sure to top up her mum's gas payments before she left for England, and had put a little money by the washing machine, as well as filling the fridge so she could be sure Jeanie wouldn't skip any meals – and she'd searched the house for twenty minutes before finding two whisky bottles secreted in the airing cupboard, tipping them down the sink before she sneaked out to the train station. Buying that last-minute train ticket from Edinburgh to Stratford hadn't left her with much to live off this month but at least Jeanie had everything she needed to get by, once she'd got over the shock of Mirren's sudden departure.

Today marked one week until her payday and she assumed she'd already forfeited that money by walking out, failing to work her notice period, and of course she'd prematurely aged Mr Angus by a decade with her home truths.

She stared at the words 'transaction pending' on the device in the barman's hand and brazened out the moment of tension, followed by instant relief as she watched the payment go through. Her jaw sent a little pang of pressure to her brain reminding her to drop her shoulders and loosen her bite.

The busy barman bustled off to serve the white-bearded, rosy-cheeked barfly in the red cravat at the far end of the bar who had been watching her since she arrived. There was a full-sized plastic skeleton draped in cotton cobwebs on the barstool beside him. She briefly thought the pair looked like a Renaissance *memento mori*, a reminder that death is always near but she dismissed her morbid thoughts as the effect of All Hallow's Eve and the worry of her increasingly dire financial straits getting to her.

She knew the barfly's type instantly. It was only a matter of seconds before he'd start asking her if she was on holiday and where she was from. She'd subconsciously resolved to ignore his eyes boring into her the instant she became aware of them, an automatic response she'd instinctively developed, like so many of her friends, as a young teen and which was now second nature.

Lifting her drink she was relieved to see a group of four holiday-makers vacating a table partly set inside a tall inglenook chimney niche. She slipped inside the towering fireplace, all whitewashed brick and cosy with cushioned benches, and quietly set to work on her drink, keeping her eyes cast down on the striped paper straw. If she didn't look at anyone, then no one could see her, she told herself, like a child hiding, eyes closed under the duvet, so the boogieman leaves them alone.

So Kelsey was feeling cooped up and tired too? Mirren had suspected as much all along of course and she'd done her best but her plan to get out of Kelsey's hair hadn't exactly worked out.

She checked her phone knowing what she'd find there. Nothing. Even her friends – fellow reporters at other papers – had stopped replying to her queries about job openings. They were probably too embarrassed to tell her that they had dutifully mentioned her predicament to their bosses and been met with incredulous looks. As if they'd hire the shouting, boat-rocking Mirren Imrie; the woman who'd accused a respected journalist of harassment. She's a trouble-maker and a liability.

A thought crept in, unwanted and bitter; she'd have to go back to her mum's and soon. How could she have fallen from being an award-nominated full time newspaper staffer with a home and a loving boyfriend to being skint, homeless, unemployable and single in the course of two months? '*Ugh!*' the sound escaped her lips as she hunched over, arms crossed, head on the sticky table, her glass pushed aside and already empty.

'Are, *uh*… are you all right?'

Snapping her head up, suddenly hyper aware there were tears in her eyes and that her mascara was filming over her vision in a greasy slick. The white cocktail napkin clung briefly to her forehead before detaching and drifting down to settle on her left boob. 'I'm fine,' she said hurriedly with as much dignity as she could scrape together.

It was not the cravat-wearing barfly at all, and not one of the tourists queueing for drinks either, but instead she was looking at the concerned face of someone not quite a stranger. She'd seen him before though only for a moment, and she hadn't noticed then his deep, dark brown eyes or the muss of near jet-black hair falling over his forehead.

'Adrian?' His name came back to her and was in the room before she could contain it.

'Yes?' He cocked his head.

'Oh, you don't know me, I just know who you are. You're from the *Examiner*, right?'

'That's right.' His full mouth twitched into a half smile that spread in a flash to his eyes. 'So, *um*, *are* you OK?'

'Well, honestly, no, but I'll be fine. Thanks.' The last word was supposed to tell him she was done talking, but he didn't move.

'See, I don't want to be *that* guy,' he lowered his voice now, 'but you had your head on the table and you seem upset. Is someone bothering you? Are you on a date from hell and you need a leg-up to get out the loo window? I can help with that.'

She begrudged the smile this prompted. 'Don't make me laugh, for God's sake. I'm being miserable and self-sufficient all by myself over here, and I'm not trying to be rude but I don't want to talk, OK?'

'I understand, I'm sorry.' He took a step back then turned away, having thrown her one last apologetic smile. Mirren had to admit she was surprised he'd backed off so readily.

He was sitting on a barstool now and she watched his back as she lifted the straw to her lips. He was all in black; a leather jacket and high-necked jumper, strapped leather boots and skinny jeans, all of which gave the impression of a French cologne model who lived off cigarettes and air. Even with his back to her, the neat stubble round his full Cupid's bow lips and the slight hollow of his cheeks beneath high cheekbones stayed in her mind. He didn't look like any guy she'd met recently and he certainly didn't behave like any of them. He was writing in a notebook now and drinking from a freshly pulled pint.

Mirren noticed he'd turned his shoulder a little on the white-bearded barfly who was loudly regaling a tourist – who had been innocently queuing to place a food order before he was accosted – with a story about how he'd acted alongside Judi Dench and they'd shared digs while on tour in the seventies. Nobody in the snug bar room could avoid hearing him. Something in the angle of Adrian's shoulder told her this old actor was a regular at the bar and he'd learned from experience not to engage him in chatter.

That's when it dawned on her she was idly sucking air through her straw. She needed another drink and dammit, if the only open spot by the bar wasn't right by Adrian, the guy she'd just sent packing. She looked at her empty glass, then at him. Her need was greater than her pride. She didn't have to sidle over tail between her legs; she could style this out. Sail in, order her JD and retreat. She was on the move.

No need for talking, don't make eye contact. This isn't awkward at all.

'Me again. Drank it all,' she found herself saying out of a horrible compulsion to explain herself and tipping her empty glass to show him. What was with her tonight?

He nodded respectfully and cast his eyes back to his notebook and his good manners only made her feel stupider. Where was that barman?

The beardy barfly was now deep in conversation with another aged luvvie, presumably an old friend, and their booming, theatrical laughter broke out every now and then. Mirren was sure she could feel Adrian flinching beside her every time it did.

'Nobody taking orders,' she muttered to herself, spinning her credit card around between her pinched finger and thumb and wondering why she couldn't stop herself speaking.

'*Hmm?*' Adrian looked up.

'Nothing, just talking to myself.' She clamped her lips, annoyed with herself.

'He said he was going down to the cellar for a minute,' Adrian remarked, keeping his eyes on his notebook but his pen was now immobile in his hand.

Her mind started working, looking for something to alleviate the awkwardness. She wouldn't have asked if it hadn't occurred to her this was an opportunity not to be squandered: 'So you're a reporter. Are there any jobs going at your paper, by any chance?'

She'd already emailed Mr Ferdinand – even though Kelsey had warned her he wasn't inclined to pay his freelancers – and of course, she'd had no reply, but maybe this guy had the inside scoop.

'*Pfft!*' He'd put the pen down now. Mirren wondered if he'd rolled his eyes a little. 'Some chance. I keep asking Ferdinand if we can bring more people on board, resurrect the paper. I mean, we've got the circulation and the advertising revenue, but he's so...'

'Crap?'

'Resistant to change.' He was frowning now.

'Sorry, I don't know him. I just heard…'

'I know what people have heard. Our reputation precedes us. But you know, we were a proper theatre paper not so long ago.' He lifted his pint to his mouth, suddenly dejected.

'I shouldn't have said anything.' Mirren reminded herself of the other very good reason she shouldn't be here saying things to him, or any guy for that matter, but especially not this one with the sharp jaw, dark penetrating eyes and fine, strong nose like a marble figure in some gallery, and she shouldn't be finding it so hard not to look at his hands gripping his pint glass, either.

She reminded herself she wasn't having anything to do with blokes from now on. She was self-protecting, hunkering down, ready to rise from the ashes of her failed relationship and career. Any day now. She just had to work at it and wait.

The barman returned and took her order. Mirren turned her attention away from Adrian and pressed her stomach to the bar, waiting in silence for her drink. Another half hour sitting by herself at her little table and she could walk slowly back to St. Ninian's. That would have given poor Kelsey at least *some* time to herself.

'You're a writer?' Adrian interrupted her thoughts.

'Yes, well, I was. I'm taking a sabbatical.'

'Doesn't that mean you have a job to go back to?'

'*Umm*, well… it's more of a career-break kind of thing. I was with the *Edinburgh Broadsheet*. Court reporter.'

'Nice gig.'

'*Hmm*,' was the best she could offer in response.

The barman offered up the contactless card machine again and she made a little prayer to the overdraft gods as her payment processed.

'There's nothing available at the *Examiner*, sorry,' Adrian said, looking at his notebook again. Mirren felt the little pang of having wounded him by telling him she didn't want his kindness a few moments ago then almost immediately changing her mind when she figured out there might be a job up for grabs.

'Look, I'm sorry. I'm not always like this. I'm Mirren, by the way.' She lifted herself onto the stool beside him at the same time as her drink was placed before her. Adrian closed his notebook, saying nothing. 'I, *uh*, I kind of made a promise to myself not to get chatting to guys in bars, or anywhere really.'

'OK?' He waited, lifting his pint to his mouth.

'I'm kind of on a sabbatical from men too.'

'I see.' A little impulse moved the corners of his lips. He wanted to smile but was holding back. 'I wouldn't want you to break your rules. I mean, they're obviously working; you looked *so* happy when I came in.' He nodded his head back to the inglenook table, which was now, Mirren noticed, occupied by a vacationing family studying their menus.

'I haven't given my rules much time to take effect yet. I'll start feeling the benefit of them any day now.'

Now he did laugh and it sounded hearty. 'You don't even know if I have a partner. Who says I was chatting you up?'

'True.'

'Well then.' He nodded self-righteously and drank his pint again, his eyes narrowed and bright with good humour.

'So, do you?' Mirren rewarded her curiosity with a mental kick at her own shins.

'Have a girlfriend? Nope. Not that you care, right?'

'Obviously.'

'So why the no men rule?'

'You really want to know?'

He'd left his notebook on the bar now and turned his body a little more towards her on his stool. 'I'm a reporter, aren't I? This sounds like a human interest story to me.'

'Well, it's hardly front page news. It's the usual story, I'm sure you can guess.' She shrugged and took a quick drink. There was no way she was about to confess what a bad girlfriend she'd been, or how even her *virtual* dating life had gone belly up. 'I just needed a break from it all. I'm going to put myself first, do some personal growth stuff.' She quirked her lips now, letting him know she wasn't moping and that she could at least keep her sense of humour about her disastrous personal life.

'Like *Love's Labour's Lost* but gender-reversed?'

'Huh?'

'The Shakespeare play? Where the king and his retinue swear off the company of women for three years in the name of their studies and self-improvement.'

'In that case, yes, just like that, but less regal.'

'They fail, you know? They can't help falling in love.'

'They're also *fictional*. And who said anything about love? As if that's an option these days.'

'Wow.' He pulled his neck back, raising his brows. 'That's really...' He hesitated.

'What? You can say it.'

'Bitter.'

'*Pfft*! OK, you *can't* say it, I've changed my mind. That was just mean.'

'You're the one sitting here telling me you won't so much as talk with a guy in case he turns out to be a rotten apple. *That's* mean. And you say you're a journalist.'

'What's that got to do with anything?'

'All I'm saying is a journalist would investigate any new potential dates properly, evaluate the evidence, carefully consider their response before...'

'But you didn't ask me on a date. There was nothing to scrutinise.'

'I might have offered you my number eventually... if I hadn't made a similar promise to myself.'

Mirren's mouth opened then closed with an exasperated huff. She was still smiling, but her eyes were wary. 'OK, it was nice to meet you, Adrian. I'll take my drink over...' She cast her eyes around the packed room. No empty seats to be had.

Why had she let herself get caught up in this conversation? She shook her head, not minding if he saw.

As she looked around for an escape route a handwritten poster at the end of the bar caught her eye.

Bar Staff Wanted. Evenings, Weekends and Dayshifts Available.

Adrian was backing off again. 'It's OK,' he was saying. 'I'll get on with my work. I didn't mean to upset you.'

'I'm not upset. I'm just looking out for myself. You'll under-stand if you really have given up on dating too.' Her eyes still lingered on the poster.

'Imagine if there *had* been a job at my paper,' he said, drawn back in and tipping his head trying to get Mirren to look at him. 'We might have ended up working together every day. With your court reporting skills and my knowledge of the town, we'd have been quite the team! *Then* where would we be?' He held his notebook up, obscuring his face as if to deflect his irresistibility and Mirren didn't even think it big-headed because he had a point; he was stunning to look at. Working with him would bring nothing but trouble her way. He was still talking, only his laughing eyes showing over his notebook. 'And then there's Mr Ferdinand. How would you have resisted *him*? He's got most of his own teeth and a nice collection of stained, beige cardigans. You wouldn't know where to put yourself to avoid the temptation.'

They both smiled and Mirren felt her armour drop a little. 'You know, on the topic of Mr Ferdinand. He owes my flatmate some money for a job she did for the paper. Any chance of nudging him for her? I promised her I'd help her get paid.'

Adrian sat up taller on the stool. 'I'm not sure I can be much help there either. He's notoriously badly organised when it comes to freelancer payments. Your flatmate will have to join the queue, or try the small claims court. Sorry to say it.'

'Really? You're saying he'll never pay?'

'I think your mate should chalk it up as a lesson learned and steer well clear of him in future.'

'But he pays you?'

'I'm a permanent staffer on payroll so that's all handled by the newspaper's parent company. We're one of twenty-eight regional papers and we're all semi-autonomous. Mr F handles the advertising revenue, the freelancer payments, bonuses, petty cash, that sort of thing, but not my salary, thankfully.' He sniffed, his expression wry and deliberate, before sipping his beer.

The old barfly behind him was getting ready to leave, throwing an inky-coloured mac over rounded shoulders and reaching for a felt fedora with a red pheasant feather stuck jauntily in its band. His elbow nudged Adrian's and it all happened so quickly after that: the beer splashing onto Adrian's notebook and across the bar and the sudden flash of anger which darkened Adrian's eyes. But Mirren caught it all.

For a millisecond she thought Adrian might swing a fist at the old man who was apologising profusely in a jolly manner, mopping at the spilled drink with the barman's towel and making even more beer run down onto Adrian's trousers.

'My good man, I must apologise,' he was booming, his cheeks rosy like Santa Claus. 'Do not reprehend. If you pardon, we will mend.' He dabbed at Adrian's legs with the beer-sodden cloth.

Mirren guessed the old buffer was reciting lines from some play or other and she wanted to smile but Adrian was grimacing and making a grab at the cloth, tossing it onto the bar with a damp slap. Surely an overreaction, even if his clothes *were* expensive designer stuff, as Mirren suspected. He was still overdoing it.

'It's not *me* you need to apologise to,' Adrian hissed.

The old man raised his hands innocently, placed his hat upon his head with a flourish and made a quick bow. 'Apologies, apologies, dear friends all.' And with that, he left, like an epilogue before the curtain falls.

Adrian turned back to his drink, cradling it, his eyes still a little wild.

'No harm done. It was just a bit of beer,' Mirren offered mildly, craning to peer at his face. *Why's he so angry? The poor old guy said sorry, didn't he?*

Adrian didn't reply. She watched him breathe deeply once or twice, obviously trying to control his frustration.

'I'd better get going,' she added, and Adrian looked up. She could read the regret on his face.

'Don't go, enjoy your drink, I'm sorry, I...'

'I'll take that number, if you don't mind,' she said sharply.

His eyes rounded until he noticed she was pointing past his ear to the job vacancy poster on the wall with the fringed scissor snips separating phone numbers. Realising what was happening, he tore free one of the strips and gave it to her, sullen now.

She looked at the paper in her hands. She wasn't thinking about Adrian, but was enjoying the warmth of a curious little glow in her chest. She'd made up her mind. She'd taken a first step towards accepting her fate. A bar job could be OK as a stop gap, if they'd have her.

She wouldn't mention it now to the barman but would ring in the morning when she'd composed herself and noted down a few things to say. She had tried to find writing work, hadn't she? *Really* tried. Her stars weren't aligned in that regard, yet. These thoughts brought a gentle kind of comfort and her lips curled into an unconscious smile.

'It was nice to meet you anyway, Mirren,' Adrian said, snapping her out of her thoughts.

He'd remembered her name, and an unfamiliar Scottish name at that, she registered with surprise. Looking at him, he seemed to have shrunk a little more. He'd overreacted and was suddenly sorry, no doubt, but he'd confirmed that Mirren's instincts had been right all along. The last thing she needed was closer acquaintance with a new guy, and least of all a guy with an obviously short fuse, even as a drinking buddy, even for an hour. Even if he was amusing, and sharp-witted, and sexy too, and her name had sounded so soft in his English accent.

In the silence between them she heard the words that had been insinuating themselves into her thoughts increasingly often lately. It was Mr Angus's voice telling her again how her 'overactive love life' and lack of professionalism impinged on her decision-making abilities, made her confused and over sensitive. Her ex-boss's braying judgement mixed with all her insecurities and every unkind thing anyone had ever said to her and she felt again the little pang of shame and embarrassment that seemed to be growing rather than diminishing the longer she spent out of the newsroom.

She packed away any feelings of attraction to Adrian. He wasn't just a handsome man, he was a reporter too, and one with a temper at that, and she'd learned her lesson on all those counts. This had been a timely warning and she took it for what it was; a reminder of her resolve.

As she walked out into the chilly darkness of All Hallow's Eve, Adrian Armadale briefly watched after her, shaking beer from his sodden notebook, his eyes full of annoyance and self-recrimination.

Chapter Eighteen

'To business that we love we rise betimes, and go to it with
    delight'
(*Antony and Cleopatra*)

The November afternoon rain was hitting the barge windows
in a loud, sleety patter. Kelsey curled her feet beneath her, as
she perched on the little padded bench by the hatch where
not so many weeks ago she and her colleagues had sold tickets
for their guided tours. Bringing her coffee cup to her lips, she
mused. It was warm in here and with the bulbs blazing in their
brass sconces the place glowed orange and cosy, and the rocking
really wasn't so bad once you got used to it, and that wooden
creaking sound like a galleon under stress in a storm coming
from somewhere in the stern had proven to be the perfectly
innocent sound of the tiller bar.

She'd enquired about the creak at the neighbouring moorings – one a holiday-maker travelling with their kids from
Napton to Stratford and back again over the course of a leisurely
fortnight; the other a retired couple who moored by the bank
permanently and supplemented their pensions by selling bags
of food for the birds on the river.

This couple, the surprisingly named Mr and Mrs Flowers,
had helped her fix the tiller bar to stop it moving and the
sound stopped too, and so she'd relaxed and spent her evenings
working busily on board, sometimes with Mirren, but less often

now that Mirren was being trained in the art of pint-pulling at the Yorick.

Kelsey had cleaned the boat's little windows inside and out, and recycled the last boxes of Norma's leaflets and custom printed tickets.

She hadn't disturbed the mallards who had set up home on the roof of the boat, reasoning that they'd been there first and had made a comfy home for themselves in what by the looks of things was once upon a time a rooftop flowerbed in a wide wooden tray but was now a mess of earth, feathers, weeds and straw.

Then the barge's bed had needed new covers and she'd splashed out on a pretty Scandi print floral set in blue and yellow. Not being much of a seamstress, she hadn't attempted to find material to match up little curtains, so she took the old red ones to the launderette then rehung them, comic in their dimensions, like those in a Wendy house.

Then she'd sprung it on Mirren. She could move in here, to the lodgings at the back of the boat, if she wanted, for as long as she needed, just to give them both some breathing space. Instead of upset or awkwardness, the friends had hugged it out like they always did and Mirren had refused to cry but she'd definitely been misty-eyed as Kelsey gave her the freshly cut key to her new waterside home.

That was five days ago on the fifth of November and the friends had snapped the pull tabs on their cans of gin and tonic sitting on the barge roof toasting to their good fortune as they watched the firework display taking place over at the rugby club for free – another perk of having a riverside bolthole.

Tonight though, Kelsey was alone. She had walked through the rain to the barge after a painfully quiet day at the studio where, now the pumpkin patch shoots were long since over, she'd done little more than snap full-length portraits of a woman applying for a job as cabin crew. Kelsey had tried not to tut at the very idea of the woman's figure being important in the application process and put it out of her mind by reminding herself she was making another few pounds to help pay the bills – and the woman didn't seem to mind one bit about having to supply the photo anyway. After that, Kelsey had emailed all the company bosses who had their staff booked in for Christmas party nights at the Osprey, letting them know she'd be there with her costumes and camera. It hadn't been her busiest day, by any means.

Now, she cast her eyes around the empty room at the front of the barge. A few large cardboard boxes lay at her feet. Apart from the sconces and the window hatch, the walls were bare. There were steps beneath the slanted access hatch, and two low, cushioned benches along the sides. It was a decent-sized room and Kelsey could stand up straight in it, just about. It was easily big enough for a dining table and a big telly if she'd wanted to extend the living quarters – and she might have done if Jonathan hadn't surprised her with his revelations about his seasickness. Instead, she had put her mind to how to use this space to enhance her photography business. Fortunately, yesterday the answer had come to her, with the help of Blythe Goode.

Kelsey had only called in to take her some library books. Blythe had asked for a biography of Vivien Leigh and something 'diverting'. She'd scoured the fiction shelves at the town's lovely little library and chosen *One Hundred Years of Solitude*, *The Bell Jar*, *Robinson Crusoe*, Defoe's *Diary of a Plague Year* and a dog-eared Daphne du Maurier with a gaudy cover featuring a long-haired pirate with his chest bared. Blythe had accepted the biography but raised a bare brow at the others, except the du Maurier.

'Funny, some people's idea of diverting. I'll keep *Frenchman's Creek* though, thank you very much. What's that one in your coat pocket?'

'Oh, that's my Shakespeare's *Sonnets*. I carry them most places, read them when I'm feeling down.'

Blythe was already reaching for it with a knowing look. 'Your beloved's an actor, isn't he? Away on tour?'

'He is. He's playing Hamlet in Ontario right now. He'll be back in town in the spring for a run of *Love's Labour's Lost*.'

Blythe kept her eyes on the little book as she turned the well-thumbed pages. 'You're missing him.' It wasn't a question and she wasn't waiting for an answer. 'My advice to you, my dear, would be to wow him.'

'Do you mean *woo* him?'

'I know perfectly well what I mean, my dear. *Wow* the man. There's a lot of drivel spoken about men wanting a woman to be domesticated and docile, but they tire of that so easily, you see, and they're soon hitching a lift on the next passing pair of frilly knickers. You need to outshine the man wherever you can, that's my advice. Surprise him constantly with your ingenuity, and don't be doing it for him either, do it for yourself. Be capable, not a wet blanket, dear. Oh, now don't look at me like that. I know you've got your business and your talents, and that's a wonderful starting point, but have you really, truly pushed yourself?'

Kelsey didn't know whether to feel offended or motivated. She settled for chastened and looked back blankly at the actress.

'You've more strings to your bow than you know of. How will you learn what you're capable of until you've struck each one? Read your sonnets as your reward *after* successes, eh? Don't go seeking solace in them and idling away the hours, *hmm*?' She was peering up at Kelsey's wide eyes and there was a challenge in the puckered set of her lips.

Anyone else might have told Blythe to mind her own business, to pack it in, but Blythe had Kelsey pinned with arrow-like precision, and hadn't the actress lived a thousand lives in her time? She ought to know a thing or two about women's ways and means.

'Make life happen? That's what you're telling me?' Kelsey said, mulling over the words.

'Get out there and find your spotlight, Kelsey. Don't wait in the wings for cues you might miss.'

All of this was like lighting a fire beneath her. Nothing spurred Kelsey on more than the weight of expectation, except perhaps the goading feeling of someone underestimating her, like Fran, her ex, had. Mari Anderson had never pushed her daughter, trusting she would eventually find her own path, and after her dad died, Kelsey spent years helping care for her baby brother and her mum when Mari was drowning in grief. It had meant that Kelsey had watched years of her youth and her potential slipping by and she'd fallen behind her peers. She was only just getting the hang of adulting at the age of twenty-nine. Certainly, she'd been lucky with all the coincidences and compulsions that had sent her down south and into Norma Arden's employ, but here was Blythe telling her to grab life and get on with it, to do *more*, and it was making fireworks spark in her chest.

'When your young man returns to you, have him find you really smiling, really accomplished. *That* is how you wow them. Have him wide-eyed in wonder.'

Kelsey didn't have any words ready in response because her mind was too occupied. Blythe was right. She was wasting time. She had two business premises and wasn't properly using either of them, and she only had three and a half months left of her peppercorn lease on the studio before she had to pay Norma the rent in full – no more mates' rates. And, now she came to think about it, hadn't *she* been in awe of Jonathan? He was the amazing one, the star. She could shine too. 'All right, then. I will,' she muttered, clutching the rejected library books to her chest.

'Come back and read your sonnets to me, won't you? When you've a great success to celebrate?' Blythe handed her treasured poems back. 'And send this Mirren you mentioned down here for a gin.'

'Course I will.' Her eyes were unfocused as she thought.

'And take those frames to the charity shop, if you don't mind. I'd ask my youngest grandson, but he's so busy at the moment.

He does what he can. He's such a good boy, and I don't like to bother him.'

Against the wall leaned a bundle of picture frames, so many that Kelsey knew she'd struggle to carry them along with the books.

Kelsey didn't want to enquire about this invisible grandson who didn't seem to do much for her at all. He must be the 'young man' she had mentioned on previous visits, surely? The one that brought the roses? Blythe seemed so fond of the idea that she had him as a helper and friend but Kelsey had never laid eyes on him. 'Been having a clear out?' she asked instead.

'I have, as it happens. Talking with you about the old days and seeing the article in the paper got me thinking about how stagnant I've been lately. Some memories you can afford to let go of, and it *was* getting a little cluttered in here.'

As Kelsey had struggled out the door, her arms full, Blythe had called out in a commanding voice, 'Wow us all, Kelsey dear!'

The idea had come to her that evening as she was washing the dust from Blythe's empty frames at the little sink in her bedsit before taking them to the charity shop. *Show everyone what you can do, make use of the spaces you have, push yourself. Wow the crowds.*

The crowds?

The glass in one of the frames glinted as she held it to the light to check for fingerprints and she caught her reflection in it, gilt-edged like a portrait. Her eyes were wild and shining.

'An exhibition… on the barge! I'll create my own photography exhibition!'

–

The rain was beating even harder at the barge windows and Kelsey was no longer sitting nursing her coffee cup. She was setting out rows of frames in every size on dust sheets, all ready to paint with the studio's leftover white emulsion. Some were

Blythe's, some were finds of her own; she'd raided every charity shop in town.

She had already set the date for the grand opening: Valentine's Day, when Jonathan would be briefly back in town to see it. That would give her a little over three months to select and print all the photos she needed, frame and hang them, and advertise the launch of the Kelsey Anderson Photography Barge Gallery and retrospective exhibition of her best work. Her paintbrush worked as the November rain fell and she was smiling all the while.

Chapter Nineteen

'My pride fell with my fortunes'
(*As you Like It*)

The lagers were easier than the cask ales, Mirren was learning.

'The glass must be spotlessly clean,' Kenneth the landlord of the Yorick had insisted multiple times. They'd worked on getting the exact angle on the tilt of the glass right, combined with the right speed on the pour and knowing when to leave off to let the head settle mid-way.

Mirren had likened pouring the perfect pint to finding the biting point between the clutch and the accelerator but Kenneth wasn't the type to appreciate analogies and had looked blankly at her. Any badly pulled pints refused by customers would be deducted from her wages, he'd told her, giving her an hour to perfect her technique.

Fortunately, the white-bearded old barfly was there to polish off any failed attempts and he had a long line of froth-filled glasses in front of him as he supped away happily.

'Practice makes perfect,' he said, eyes aglow and cheeks pink, as Mirren slid yet another disaster towards him. 'Must be my lucky day. The lass who worked here before you got the knack instantly, didn't get so much as a snifter on *her* first shift.' His voice was jolly even though it was boomingly loud and Mirren wished he wasn't so meticulous about broadcasting each failure to the entire bar which was surprisingly busy for a wintry Wednesday afternoon.

She smiled back when he threw her a compassionate wink and she quickly looked back at her grip on the glass and the beer tap, exhaling through pursed lips, her brow furrowed with concentration as though she were about to pilot an Apollo rocket instead of pulling a dribbling pint of Bottom's Bobbin.

'After that you can try the Fair Youth,' Kenneth was instructing. 'Needs a slower pull than the Dark Lady.'

So it had come to this. Her degree at journalism school and all those years of training, covering charity bazaars and stories about the village fair's prize-winning fruit pies, and her long apprenticeship under Jamesey on the court stories at the *Broadsheet*, all that grafting and climbing. Just when she'd been on the cusp of a breakthrough it had all fallen apart. She refused to believe all her hard work had been for nothing.

She'd picked up resilience beyond measure for a start, and she'd held on to some of her professional pride even if she couldn't practise her literary art at the moment. Her command of words, her investigative talents, her coolness under pressure in a bustling environment, all of these she could store up for when her big break came, and that wouldn't be long, surely? She was on the edge of the next stage in her journalism career, she could almost feel it.

'Packet of pork scratchings please, love,' a tourist was asking, bringing her round from her reverie.

'Kenneth, can you show me how to work the till please?' Mirren asked in a small voice as the pre-theatre crowds began to pour in and she lost herself in the sudden rush and clamour, all thoughts of her old career banished.

–

'It's you!' the voice exclaimed from the end of the bar. Mirren barely registered it. It was ten minutes until last orders and she was looking forward to ringing the brass bell for the first time. The hours had flown by in a noisy blur of orders shouted out across the hubbub, mixer bottle tops clanking into the pail below the bar, bubbling optics and overflowing froth – and she'd actually enjoyed it. Her feet ached even in her flat boots, but there were tips in the jar, happy punters talking loudly and huddling together, full bellies, and empty plates being cleared away by the kitchen staff.

She glanced over to find Adrian smiling, learning with his arms crossed on the bar.

'I've been keeping an eye open for you all over town,' he said. 'Should have known the Yorick would snap you up. You doing OK?'

'I'm good actually.' She was surprised to find she meant it too. 'Why were you looking for me?' She took the opportunity of a lull in orders to wipe her cloth along the bar towards him. 'Drink?'

'What are you having?' he said.

'Nothing, I'm working.'

'OK, what would you *notionally* be having if you weren't working? JD and Coke, right?'

She hid her surprise about him remembering, telling herself this was the oldest trick in the chat-up line book; remembering a small detail about a girl and hoping her self-esteem's so low she'll be bowled over. *Not anymore*, she thought. *Bet he can't even remember my name by now.* 'Is that what you want? Jack Daniels?' she asked.

'Sure, and have one for yourself after work, Mirren.'

Anyone can remember a name. What of it? 'No, I'm good, thanks.'

Kenneth had told her to always accept the offer of a drink and to put the money in the jar for splitting with the team and she had been saying yes all evening but nothing could induce her to accept in this instance. Perhaps if he wasn't looking at her like that, with the wolfish smile and something daring in his eyes that her very blood cells responded to…

She worked the optic and handed him his drink, followed by the card machine. He was shaking his head and blowing an exasperated breath as he paid up.

'Wish I hadn't bothered now,' he said in a wry tone.

'Bothered with what?'

'Asking Mr Ferdinand if he'd see you.'

She glanced around, hoping Kenneth wasn't in earshot. Luckily he was wiping today's specials from the board. 'Mr Ferdinand? What did he say?' she asked surreptitiously, fiddling with the plastic drink stirrers in the jar, still trying to be aloof.

'December the first, lunchtime, you've got ten minutes.'

'Really? Oh my God,' she gasped and watched his mouth twitch in response. Mirren regretted her broad smile instantly. That was exactly the kind of thing that gave men the wrong idea; what Mr Angus would call 'letting your overactive love life interfere with your professionalism'. She rearranged her face into something more neutral. 'I mean, that's very kind of you, thank you.'

Adrian was still smiling, charitably under the circumstances. 'Look, I don't meet many reporters around town. You seem like a good person, even if you are prickly as hell.'

'Hey!'

'We should be friends.'

She drew her neck back at his bluntness. Mirren was ready to speak but he knew what was coming, another knock-back.

'Hear me out. It would be nice to talk shop with someone in the same line of work, you know, as friends and hopefully future colleagues. If you impress Ferdinand and convince him to bring you on board you'd be doing me a huge favour. Sometimes working alone with him is frustrating. *All* the time, in fact.' His expression was so open, it was hard to rebuff.

'Friends?' she said, in spite of her brain screaming for caution.

'Nothing more. I told you I'm taking a break from dating too after—'

Mirren flinched at the bell ringing loudly behind her and turned upon Kenneth. 'I was looking forward to ringing that! Isn't it the new barmaid's rite of passage?'

She was met with a staid look from dour old Kenneth. 'You'll have a thousand more shifts to ring the bell, Mirren.' Then he called across the room, 'Last orders please.'

Mirren met Adrian's eyes and she knew he understood her thoughts. *A thousand more shifts?* She hoped not, and so did he.

Mirren was still thinking about Adrian's single status and what might have brought it about when a booming voice called over the crowd: 'One for the road if you don't mind, my lovely,' and both Mirren and Adrian knew who it was.

'That old Lothario's always in here,' Adrian complained, seeing the actor who'd doused him in beer.

'That's my favourite customer you're talking about,' replied Mirren *sotto voce* as she waved and pulled his drinks, always the same thing, she'd learned – a pint of ale, and a glass of Spanish sherry which he referred to as 'sack'. The request had confounded her at first, but Kenneth had nodded to a bottle on the shelf saying, 'That's his; only one that drinks it. I bring it in special from Malaga, just for him.'

Adrian was glowering at the old fellow through narrowed eyes.

'What have you got against him?' Mirren whispered. 'He's lonely, that's all. So what if he's a bit… boisterous? I'm sure half his stories are made up but he's entertaining when you get to know him. He's got no family, you know…'

'Oh, it's all true,' Adrian interrupted. 'He's a big star round here. Well he was. An old-guard luvvie. He was in loads of seventies sci-fi too, even *Star Wars*.'

'No!'

'Yeah, don't you recognise him?'

Mirren plumped a lip. 'Nope.' She was aware of Adrian's critical glances as she gave the old man his drinks and took his money which he picked out in coins from a little leather purse like her late grandfather had. That wasn't the only thing about the old man that reminded Mirren of her grandfather. The beard, the jolly round cheeks and his twinkling eyes took her back to happy days as a child when her mum's father had wrapped them both up in his love and devotion. Happier days, when her mum wasn't wracked with addiction and her dad still lived at home. But she didn't want to think about that.

As soon as she could, she was back beside Adrian. 'You'll strain your face gurning at the poor old fellow like that. Seriously, what's wrong with you?'

Adrian said nothing, drained his drink and made ready to leave. 'Twelve o'clock on Tuesday the first, remember? Don't be late, you might keep Ferdinand from his lunchtime nap.'

'I'll be there.'

He nodded, pulling his black jacket on and flattening his hair under a black peaked cap that framed his dark brows and cheekbones in a way that made Mirren want to sigh.

'Adrian?' Their eyes met for a beat she wished she could sustain. 'Thank you. I mean it. You're a good friend.'

'Yes, I am.' The flash of his teeth in a stunningly squared smile called to a traitorous place inside her and she fought to control muscle and nerve telling her to smile back, to lean across the bar and reach for his lapel, to speak to him in a low voice about wanting him. The old Mirren would have done all these things, but thankfully her resistance wasn't put to the test because he was suddenly gone, leaving her watching in his wake as the crowds parted to let him pass then closed in again.

Chapter Twenty

'O, how shall summer's honey breath hold out
Against the wrackful siege of battering days,
When rocks impregnable are not so stout,
Nor gates of steel so strong, but Time decays?'
(*Sonnet 65*)

The courier van had only just pulled away from St. Ninian's but Kelsey was already cross-legged on her bed pushing aside the clutter of books and catalogues all explaining the finer points of curating photographic exhibitions which she'd spent the morning poring over. She tore at the cardboard packages and pulled free the large glossy prints in their protective cellophane.

It had taken days for her collection of negatives and contact strips to arrive from her mum in Scotland and then she'd gone through the careful process of selecting the perfect images to send to the developers. She wouldn't let herself think about how much it had cost; it was an unavoidable expense and an investment in her business. These images wouldn't just be *displayed* in her new floating gallery; they'd be on sale too. The shots had to be perfect, and they were.

Every photographer has one; a list of those stand-out images where their skill, the lighting conditions and their subject come together to create something magical, the very best examples of their craft stretching back years. Kelsey had drawn her greatest hits together for the first time and the sight of them in her hands now made her heart soar.

The first out the packaging were old images from the only other exhibition she'd taken part in, back when she was in the university camera society, back when she had a group of happy, creative mates endlessly talking about f-stops, film-processing and double exposures, way back before she met Fran and let all her dreams slide, prioritising instead his ambitions.

These Scottish semi-rural landscapes, taken ten years ago now, captured where she was from, the very heart of her. A fisherman repairing his nets on the quayside near Mirren and Preston's old flat; shining, striped mackerel in their iced trays fresh off the morning boats on the Firth; a combine harvester in the fields throwing dust and chaff into a clear August sky with the ruins of the Victorian pit head in the far distance. Then there was a black and white shot of a younger version of her mum standing in her kitchen behind Grandad in the chair, a towel around his shoulders, having his hair cut. Another taken in the little ice cream parlour at North Berwick she'd visited with her grandparents, the flavours laid out in their tubs like a pastel paint palette. Looking at it now she could almost taste the mint choc chip ice cream and feel the summer sun making it melt in her cone.

Photographs could always do that for her; send her right back to the moment they were taken, preserved forever. A lens makes everyone a traveller in time.

She was looking now at a shot of Mari pushing Calum in his buggy outside John Menzies on Princes Street and could swear she detected her mum's Chanel No. 5, and somehow this shot of Mirren's back as she looked out over Edinburgh castle ramparts had conjured up the distinctive smells of roasted malt from the North British Distillery and the smoke from the castle's one o'clock gun.

She peered closely at another familiar old image and smiled; a picture of an English garden. She'd only ever seen the photo in nineties' five-by-four gloss but as a ten-inch matt enlargement she noticed for the first time the slightest blurring at its furthest depths. It was hardly surprising it wasn't perfectly focused, since this was the very first shot she ever took, with her dad's camera, under his instruction, standing peering over the hedge at the boundary of Shakespeare's birthplace as a thirteen-year-old Anglophile, already lost to the romance of theatre and history and, unbeknown to her, about to become a vintage camera enthusiast.

Her father wasn't in the picture, he wasn't in any of the exhibition shots in fact, but he was present in every single depression of the shutter button and in the very light itself as it worked in chemical reaction upon sensitive film. All of these early pictures recorded her love for him and how it was the very makings of her.

Then there were the newer ones. Confetti thrown in the air against a blue sky at Norma's wedding, abstract and colourful. A number of pictures of Blythe from the day they met, her violet eyes contrasting wonderfully with her white hair and the pink paper flower at her ear. Kelsey knew these would look just right hung alongside the headshot of Jonathan in silky monochrome which she stalled over now, wanting to press her fingertips to his accent mark eyebrows and the strong lines of his temples and jaw.

She grabbed for her phone and typed.

> **Only twenty-three sleeps! I'll be opening the first door on the studio advent calendar tomorrow. I can't wait to see you! Not long now. I love you, x**

Off flew the words into the ether. Even though she was missing Jonathan, she knew how to love someone she couldn't see every day; her dad had taught her a little about that.

Just as she was opening another text box to send a chaser of a love heart emoji, she heard Mirren's knock on the door. Actually, it was more of a kick somewhere near ground level.

'Coming! Don't you have your key?' Kelsey called. It had been two days since they'd seen each other, Mirren was so busy at the Yorick and had seemingly settled in to the barge's living quarters very happily indeed. The tension of being cooped up together was long forgotten now they each had a little more space and a lot more privacy. Kelsey greeted her with a grin as she let Mirren in. 'Woah, what's all this?'

Mirren's arms were piled with books and two carrier bags swung from her wrists. Only her eyes showed over the load.

'I met your neighbour at last. Blythe? She gave me these. Said she was having a clear out and thought you'd like them. She also made me down a shot of eighty proof alcohol that tasted like hand sanitiser and hedgerow.'

'That's Blythe for you.' Kelsey rescued the books and piled them on the floor, then safely packed away the exhibition photographs from the bed, keeping only Jonathan's head shot out and placing it on top of the pile.

'And I got us some dinner,' Mirren was saying, emptying the carrier bags of the two portions of bangers and mash with onion gravy in their foil containers which Kenneth had given her from the kitchens, along with a shiraz to celebrate her joining the team and in honour of her first pay cheque. 'These were on the house. Maybe my new boss isn't so bad after all.'

Mirren set about reheating the food and pouring the drinks while Kelsey sorted through the books, fascinated.

'Nice one, Mirr!' She smacked her lips approvingly at the takeaway. 'So... Blythe didn't want any of these books?'

'Nope. When I let myself in she was peering through the chain at her flat door; she must have been watching for someone passing. She said she knew you'd appreciate some of the Shake-speare text books, and there's some old acting handbooks too...'

'Ooh, perfect Christmas presents for Jonathan.'

'I thought that, and that one's on theatrical costume design...'

'I could give that to Myrtle and Valeria for their shop!'

'And she practically threw that one there out the door.'

'What, this one?' Kelsey held up the slim volume, reading aloud the title. '*An Actor's Life* by John Wagstaff.' The inside jacket told her it was one of a one-hundred-copy print run from a small local press, probably long since defunct. 'I'm not surprised she didn't want to keep this one. Seeing it must bring back bad memories for her.'

'*Hmm*?' Mirren was busy finding cutlery.

'This guy, John Wagstaff, was mentioned in her newspaper article. He was her co-star and got so drunk before the opening night of *Cleopatra* he fell off the stage and broke his legs, ruined the run for everyone, and if my instincts are right, that's not all he ruined.'

Mirren handed Kelsey a wine glass. 'What do you mean?'

'Well,' she lowered her voice as if somehow Blythe could have made it up two flights of stairs and was listening at the door. 'Blythe had a baby and the theatre bosses didn't like her being an unmarried mum. Eventually they pushed her out of the company, ruined her career. I reckon the daddy was this guy.'

'Old scoundrel, let's have a look at him.' Mirren flicked through the illustrations while the microwave droned from the corner. The cover didn't give much away, featuring only a drawing of the comedy and tragedy masks, but inside there were black and white pictures of the man at work. 'Tights, codpieces, the usual stuff...' Mirren said as she flicked. 'Oh, hold on, there's his face... God, he's gorgeous! Nice one, Blythe!'

'Pass it here,' Kelsey took the book and studied the images, turning the pages with increasingly quick flicks. 'That is *so* spooky.'

Mirren began serving the steaming food onto plates. 'What is?'

'Look at him! He's the double of Jonathan.'

'Oh yeah.' Mirren peered over. 'That is a bit weird.'

Kelsey couldn't push the images from her mind as she and Mirren sat together on the bed, eating quietly. Throughout the meal she kept returning to the book, flipping its foxed pages until she came across a head shot that made her stomach convulse. The heading told her it was taken in nineteen sixty-eight and that Wagstaff was pictured in his stage make-up for *Antony and Cleopatra*. Kelsey reached for Jonathan's headshot and compared the two for a long while.

'Mirren?' Kelsey's tone was ominous. 'Did I ever tell you the story of Jonathan's dad?'

'*Umm*, not really… I remember you saying he doesn't know who he is.'

'That's right,' Kelsey said. 'I mean, his mum knows, obviously, but out of respect for her and his stepdad Jonathan never wanted to know anything about him, not even his name. He said his mum tried to tell him when he was a teenager but he couldn't stand it. You know, his mum's story is strikingly similar to the one Blythe told me, now I think about it.'

'Spill.' Mirren's lips curled over the rim of her glass and her eyes crinkled. She was enjoying this.

'Jonathan's really private about this kind of stuff, and Blythe probably believed she was telling me in confidence. You won't repeat it to anyone, will you?'

'Kelse, I've got nobody to tell.'

'Well, OK. Jonathan's mum was an actress here in town and some guy in the company got her pregnant and ditched her. She went back to Oklahoma and raised Jonathan on her own, never had a penny or a sniff of fatherly interest from whoever he was. Anyway, Blythe fell pregnant to some guy in the company too! And she said he was really handsome, like… irresistibly.'

They both turned their eyes back to the book lying open at the portrait as though the spine had been flexed there many times. It was so patently like Jonathan's image staring back at them, even in the heavy stage make-up – though Jonathan's features were more refined, his mouth more delicate and curving and he had the unmistakable ruddy health of an actor who spends a lot of time in LA and even more time in the gym.

'Are you thinking what I'm thinking?' Kelsey had noticeably paled.

'Look, it's a grainy picture, and all these guys look the same in that ridiculous stage make-up with their floppy wigs, pointy-toed shoes and their codpieces… and there must have been *hundreds* of hot male actors passing through town. One guy can't be responsible for every surprise baby.' Even as she spoke Mirren was already on her phone, Googling. 'Let's see where this guy is now before we jump to conclusions. He's probably been happily married to his husband for the last twenty years and living in some luvvies' retirement community. Oh, Jesus!' She turned the search results to Kelsey. 'It's him. John Wagstaff is the barfly from the Yorick. I *know* this guy.'

'He lives in town?' Kelsey gasped.

'Yeah, and he's always talking about how he drank champagne from a satin slipper with Dickie Attenborough or danced a conga at Princess Margaret's birthday party with John Gielgud and Elizabeth Taylor. I always thought he was lying but…' Mirren paused, struck with sudden understanding.

'*What*?' Kelsey's eyes bulged.

Mirren's mind flitted to Adrian. 'Somebody told me his stories were all true. He's a proper celeb around here and he was a big star in eighties sci-fi. Your wee brother would definitely know all about him. But how old is Jonathan?' Her thoughts raced.

'He'll be thirty-three this year.'

'OK, so it's feasible Wagstaff was still hot as hell and seducing every young actress in town in the late eighties, right? He'd be in his late forties by then…'

'And in his twenties when he acted alongside Blythe?'

'You'd think he'd have learned a thing or two about destroying girls' lives by the time he met Jonathan's mum though,' Mirren added, bitterly. Her mind ticked on. *It would be easy enough to do a bit of digging and find out more. With the right help from a local, an insider who knew the town and its people... someone like Adrian Armadale.*

'What are you thinking?' Kelsey's eyes narrowed suspiciously.

'Nothing. Do you really think this could be Jonathan's dad? You *have* to tell him.'

'No. No, I don't. Not without some proof. You can't spring something like that on a person.' Kelsey swigged at her wine, her eyes darting as she thought. 'I can't possibly ask Blythe if there were other actresses after her... I mean, she did mention girls leaving their jobs at the theatre in the sixties because of unplanned pregnancies; she told me some of them disappeared entirely...'

'Like Jonathan's mum going back to Oklahoma?' Mirren cut in.

Kelsey worried her bottom lip. 'I could never ask Blythe about any of that. That would be unforgivable.'

'We have to do something... Jonathan could meet his real dad as early as Christmas! And old Wagstaff's not exactly getting any younger – the way he can put away those glasses of sack and ale he's probably approaching his sell-by date—'

Kelsey interrupted, her cutlery now abandoned by her half-eaten meal. 'His step-father, Art, is his real dad. That's what Jonathan says. If Wagstaff is his father, and it's a big *if*, he was nothing but the sperm donor.'

'You said Blythe had a son, and she mentioned having grand-sons?' Mirren's eyes were aflame now. 'Jonathan could gain a dad *and* a half-brother *and* nephews...'

Kelsey tamped down Mirren's excitement, feeling the panic rise in her own chest. 'No, don't. We're getting ahead of ourselves. Jonathan would be devastated if he thought we'd been snooping into his mum's secrets. She left England to get away from them. Neither of them would appreciate us throwing this in her face... and we're most likely wrong anyway. I haven't even met her yet, for goodness' sake.' Kelsey mimed a hand-shake. 'Pleased to meet you, Mrs Hathaway. Remember that actor who knocked you up in the eighties and abandoned you both, is it *this* guy by any chance?' She held up the book. 'It's not exactly the best plan for a meeting-your-boyfriend's-mum scenario, is it? Besides, maybe some dads aren't worth finding?'

These last words rocked Mirren like a gunshot near her ear, but she tried to hide the flinching feeling. She took a long drink, trying to swallow the memories of her own dad walking out when she was so tiny, and all the waiting and worrying, watching her mum sinking deeper into the bottle. Yes, maybe some dads weren't worth looking for. It had been almost two decades since she last saw her own father. He hadn't even called on her birthday this year, even though she had been careful to always keep the same number and to have her phone charged on the day in case she somehow missed him. Her brain dredged up deeply buried memories of his calls on her childhood birthdays – the dread of the phone ringing, then the stilted conversation with the stranger. He'd always phone so late at night that she'd have to wait all day, the nerves spoiling her appetite for jelly and cake and making her little parties with the neighbourhood kids fraught, unhappy, tearful things. No child should hate their own birthdays.

Mirren's tone had cooled considerably. 'OK. I promise I won't say anything to Jonathan, but if we uncovered the truth, you'd *have* to let him know, right?'

'He doesn't want to know or else he'd ask his mum. This is a sleeping dog that really needs to be left well alone.' Finding she couldn't sit still any longer, Kelsey scraped the plates into the little kitchen bin, keeping her back turned to Mirren. She didn't want to admit she simply couldn't guess how Jonathan might react if she told him their theory; she didn't know him well enough to be sure, and that irked her. He might be relieved.

Maybe his mysterious paternity had been a weight on his mind for a lifetime and now it had become one of those silent sore points he couldn't discuss at home anymore, too risky to bring up.

Maybe he was just hoping his father would reveal himself to him one day like those adult children you see on *Long Lost Family* where they meet for the first time and fall into each other's arms? No. Jonathan was too proud and protective of his mother for that, surely? That's the impression Kelsey had from the few times he'd spoken of her anyway. The only thing Kelsey was certain of was that he could get hurt, and the thought of causing him a moment's pain nearly winded her.

'Let's leave it,' Kelsey said, meeting Mirren's upturned face. 'We need to get rid of that book, make sure he never sees it.'

Mirren picked it up from the bed, slipping it in her jacket pocket. 'Consider it gone.'

Kelsey tried to focus on the wine and Mirren's company for the rest of the evening but everything felt burdened and heavy now. Soon they were saying their goodnights and Mirren was telling Kelsey not to let it worry her and promising again she'd keep quiet about the whole thing. Zipping her jacket, she walked out into the chilly darkness for her journey towards her cosy bed in the back of Kelsey's exhibition barge, planning to read the Wagstaff biography from cover to cover as soon as she climbed aboard. It couldn't hurt to find out a little more about the old actor, and as a reporter, the mystery was irresistibly attractive, even if she would have to keep any findings to herself, for now.

Chapter Twenty-One

'At Christmas I no more desire a rose
Than wish a snow in May's new-fangled mirth;
But like of each thing that in season grows'
(*Love's Labour's Lost*)

Advent. The days passed in quick succession like colourful paper doors opened each morning, every day revealing a different charming scene.

Stratford assumed a new shining mood during these increasingly cold and dark days as midwinter drew nearer. The Christmas tree on the roundabout by the bank towered and glittered, the streets were strung with jewel-like lights; hoar frosts turned the mornings sparkling white, and the water in the marina slowly became frigid and slushy.

Christmas markets lined the riverside weekly, chestnuts were roasted at smart braziers under striped canopies on street corners, and the theatres burst into life each afternoon and evening with sell-out Christmas shows.

Every restaurant window was aglow with happy revellers celebrating the season huddled up close to family and friends. The streets bustled with shoppers shoulder-to-shoulder, with peppermint hot chocolates conveyed in paper cups. Kelsey took delight in every second of Stratford-upon-Avon in its December finery even if she was too busy to stop to admire it for very long.

Her Christmas party nights at the Osprey Hotel were in full swing and Kelsey had been glad to find William Greville's father – just as redheaded and suave as his son – waiting for her on the first night with her empty tables already set up for her beside the bar and DJ booth, just as Will had promised.

She had quickly learned the knack of letting the corporate party-goers part with their Christmas bonuses: let them drink and dance until they've lost their inhibitions and simply wait until they come to her, stumbling and grinning, only too happy to Velcro themselves into Henry VIII and Anne Boleyn costumes and pose for drunken, grinning shots, handing over their credit cards and paying upfront, generously springing for five or six images in one fell swoop, all to arrive by morning in their inboxes and on their doormats within a week.

Each December Monday morning she'd call in to see Myrtle and Valeria to refresh the costumes, sorting out the ones that wanted dry-cleaning or repairing – the revellers weren't careful with their dressing-up games – and each Monday she'd find the women blasting Bing Crosby and enjoying a busy first rental season.

'Who knew there were so many am-dram pantos and fancy dress parties in town?' Myrtle had said, showing Kelsey their ledger with a grin.

They weren't the only ones finding themselves suddenly in demand. Kelsey's weekdays were livened up with a few festive photoshoots in her studio as she discovered the family Christmas card shoot was very much A Thing in Warwickshire. Like the Christmas parties, those shoots had been nothing but fun and her heart swelled with pride every time she entered her profits on her spreadsheet.

As the days passed and Jonathan's visit grew closer Kelsey found herself less and less preoccupied with the John Wagstaff theory – whenever she did think back to that night at her bedsit with Mirren she felt increasingly sure they'd both overreacted. What with the wine and the excitement of her exhibition taking shape she'd got carried away. Her mind must have been playing tricks. Of course she would see Jonathan's handsome features – which she'd only moments before been poring over in his headshot – replicated in the romantic old images of the older classical actor. She'd been mistaken. Didn't she see Jonathan everywhere? His presence was like a ghost in all their old romantic haunts, places they'd shared a kiss or intense, longing looks. She often imagined she heard his voice in the crowds and caught a hint of his scent – peppermint gum, fabric softener on cotton and soap – on the air, and she'd torture herself by turning her head to look for him, knowing he was far away overseas. Of course she saw Jonathan in Wagstaff's book images.

She had by now firmly resolved never to mention her over-heated, flighty ideas about Wagstaff – stupid, hurtful, dangerous ideas. Instead, she smothered them until they were almost gone and told herself nothing was going to spoil her precious few days with Jonathan.

This resolution gave way to a little pang of anxiety. She may well have spotted spectral glimpses of him all over town but could she remember what it was like to be near him? Not even in her most vivid daydreams could she conjure up that feeling of true proximity. They'd only spend four days close together before he left town. What would it be like to touch him again? Would it feel the same? Would it be awkward to reach up on tiptoes to kiss him once more? Was Jonathan thinking these things too?

His run of *Hamlet* would be over soon and he'd be getting on the plane ahead of four days of rediscovering one another, and now that Mirren was happily installed at the barge – albeit a little more cramped in there, what with the exhibition photographs in their frames lined up and ready to hang in the new year – they'd at least have some privacy.

Something else niggled at her though. She should be happier than this. There was something more causing her discomfort and it had begun when she'd called home recently and Calum had joked with her when he answered the phone that their mum had bought a red lipstick and was walking around with a smile on her face. Mari had laughed and snatched the phone and Kelsey could imagine her pretending to smack her cheeky son around the head for teasing her, but when Kelsey had asked about her mysterious nights out at the Bonnie Prince Charlie she'd found Mari reluctant to talk and she'd wished herself there in her mum's little grey house by the even greyer sea so they could drink tea and talk it over.

If she hadn't been feeling the miles between them in her very bones and blood at that moment she truly internalised the great distance when her grandad took the phone and asked in a shaky voice whether she was coming home for Christmas and she'd not known how to break it to him that no, she wasn't. He'd been told umpteen times but had forgotten again. She felt each of the three hundred and thirty miles of motorway that separated them and she gulped to hold back the tears.

Just as her business was starting to take shape she was losing her grip over the other parts of her life and feeling more untethered from home than she ever had. Even Mirren wasn't around for a hug and a cuppa, she'd been so busy working Christmas shifts at the Yorick.

That wasn't all Mirren had been up to. Unknown to Kelsey, she'd followed in her footsteps up the stairs at the *Examiner* office recently for an audience with Mr Ferdinand.

–

Mirren hadn't wanted to mention the interview for two very good reasons. Firstly, Kelsey would roll her eyes and remind her that getting money out of Mr Ferdinand was like dowsing for water in the Atacama Desert; and secondly, she didn't want Kelsey to think her single-girl resolve was weakening just because a gorgeous model-like journalist with a wolfish grin had done her a favour by setting up the interview, especially when Kelsey had, not so long ago, teased her about her apparent imperviousness to his good looks.

Climbing those stairs in her best black suit and red silk blouse Mirren told herself Adrian may as well be as fusty and grey as Mr Angus for all she was interested in men these days, and she believed it too, until she caught sight of Adrian at his desk through the door on the second floor landing and she froze, staring at him.

His dark eyes reflected the intense blue of the computer screen he was glaring at, his hand moving the mouse on the desk. He was in a crisp white shirt open at the neck, its textured cotton stretching beautifully over muscled shoulders, his sleeves rolled up to the elbow revealing the kind of forearms that usually made her bite her lip, and worst of all, Mirren gulped, he was wearing chunky black-rimmed glasses she hadn't seen him in before and they looked so good with his wild black hair. The whole effect screamed smart, elegant, and sexy – as if she didn't already know that about him. *Dammit.*

She slipped past the door and carried on her ascent to Mr Ferdinand's office, all the while having a serious word with herself. *I definitely do not fancy Adrian Armadale – not even one iota, nope, not one ounce of attraction. I'm totally not thinking about him wrapping his arms around me or him wearing those specs while he kisses me. Argh! Nope. This is fine. I've got this.*

She was so absorbed in her thoughts she found herself committing the huge faux pas of knocking on Mr Ferdinand's door and walking straight in, just as she'd used to do at the *Broadsheet.*

The horror of realising what she'd done was compounded by the look of shock and ire on Mr Ferdinand's face as his head snapped round and he yelled a fierce 'Get out!' from the corner of the room.

She found herself red-faced and cringing behind the door again, shouting her apologies through the smoked glass, replaying what had just happened.

He'd been hunched over a small safe, stuffing notes inside, his back curved and his hands busy, and when he noticed her intrusion he'd snatched the money to his chest and shielded it like a child protecting a prized toy.

From the look on his face and the anger in his voice Mirren already knew the interview would come to nothing. He called her back in after a few moments of clattering about and muttering curses and was surprisingly accommodating, listening to her talk about her experience and her qualifications but his smile was that of a man not used to smiling, forced and unnatural, and behind his eyes and in the twitch at his cheek there smouldered a little livid streak that confirmed her fears that he'd dismiss her in a minute or two once this perfunctory chat was over, and that's just what happened.

'Thank you for coming in. There's nothing for you at the moment, but I'll keep your CV on file in case anything comes up.' He stood up in his beige cardigan and brown tie, the colours doing nothing for the pallor of his skin, a pale sickly green like last week's lettuce.

Mirren tried to stall her dismissal but it was no use. He offered her his hand and they shook limply, and that was it.

She didn't stop by Adrian's office to show her gratitude for his help or to tell him how she'd blown it; she didn't even glance in at the door as she bounded down the stairs thanking her lucky stars for her shifts at the Yorick.

The *Examiner* had been the only interview she'd managed to line up since her epic resignation in Mr Angus's office – which she'd come to think of as being less like the triumphant clarion call for feminism in journalism that she'd hoped it was and more like an embarrassing, irrational rant and a catastrophic, career-ending error in judgement. She couldn't think about it without wincing and every time she did, Mr Angus's words rang louder in her mind. 'You need to ask yourself if you're really cut out for a career in journalism,' he'd said, and she'd gone and proven him right by screeching in his face like an angry teenager.

The only way to drown out the mortifying effects of his words was to berate herself with a few of her own, and so she did. She'd always felt like an imposter in the newspaper industry but nobody else had noticed until she'd stupidly outed herself that day. Now everyone knew Mirren Imrie was an unemployable trouble-maker.

Thank God for dour old Kenneth at the bar. He'd hired her with no questions asked and she was at least supplementing her minimum wage with nightly tips. With no writing jobs forthcoming she could stay in town for a little while, pay her way, and help Kelsey out by being a security presence on the boat at night as well as contributing to Norma's rent, even if the barge wasn't ideal, with the drunks passing by noisily after midnight.

She reminded herself as she left the *Examiner* offices that she still had a place to lick her wounds and time to figure out where in the world she was supposed to be and just exactly what it was she was destined to do with the rest of her life.

Chapter Twenty-Two

'Some say that ever 'gainst that season comes
Wherein our Saviour's birth is celebrated,
The bird of dawning singeth all night long'
(*Hamlet*)

December the twenty-third and the morning was dark. Kelsey had found she couldn't sleep any longer and had climbed up to the roof terrace to keep watch for Jonathan's arrival.

The streetlights shone on roads wet from the sleet showers overnight. The wind was bitingly cold though her grey flannel pyjamas. She switched the summer fairy lights on and the coloured bulbs sparkled all around the low wall that enclosed the little patio high up over St. Ninian's Close. An early bird on the lawn below sang out alone and no lights came from any of the surrounding houses. The commuters would still be asleep for another few hours.

Wrapping her arms around herself, she was beginning to think this wasn't her best idea – she'd be greeting Jonathan with knotted, windblown hair and a frostbitten nose – when she saw the yellow light of the cab as it crawled along the narrow residential street lined with parked cars.

Her heart had already skipped beats at two other approaching cars and one milk float this morning but this time she was sure it wasn't a false alarm. It was him. He'd come back to her.

They'd planned, back in the summer, to meet again at the pink café by the marina where they'd first laid eyes on one another, and it had burst Kelsey's romantic bubble to realise Jonathan's flight would land in Birmingham at two a.m. so it wouldn't be possible. Jonathan had reassured her that it didn't matter where they met as long as they were together again, and so she'd devised a plan B and waited romantically for him by moonlight, like she had the day they finally declared their love for each other and Norma had delivered him up to her in a cab and then driven away, leaving them alone together.

The cab was now pulling to a stop and its door swung open in slow motion. After a moment, the unmistakable shape that was Jonathan Hathaway emerged into the gloomy December morning. She would recognise him anywhere and from any distance; he fitted the exact shape and dimensions of all her desires, and her nerves thrilled with the recognition.

No thoughts ran through her mind, only feelings moved her as she watched the cab pulling away leaving Jonathan to drag his suitcase to the side of her building. When he stepped into a shaft of light from a streetlamp she saw he was looking up at her and smiling with wet, sparkling eyes.

She let the key fall from her hand and without hesitating he caught it in a fist as though he'd known that's what she'd do, and then he was gone, lost in the dark shadow of the building wrapped in its blanket of ivy.

Her breathing stalled as she listened to the sound of the key in the lock downstairs followed by the bump of his case over the step, and she found she was moving too, padding down the ladder from the roof terrace, pulling the hatch closed behind her, and listening for his feet bounding three at a time up the unlit staircase.

She stood rigid by her door, consumed with her body's answering awareness of his approach until there he was in front of her like an apparition, his hair falling over his forehead, his sharpened eyes penetrating hers, and his arms already reaching for her.

Wordlessly, he pulled her close to him with strong hands and his mouth claimed hers. Relief flooded her frame. They'd spoken enough these last months and there were no words more pressing than the hard kiss he was giving her.

As he half-walked, half-lifted her through the door into her apartment, still feverishly kissing her, she couldn't help but moan against his lips. The effect of the sound upon him was like lightning bursting from the heaviest storm cloud. He exhaled a deep primal moan into her mouth and her very core tightened in response. Toppling him onto the bed Kelsey fell with him. She had him wrapped in her legs in an instant.

'Oh God, I've missed you,' he said breathlessly into the hollow between her neck and collarbone where, as he brushed his lips in a slow sweep over her skin, a thousand nerve endings prickled and sparked. Kelsey bucked her hips beneath him, grinding against the hard answer of his arousal through their clothes.

'Take all of this off.' Her voice was low and insistent as she pulled his thick woollen jumper over his head followed by his t-shirt. The sounds in his throat quickened at the touch of her hands and her nails running over his bare back.

'I want you so bad,' he said, bringing her eyes into focus.

She found her vision swam dizzyingly with the sense of his weight upon her. For a brief moment they held each other's gaze and their swollen lips broke into breathy smiles. Together at last.

Kelsey wasn't going to waste a second of their reunion and was already wriggling out of her pyjamas. In the twinkling white light from the little Christmas tree by the bed she saw his neck and cheeks blushing red before he brought his mouth down soft and slow to her throat, moving in a trail of hungry kisses along her clavicle, lingering over the sensitive dip between her collar bones then down over her breasts. The great shattering groan he gave at the sensation of her nipple between his lips drove her nearly to madness and sent her hands searching for his belt buckle. She wouldn't wait a moment longer; there was time enough for leisurely, painstaking love-making, but this wasn't the moment. His eyes followed her hands yanking his jeans down over his hips. When their gaze locked again his mouth panted and his eyes burned with wanting.

She saw the fight in him as he forced himself to pull away, never dragging his eyes from where she lay on the bed completely naked, completely his.

He was reaching into his jeans pocket and, rifling through his wallet, cards and coins spilled over the bed, making them both laugh at his eagerness to locate the foiled packet now between his fingertips.

The moment's pause where Kelsey bit at her lip and Jonathan searched her face for consent contained all one hundred and ten days of impatient waiting. She nodded almost imperceptibly and he was inside her, her calves wrapping around him, driving him on, the muscles in his shoulder blades flexing and moving, their names on each other's lips, their cries building in the quiet of the midwinter morning.

Chapter Twenty-Three

'The morning steals upon the night,
Melting the darkness'
(*The Tempest*)

'No point asking how your reunion with Jonathan went then?'
said Mirren, placing the frothy cappuccino on the bar and
smirking. 'Did you even brush your hair this morning?'

Kelsey just grinned and sipped the coffee.

'Can you at least stop leering like that, it's putting the brunch
crowd off their eggs Benedict and it's making me feel like the
old crone of the village who only distantly remembers what sex
was like. Seriously, woman!' Mirren flicked the tea towel on the
bar.

Kelsey laughed contentedly. 'I can't help it, can I?' She
lowered her eyes and tried hard to suppress the blushing grin.
'Besides, nobody's even looking. As if they could tell anyway.'

Mirren raised an eyebrow at Kelsey's bedhead hair and
smiled. 'So where is he? Sleeping off the shock of the ravishing
you gave him?'

Another laugh. 'No he's at the Willow Studio Theatre,
remember? They've only got today to block out *Love's Labour's
Lost* and get him fitted for his costume ahead of opening in
April, and then he's meeting the dramaturg this afternoon to
talk over his lines.'

'Sounds glamorous.' Mirren wiped around the beer taps then
set about erasing the brunch specials from the board, replacing

them with the turkey and trimmings lunch the Yorick was famous for at this time of year.

'Not if you'd seen the poor guy this morning; the red-eye flight from Canada's left him exhausted.' Kelsey took advantage of Mirren's turned back to smile indulgently to herself and replay the moment she'd woken after dawn and remembered Jonathan was there in her little bed and she'd pulled him closer.

'Oh, hello,' he'd said, his sweet, slightly lop-sided smile revealing the tips of his white teeth in a way that made her go weak. 'You're here too, are you?'

'I am. Fancy meeting you here.' And they'd laughed like theirs was the most original comedy and looked at each other, dopey and shy in the morning light. Inevitably, they found themselves kissing again, Kelsey clambering onto Jonathan's lap so they could rediscover each other all over again but this time slowly and with the deep, sleepy warmth and intensity of morning sex when the world outside is chilly and indoors the Christmas lights glow bright.

She'd been shocked at how visceral their attraction was now they were together in the flesh again, how real he was. His hot breath and the wet noise of his mouth and tongue crackling close to her ear as he kissed her lobes had made her delirious. She'd loved the smell of his shampoo and the way his hair had grown longer and he'd occasionally draw back from kissing her to toss his head and flick the floppy fringe aside and every time he did it he looked even more like a matinee idol than she'd remembered. She'd been held enthralled by the physical reality of the textures of his skin and the goosebumps and soft hairs raising on his arms when she kissed him. That was the kind of spellbinding closeness she'd missed, the kind you can't feel through a screen.

'Seriously, you're scandalising Kenneth,' Mirren remarked, cutting through the lovely daydream, and the poor landlord at the other end of the bar folded away his newspaper before shuffling off to see how the giblet gravy was coming along in the kitchens.

'So what are your plans for today?' Kelsey asked.

'Well, let's see; there's clearing away the breakfast dishes, serving all the pre-matinee drinks, and we've got three lunch sittings before grabbing a bit of dinner sat out the back on the laundry baskets, and then evening bar service starts. There's a singer in tonight too, so the place will be packed. Lucky for me, I knock off at seven so it'll be a Pot Noodle for one back at the barge. No sympathy please or I might actually cry.'

Kelsey checked the pitying crumple of her mouth, but Mirren had already moved on. 'What have you and Jonathan got planned for tonight?'

Kelsey shrugged sheepishly, trying so hard not to grin but failing.

Mirren tutted and rolled her eyes playfully. 'What a time to swear off men. Christmas is the worst time of year to be alone.'

'You're not alone,' Kelsey cried. 'You're single. That's different.'

Mirren arched a brow.

'Listen, how about we all have dinner tonight? Jonathan's dying to see you.'

Mirren poured herself a coffee from the machine. 'No, you guys get reacquainted. He's only here for a few days. I'll be fine.' She brought her cup back to the bar, planting her elbows and cradling her face between her fists. 'I'm just a bit homesick really.'

'You are?'

'I've been wondering what Mum's up to, hoping she got the presents I sent... she doesn't always answer when I call, so...' Mirren shrugged her shoulders and her fists squished her cheeks.

'You could always invite her for a holiday on the barge in the new year?'

'*Hmm*?' Mirren tipped her head. She hadn't considered that. In their few brief phone calls lately – Mirren always rang her, never the other way around – they'd established a new kind of gentle civility. Sometimes, their conversation was even friendly and she'd made her mum laugh a few times with her exaggerated tales about life by the river and the ducks that still lived on the roof, but she couldn't help the sneaking awareness that her mum could stomach her precisely *because* they were far apart. Still, anything was an improvement. 'You wouldn't mind if she came for a couple of days?'

'*You're* the one renting the barge living space...'

'Hardly! I'm paying a quarter of what the rent should be. If that.'

Kelsey waved a hand. 'I already told you I didn't want any money, but you did insist. Besides, the barge will soon start paying its way once the exhibition's up and running and it'll all be academic then.' Kelsey crossed her fingers.

'You shown Jonathan the framed prints yet?'

'Not yet. There isn't a lot of time on this trip. Maybe tomorrow though.' Kelsey sipped her frothy coffee. 'I know what you mean about missing home. It's especially hard at Christmas. I thought what with Jonathan arriving I'd be made up, and I am, don't get me wrong, but when Calum's Darth Vader in a Santa hat Christmas card arrived this morning I just felt so...'

'Far from home?'

Kelsey's look confirmed it and they both fell to drinking again.

'Did you, *um*, say anything to Jonathan about...' Mirren looked around the room as though someone might be eaves-dropping. Kelsey caught her meaning.

'No, and I won't be either. Christmas is hardly the time to mention runaway dads...'

'He was in again yesterday, you know? Old Wagstaff.'

Kelsey gave Mirren a stern look. 'No concrete evidence; no telling, remember?'

'I remember. Look, I'd better clear some tables.' Mirren left Kelsey to her thoughts and soon the bar was so busy there was no time for chatting. They barely had the chance to exchange a hug when Kelsey left, and before Mirren knew it, the day had passed in a blur of Christmas-jumper-wearing happy customers, the clinking of the tips jar, and at least sixty turkey dinners demolished, and her shift was over.

–

'Hey! How did the interview go?'

Mirren was crossing the little bridge over the Avon in the dark, clasping closed the collar of her black faux fur coat with a gloved hand, trying to retain some of the heat of the Yorick when she flinched at the voice. Adrian was behind her, laden with wrapped gifts in two big bags.

'Oh, hi,' she said, surprised how happy she was to see him. 'Do you live over this side of the river?'

'My brother's family do. I'm taking them their presents before they fly off to Disneyland for Christmas; they're surprising my little nephew.'

'No way? Lucky kid!'

'Right? The closest I came to the magical kingdom as a boy was Mum taking me to sit on Father Christmas's lap in Woolworths.' They shared easy smiles. 'You going home?' he asked.

'*Umm.*' The barge was only a few yards along the riverbank; she could see the frost sparkling on its roof in the half-moon light from here. She couldn't bring herself to point out this *was* her home. She was keeping her distance. The less he knew about her, she reasoned, the harder it would be for them to talk intimately, to get closer; and the easier it was for her to stick to her plan of feeling nothing at all for a while, of rebuilding herself from the inside out. 'No, I'm just taking a stroll after work, it's been a long day.'

'Mind if I stroll with you for a bit?'

She shrugged as breezily as she could and let their pace synchronise, trying to suppress the sinking feeling of her resolve weakening.

'I'm guessing Mr Ferdinand didn't mention my interview?' Mirren said in a droll tone.

'He's so secretive, we barely communicate outside of emails,' Adrian said cagily.

'It's safe to say you and I won't be sharing an office any time soon.'

'*Aww*, that's a real shame. I read your piece... the Scottish Brexit story?'

'How do you know about that?'

'I might have... seen your CV while *umm*... filing it?'

'You do Mr Ferdinand's filing?'

'Technically I was taking it out of the bin, but...'

'Why would you tell me that?' Mirren pretended to be wounded, but she'd known full well that Mr Ferdinand had binned her CV, just as he'd binned her last hope of a job in newspapers. 'So you *did* know I didn't get the job, then? Rummage through bins often, do we?'

'I can't say I make a habit of it, no. I rescued it and couldn't help seeing your article listed and, well, I looked it up online.'

'You actually read it?'

'Of course I did. It was really good, and I mean *really* good. No wonder you were nominated for that award.'

'I wasn't shortlisted or anything,' Mirren found herself saying, struggling with the admiration.

'You're a great writer, Mirren, even without an award. Anyway, I needed some evidence to help plead your case with Ferdinand, see if he'd reconsider. I printed it out for him and left it on his desk.'

'And?'

Adrian grimaced.

'Didn't even read it, did he?'

'No, but that's his loss, isn't it? And mine.'

Mirren's words faltered at this. 'Th-thanks anyway. We tried.' Flustered, she looked out over the water, avoiding his sidelong glance. They fell silent for a moment as they came up alongside the barge and passed it. All the while Mirren was becoming increasingly aware of her aching feet after her long day at the bar, but she matched Adrian step for step.

'I was really looking forward to working with you,' he said at last. 'You'd certainly liven up the office. Some days I feel like I'm running the place; Ferdinand's so quiet, hidden away upstairs all day, most likely snoring.'

'God knows, I needed that job.' The voices in her head were singing in chorus, *But you messed up the interview. Typical Mirren, always spoiling things.* 'It's all right. I'm determined to enjoy the Yorick. It's not so bad, actually, and these long shifts certainly beat awkward Christmases back home.' She didn't elaborate even though Adrian raised his brows encouraging her to go on. 'I have a feeling me and your Mr Ferdinand wouldn't really have got along anyway.'

'I guess I'm trapped with the old stick insect then. You'd never guess he used to be an actor, would you?'

This surprised a laugh from Mirren. 'No, you would not!'

'That's why Clement Dickens, the old editor, hired him, to get the gossip straight from the rehearsal room, but when Clement died the editorship went to Ferdinand and that was curtains for the paper. Ferdinand wasn't much interested in theatre by that time, a touch of failed actor complex if you ask me, so the paper ended up going back to its old pre-Clement ways; it's theatrical focus went out the window and it became a run-of-the-mill local rag again.'

'That's a pity. We could have written up a storm together.' Mirren checked her smile, realising Adrian had stopped walking and they were now well on their way out of town on the opposite side of the bank from the magnificent Holy Trinity Church, its stained glass aglow and its spire disappearing into the dark sky.

'Mirren?' he said cautiously.

She jammed her hands into her pockets, not quite trusting them to stay there. 'Uh-huh?' She tried to sound casual.

'I know you said you weren't interested in dating and I get that, but I wanted to say that... *umm*,' he cleared his throat, aiming his gaze intently at her eyes. 'I'll wait.'

She stared back. 'You'll *wait*?'

'In case one day you change your mind. I'll be here, waiting. We could get a drink or—'

'We can get a drink any time, we're friends, remember?' she interrupted with false laughter. 'Anyway, I thought you were done with dating too?'

He looked sheepish at this.

'Besides, I wouldn't be a great girlfriend, trust me. You're dodging a bullet.'

His expression said he wasn't buying any of that. 'Of course we're friends.' He nodded, looking down at the ground, trying to hide the defeat, and failing.

Scuffing her boots on the path, Mirren felt the awkwardness set in. 'It's getting really cold, I'd better head back to my place.' She thumbed the way along the river behind her, hoping he wouldn't follow or she might be spending the rest of the evening having to keep up her pretence of living in a real house like a real adult and not camping out in the back of her friend's boat.

'Sure. It is chilly,' he agreed. The moonlight on his dark hair and lashes gave them a sapphire sheen. Mirren blew out a sharp exhalation at the sight of him, crestfallen and so handsome. She tried to congratulate herself for resisting his offer but, deep down, she just felt unkind and self-defeating.

'OK, goodnight,' she said, determinedly.

'See you at the Yorick? I'll drop in for a Christmas drink.'

'Right-o, I'm working all Christmas.' She wondered when she'd last used the phrase 'right-o' and whimpered. The impulse to close the gap between them and press a conciliatory kiss to his cheek was overwhelming. Instead, she took a stumbling step backwards, somehow tripping on her own feet but quickly recovering.

He watched her walk away before letting his chin fall to his chest, shaking his head, but he was smiling with the look of a man who had bared his feelings and wasn't all that sorry he'd tried.

Chapter Twenty-Four

'To me, fair friend, you never can be old,
For as you were when first your eye I eyed,
Such seems your beauty still'
(*Sonnet 104*)

'Woah, please let me help with that,' Kelsey called out at the sight of Blythe teetering on a kitchen stepladder, reaching up to the larder shelves and directing some particularly fruity language at some jars of fruit jam.

'Can't reach the bloody things,' she muttered, stepping down again and watching Kelsey reach up with ease.

'How many do you want down?'

'Depends. Do you like gin jam? Six ought to do it.'

'*Gin* jam?'

At that moment the toaster on the work surface popped. 'I made some raspberry gin back in September, couldn't bring myself to waste the booze-soaked raspberries, so *voilà!* Gin jam.'

'It's cocktail hour even at breakfast time?' Kelsey grinned, placing the jars two at a time on the table by the copper still.

Blythe said nothing but waggled her bare brows proudly.

'Pop one open, dear.' Blythe buttered the toast and pulled out a plate for Kelsey. 'You can sample it here first, let me know if you like your Christmas present.'

Kelsey eyed the six jars and hoped Blythe didn't mean to give them all to her, until, that is, she took her first bite. Sweet strained raspberry juice and bitter gin had combined in a perfect not-too-firm jelly-like set. 'Oh wow!' Her taste buds zinged.

Blythe chuckled and poured water from the whistling kettle into an antique silver teapot. It looked like Kelsey was staying for breakfast. She'd only meant to pop in for a moment to ask her a question.

'I was wondering whether you wanted to come and see the Christmas lights today with me and Jonathan? You haven't met him yet and you can talk Shakespeare all day, and maybe we could get some lunch in town? You haven't been in town for a while, have you? Be nice to get out.'

Blythe's eyes dimmed. With a nod at the tray of cups and saucers she shuffled away to her salon, leaving Kelsey to load the jam, toast and teapot and carry the tray in her wake, calling behind her, 'Obviously, you don't have to, I just thought it might be nice to do something festive?'

Blythe lowered herself wearily onto her pink chaise, still silent.

'Can I get you any groceries then?' Kelsey pressed. That was when she noticed the fancy white box of almond turrón on the table by Blythe's elbow and the bottle of fino still sitting upon their torn Christmas wrapping.

Blythe followed her eye line. 'I've everything I need for a lovely Christmas, thank you dear.'

'You've been getting presents?'

'Mm-hmm, my favourite. Spanish turrón and sherry. Every Christmas my son sends them.' Blythe sipped her tea. 'Eat up, toast's getting cold.'

Kelsey wouldn't be put off. 'You've got a wheelchair, haven't you? I saw it folded up in the hall. Maybe we could take a walk along the street, have a good old nose in all the windows at people's Christmas decs?'

'Darling, I appreciate you asking, I do, and my grandchildren ask me the same things and I see them tutting and shaking their heads at me being a stubborn old bird, but Kelsey, you lose confidence after being sat indoors for a long time; even the shortest stroll feels a little frightening. You tell yourself, I'll go out once I'm over this cold, but when that's gone, you've got a twinge in your back, and then the weather's not good enough and the pavements are slippery and before you know it a year's passed and you've not set foot over your threshold. You'll see. The world's your oyster when you're young and mobile...'

'*Knock knock?*'

Both women turned to the sound of the voice in the kitchen. Kelsey had been listening and nodding along, feeling as though she was finally getting a glimpse of the real Blythe beneath her glamourous bravado and she regretted the interruption even though it was her favourite person. 'That'll be Jonathan. I told him to come down when he was done talking with his parents in the States.'

'Ah, the famous Jonathan Hathaway. Let's be seeing you then,' Blythe trilled, and Kelsey watched her elderly neighbour with all her worries about her mobility and independence, the woman who struggled to reach her shelves and hated admitting that struggle, suddenly assuming her actress's posture again. When Jonathan's head appeared around the salon door frame, Blythe was already sitting taller and stretching her neck, elegant and poised. That was all about to change when she saw Jonathan.

'Oh! Goodness!' Blythe cried out, raising a hand to her mouth, her eyes narrowing to focus on his features. 'You... you...'

'Blythe, are you all right?' Kelsey was on her feet in an instant, making her tea slosh in the saucer.

She watched the woman do battle with herself, gaping open-mouthed, seeing the look of bewilderment cross her face before it was erased by a forced, friendly smile, but the panic still showed in Blythe's eyes. 'I'm fine dear, fine. I thought for a moment you were someone else... I couldn't account for it... oh, dear.'

Jonathan was now kneeling by her side. 'It's just me, Jonathan Hathaway, Kelsey's... boyfriend.' He'd never used the word before, not in front of Kelsey anyway, and their eyes widened and met for the briefest moment of smiling surprise before turning back to Blythe who was now a picture of poise again.

'You two had better get going if you're to make the most of the daylight. The days are so short now midwinter's here,' she was saying, running her napkin over the invisible toast crumbs on her muted gold pleated skirt.

Blythe always dressed as though she were expecting company – Burton and Taylor perhaps – and she'd stepped her dressing up a notch for the festive season by matching her cream blouse, cardigan and pink river pearls with a winter-white fur stole which Kelsey just knew was as old as the hills and definitely *not* faux. Her crystal earrings glittered in the light and her smile said she'd pulled off a spectacular recovery from her little moment of discomfiture.

'Go on, off you go. Don't want to stand in the way of young lovers. Besides, they're showing *Lawrence of Arabia* at ten and I like to see my old pals at Christmas time. Oh, Peter O'Toole was a lovely man, such a twinkle in his eye and always a delight at parties.'

Jonathan was looking warily at Kelsey who was staring, concerned, at her neighbour, uncertain quite what was happening. Blythe was always dramatic, but this morning she was off the charts.

'Before you go, give that cloth a tug, will you?' said Blythe, and Kelsey was surprised to find she kept an ancient television in the corner covered over with an embroidered cloth as though it were a mouthy parrot in a cage.

'Lovely, dear. Toodle-pip.'

'*Umm*, OK, well, merry Christmas?' said Kelsey, only to be met with Blythe's studied silence. She was jabbing at a clunky-looking remote control.

Jonathan had better luck. 'It sure was nice to meet you, Miss Goode,' he said in his charming Tulsa accent. Blythe nodded courteously at that and let him take her hand, but there was a hint of unsteadiness in the way she held her head when she looked at him.

It had taken another ten minutes of reassurances from an increasingly annoyed Blythe to get them out the flat, both of them clutching three jars of gin jam to their chests.

'Do you think she's OK? She looked like she'd seen a ghost,' Jonathan said as they dropped the jars off in the bedsit upstairs.

'She's not normally like that, she must have got a fright when you came in. She was busy telling me about how she's practically housebound. It can't be easy for her to let her guard down, she's so proud, you know? If I ever see those grandsons of hers I'm going to have a stern word with them. She needs someone to take her in hand.'

Jonathan laughed. 'I met her for precisely fifteen minutes and I can already tell she'd not make that easy for anyone. She's feisty as hell.'

Kelsey laughed and locked her bedsit door.

'She's obviously not completely starved of company. There were Christmas presents there, and she mentioned a son? I heard you talking when I arrived,' said Jonathan taking Kelsey's hand on the stairs.

'She has a family, yeah. I don't know much about them though.' Kelsey's words tailed off into silence as she tried to tamp down the thoughts rushing in. *Was Blythe startled by Jonathan's similarity to Wagstaff? Had she seen the resemblance too? How else could that reaction be explained? And those grandsons Jonathan mentioned so casually could be his own relatives if my half-baked theory's right and Wagstaff really was Blythe's lover twenty years before Jonathan's poor mum was seduced by the old rogue… if indeed, that's what happened.*

Down in the hallway Jonathan pulled her close. 'Now you're the one freaking me out. You're so pale. What is with everyone today? Come on, let's go chill out in town, see some sights. It's been an intense few days; I feel like we've barely had a chance to draw breath. What say you just hold my hand, walk beside me, and we'll have a proper date to make up for all the ones we missed over the autumn?' His kiss sealed the deal and they walked out of St. Ninian's and through the chill winter winds towards town.

Chapter Twenty-Five

'My bounty is as boundless as the sea,
My love as deep; the more I give to thee,
The more I have, for both are infinite'
(*Romeo and Juliet*)

One of the many things Kelsey loved about Jonathan was how he was exactly the right height to deliver forehead kisses and that's just what he was doing now as they stood, hands clasped in the small of each other's backs through cosy layers, smiling dopily at one another in the middle of the bustling Christmas market by the riverside while a group of buskers with guitars and a keyboard sang about chestnuts roasting on an open fire.

Jonathan crooned along and between lines he'd dip his head and press kisses along the smooth spot between his girlfriend's brows and her bobble hat.

A Father Christmas ringing a bell and holding out his collection tin smiled at them indulgently as he Ho-Ho-Ho'd past them, no doubt seeing what everyone else could see; two young people stupidly in love, getting in everyone's way, totally unaware of the world outside their love bubble.

'Me-rry Christ-ma-as, to yoo-oo-ooo,' Jonathan sang, really going for the big finish, and Kelsey grinned helplessly up at him as the last-minute shoppers bustled by and the band burst into a Mariah Carey Christmas number complete with jingle bells ringing.

'We should probably, like, look around at these stalls?' Jonathan said, still planted to the ground holding Kelsey close, and they grinned at themselves for being like this.

'We really should move along,' she agreed.

It took another few moments of gazing and at least twenty soft kisses at her temples for them to link hands and start walking, still more absorbed in each other than they were in the beautiful scenes around them. The Christmas lights high above the market were shining even though it was only ten in the morning and the sky was a dark, looming grey. Blythe had said earlier on it looked like it might snow but so far not one flake had fallen.

Rich foody smells swirled in the cold air from the pulled pork stall, a candyfloss machine, and a van with a queue snaking right down to the river's edge popular with visitors hungry for foot-long unpronounceable German sausages.

The first stall they came to was laid out beneath its green awning with vintage jewellery, old books and kitschy knick-knackery. Jonathan pulled Kelsey closer to it. 'Do you like anything here?'

'Oh, I don't need anything.'

'Nobody *needs* cute stuff, no, but do you *like* anything you see?' He understood her love of vintage things and the way old objects could recall lost worlds and forgotten stories. Her eyes sparkled as she looked over the items in a voracious way that made the stall owner mentally rub his hands together.

Kelsey had a copy of an old book in her gloved hands already. 'This is nice.' She gave the black leather and gold embossing a little sniff before flicking through the pages. 'It's a nineteen-fifties copy of the plays of John Webster.'

'Can I buy it for you?' Jonathan reached for the book. 'I already have something special for you but it's nice to unwrap lots of little things, right?'

'Actually, I was thinking maybe for Blythe? She played Webster's Duchess of Malfi once, you know? But I'll pay for it.'

Soon the book was wrapped in tissue paper and in Kelsey's trusty satchel and they were on their way to the next stall, which was laden with gingerbread biscuits. The scent of cinnamon, ginger and brown sugar hit them hard.

'*Now* it smells like Christmas. My wee brother used to love these,' Kelsey smiled.

'My sisters love 'em too. Mom always baked cookies on Christmas Eve and we'd leave some out for Santa Claus. The thing about having four baby sisters is they need a *lot* of Christmas cookies. She'd be baking most of the holidays. At least that's how I remember it. In fact this stall looks kinda like Mom's kitchen. Cookies everywhere.' He was smiling and gripping Kelsey's hand. 'Can you fill up a bag for us, please?' he asked the baker before turning to Kelsey. 'You want angels or reindeer?'

'I like the love hearts,' she replied, drawing Jonathan's focus back to her rosy cheeks and smiling lips. The poor stall owner had to navigate their lovestruck, goofy distraction to get Jonathan to remember to actually pay for them.

On they strolled, talking all the time about their respective family Christmases, sampling the gingerbread and not minding the bitterly cold north wind.

'Hey, look at that!' Jonathan suddenly pulled Kelsey to him and pointed through the crowds on the marina. Kelsey spotted it too and they instantly broke into an awkward slow run through the thronging masses.

There was one table unoccupied at the busy little pink café with the candy-striped awning where they'd first met: *their* table, with two chairs arranged just as they had been on the very day they first bumped into one another, and yes, they were going to reclaim their spot.

They skipped through the crowds, dodging the shoppers, and crossed over the road through the end-to-end crawling cars, their eyes fixed on their prize and already celebrating their victory, but just at the moment they stepped onto the pavement and were reaching for their table a woman threw herself into one of the chairs with an exhausted sigh, letting her shopping bags fall to the ground, the gift-wrapped contents of one spilling onto the pavement at her feet.

Kelsey and Jonathan drew up short just as a man passing the woman stopped and helped her bundle the gifts back into the bag. The strangers were oblivious to them watching them with their mouths crumpled in confounded surprise; already absorbed in what any passing fool could see was their split-second attraction. They overheard the man asking the woman if she was meeting someone before he claimed the spare chair, even though less than sixty seconds ago he had been bustling past with no intention of sitting.

Astonished, Kelsey smiled at Jonathan. 'Cute,' she whispered, and they both diverted inside the café doors shaking their heads with amusement.

Once inside the cosy, shockingly pink café where condensation steamed up the windows and a white Christmas tree twinkled at its centre, Kelsey told Jonathan to sit down and ordered two hot chocolates at the counter, not even having to ask Jonathan if he wanted one.

Soon they were pulling their chairs closer to each other, taking the first sips of their drinks and laughing at the whipped cream on their noses and lips.

'Aww, man, we really are *that* couple,' Jonathan laughed, swiping a slow thumb over Kelsey's mouth. She just knew he was going to offer it up for her to lick away, which he did.

'Sickeningly in love, you mean?'

'Infuriatingly so.'

'I love it.' Kelsey grinned.

'Me too.'

No one in the café minded their laughter as they hunched their heads closer and talked over the sounds of Brenda Lee's 'Rockin' Around the Christmas Tree' from the café radio.

'My sisters would love this place, especially Daisy,' Jonathan said.

'She's the littlest, right?'

'She's fifteen. I think she's a budding actress. Someone should really have a word with her about that,' he said in his drollest voice, deep and crackling with humour, as he stirred the candy cane in his drink. 'It's no life, pretending to be someone else half the time. Then there's the stage fright and the late nights and the being away from the people you love.' Another kiss pressed to her lips; this one tasted of peppermint. 'I guess you'll get to meet them all in April.'

'Are *all* your family coming to see you in *Love's Labour's Lost*?'

'Sure are. Opening night. Dad's already booked the flights so there's no getting out of meeting the entire family.'

'I can't wait.'

Jonathan called Art his 'dad', of course, Kelsey thought. Because he was his dad, the only one he knew, and the warmth and affection with which he spoke about him lit his face.

'Jonathan... did you even want to meet your father?' Kelsey blurted it out, eyeing him warily.

He returned her stare with a look that asked *where did that come from?* 'Nope. Never,' he replied. 'I have my family back in Tulsa, they're all I ever needed.'

'OK,' she nodded. 'You're right, I shouldn't have brought it up.'

'Hey, we can talk about anything. I don't know the first thing about whoever that guy was and I don't wanna know. I've made it to the age of thirty-two without knowing him, I think I got it from here, don't you?' He winked to show he didn't mind. 'Hey, don't look so sad. Art is a great dad and he makes Mom happy, and you know he raised me since I was seven, so...'

'He's your dad.' Kelsey was nodding. She'd done the right thing. Keeping schtum, not spoiling things. This was further confirmation, if she needed it, that she had to respect Jonathan's wishes in this.

'Are you thinking about your own dad?' he was asking.

'Oh, no, not really. I mean, I'm always thinking about him one way or another. It's worse at Christmas, you know, the car accident happened just after New Year… I'm missing all of my family, really.' She took a sip of chocolate and shrugged. 'Never mind, can't be helped.'

'Like heck it can't!'

'What?'

'Let's go see them.' He said it as though it was the simplest thing in the world.

Kelsey's eyes bulged.

'They won't mind us showing up, right?'

'Mind? They'd be over the moon. Are you talking about surprising them? Just turning up for Christmas?'

'Sure! You've got a driving licence, right? I do too. What is it, like a ten-hour drive? There's a car rental place nearby?'

Kelsey was nodding. 'Six hours, maybe seven? We'd be there by bedtime. Oh my God, are we doing this?'

'As long as we're back for my flight to LA on the twenty-sixth.' Jonathan looked at his watch before calling for the cheque and reaching for his wallet to pay. 'We're doing this.'

As they left the café, Kelsey suddenly remembered to look back at the two strangers who had thwarted their re-enactment of the day they'd met. They were standing by their empty coffee cups now and sheepishly swapping numbers into mobile phones.

She grinned and nudged Jonathan to look around. Another chance meeting had taken place. Another couple were about to embark on a new love affair. Good old Stratford-upon-Avon, the home of English love poetry, was working its romantic magic once more.

Jonathan swung his arm over Kelsey's shoulder, locking her in tight to his long body and they bustled happily home to stuff bags for their Christmas Eve journey north.

Chapter Twenty-Six

'Now I see the mystery of your loneliness'
(*All's Well That Ends Well*)

The text had been left on 'read' for three days when Mirren woke that Christmas Eve morning. The little tick confirmed Preston had seen it. She was just beginning to accept the fact that he wouldn't be replying and that she'd made yet another error of judgement and no doubt hurt him all the more when the notification sound pinged. She'd just been getting out of bed and reaching for the frying pan for the festive bacon-wrapped-sausage on a roll she'd promised herself when she grabbed the phone and read feverishly.

> **Merry Christmas! It was good to hear from you. I'm good thanks. We're out on tour at the minute. Listen, you don't need to apologise again, OK? You're not the big bad wolf you think you are. I thought a lot about what happened and you know we would have broken up somewhere along the line, right?**

> We should have split as soon as you knew the magic was going but in the end I guess we did our best. I'm glad you messaged actually. I've felt weird not letting you know I've been seeing someone. She's our new drummer. I hope that doesn't hurt you. I don't want it to. I hope you can move on and find someone really special too. Go and have yourself a merry little Christmas, miss you, P, x

At first his message had made her smile – once she'd stopped shaking, that was. After the adrenalin burst of hearing from Preston again faded she was left with an ache inside. One line stood out more than the others. 'We should have split as soon as you knew the magic was going.'

He was right, of course. She should have had the courage to break it off there and then, all those years ago, but she couldn't bring herself to.

'*Ugh*,' she grumbled into her hands, standing by her unmade bed. Even his texts to his ex-girlfriend were considerate and sweet. Suddenly she'd lost her appetite for the breakfast she'd been looking forward to alone in the silence of the barge, by the light of the little coloured bulbs she'd strung around the galley kitchen window.

She poured a long glass of water, thinking of Preston's message and hearing all the while her mum's voice telling her how cruel she'd been, how skittish and disloyal all those years. Typical Mirren.

The voice, and Preston, were right. She'd stayed with him and tried to pretend things were fine, hiding her deepest wishes – for change, a little adventure, a lot of passion – and hoping they'd go away, senselessly redirecting them towards brief bursts of something that felt daring – the cheating – and every time finding she felt even worse afterwards. Then she'd be consumed with the effort of burying all that guilt, along with all her desires, until there was very little left of the real Mirren; instead she had been a knot of remorse and self-loathing, and yet somehow all it took was a plastered-on smile and a bit of swagger to cover it up.

Another text pinged onto her screen and she almost choked on her water.

> BTW, did your mum mention I dropped by with some of your old clothes? I was really there to give her the leaflet. Did she mention it? I'm guessing no? Remember my uncle is in that alcohol dependency support group? It was one of their leaflets. Anyway, you might want to mention it? Follow it up, if you want? You know what to do for the best. OK, got to go, we're playing in Birmingham tonight. X

Mirren felt the tears welling. Kind, loving, wonderful Preston. She'd forgotten what a relief it was to have somebody know her and understand her life. Preston knew, even better than Kelsey did, what growing up with Jeanie had been like, and he knew she kept it secret from everyone she encountered. He'd cared enough even after they'd broken up to visit her mum. Jeanie was right; she hadn't deserved him. She pulled the duvet over herself and cried until it was time to leave for her shift at the Yorick.

–

Mirren tried to get a good look at John Wagstaff's face. He was right under the bar lights ordering his usual ale and a glass of sack so it was the perfect opportunity to get him chatting and scan his features for any hint of Jonathan Hathaway in them, but her eyes were tired and gritty from crying and the old man's whiskers hid most of his face anyway.

'Not spending Christmas Eve with family?' she asked, focusing on his eyes, ice-blue, just like Jonathan's.

'Not I. I'm a solitary swan, always have been,' he said, almost sadly. 'May I enquire about your plans, far from home and hearth, what will you be doing tomorrow?'

'Hah! I'll be here. At least for the afternoon shift. Can't have the people of Stratford going without their Christmas drinks, can we?'

Maybe something in the set of his mouth, she thought, looked familiar too, but age, booze and the bachelor life had done a number on old Wagstaff's handsome face. She knew he was telling the truth about being a solitary swan, his autobiography had confirmed it; never married, no mention of any children, and he'd lived itinerantly after his infamous leg-breaking fall from the stage at the end of the sixties, going from regional theatre to film set to whichever hostelry was nearest the stage door.

The book had been an interesting enough read, written in Wagstaff's own bright and witty words but not exactly a tell-all exposé. A part of her, the part that didn't like the idea of stalking elderly men, told her to give her curiosity a rest and she turned for the till.

Kenneth appeared by her side, settling a glass of bubbly in front of her. 'Compliments of the Yorick. Drink it up girl and get your Christmas spirit back, you look like a damp dishcloth draped over the beer taps.'

'Charming,' she said with a roll of her eyes, throwing a smirk at her boss who she had warmed to a little more with each shift. He was staid and quiet, yes, but kind too, just a no-nonsense kind of bloke; all that mattered to him was that everyone was happy in his little kingdom, and that started with his staff. He had already disappeared into the little snug bar to clear glasses so Mirren clasped the champagne flute and raised it to Wagstaff who had settled himself by the bar to read his newspaper.

'Cheers,' she said.

'No, no, no,' Wagstaff blustered, reaching out a hand to stall her. 'That's no Christmas Eve toast. Try this one.' He lifted his own drink in salute. '*Heaven give you many, many merry days.*'

'I'll drink to that.' She threw back the champagne and when she lowered the long-stemmed glass again the vision before her made her splutter.

Adrian Armadale was by the bar in an oversized cream fisherman's jumper – not a woolly snowman or knitted reindeer in sight; she bet he'd never once known the itchy discomfort of a tacky Christmas jumper. He had one hand stuffed into the pocket of his black jeans, the other grasping a bountiful bouquet of roses with petals the colour of antique lace. He was wearing those spectacles again with his hair ruffled and jaw lightly stubbled, giving the impression of a Dior model off duty for the holidays.

'Hi,' he said, smiling unassumingly.

She warily eyed the flowers and when he caught her expression he brought them abruptly down to his side. 'Oh! Sorry, I didn't bring these for you, they're for someone else.'

Mirren could feel her colour rising and wished the cellar door beneath her feet would fall open, taking her with it.

'I'm paying a visit to family after this, these are for… anyway, look, I was just passing and… *uh*…' he rambled.

Mirren took the opportunity to swig the last of her bubbly and pretend this wasn't horribly awkward. She thought of his words last night by the river: 'In case one day you change your mind. I'll be here, waiting…' Is that why he was here on Christmas Eve when he had better things to do and other people to be with? Was this a reminder of his promise to wait for her?

'*Ah!*' John Wagstaff boomed in interruption, gesturing to the roses with expressive hands which told Kelsey they were in for another of his frequent dramatic monologues, and she was right. '*Let thy love be younger than thyself, or thy affection cannot hold the bent,*' he orated, making half the bar turn to look around. '*For women are as roses, whose fair flower being once displayed, doth fall that very hour.*'

The look this drew from Adrian reminded Mirren of how angry he'd been the night of the spilled pint. In an attempt to intercept some of Adrian's ire and to prevent Wagstaff proclaiming any more dubious guff about women displaying their flowers, she threw the actor a free bag of scratchings by way of applause – which he greedily tore into – and hastened Adrian to the furthest end of the bar.

'I've told you before, you have to leave him alone.' She almost said 'he's harmless' but she'd been told this once herself and it hadn't ended well.

'Are you drinking on duty?' Adrian said with a smirk, ignoring her warning.

'It *is* Christmas Eve.' She looked at her watch. 'Every journalist I know back home would be up to their eyeballs in empties by now. Are you having one?'

'Coke, please.' His phone rang as Mirren was pouring his drink and he stepped away into the inglenook to talk. She heard him saying, 'Mr Ferdinand? I've got today off, remember?'

At that moment the brass bell over the door rang out through the sound of chattering diners and the pulling of crackers. Mirren was astonished to see Jonathan Hathaway bounding in with a very flustered-looking Kelsey behind him.

'Wait a sec, Jonathan. I'm sure Mirren'll be busy…' she was saying in a pitchy voice.

'She's right here,' said Jonathan, coming round to the side of the bar to wrap her in a quick hug. 'Good to see you, how are you?'

Over his shoulder Mirren looked from Kelsey's startled eyes to the oblivious Wagstaff still sitting by the bar absorbed in his paper. Kelsey was shifting from foot to foot and Mirren realised no one was talking but Jonathan.

'We wanted to let you know in person… we've hired a car. We're heading to Scotland!'

Kelsey took over now, coming to stand by Jonathan's side. 'I told Jonathan we should just ring you and get going but he wanted to see you.'

'Didn't want to skip town on Christmas without letting you know first. Sure you can't come with us?' Jonathan threw in, still grinning with the excitement of heading north.

Mirren took them both by the shoulders and turned them for the door. 'What a great idea, getting away to Scotland for a while. You should really get going or it'll be dark by the time you hit the Borders.'

'You don't mind?' Jonathan was asking as Mirren yanked the door and bustled them out into the chill.

'Me? No, I'm working, can't leave Kenneth in the lurch. Have a few of Mari's kilties for me, OK?'

Jonathan was looking at Mirren perplexed but still letting her shove them both down the pub steps to where their hire car was parked.

'Is that yours?' Mirren asked. 'In you get then. Get out of this cold.' She rubbed her arms and gritted her teeth with an exaggerated, '*brrrr!*'

'*Uh*, OK, well, happy holidays, Mirren,' Jonathan said, unlocking the car and getting into the driver's seat.

When he was out of earshot Kelsey gripped at Mirren's arms and whispered urgently, 'Oh my God, that was a close one. I tried to dissuade him but he's surprisingly determined when his mind's set on something. He wasn't going to go without making sure you didn't mind us leaving town first.'

Mirren was dismissing his concerns with the wave of her hand. '*Pfft!* I'm fine, never mind all that. Did you see him? By the bar? *Wagstaff.*' The whispered name was barely audible over the hire car's engine starting up.

Kelsey nodded rapidly. 'I saw him. I just *knew* he'd be there the minute Jonathan suggested visiting you, but how was I supposed to put him off without looking suspicious? What if they'd had a father-son recognition scene like in a Shakespeare play? Can you imagine? My heart's pounding!' Kelsey had her hand over her coat lapels trying to settle her breathing.

'They didn't even notice each other. Why would they? They're strangers.'

'I know, but still, I thought maybe they'd see something in one another...' Kelsey had a faraway look in her eyes that betrayed all her hopes for a reunion between them.

'We don't even know if they're related. You're the one who told me not to push it...' Mirren cautioned.

'I know but... maybe if you did a *little* digging?'

'I tried, but Wagstaff's pretty tight-lipped, said he didn't have any family. That's all I got from him.'

Jonathan was rolling the window down which silenced them, and the exhaust fumes made it impossible to stand by the car any longer.

'Go on, get in. Give your mum a hug from me, OK?' Mirren told her.

Soon they were pulling away, Kelsey waving frantically and Jonathan tooting the car horn, leaving Mirren waving from the pavement. Kelsey's shoulders slumped and she mentally weighed up her feelings; mainly relief that drama had been avoided, mixed with some regret that a reunion hadn't been possible.

'Are you all right, Kelsey? You were kinda jumpy back there?'

'What? I'm great!' she replied, a little too quickly. 'Mirren doesn't like to be disturbed at work, that's all.'

'So are you going to tell me?' He glanced at her, suddenly serious, as he navigated the narrow riverside streets heading for the main road out of town.

Kelsey started in fright, fixing round eyes on him. Had he overheard everything? She gulped. 'Tell you what?'

'What exactly a *kiltie* is?' Jonathan grinned.

–

Back at the Yorick, Adrian was hanging up his phone with a glower and looking for Mirren who was now standing by the bar pouring herself another glass of bubbly before downing it in three big glugs. Wagstaff had lumbered away unnoticed in all the excitement and his barstool sat empty.

Seeing Adrian approach she felt strangely comforted by his presence. 'Mr Ferdinand? What did he want?' she asked, nodding towards the hand that held his phone.

'Who knows, mad old stick insect! He kept asking what I was doing today, whether or not I'd be in the office. I told him I was busy. He'd probably forgotten some job or other he wanted me to do before the break. Well, it's too late. I'm on holiday now.'

Mirren eyed him, considering something for a long time. Adrian let her look, his head tipping.

'Penny for them?' he said.

'I was just thinking... old Wagstaff. Do you know much about him?'

Adrian tightened his lips just as he always did when Wagstaff was mentioned, but it gave Mirren the impression he'd hoped she'd been thinking about something quite different. In fact she'd been weighing him up, wondering whether she really could ask him for help. They were friends now weren't they? Friends can ask a favour.

'I know a bit, why?' he said.

'Those people you saw me with?'

'Jonathan Hathaway, the actor?'

'That's right! I'd forgotten he was a bit of a celeb. Well, he's dating my friend and, look, it's a bit delicate, I shouldn't really say...' She thought of the tiny hint of crushed hope in Kelsey's eyes and how it felt utterly wrong for Jonathan to be standing five feet away from the man who might have given him life and neither of them even knowing it... and then there was poor

Wagstaff heading home for a solitary Christmas Eve. Surely, she had a duty to discover the truth? Kelsey had practically instructed her, hadn't she? The champagne in Mirren's empty stomach was helping to convince her too. 'I think Wagstaff might be Jonathan's dad and he abandoned Jonathan's mum when he discovered she was pregnant. She was a young actress in town you see...'

A dark brooding look transformed Adrian's face. 'That old rogue. I wouldn't put it past him.'

'You don't like him much, do you?' She thought of Adrian's strong sense of responsibility. It was sort of noble, and she liked him all the more for it.

He shook his head. 'So what are you asking me?'

'For proof? You must know someone who knows someone... this town is legendary for its theatre gossip. You can't blow your nose backstage at The Other Place without someone at The Swan knowing about it.'

Adrian's eyes narrowed. 'Hathaway?' he said to himself. 'His mum was *Olivia* Hathaway? *Hah*!' he exclaimed in surprise. 'I've heard a little about her from Ferdinand. She was a real star for a while.'

Mirren watched his thoughts consume him.

'I can do better than uncover some old gossip,' Adrian said, rising from the bar leaving his Coke untouched. 'When do you clock off?'

'Six.'

He grabbed his bouquet of roses once more. 'Then I'll be back at six.'

Mirren watched him leave, hoping that by some Christmas miracle, for once she'd done the right thing.

Chapter Twenty-Seven

'There is a world elsewhere'
(*Coriolanus*)

Brake lights and headlights shone all along the dark December motorway. Chris Rea's gravelly voice was celebrating the joys of driving home for Christmas on the car radio, while Jonathan clutched two red takeaway cups of gingerbread spiced latte and surreptitiously side-eyed Kelsey as she drove.

'Stop watching me,' she said, her jaw tense but still amused, as she ground between gears. 'I'll be fine once I get used to it.'

'When did you last drive?'

'About six years ago when I passed my test.'

'Six years? We're gonna die,' he mugged.

'Hey, I'm not the one who'd never used a gear stick before, OK? Anybody can claim they're a good driver if all they have do is push a lever and steer! You were pretty bumpy when we first set off from Stratford, you know?'

'OK, I know, I know,' he laughed.

Kelsey pretended to sulk, adding in a low voice. 'I only stalled it twice back at the services, and you won't catch me going over seventy, *unlike some people.*'

'Hey, that was a momentary lapse in concentration when you were feeding me that gingerbread heart.'

'Tell that to the motorway police.'

She laughed, surprised they had slipped into this new, easy way of talking. When had that happened? It must be a good thing, a sign that they were relaxed with each other, she thought. She could feel Jonathan tensing beside her again as she accelerated to overtake a lorry.

'Careful,' he cried, as his foot automatically stretched into the footwell, looking for a non-existent brake to pump.

'You're doing it again. Just relax and listen to Chris; he *loves* driving on dark, icy, overcrowded roads. I'd never have guessed you were a nervous passenger.'

'I'm not nervous, I'm having a great time.' Jonathan sipped his coffee and set his eyes on the cars' lights snaking in a chain on the road ahead. 'How much longer?'

'*Hmm*, couple of hours. It's nice just puttering along with you.'

'I liked the bit at the services best,' grimaced Jonathan.

'You're going to have to distract yourself... tell me a story or something.'

'OK, t'was the night before Christmas...'

'Tell me about your mum,' Kelsey urged.

'Oh, well, OK. Let's see. She's real dainty, like my sisters. I guess I don't get my height from her. She works one job these days but when I was a kid and it was just us two she worked all the time. I'm not kidding. I'd be looked after by all these aunties on my street – none of them were my real aunts – while mom worked the cash register at the 7-Eleven, or taught her art and acting classes, and she was a cleaner in this old lady's house for a while. Yeah, she's amazing. You're gonna love her.'

'I know I will.'

'Once she met Art things got easier. He's an English professor. Now Mom teaches her drama classes and that's it. She's thinking about retiring soon though. Yeah, you're gonna love her. Do you, *uh*, think your mom's gonna like me?'

'Hah! Well, be prepared for the loudest scream you've ever heard when she sees us. If that doesn't frighten you off, you're definitely going to get along. All she ever wanted was for me to be happy like she was with Dad.'

She threw a quick glance at Jonathan listening starry-eyed beside her. He reached for her hand on the gear stick and squeezed it gently, and they fell silent for a while.

'Look, there it is!' Kelsey called out, pointing to the roadside.

They both stared at the sign, a huge saltire cross in blue and white with the Gaelic words, '*Fàilte gu Alba*' in bold letters.

'Failty goo alba?' He squinted as they passed.

'Welcome to Scotland,' she said, and the words caught a little in her throat as she was hit by the same sudden wave of sentimental pride every Scot making their homecoming journey ever felt, the feeling made all the stronger because this time she was bringing Jonathan with her. 'Welcome to Scotland!' she said again, pressing the pedal a little harder, carrying them off into the night, so close to home.

Chapter Twenty-Eight

'She never told her love,
But let concealment, like a worm i' th' bud,
Feed on her damask cheek.'
(*Twelfth Night*)

As Mirren left the Yorick the last of the Christmas Eve audiences were swarming into the theatres on the riverside buzzing with excitement for the last performances before the break.

It had been an exhausting shift but the sight that greeted her as the crowds thinned made up for every empty pint pot she'd hauled out of the steamy glasswash trying to keep up with demand at the bar.

Kenneth had helped her serve all afternoon, his shirt sleeves rolled up, and she'd barely had a chance to stop, even missing the free turkey and trimmings Christmas Eve lunch she'd been so looking forward to.

There had been the added distraction of thinking of Kelsey driving north with her boyfriend and she thought about them often as she worked; no doubt they were holding hands on the gearstick and grinning soppily at each other like two gigantic nerds in love.

The single life was hitting her hard just as much as it was fuelling her pride at keeping her promise to herself. There would be no cosy boyfriend-for-Christmas moments and no visit home for her this festive season.

It's always nice to have someone to kiss at Christmas, she'd pined as she served the happy couples in town on seasonal mini breaks – all sexed up and gorging on Shakespeare and champagne – and her heart cracked a little when she told herself it might actually have been quite nice to see her mum who was all alone in her little house with the telly blaring and the temptation of the off licence just around the corner. Maybe she should have tried to get home for Christmas after all?

She'd sighed so much during her shift even Kenneth had been worried. Putting a fatherly arm around her shoulder, he'd told her she could knock off early if she needed to, but – partly thinking of the quiet, lonely barge waiting for her and partly spurred on by her loyalty to the Yorick – she'd persevered and time had passed as it always does.

But now, like a reward for her efforts, Adrian Armadale was waiting there in the shadows of the high wall that contained the pub's front garden, his black hair shining metallic blue in the coloured festive bulbs strung high above them. It was cold and dark but the people walking home with last-minute shopping ready to settle in for Christmas meant the town was alive with laughter and chatter. The whole scene lifted Mirren's spirits.

'You made it back. I didn't know if you would,' she said to Adrian. That was when she noticed his preoccupied, slightly deflated look.

'I spoke to my contact. I thought they'd have a lead but they said what everyone else around here knows; Wagstaff was a playboy all through the sixties and seventies, always had a beautiful woman on his arm, but that doesn't confirm anything about him knowing Jonathan's mum or having a relationship with her in the eighties.'

Mirren could see he really had a bee in his bonnet. 'You've been chasing it up all afternoon? Didn't you have family to see?'

'Oh I saw them,' he said distractedly. 'I'm not giving up yet. I know where we can find concrete information about Olivia and Wagstaff. Are you free now? Want to come?'

Mirren thought about the evening she'd had planned, having been too proud to accept Kelsey's invitation to eat takeaway food at the bedsit with her and Jonathan – irrelevant now they'd made a dash for Scotland. There was *It's A Wonderful Life* primed to watch on her laptop and a big, tartan tin of shortbread – Mirren's favourite – her mum had sent post restante to the local post office. Mirren and Kelsey had been surprised to learn the postie didn't deliver to riverside moorings and had hastily set up the barge's mailbox. The shortbread had been Mirren's first and only mail since moving-in day.

'I've got nothing planned,' she told him.

'Great. Are you hungry? You should probably eat first.'

'I'm not hungry,' she lied, too impatient to find out where they were going.

'Not even for these?' He produced a box of beautifully beribboned chocolates from behind his back, the fancy kind from the little chocolatier in the arcade.

'OK, maybe I'm a little peckish.' *Why am I grinning so much? And what's with that rush of adrenaline?* She scanned his face, wondering if he was feeling it too and trying to fight the excitement bubbling up within her, but it was too late because he was smiling at her and wishing her a happy Christmas under the streetlights and every pound of her flesh wanted to betray her vow and kiss him.

'Merry Christmas,' she said, forcing herself to be sensible. 'Here, I have something for you too.' From her pocket she produced the John Wagstaff autobiography, which he took with a wry laugh.

'Our mark?'

'That's right... and there's this as well.' Her other hand grasped a bottle of champagne from the bar fridge. It had cost her week's tips but it was Christmas Eve after all and she'd wanted to give him something nice. *Because that's what friends do. Platonic, chummy friends who don't fancy each other.*

'Come on, we can pop that cork where we're going,' he said, taking the bottle and jamming his free hand into his long coat, his black cashmere scarf flapping in the cold breeze. 'Follow me.'

There were no signs of life at the *Examiner* officers as they crept up the dark, creaking staircase past Adrian's office, neat and tidy with his Christmas cards displayed on the wall.

'Is this breaking and entering?' Mirren hissed quietly.

'Why are you whispering?' Adrian whispered back, breaking into a laugh and flicking the lights on as they climbed up to the top floor. 'It's not breaking in if you work here and you have a key.'

'Fair enough. So what are we looking for?'

Adrian led the way into the room next to Mr Ferdinand's dark office. The whole building was silent and surprisingly warm. The heating system worked even if the Editor in Chief didn't. Mirren couldn't control her feelings of defeat as she glanced around the shabby, haphazard offices on the upper floors, comparing them to the sleek and modern *Broadsheet* building. If she couldn't even get a writing job here, she really had hit rock bottom.

The lights flared on revealing what looked like a cross between a store room and a library, but the cabinets that lined the walls held little white boxes instead of books and there, taking up a quarter of the room and up against the far wall, stood a great grey machine with a chair in front of it.

Adrian walked over to it. 'So this is the…'

'Microfilm reader,' Mirren cut in. 'For looking through old newspapers archived onto reels. I know exactly what it is and how to use it. I did my journalism degree in the days before newspaper archives were digitised, remember?' She was already crouching by the plug and switching it on at the mains, leaving Adrian raking a hand through his hair, smiling at her enthusiasm. 'Where did you study?' she asked as the machine whirred into life and the bulb behind its screen glowed dimly. Mirren had used these contraptions, once the height of data storage technology, time and again searching old newspaper archives and she loved its clunking simplicity.

'I didn't study anywhere,' Adrian replied. 'I joined the staff here as the Saturday tea and photocopying boy when I was fifteen, then I moved up to being a junior reporter straight out of school with my A-levels in English, Art and Fashion.' He looked a little sheepish at the admission. 'Nothing like a fancy journalism degree for me, I'm afraid.' His look suggested he expected Mirren to be disappointed somehow, but it didn't dim her view of him in the slightest.

'I knew you were a bit of a fashionista,' she grinned, trying not to run her eyes over his smart outfit – or more specifically, she was avoiding thinking about how his clothes spoke of the perfectly defined model-like frame beneath. *Dammit*, if he wasn't smiling shyly now with a hint of red in the apples of his cheeks beneath those specs. She snapped her eyes back to the screen. '*Umm*, so Mr Ferdinand was your mentor, then?'

'He taught me everything he knows about the industry, shame half of it was fifty years out of date.' Adrian looked around at the dusty clutter of the archive room. 'We're losing advertising revenue every year. I'm not supposed to know this, but our parent company, Eagle Media, are sniffing around again. I'd be surprised if we were still open next Christmas.'

'What would you do then?'

He shrugged. 'All I ever wanted to do was work at this paper. Well, I used to want that, and I was proud of it too. Back when we were famous for our theatre coverage. That was fifteen years ago now, can you believe it? I still review every play that comes to town; sometimes I interview the directors or actors, but I get the feeling nobody reads my columns anymore. We're the paper you pick up if you've got kittens to sell... or you're looking to line your budgie cage.' There it was again, that dark, brooding look she'd seen him fight so many times now. 'Maybe the big bosses will move me to the *Honeybourne Gazetteer* or the *Alcester Bugler* when this place closes.'

He was looking up now at the ornate yellowing cornicing and the stained glass and leading on the skylights. There was still the shell of a fine building to admire and, if you looked past the mess, it hinted at the glamour of a lost age of reporting. The sheen over Adrian's eyes told Mirren he was picturing it now, back when he was a teenager at the end of the *Examiner*'s long heyday, before the rot set in.

'Anyway,' he forced out a big sigh. 'What year are we looking for?'

'Oh! Of course!' Mirren awoke from the hazy pleasure of watching him. 'Jonathan's thirty-two, so he was born in...'

'Eighty-eight,' they both said at once, and Adrian searched the cabinet.

'Eighty-four to eight-six... eighty-seven to eighty-eight. Got it!' He pulled out two white boxes tied with string. 'Here we go.'

He watched her, impressed, as she unwrapped the roll of film and set it upon the machine's spinning spool, threading the end of the reel into the clamp and starting the slow scroll through the archived pages projected and enlarged on the screen, every page of the original editions long since disintegrated or destroyed and captured for posterity decades ago on the celluloid spool.

Mirren scrolled, searching for any mention of Wagstaff and Olivia Hathaway. Had the pair ever acted together, or even worked together in the same season of plays? Had they been photographed out on the town together at some premier or at a cast party? Had they done a press call together, or an interview? She relished hunting through the reel for evidence. This was what she was good at; finding the story, sifting through resources to get to the truth, with sharp eyes and sharper wits. The thrill of reporting was coming back to her, something that had been dulled writing up magistrates' proceedings at the *Broadsheet*.

Adrian, Mirren noticed, had left the room, so she worked on, hoping she wouldn't stumble upon any mention of Blythe and Wagstaff. She'd blurted out the mystery of Jonathan's paternity to Adrian; she didn't need to add details about Blythe's potential love affair with the old rogue too. Jonathan's story was delicate enough without adding another layer of intrigue and Blythe's controversial pregnancy was no one's business but her own – everyone deserved to keep their secrets, didn't they? Her excitement ebbed a little at this.

She thought of how even the national papers would love this scoop. Famed TV and stage actor, John Wagstaff – the man who (probably) ruined Blythe Goode, sixties stage siren – reunites with his long-lost American son, also an actor reaching the height of his career and returning to the English stage for another triumphant season. She could see the salacious head-lines and the clickbait sidebars already.

The thought of it was enough to make her hands fall to her lap, just as Adrian was returning with two empty mugs.

'Let's open that bottle, shall we?' he said. 'Hey, what's the matter?'

'Are we doing the right thing? What if we find out Wagstaff *is* Jonathan's dad? That kind of information in the wrong hands could ruin his life. If it got out and in the news there could be a scandal all over again; we could hurt his mum's feelings, humiliate them both. Is it worth it?'

'Whatever we discover, nobody needs to know,' said Adrian, pulling up a chair beside her. 'You're looking for proof, right? If we find it, your friend can break it to her boyfriend and then it's up to him how he proceeds. He doesn't have to act on it, but at least he'd know.'

'If he wanted to know he'd ask his mum.'

Adrian swallowed, setting the bottle of champagne down again, thinking hard. Eventually, he made up his mind. 'You're right. Nobody likes to be reminded of family secrets left buried for generations. It's not our place to interfere. We *should* leave it.'

'Working late?'

They both quailed at the voice from the doorway. Adrian drew a martyred breath before he turned to face its source.

'Mr Ferdinand? I was just showing Mirren the archives.'

'Got a news story, have you?' The editor peered at them, his nose raised, sniffing out an exclusive.

'Nope, I'm just really into archives,' Mirren said hurriedly.

'Anything I can help you with?' He wasn't going to let this lie.

'We were just leaving actually, weren't we?' Adrian said, surreptitiously placing the mugs on the floor where his boss wouldn't see them.

'Did I hear you mention Olivia Hathaway?' Ferdinand pressed, leaning across the doorway and looking as frail and as sticky as a spider's web.

The young reporters turned to one another, plumping their bottom lips in fake confusion. '*Uh*, nope, don't think so,' Adrian said, while Mirren shook her head innocently. 'Grab those chocolates, Mirren, let's get out of here. We'll be off now, Mr Ferdinand.'

Mirren wound the film back onto its spool as Mr Ferdinand approached the machine. He was still talking in his nasal tones. 'Because you know old Wagstaff got Olivia in a compromising position? She left town after that. Haven't heard her name in years, actually.'

'You knew them?' Mirren blurted, giving up the pretence.

'Everyone knew them. At least everyone in the theatre world. It was a minor scandal, I suppose, but soon forgotten. I was a handsome young lad at the time, of course. I was Brutus' page in *Julius Caesar*. I got to hold the dagger, you know? On a little cushion.'

Mirren humoured him with widened eyes and an interested smile, all the while thinking it was easier to picture Ferdinand wielding a murder weapon than it was to imagine he was ever a handsome young lad. 'Were they... in love?' Mirren hazarded.

Mr Ferdinand pulled a face as though this were the oddest of questions, then ignored it. 'So you *weren't* researching a story?' Mirren saw the quick lick at his thin, parched lips like a lizard tasting the air.

'Goodness, no. Well, it was nice to see you again, Mr Ferdinand. Merry Christmas.' She stood up tall in front of him, allowing Adrian to slip the reels back into the cabinet, making sure to smooth the row so nobody could know which boxes they'd picked out.

Mr Ferdinand, cowed by Mirren towering so close to him and smiling with her red-lipsticked mouth, took a step backwards. She'd known he'd be intimidated by the proximity – Mr Ferdinand didn't look the lascivious, grab-a-handful-while-you-can type – and he'd slunk out the room, calling behind him something about making sure they didn't leave a mess.

They followed him from the archive room, hearing the microfilm reader's fan whirr down into silence again. Mr Ferdinand was standing awkwardly in front of his office door. 'xI'm leaving now too. I was just, *eh*, making sure we'd locked up properly for the holiday. See you early on the twenty-eighth, Adrian.'

'*Uh*, sure. Merry Christmas.' Adrian reached for Mirren's hand and she instinctively clasped it, making their way from the building while casting cautious glances at one another until they were on the street and out of Ferdinand's hearing.

'He heard us talking about Olivia and Wagstaff; do you think he heard the bit about Jonathan?' Mirren asked.

'I don't know. He's deaf as a post when I'm asking him for petty cash or help with an article, but he definitely knows we were up to something.'

'*Hmm*,' Mirren worried her lip. 'So that confirms it. John Wagstaff is Jonathan's dad.'

'I think so.'

'What do we do now?' Mirren asked.

Adrian cast a glimpse back at the *Examiner* offices just as the gap held open in the blinds in Mr Ferdinand's office rattled shut. 'Let's get out of here,' he said. 'Find somewhere to drink this bubbly?'

Mirren was too shaken from Mr Ferdinand's bombshell and from the heat of Adrian's hand still clasping hers to stop the words flying from her mouth. 'You can come back to mine if you like?'

—

Three hundred miles north, Kelsey and Jonathan were stepping out of their car into the moonlight and smelling the cold, salty air of the Scottish East coast.

The lights on the Forth bridges lit up the sky over the Firth towards Edinburgh. Inland, the fallow winter fields lay frosted and black and the gentle Lammermuirs lifted upwards into the dark sky, their roads barely passable in these icy conditions. Unknown to Kelsey and Jonathan, linking arms on the doorstep of Mari Anderson's little grey stone house by the sea wall, the first snowflakes of winter were falling there and soon they'd make their way here too to the water's edge.

For now, all that concerned Kelsey was greeting Mari, Grandad and Calum and letting them take their first look at the newest member of their clan.

The door pulled wide open, the light and warmth spilled out and they stepped inside, screams of delight and hurried footsteps on the stairs drowning out their greetings.

Chapter Twenty-Nine

'Let us once lose our oaths to find ourselves,
Or else we lose ourselves to keep our oaths'
(*Love's Labour's Lost*)

'Cheers,' Adrian and Mirren clinked the steaming mugs together and settled back onto the bed at the back of the barge, making sure to keep a space between them.

'No sofa,' Mirren had informed him awkwardly as he cast his eyes around the low room following the even more awkward revelation that she lived on the boat they'd walked past only the night before and she hadn't let on. He'd been generous enough to just smile at her embarrassment and didn't probe her reasons. He'd even kept his sense of humour when she asked him not to pop the cork on the bubbly that he'd began peeling the foil from, and instead she'd flicked the kettle on. If they were going to hang out together she wanted to keep a clear head.

Adrian now sipped his tea, his boots and coat left by the little hatch in Kelsey's gallery area, now cluttered with framed photographs waiting to be hanged. 'Can we at least open the chocolates?'

'Oh, go on then, let's live dangerously,' Mirren quipped, pulling at the ribbon on the box and all the time trying to sound matey and calm, even if her insides were fizzing like popping candy.

'I can't believe you've never seen this film,' Adrian remarked as Mirren hit 'play' and *It's A Wonderful Life* burst onto the laptop perched on the little shelf at the end of the bed and a bell tolled on screen and the jolly, festive title music played.

'It always looked kind of sad to me, so I avoided it. I'm more of a *Muppet Christmas Carol* kind of woman.' Mirren offered up the chocolates and Adrian took a soft centre, which she wasn't going to read anything into.

'Can't argue with that. You've got to love Kermit's Bob Cratchit, it's the little guy's best work, but honestly this is a great film too. I watch it every year. It is sad though, you're right, but don't worry, I won't blub this time. At least I'll try not to.'

'I won't judge,' she laughed. 'Tissues are just over there.' She popped her choice of chocolate, the peanut brittle square, into her mouth and crunched happily.

The titles finished turning and the orchestra swelled and for the first time Mirren thought it actually felt like Christmas. In fact, it felt surprisingly like the kind of cosy Christmas evenings she used to have with Preston, warm and comfy, just a movie and some snacks, never anything too intense, just companionship. Yet there was a little something troubling her, keeping relaxation at arm's length.

'Adrian?'

He was intently watching the opening scenes. '*Hmm*?'

'Are you sure you can keep Wagstaff's baby-daddy news to yourself, even after I tell Jonathan when they get back to Stratford on Boxing Day? It's a secret only Jonathan needs to know, right?'

'Of course.'

Mirren took her eyes off the screen and quickly glanced at Adrian, who smiled back. 'And you don't think Ferdinand suspected anything?' she added.

He hesitated before answering this time. 'I don't think so. If he says anything I'll just act innocent.' Seeing the crease form between Mirren's brows he was spurred on to say more, turning a little to face her. 'I promise I'll keep it to myself, OK? I pinkie

230

swear.' He offered her his crooked little finger and, smiling, Mirren hooked her own around it.

'OK. We'll let Jonathan deal with the news in as dignified and private a manner as he can; it's his news, no one else's,' she said solemnly, before pulling her hand back.

Adrian seemed satisfied with that and offered her another chocolate, rubbing his shoulders into the pillows behind him.

Maybe Mirren wasn't aware of it but she too shifted so she was more comfortable, moving a little closer, cradling her mug of tea in both hands, her eyes now fixed back on the screen. 'So what's this movie about then?'

'It's about an angel sent from heaven to help this guy who thinks his life is a mess. He shows him what life would have been like for those around him if he'd never existed.'

'Oh.' Mirren took that in for a moment.

'Am I talking too much?' Adrian said suddenly, in a strange, slightly slurred accent.

'What?' Her eyes snapped to his, amused. 'What the heck was that supposed to be?'

'It's James Stewart.' He nodded at the screen. 'Didn't it sound like him?'

'If he was doing an impression of Sean Connery, maybe. That was terrible.' She couldn't help laughing.

'Aww, come on, it's one of the most famous lines in the movie. I sound just like him.' To prove it he tried again. 'Am I talking too much?'

She screwed her face up playfully, but he was determined to go on, switching characters now.

'Yes! Why don't you kiss her instead of talking her to death?'

They both laughed but Adrian's eyes darted back to the screen again, having fallen, just for a second, to Mirren's mouth.

Excruciating silence followed; even the film score was quiet for an agonising moment.

Mirren couldn't help smiling when she realised Adrian's eyes were boring into the screen and he was smirking, both of them feeling the awkwardness dragging on until it was impossible not to acknowledge it with a sniffed laugh.

There was no hope of concentrating on the movie now. Mirren glanced at him. His thick, black-rimmed designer spectacles reflected the moving images on screen and she watched the soft blink of his dark lashes, long from this angle, longer even than her own. His lips were parted as he pretended to be rapt in the film.

'You're watching me,' he said, still avoiding her eyes, and his lips tugged into a smile.

'I was just thinking…' she began.

This made him turn his head.

'You told me you weren't dating. Why is that?'

He reached a hand into his thick hair and mussed it with a deep exhalation, shifting to face her properly. '*Umm*, well. Let's see. My ex told me I'm not great at being a boyfriend. In fact, not just one ex.' He inhaled through gritted teeth like the words stung but his eyes were still full of humour.

Mirren tipped her head, listening.

'Apparently, I'm a lot like my dad in that regard. My parents divorced when I was eight. They married *really* young and it just wasn't going to work. Mum said he'd always been bloody-minded, focused on himself and his work and, I don't know, based on my past relationships and my girlfriends' helpful feedback maybe I take after him. In Dad's defence I think he's changed a lot. He remarried – so has Mum, by the way – and they're both pretty happy now. Maybe Mum's still a bit bitter about it. But I can't help thinking that recently I *have* been too focused on work, you know? But I really thought the *Examiner* was worth saving. I'd do anything to keep that place going and make it the theatre paper it used to be. It's too late now though.' He shrugged, absorbed in his thoughts. 'After my last girlfriend broke things off I decided to stay away from relationships for a bit. It was easier to be alone and just… work.' The glaze over his dark eyes disappeared and he fixed Mirren with a penetrating look. 'But then I met you and…'

They weren't laughing any longer. Mirren's hand strayed from the mug she'd been clasping for dear life and she touched her fingertips to his wrist and what felt like sparks burst from their touching skin.

'Will you tell me about you, and why you're avoiding love?' Adrian said softly.

She shook her head at that word. It wasn't love she was avoiding; it was herself, the very worst bits of herself, and the situations that brought out the worst in her, but right that second her vow didn't seem as pressing as it had in the days before. This didn't feel like the kind of situation she'd ever been in, the kind that made her feel scared, or stupid, or both. Right now all she felt was warmth, so she put her mug on the windowsill by the bed and leaned closer to Adrian in his soft jumper and he lifted his arm so she could snuggle into his side.

'This isn't breaking your rules, then?' Adrian said, as their eyes settled on the movie once more. Mirren didn't answer but curled her legs up and let Adrian rest his hand over her hip. 'You're going to love this film,' he said, smoothing his hand in a slow circle against her side. 'Everyone gets a second chance at Christmas.'

For one drawn out thunderbolt of a moment Mirren listened to Adrian's breathing before gathering a handful of his jumper across his chest into a fist and pulling him gently down the pillows until they were face to face. There was a disconcerting moment where Adrian nearly spilled his tea and Mirren had to rescue the mug, but somehow it didn't matter because he was smiling with shining eyes, and it was Christmas Eve, and they were so close to kissing, and maybe this was *her* second chance. So she closed her eyes and let him hold her close to him, their mouths brushing with irresistible softness that felt like melting.

Chapter Thirty

'Eat and drink as friends'
(*The Taming of the Shrew*)

It had been a perfect Christmas day, even though they'd both awakened stiff and uncomfy on the sofa after a night bundled in each other's arms listening to the clanking of the radiators and Grandad snoring upstairs in what had been Kelsey's childhood bedroom.

Mari had helped Grandad downstairs that morning and they'd all sat in dressing gowns and slippers drinking coffee and eating hot, buttered bran scones. Jonathan had never seen the rough brown savoury scones before but happily devoured two while everyone watched Calum tear open his presents.

'That'll be the last we hear from him, then,' Grandad said as Calum unboxed the games console he'd been hoping for all year long, and Mari agreed with a wistful laugh that had all of her memories of earlier Christmases when her children were still little wrapped up in it.

Everyone else's gifts were modest – new pyjamas and slippers, chocolates and smelly stuff, and Kelsey had taken the opportunity to redistribute her wealth of Blythe's gin jam – and the unwrapping had been happy and relaxed now theirs was a house full of adults adjusting to what Christmases would be like from now on now Calum was growing up.

Kelsey had been thrilled to unwrap Jonathan's gift to her, a box of vintage, coloured glass filters – attachments for her dad's camera. She'd scoured eBay for something similar over the years and never found any. How had Jonathan known, she'd wondered, wide-eyed and delighted.

'Dad gave me them the second I told him you were a camera enthusiast. They were from his old Canon camera so I think they'll fit, right?'

Kelsey attached them to her camera's lens straight away, snapping tinted images in pink and orange, red and green, exclaiming all the while how thoughtful Jonathan had been.

'Thank Art, it was his idea,' he said.

Christmas had always been a cosy affair at the Andersons, a day for Buck's Fizz well before noon and musicals on the telly. Lunch was always plentiful and hearty. Mari traditionally hosted the whole family as well as her closest friend Ted and his husband Alex, and it wasn't unusual for Grandad to be there early in the day to help peel the sprouts, and that's just what he'd done that morning while the turkey cooked in the oven and everyone lounged on the sofas looking at the *TV Times*, catching up on the details of Kelsey's new life and hearing all about Jonathan's closing night as Hamlet.

Ted and Alex arrived at twelve with their toothless rescue mutts, George and Mildred, and the revelry increased by a few hundred decibels as everyone shouted over the dogs' yapping every time Calum's console gargled and beeped with the sounds of the rebooted retro arcade games he was already mastering.

'Is Jonathan enjoying himself, do you think?' Mari had whispered during a quieter moment before lunch as she decorated the kitchen table with trailing ivy and holly from the garden all wrapped around a thick red pillar candle that only came out once a year. Kelsey stirred the gravy and kept an eye on the steaming veggies.

'He's fine, yeah, just look at him.'

They peered through the doors leading to the living room framing Jonathan sitting beside Grandad helping him with a *Polar Express* jigsaw, both men talking through their strategies ('build the edges first, then find all the black bits of the engine') and frowning with concentration. Mum and daughter smiled and carried on with their preparations while the Robbie Williams Christmas album played from the ancient stereo that had been Kelsey's dad's.

'Love, there's something I need to tell you,' Mari said as she finished setting out the holly leaf paper napkins, glancing nervously at the kitchen clock, but there hadn't been time to say anything else because the doorbell rang and Mari opened the door to a stranger in a shirt and tie under a gaudy Christmas jumper and she ushered him into the kitchen.

'This is Rory,' Mari said to Kelsey over the man's shoulder.

'I've heard so much about you, Kelsey,' he'd said gently, his freckled cheeks glowing pink from the cold outside. The wide-eyed look Kelsey threw over Rory's shoulder at Mari as she gave him a quick hug said *that was funny because she hadn't heard anything about him.* Mari only blushed.

'Looks like you're about to serve up, do you need a hand with that?' Rory offered and he and Kelsey worked together on the last of the preparations.

'Your mum tells me you're planning an exhibition at your very own gallery?' he said as he drained the potatoes and his glasses steamed.

'That's right, on my little barge.' It sounded almost comical but there it was. In less than two months she'd be opening her very own gallery.

'Your mum's so proud of you. She can't wait to see it.'

'You should come to the opening too.' Kelsey had said it before she'd thought it through. Rory and Mari were smiling and making gasping, surprised laughs across the kitchen as Mari spooned cranberry sauce into a little glass dish. 'Or, *uh*, sorry, is that a weird thing to say? You'll probably be busy working… at your, *um*…'

'Opticians?' he offered.

'Ah! Yes, you might be busy at the opticians.'

'Never too busy for your mum. That's where we first met, actually; when she came in for her sight test.'

'You didn't meet on a dating app?' Kelsey was surprised.

'*Uh*, no, I wouldn't know much about that sort of thing.' Rory's ears were turning pink and he focused hard on buttering the carrots.

Mari untied her apron, coming to Rory's rescue. 'You know, Rory, it *would* be nice to take a trip somewhere together.'

Kelsey slipped away, peering into the fridge, trying to make herself look busy.

'You wouldn't mind if I came along to the gallery opening?' Rory said delightedly.

'We can make a weekend of it… if you wanted to? It'll be Valentine's weekend…' Mari said.

Kelsey listened to the shy, relieved laughter behind her; the kind that betrayed how new and tentative their relationship was, and she heard the little kiss Rory placed on her mum's cheek and her soft laugh in response.

'Right, well, we should probably eat then. Do you want to sit down, Rory? I'll call the others,' Kelsey said at last, breaking the blushing buzz in the air, mainly generated by a starry-eyed Mari who somehow looked about ten years younger than Kelsey ever remembered her being. Kelsey was surprised to find she wasn't a bit put out about Rory joining the family for Christmas lunch, in fact, it felt exactly right. Her lovely Dad would have wanted this for Mari and the thought made her smile as well as a little misty eyed.

The kitchen windows were steamed up and rich foody aromas filled the air as Mari and Kelsey carried dish after dish to the table. When they were finished, Rory had stood up to pull a chair out for Mari and bowed his sandy head to kiss her as she sat down while her mum flustered like a schoolgirl.

Soon they'd all settled around the table and piled their plates high. Jonathan was happily wearing the tasteful Christmas jumper Kelsey had given him that morning – Shakespeare in a

Santa suit with drooping red bobble hat on his bald pate. They'd all laughed as they pulled their crackers in a circle with crossed arms and Grandad had joked about how that was enough exercise for one day and asked for extra roasties to make up for the calories burned.

Jonathan had been surprised to learn that the pigs in blankets he'd already eaten three of were in fact the 'kilties' that had confused him the day before. 'Let me get this straight,' he'd laughed. 'It's a sausage, wearing a little bacon kilt?'

'Aye, what else would it be?' Grandad had replied matter-of-factly, making everyone laugh again.

There had been wine and cracker puns that made everyone groan and a Christmas pudding that wouldn't light until Ted took over heating the brandy in a ladle over the gas ring before taking a match to the liquid and pouring the licking blue flames over the pudding, immediately setting off the smoke alarm.

That evening, as Jonathan dried the dishes and Mari made the turkey sandwiches, Kelsey watched them together from the kitchen doorway. They were talking, heads bowed and conspiratorial, and she'd smiled to see how easily her American boyfriend had fit in and how welcome everyone had made him.

–

Now it was late and Christmas Day was almost over. Everyone had gone to bed. Kelsey yawned on the sofa in her new pyjamas and dragged the duvet around her. Jonathan had showered and wore nothing but a towel around his waist, his hair occasionally dripping as he flicked through the pages of the acting manual of a nineteen-thirties stage star – pictured in tights and codpiece on the cover – that Kelsey had given him that morning, one of Blythe's donated book haul. As he stood over her, reading aloud, he seemed strangely agitated and in high spirits after the long, exhausting day of eating and merry-making but she didn't think any more of it.

His hammy, faux-English accent rang out. '*Ensure to raise one's voice without elevating the pitch. Consistency of tone is everything and one must employ Received Pronunciation at all times in order to make the Bard accessible to the common theatre-goer. Assume a grand attitude with shoulders and chest broadened. Stretching the throat will create the resonant boom required in large auditoria…*'

Kelsey giggled as Jonathan adopted an exaggerated stance, his legs comically wide and face contorted like a *Carry On* film actor.

'This stuff is so dated,' he laughed, folding the book shut. 'I wear a tiny microphone in my hairline now. Stage acting's more like TV acting these days, so much smaller and quieter.'

'So less chest-puffing and booming then?'

'And less occasion to wear tights.'

'Shame, that.' Kelsey lifted the hem on Jonathan's towel with her foot and waggled an eyebrow mischievously.

He threw the book aside and leaned over her, clambering onto their nest of duvets and pillows on the sofa and kissing her softly on the temple.

'You should write an up-to-date actors' handbook,' Kelsey mused.

'*Hmmm.*' He was kissing her neck now.

'You are, after all, the greatest Hamlet of our generation.'

'Never forget it,' he spoke in a low tone near her ear, pulling the covers and enveloping them both in warmth. 'Actually, that's not a bad idea,' he said, lifting his eyes to hers. 'I could do with another source of income when I move to England permanently in April.'

'Meeting my family wasn't enough to send you running for the airport then?'

'Not nearly enough. You'll have to do much worse than that to get rid of me. Even your mom's boyfriend was nice.'

'Rory? Yes, he was.' Kelsey smiled, a little wistful. She'd never seen her mum so transformed. She'd been more carefree than she'd ever seen her.

'Was it strange seeing her with someone else?'

Kelsey thought for a minute. 'No, it was nice actually. I hope he sticks around.'

'I didn't think he was ever gonna leave, they spent so long saying goodnight at the door earlier.'

Kelsey laughed again. 'Love, huh?'

'It's catching.' Jonathan pulled her closer. 'Come here,' he said in a low murmur before he kissed her again, oblivious to the snow falling in fluffy flakes outside and the sounds of the waves, tempestuous and cold, hitting the sea wall just over the road from the cosy little house where they'd spent the happiest Christmas of their lives.

Chapter Thirty-One

'In nature's infinite book of secrecy, a little I can read'
(*Antony and Cleopatra*)

Back in the earliest hours of Christmas morning the barge rocked queasily on the Avon. Mirren sat with her legs drawn to her chest at the end of the bed watching Adrian asleep in the twinkling light from the coloured fairy-strand along the galley kitchen wall. Mirren didn't know what time it was other than it was well past midnight.

They must have kissed for hours, slowly at first, then hungrily like teenagers, hands fumbling, pulling jumpers over heads like they'd been unwrapping Christmas presents – real, deep moaning kisses that shook Mirren with their heat.

Eventually, they'd pulled apart, still mostly clothed, before they could get too carried away, and they'd sunk down onto the mattress and Adrian had trailed lazy fingertips up and down her spine, smiling like a sleepy wolf as they'd both grown drowsy.

Now her eyes were wide, her hair hanging messily over her shoulders and down her back. She couldn't find her top or bra in the low light. Letting him cover her in heated kisses hadn't been part of the plan at all. *What happened to a movie and cosy cuppa?* She cursed herself under her breath, disappointed.

Could she reach her pyjamas shoved under the pillow? She wanted to be covered up again, even though she could still feel the pressure and suction of his full lips as he mouthed her breasts and stomach and told her it was OK, she could relax, he didn't expect more, and he'd checked and rechecked she was still happy.

Of course she'd been happy, she'd been delirious. Theirs hadn't been any old kisses. They were incendiary and had stolen her breath, made her groan his name, and he'd drawn back to look at her in gasping wonder before bringing his mouth down onto her skin again.

The soft spot under her ear, the most sensitive places on her belly and sides, new delicate patches of skin where her nerves had fizzed and thrilled and where she didn't even know she had wanted to be kissed; he'd found them all.

But now the barge had grown cool, and she didn't know it but the spiral had already begun.

It crept up so invisibly she didn't recognise it for what it was. First came the recoiling, then the examination of how exactly she'd let it happen. She replayed the moment they'd first kissed and yes, it had been *her* pulling at his clothes, reaching for his mouth.

She watched herself now on the bed in his arms and she shook her head to stop the memories. She'd been frantic and greedy. What was it about this lovely, patient, sexy guy that he could do this to her? What was wrong with him that he wanted to?

Then the reprimands lined up in her mouth, so she scolded herself under her breath. Her own words came out first, quietly so that he wouldn't hear. 'What have you done? So much for your resolve. Stay single, focus on yourself, stop messing up other people's lives. Fuck's sake, Mirren.' Then she heard the other voices piping up right on cue and the loudest was Jamesey Wallace, salacious and lip-smacking, sneering the words, 'You women are all the same. You pretend like you want the nice guy who cooks for you and picks you up when it's raining and all that, but deep down all you really want is a good fucking.'

Her scalp prickled hot and cold with resentment, regret and panic. Jamesey'd had her pinned all those months ago. Her mum saw right through her too. Mirren could picture Jeanie shaking her head and throwing cutting remarks at her.

Mirren didn't know she was breathing sharp and shallow but the lack of air was making her head ache. For a second she considered waking Adrian and asking him to leave, then immediately she felt even worse. No, he didn't deserve to be thrown out onto the dark marina in the middle of the night. Maybe if she pulled some clothes on she could walk the riverside until morning when he'd leave?

The spiral had somehow conveyed her to the little bathroom and she found herself scrubbing her teeth with her pink toothbrush and only just realising her gums were bleeding and she was crying. 'Stupid cow,' she told her reflection in the mirror, her mouth set in a crumpled, tearful line.

Without thinking, she found herself reaching for the bleach bottle under the toilet and pouring the thick liquid into the sink and setting about scrubbing it with the very same toothbrush. Brush, brush, brush at the taps then onto the row of tiles above it, all the time repeating the insult. 'You stupid bloody tart. Couldn't help yourself, could you?'

'Hey, *woah there!*' The look on Adrian's face as he peered round the door and the concern in his voice shook her from her state enough to drop the toothbrush and hurriedly pull the plug, sending the bleach down the drain. She turned away from him and let the tap run.

'You should go,' she said quietly.

'*What*? What's happened, Mirren? Are you OK? Come out of there, it stinks of chemicals, you need some air.' His hand wrapped around hers and he pulled her through the narrow door. He dashed for the bed and returned with his woollen jumper which he hastily pulled down over her body. It was soft, like his voice now.

'I got up to get us some water and thought you'd beaten me to it, then I find you in here calling yourself awful things. What happened between us falling asleep and now? Did I do something wrong? Is there something you need?' He held her firmly by her arms which she let hang limply by her sides.

'I'm sorry I woke you. I'm fine, honestly. I'll sleep in the front of the boat, you go back to bed...'

'No way. Uh–uh.' He shook his head. The shock on his face had settled into a smile. 'Come on, I'm putting the kettle on.'

After he'd pulled his t-shirt back on and placed two steaming mugs before them on the little galley kitchen table he sat down, not at the opposite side of the table but right by her so he could hold her hand. 'Do you often talk to yourself like that?'

'Everyone talks to themselves, don't they?' Mirren had washed her face and put her glasses on and was hoping she could brazen it out until he fell asleep again. Making light, that's what she did best.

'Sure they do, but they don't call themselves names like that. Whose voice was that? Who first said those things to you? Because you sure as hell weren't born thinking about yourself that way.'

Mirren's eyes snapped to his. He knew. Somehow he knew. She could see it in his eyes, pity mixed with kindness. Just when she thought he couldn't read her any better, he reached over to the packet by the kettle and grabbed the chocolate digestives, turning the open end towards her. 'You talk, I'll listen. And we'll smash this whole packet, yeah?'

It was enough to make her laugh and to feel a little spark of warmth between them again. It wasn't easy at first, but once the words started to form into stammered sentences she found she couldn't stop.

So she talked, telling him everything; about walking out on her job, and about her poorly mum and what the alcohol had done to her. How it made it impossible for Jeanie to resist her cruellest urges, but how when she wasn't tortured by the addiction she was bright and smart and good company.

She'd cried hearing the words coming out of her mouth, and she'd admitted with shame that some of the worst things she'd ever heard herself called had been said by her mum. But it wasn't all Jeanie's fault, she insisted. She'd been hurt too, horribly let down when Mirren's dad ran off leaving her to cope alone, and so soon after Jeanie's own, loving father passed away. Jeanie's family had disintegrated within weeks. It hadn't been fair and the shock had sent her into a spiral of her own, trying to numb her pain and finding Mirren so easy to blame when things got difficult.

Then Mirren told him about Preston and how she'd loved him since school and they'd moved in together and been happy, but when she was an undergrad away at university, at first she'd stay in halls during term time and she wasn't above snogging other Freshers in the uni bars, but at the time she'd excused this by saying she was only trying to figure out why things with Preston didn't feel right. She told Adrian how, once she graduated, they had really settled down, like an old married couple, and it was nice and chilled for a long time, but five years ago things started to go wrong again and last September she'd let Preston down for the last time by sleeping with Will on the night at the theatrical gala. Then she'd faltered over the worst part, the part that hurt most. It had taken a great, deep breath to get the words out. She'd never, ever said it aloud before.

She filled him in on what happened on the night of her first Christmas party at the *Broadsheet* when she'd covered her nerves by drinking too much and she'd not said no when Jamesey wanted to kiss her in the print room. Even though it had only lasted a second and the feel of his mouth turned her stomach instantly and she'd run for her bus, listening to him laughing in triumph as the door slammed, she could never forgive herself.

'That was the first time I'd cheated on Preston when we were both grown-ups, after years of faithfulness and cosiness at home,' she said, tears falling over her cheeks.

'What you described with Jamesey doesn't really sound like cheating to me, somehow?' Adrian said, topping up her mug from the teapot.

'Part of me wanted to do it. Maybe if I could get him under my power, bend his will, I'd have won, and he'd stop harassing me all the time. I don't know, I wasn't really thinking clearly. All I know is I hated him before that kiss and afterwards, I hated myself. I couldn't tell Preston. Maybe I should have, because after that I couldn't stop pressing the self-destruct button on our relationship. Deep down, I knew I didn't deserve him, and I didn't have the guts to leave our little comfortable bubble I'd been in since school… and somehow after that I kept doing it – cheating, I mean.' She let her eyes fall to Adrian's thumb circling over the back of her hand as he held it.

'Must have been the guilt, it does funny things to people,' he said.

She shrugged. 'So you see, I'm no good as a girlfriend, I'm a shitty daughter – sitting here bad-mouthing my mum and she's all alone with nobody helping her in Scotland – and I'm an absolutely awful friend. Just think what I'm about to do to Jonathan. I'll have to tell him about Wagstaff when I should have kept my nose out of his business.'

'No. I'm not having that.' Adrian put his empty mug on the table with a look so simultaneously indignant and comedic she smiled in surprise. 'You're the best person I've met in, oh, easily a quarter of a century. I see that you're good and kind, but you beat yourself up horribly, and you shouldn't. Don't let yourself. Now I'm not here trying to be a white knight on his charger wanting to fix your problems, but I am a smart, switched-on guy and I know good people when I see them. And you're good people, Mirren Imrie. This Mr Angus and Jamesey, they've been gaslighting you; trying to convince you you're wrong about all the awful things they put you through, and look, it's worked. You're blaming yourself, exactly what they wanted to happen. If you're hiding away in England blaming yourself you're not exposing their creepy behaviour and their sexist organisation, are you?'

Mirren blinked, her mind whirring. She'd seen gaslighting before. Fran had done it to Kelsey, making her feel guilty about wanting more from her life – other than watching him excel in his teaching career and tending his house for him – and he'd made her doubt she could ever make money from her photography. He'd *convinced* her too, made her feel like she was in the wrong for wanting a career of her own and a life outside of his ambitions, but now Kelsey was here in Stratford, living her best life, and proving him wrong.

'You're right. Why did I need someone else to see it?' Mirren said, eyes wide.

'Because you're too busy beating yourself up?'

Mirren shook her head in wonder, replaying Mr Angus and Jamesey's words and feeling the constricting power they had over her loosening, and in its stead the anger came flooding back in. 'Jesus!' she mouthed. 'You're so right.'

Adrian passed a hand over the back of his neck and seemed lost in thought for a moment before he spoke again. 'Am I? Well don't thank me. I'm just as bad as them. You *told* me you didn't want a boyfriend, and I didn't listen. I'm sorry for that. I shouldn't have pursued you. I won't anymore if you really want me to stop, but I do really, really like you, and I respect you, and I think you deserve to be happy. Please don't add me liking you to the list of things you beat yourself up about.'

Mirren scanned his face looking for the truth in his words. He was fired up now, still talking, his cheeks a little flushed.

'And you know, while we're on the subject, I'm no angel either. I hurt girls in the past, wasn't careful with their feelings, and I wasn't exactly living like a monk in my early twenties. I made the most of the clubs and met loads of women and I know I messed around behind one girl's back. But you know what? I don't beat myself up about it now. And why's that? Are the rules different for me because I'm a guy?'

Mirren shrugged, 'They shouldn't be.'

'Exactly,' he was nodding emphatically. 'So when, precisely, are you going to forgive yourself for doing the same things I've done, for making mistakes, for having *fun*? *Hmmn*? At New

Year's?' He searched her face. 'Nope? In five years, maybe? Ten? Or are you going to live like this forever, because that's no life.'

Mirren only listened.

'Do the people you hurt forgive you?' he pressed.

Mirren thought hard. Preston had told her not to apologise any more and he was happy now, already moved on; she'd learned as much from his texts.

'Guilt be damned,' Adrian said. 'You *have* to live your life happily, Mirren. With me. If you'll let me?'

As he spoke, the bells of Christmas morning rang out from Holy Trinity church. Outside the darkness was stealing away, leaving a crisp, frosty morning. The barge was surrounded by chilly winter mist and the white swans gliding by. Mirren felt all her armour fall away.

'You told me the king and his men give up their oaths, and they fall in love?' Mirren said.

For a moment Adrian didn't understand. 'In *Love's Labour's Lost*? That's right. They realise what matters in life – love and company and happiness – and they give in to it. They let themselves be happy and they never regret it.'

'Well then.' Mirren stood on unsteady legs and Adrian did the same. She led him by the hand back to the bed and they both climbed under the covers once more.

Chapter Thirty-Two

'That you were once unkind befriends me now,
And for that sorrow, which I then did feel,
Needs must I under my transgression bow,
Unless my nerves were brass or hammered steel'
(*Sonnet 120*)

Late Christmas morning on the marina was bright and crisp. They'd slept until after dawn and awakened naked in each other's arms. Adrian had begged Mirren to join him for Christmas lunch at his mum's, telling her there would be plenty of room at the table, especially since his little brother was in Disneyland with his wife and kid. Although she'd wanted to, she still had her shift at the Yorick and she couldn't let Kenneth down. He'd be there already in his Rudolf tie and paper crown getting ready for the first lunch service.

Mirren kissed Adrian all the way out the barge and onto the riverside, trying to prolong their goodbyes and he'd promised he'd ring her tomorrow. As he walked away, he turned back to blow her kisses too many times to count.

After showering she put on her red, sequinned party frock, because why not? It was, after all, Christmas day. As she walked over the theatre gardens towards the Yorick she dialled her mum's number, a little more nervous than usual, and not just because she didn't know what state she'd find her in.

'Mum?'

'Merry Christmas,' Jeanie replied, sounding cheerful and alert.

'Are you OK?'

'Yep, fine thanks. I'm just away to put my Christmas dinner on.'

'Sorry I'm not there,' Mirren said with a pang. 'Listen, I promise we'll spend next Christmas together, OK?'

Jeanie sounded surprised when she replied. 'That would be nice.'

'I feel like… we could have a better year, maybe? Us, I mean.'

There was silence on the line for a second. 'I hope so.'

'And maybe you could come here for a visit in the New Year? Stay on the barge with me? It would be nice to spend some time together?'

'It would. I'd like that.'

Silence fell again, full of emotion.

'Mirren?' Jeanie said. 'I'm trying. I'm really trying this time. I've joined a new group and…'

Mirren heard the tearful shake in her mum's voice. 'And I'm here to help,' she said, now reaching the steps of the Yorick.

'OK, then.' Jeanie sniffed. 'We'll have a better year.'

'OK. Mum, I'm at work now. I'd better go in. Thanks for the shortbread.'

'Mirren? Did your dad ring you?'

'Not yet.' They both knew he always phoned on Christmas Eve, every year at pub closing time, but not this year. Mirren knew what it meant. No birthday call, and no Christmas call. This must be the year their stilted, barely-there connection was severed entirely. He'd lost interest at last. 'It doesn't matter,' Mirren told her mum.

'You've got me,' Jeanie said hurriedly, and the words sounded unfamiliar but so welcome.

'OK,' Mirren was smiling now, with tears spoiling her mascara. 'So, I'll see you soon then.'

Anyone listening in might have thought nothing of the conversation, but to Mirren and her mother, these were entirely new sentiments. Simple, caring words that they'd never spoken aloud, but at last they'd made a tiny breakthrough. Maybe Jeanie's sobriety would last – neither of them knew for certain – but Mirren had it in her power to make sure their connection lasted, even if it wasn't always perfect. They had a chance to start over. Maybe there had been other chances over the years but she hadn't taken them. This one she was grabbing with both hands and for once, there was a little hopefulness and forgiveness connecting them.

That night, as she walked home from the Yorick, exhausted, physically and emotionally, with her cling-filmed Christmas dinner plate in hand, she thought how simple the day had felt, and how calm. *This must be what happiness is like*, she'd thought.

She'd texted Kelsey with her good news about her mum and about Adrian and to wish her a happy Christmas in Scotland. She didn't mention Wagstaff; no need to throw the cat amongst the pigeons today, not when things were peaceful for once. She'd tell them both tomorrow, with Adrian by her side hopefully, and they could talk it all through before Jonathan flew off to LA.

Back on the barge with her fairy lights shining, Mirren microwaved her dinner and quickly texted Adrian.

> **Merry Christmas, I hope you're having a lovely time. See you tomorrow? Night night, x**

As she threw her phone on the bed and pulled off her boots she heard the little pinging sound from under the kitchen table and was surprised to discover Adrian's phone on the floor. He must have left without it. He *had* been a little distracted this morning when he was leaving, as they'd kissed and giggled and waved soppily to one another. It was too late now to do anything about it. Hopefully he'd call round for it in the morning. So she settled in for the night with her food and the festive TV programmes, and true warmth in her heart. Life was indeed wonderful.

–

'Morning, *umm*, is that Adrian's mum?' There was only one number stored in the phone, so she'd rung it.

'It is?'

'I'm Mirren, Adrian's friend? He's left his phone here.'

Mrs Armadale didn't seem to recognise her name. Maybe Adrian hadn't mentioned her yet. She refused to be rattled by that.

'Ah, he's not here at the moment. He stayed for Christmas but then left this morning in a bit of a hurry. He said he had work to do. I expect he's at the *Examiner* offices.' Her tone was weary.

'On Boxing Day?' Her mind ticked over. *Mr Ferdinand told Adrian to come back to work on the twenty-eighth, didn't he?*

'He said he had to go in, something he needed to investigate, apparently.'

'Really?'

'You know what he's like when he's got the bit between his teeth with a story, it's all he can think about. It's all work, work, work with that one. Just like his father.'

'A story? Did he say what it was?'

The woman became guarded now. 'What did you say your name was? Shall I tell him to ring you if I see him?'

'It's all right, I'll take the phone over to the *Examiner* offices now.'

–

As Mirren put the phone into a padded envelope and made her way across Stratford – now packed with families on their Boxing

252

Day walks – she tried to resist the compulsion to catastrophize. *So what, he's gone in to work? He has some story to work on. I'm sure it's perfectly innocent. Maybe he often works over Christmas? He did say he'd do anything to save the newspaper he once loved and he's at risk of losing his job if the parent company shut it down. He's probably busy getting the New Year edition ready while Mr Ferdinand sleeps off his turkey and trimmings and doesn't care a jot if his business is going under. That's all it is.*

When she reached the doors of the *Examiner* she found they were locked but there were lights on up on the top floor where the microfilm room was, and when she rattled the letter box and pressed the bell, she caught a glimpse of the blind in Mr Ferdinand's office cracking open and an eye peering down at her, but it was gone in a flash.

She called for Adrian through the letter box, not minding if she looked a bit mad hollering in the street, but no one came down. Thinking quickly, she opened the envelope and punched her number into Adrian's phone, saving it as a contact, before posting it through the letter box inside the envelope. She'd been sure to save his number into her own phone too and she quickly rang it and left a voicemail.

'Adrian, are you in the offices? It's me. Listen, I don't know if you're working today or… maybe you've got a big story you're working on…' She couldn't quell the doubts circulating in her mind now. 'Just, please remember what we promised about Wagstaff, OK? It's Jonathan's business, nobody else's. I'm sorry I'm saying this. It's not that I don't trust you or anything…' Her words tailed off. 'Call me when you get this? OK? Bye then.'

She cast one last look up at the building. What was going on in there that meant someone was working on Boxing Day, and why hadn't Adrian come back to the barge when he realised he didn't have his phone? Was his mum right? Was he so distracted by a new scoop that he wasn't thinking of anything else? He wasn't thinking of her?

With flutterings of anxiety in her chest she made her way to St. Ninian's Close. She had to tell Jonathan, right now.

Chapter Thirty-Three

'Alack, what heinous sin is it in me
To be asham'd to be my father's child!'
(*The Merchant of Venice*)

'Kelsey, will you do me the honour of… no, no, gotta get this right.'

Jonathan kneeled down in front of Kelsey's bedsit door, murmuring the words in rehearsal, his hand nervously patting at his pocket. 'Will you be my wife? *Argh*! No. Will you let me be your husband, and I'll love you 'til…'

He heard the footsteps on the stairwell. They'd only just returned to Stratford after the long drive and having dragged their luggage back upstairs together, Kelsey had remembered her camera in the boot and run out to the hire car to get it. He swallowed hard at the sound of her approach.

He'd failed to pop the question by the pretty lake on the roadside that morning, thinking how their grandkids should be able to tell a better story about their grandparents' engagement than it taking place over takeaway sausage rolls and lattes at a motorway services no matter how deep the snow on the roadside or how many fancy ducks were gliding by at the time. He'd considered doing it first thing when they woke up so all the Andersons could celebrate with them but Calum was determined to drag a half-asleep Kelsey outside for a snowball fight and then the moment was gone.

He had to do it now. His flight was leaving just before midnight and he had to set off for the airport soon. 'Come on Jonathan, screw your courage to the sticking place...' He was on his feet and running his palms against his sides when he heard the voices – *two* Scottish voices – behind the door.

Kelsey was asking what she'd been up to over Christmas day and Mirren was muttering something about it being just a quiet one and trying to stop Kelsey going through the door. 'I need to talk to you...' Mirren said.

Kelsey let the door swing open and greeted Jonathan with a quick kiss. He was pale and flustered and still standing limply in the middle of the room. 'Got it.' She held the camera case up by its straps. 'And I found Mirren outside, too! Mirren, do you know it's snowing in Scotland? But it had cleared up by the time we drove through Northumberland.'

'Kelsey, can we have a word, just us?' Mirren sounded desperate.

'Actually, there's something I need to show you.' Kelsey looked as nervous as Mirren and Jonathan now. 'Jonathan, where is it?'

'*Hmm*?' For a moment he was blank. 'Oh, the paper? Here.' He pulled a copy of the *Edinburgh Broadsheet* out of the suitcase.

'I think if you've got bad news to tell you should just come out with it, right Mirren?' She took the paper from Jonathan and opened it at the centre pages. 'Mum kept this to show me. It's the fourteenth of November edition. She wasn't sure if I should tell you or not, but... look...'

Mirren's face lit up. '*Festive Theatre Minibreaks That Won't Break The Bank?* It's my article. They ran it! I don't believe it. I submitted on the Friday before that stuff with Jamesey happened so it's only right they run it, actually. They've changed some of my wording and cut it a bit but, still. Ooh, look at the pictures, they're lovely.'

Kelsey stepped closer to her friend, speaking softly. 'Mirr, they didn't put your name on it.'

Mirren scanned the by-line, recoiling as though she'd been shot. 'By James Wallace, Senior Reporter? What the...?' Her mouth opened and closed and her eyes flickered in disbelief. 'They published it with *his* name on it? But these are my words!'

'I know. I don't know how they had the brass neck to do it,' Kelsey commiserated.

'I do,' said Mirren, gravely. 'It's a sign, if a sign were needed, that they hold all the cards, and that they don't care about me or my feelings. It shows they've got all the power and I'm irrelevant to them, they'll do what they want without fear of consequences, and they'll champion Jamesey no matter what.'

'I'm so sorry,' Kelsey said, rubbing Mirren's arms. 'I thought it was better that you knew... but now I'm not so sure. Are you OK?'

Mirren shook herself alert at Kelsey's words. 'No, you were right. It *is* better to get things out in the open... even if they hurt a bit, right?' All her instincts were yelling at her that no, it wasn't better at all. *Turn around and leave them to say their goodbyes and let them live in blissful ignorance for the rest of their lives*, her nerves screamed, and she would have left if it wasn't for Kelsey staring piercingly at her and stepping even closer, lowering her head inquisitively. Mirren tucked the newspaper under her arm. She'd have plenty time to weep over it later. She had a job to do.

'Did you... did you find something?' Kelsey's voice was slow and cautious and she turned twice to look at Jonathan as she spoke. 'You said there was something you wanted to tell us?' The alarm coloured Kelsey's cheeks. The sense of there being no going back now was already in the room between them all.

'Something up?' Jonathan asked.

'*Um*, Jonathan, you should sit down,' Mirren said.

'Why?'

'I don't know. On films they always tell you to sit down when there's news...'

'OK,' Jonathan laughed but his eyes were questioning. He did as he was told and sat on the bed. Kelsey slipped in beside him, clasping his hand and making him even more confused.

'Has something happened? Look, you'd better tell me quick before I really start to freak out.'

'OK, *um…*' Mirren flustered. 'Well… we think… we found your dad.' She jumped at her own words.

Jonathan didn't react other than drawing his neck back an inch.

'We found out who he is and he still lives in town and…'

At this Kelsey made a squeaking sound and clamped her hand to her mouth. 'You know for sure?'

Jonathan was looking between them both, squinting, his mind working.

Mirren couldn't stop now, not with the tale half told. 'He… he's an actor too, well you already knew that, didn't you? He's called Jonathan Wagstaff.'

'Who is *we*?' Jonathan asked in a dry monotone.

'*Huh*?' Mirren started.

'You said *we* found out who he is.'

Kelsey watched Jonathan's eyes darken and his profile harden into an expression she'd never seen before.

'Me and Adrian Armadale,' Mirren said ruefully.

'Who the hell's that?' Jonathan snapped.

Kelsey, sensing danger, took over. 'He's a reporter. He works at the *Examiner*. You can trust him. I'm sure he's not going to tell anyone, right, Mirren?' Kelsey added hurriedly.

Mirren had texted Kelsey to tell her about the night she'd spent with Adrian and how sweet and kind he was and how she might actually have turned a corner, but Kelsey knew nothing about him disappearing since then. There hadn't been time to let her know. Mirren was looking at her now with sorrowful, guilty eyes.

Jonathan processed the information. He dropped Kelsey's hand and clasped his fingers together, his knuckles whitening.

'Adrian Armadale? I know who that is. He's the hack who wrote that hatchet job exposé on me and Peony. The whole damn thing was lies! He said we were getting married, talked about Peony like she was trash. Do you know how much *hurt* that article caused us? And all for some front page gossip.'

Kelsey gulped. 'No, it can't be!' She still had that newspaper shoved somewhere under her bed with the rest of her books and magazines and she rummaged for it now, pulling it out and scanning the front page. 'He's right,' she said slowly. 'Look. It *was* written by Adrian Armadale. There's his name. I'm so stupid. I should have remembered that name, remembered he was a two-bit hack.' She turned the front page towards Mirren who peered at it with growing dread.

'*This* is the guy you trust to keep it a secret?' Jonathan raised his voice and Mirren stepped back against the kitchen cabinet. She knew her tears were on their way, but Jonathan wasn't done yet.

He turned on Kelsey now. 'You *knew* about this? And you didn't tell me?'

'I didn't *know* know. I just had an inkling and… I asked Mirren to investigate.'

'How did you get this *inkling*?'

'Show him the book, Mirren. Wagstaff's biography with the pictures in it. You looked so similar, it got us wondering…'

Mirren was shaking her head, blanching horribly. 'I don't have the book. I gave it to Adrian.'

'And where is he now, this Adrian guy?' Jonathan practically growled the words.

Mirren still didn't know and her blank look said as much. It also signalled to Kelsey there was more to tell about how Mirren now stood with Adrian Armadale after their cosy Christmas Eve together.

Jonathan forced an exasperated breath.

'It's not Mirren's fault, it's mine.' Kelsey was standing now, spreading her hands pleadingly. 'I didn't want to tell you until we had some real proof – other than you two looking identical.' Her eyes welled with tears.

'What proof *do* you have?' Jonathan asked, his voice increasingly terse.

All eyes fell on Mirren and she tried to explain. 'It *um*... it was Adrian's boss who told us. He used to know your mum and Wagstaff and he remembered...'

It was Kelsey who snapped this time. 'Mr Ferdinand knows? Oh my God, Mirren!'

'No, he doesn't know; not about Jonathan anyway. He only mentioned the pregnancy. He doesn't know you're the son.'

Jonathan sprang to his feet. 'You're talking about *me*,' he jabbed at his chest, 'and my mom like we're some trashy newspaper story!' Distraught, his jaw softened and tears fell fast down his cheeks. When he spoke again his voice was curt and suspicious. 'Why did you *really* want to know?' He was feeling the pain and finding his voice now. 'You lost your job recently, didn't you, Mirren?'

'Jonathan, please don't,' Kelsey begged, to no effect.

'A scoop like this is just what you needed to impress Mr Ferdinand and this Adrian and get yourself back in the game, isn't it? I can't believe you'd do this to me.'

Mirren was silent.

'Jonathan, you're wrong,' Kelsey cried out through her tears.

'And *you*!' He turned his burning eyes on Kelsey. 'You let them do this. You didn't even *think* to mention it to me first!'

'I did, I tried. You said you didn't want to know the truth, but I...'

'*What*? You *what*?' he barked.

'I thought everybody deserves to know who their dad is.' She gasped a deep breath. 'Everybody should be able to talk to their dad if he's out there somewhere, missing them. And I thought...'

'But he's not missing me. He's never missed me. He broke Mom's heart, he ended her career, and he abandoned us both.' His face was wet with tears.

Kelsey couldn't help herself. 'He's old and he lives right here in town. If you're going to meet, you should do it soon. I know he'll love you and...'

'Meet?' Jonathan pushed a hand through his hair. '*Meet?*'

'I don't even have *one* dad,' Kelsey sobbed. 'You've got two, Jonathan! I thought you'd want the chance to at least know about your other father, and maybe you could talk...'

'This isn't about you, Kelsey, or your dad.' He drew up short at the shock on Kelsey's face.

There was so much at stake that Kelsey knew she had to go on. 'It's not only your dad I thought you deserved to meet; there's others too. You might have half-brothers, nephews as well. You could have a whole family if we're right about Blythe having Wagstaff's child in the sixties...' Her voice broke when she saw his anger. Now she really was afraid.

Jonathan was deathly pale and shaking from his shoulders to his knees. 'These are people's lives you're interfering in!'

'I know, I'm sorry,' Kelsey said unsteadily. 'I thought you might like the idea once you had time to get used to it. You could double your family in an instant...'

Jonathan made a grab for his coat and threw it on before angrily pulling on his scarf.

'I only wanted to increase my family by *one person* today and it wasn't with the addition of some old soak who didn't want me when I was a child. What am I going to tell Mom? How is she supposed to take this? We had nothing growing up, you know? *Nothing!*' He yelled the last word, making the women flinch. Kelsey grabbed for his hand. He dodged away, knocking the bedside cabinet and sending books and photo frames tumbling to the floor.

'I'll take the car back to the hire place now, then I'll get a cab to the airport. I can't even look at you two now.'

'Jonathan, I'm sorry,' Kelsey cried out as the door closed behind him.

The friends turned to face one another wordlessly, Kelsey distraught, Mirren wiping away tears and reaching for her mobile.

'I'll try to call Adrian again, find out what he's up to.' She had the phone to her ear, listening to it ring straight to voicemail.

'How can you trust him, Mirren? When he stitched up Jonathan and Peony like that? His article – his *lies* – were responsible for keeping me and Jonathan apart all summer. What do you even know about this guy, Mirren?'

She hung up and let the phone slide to her side. 'I thought I knew him.'

Kelsey slumped onto the bed, reaching to the ground to pick up the framed picture of her and Jonathan taken at Norma's wedding in September when they were grinning and doe-eyed in love. A little velvet box she'd never seen before lay amongst the mess on the floor, it caught her eye and she grabbed for it, flicking open the top.

Gold bands entwined in an Elizabethan love knot and dotted with tiny faceted sapphires sparkled in the artificial lights of the bedsit. Her voice shook. 'He was going to *propose*?'

'Oh my God, what?' Mirren seemed to forget that Jonathan had stormed out seconds before, momentarily wrapped up in the revelation that her best friend had come so close to getting engaged. 'Surely, that's a sign he'll be back any minute now, once he's cooled off a bit?' she enthused. 'Wow, it's so beautiful, Kelse!'

Kelsey looked at Mirren, incredulous, and snapped the box shut. 'Please, just leave.'

'But...' Mirren was going to argue, but the look on Kelsey's face – of fury and heartache – frightened her, so she quietly closed the door behind her, while Kelsey strained her ears to listen to the sound of Jonathan's hire car pulling away from St. Ninian's Close.

When she was alone, Kelsey doubled up as if in pain and wept over the beautiful engagement ring Jonathan had abandoned in his haste to get away from her.

Chapter Thirty-Four

'That time of year thou mayst in me behold
When yellow leaves, or none, or few, do hang
Upon those boughs which shake against the cold,
Bare ruin'd choirs, where late the sweet birds sang'
(*Sonnet 73*)

The phone call home that night hadn't helped at all. Mari had
tried to soothe her daughter, who was frantic and shaking with
great sobbing convulsions as she told her the news.

'He dropped a ring on the floor when he raced out, Mum.
An engagement ring.'

Mari hadn't been as surprised as Kelsey expected.

'Kelse, love, on Christmas Day when we were doing the
dishes together Jonathan asked me if he could propose to you.'

'He did? That's so like him.'

'And he asked your grandad. He even asked Calum.'

His respect for her family's wishes made the discovery hurt
all the more. 'That's why Jonathan was so jumpy on Christmas
night, he was nervous about asking? And that's why he was so
keen to come to Scotland to meet you all!'

'If he went to the trouble of finding you that beautiful ring,
and asking us for your hand then I know he'll come round.
Don't cry, darlin'.' Mari was close to tears herself.

'Will he? If I hadn't interfered and kept secrets… If I'd
just talked to him we'd be engaged, but now he's on airplane

mode above the Atlantic and he won't be back in Stratford 'til Valentine's Day. I can't wait that long to see him.'

'Have you spoken at all yet?' Kelsey knew Mari was holding it together but there was a distinct wobble in her voice.

'No, he texted when he was about to board the plane, saying he needed time to think. Think about what? I don't know. His dad being Wagstaff? Or proposing to me? And now I've got to break it to Blythe. She has grandkids too, surely they deserve to know they've a secret uncle, right? Oh, I don't know.'

'Why don't you sleep on it and go and talk to her in the morning, tell the truth, and Blythe can decide what's best for her own family.'

After a lot more consoling Mari finally wished her daughter goodnight, and Kelsey lay down, still dressed, upon her little white bed, clutching the velvet box which had until this afternoon contained all Jonathan's hopes and dreams for their future life together.

He'd wanted her for his wife, and she'd been too self-absorbed to know it was coming. *If only* she'd been focusing on Jonathan's feelings like he always had hers in mind; instead she'd been distracted by the idea of him reuniting with a wayward, uncaring father who had never even held him as a baby, when in reality he already had a loving dad.

Deep down, she knew Jonathan was right. The search for Wagstaff *had* been about her all along. She didn't have any dads at all, and the idea of being presented with two had overwhelmed her. *Imagine that*, she'd thought. *Two fathers to love! Two dads to adore him!* Her judgement had been thrown off by her own desires and her overactive imagination, and now Jonathan was hurt, betrayed… and gone.

She cried herself to sleep that night, her phone and the engagement ring clasped in her hands.

–

The sapphires shone in the light from Blythe's pink tasselled standard lamp as the actress inspected the ring.

'Nothing? You've got no advice for me?' said Kelsey, her eyes red from crying away a sleepless night.

'No, dear.' Blythe shook her head with the smiling air of a mystic sage about her.

'But, you're so good with advice normally; "wow your bloke", "grab the spotlight", but now you've got nothing?'

'Never, ever pluck your eyebrows?' Blythe asked solemnly.

'Thanks.' Kelsey slumped on the little stool at Blythe's feet.

'Always moisturise your neck?' Failing to get a rise out of her young friend, Blythe took a different tack. She motioned for Kelsey to lean close to her and gently pulled her head onto her lap. 'You don't need advice, darling. You simply need a bit of cherishing.' She raked her fingers across the baby hairs around Kelsey's temple.

'Oh, I've spoiled everything. Then there's Mirren. I was the one that told her to go hunting for clues and then last night when she'd told us all what she'd found I chucked her out!'

'You should have asked me in the first place,' Blythe said.

Kelsey tensed as the thought struck her. 'You didn't look very surprised just now when I told you Wagstaff is Jonathan's dad.'

'I wasn't. I knew the minute I saw him on Christmas Eve. Like twins, they were. I thought I'd had one too many gin jam scones and finally flipped my wig. There he was, John Wagstaff, standing in my *salon*, transformed from his baggy old self into the handsome boy he used to be.'

'I'm sorry. I should never have let that happen. I know that you used to know him, back then, and that he spoiled your career by falling off the stage drunk and... obviously what happened with your baby and everything.'

Blythe stopped stroking her hair. Kelsey raised her head abruptly and made panicked goldfish mouths at the older woman. 'I mean, I figured out what happened and I... at least

I thought I'd figured it out… you must have got *such* a fright, suddenly confronted with your son's half-brother…'

'Lorcan's half-brother?' Blythe wrinkled her brow.

'Lorcan? Is that your son's name?'

'Yes, but he's not Jonathan's half-brother or any other relation.'

'You and Wagstaff… you weren't…?'

'Good lord and all his ministering angels, no! What a notion. Wagstaff was handsome and impressive in his own way, but an utter philanderer and a cad. I would *never*!'

'Oh!' Kelsey was sitting bolt upright on the floor.

Blythe huffed a laughing breath and pointed a finger towards the kitchen. 'Get the kettle on. We've some tangled webs to unweave.'

–

Blythe joined Kelsey at the table, dragging her walking frame as she moved, her hand clasping a photograph against the grey rubber handles.

Kelsey had already given Blythe her Christmas present, the book of Webster plays, and Blythe had kissed her forehead in thanks and it sat now on the kitchen table by the teapot still on its white tissue paper. Kelsey had poured the tea while Blythe was rummaging in a black lacquer box on the oak dresser looking for a photograph.

'*This* is the father of my child,' she said, presenting the photo to Kelsey, and taking a slow seat at the table. 'My one true love, my Laureano.'

The picture could not have been more different to the images of Wagstaff Kelsey had worried herself over. The man smiling into the camera was slender-waisted, broad-shouldered, svelte and deeply pretty.

'This was taken at our little olive garden at Valladolid, nineteen seventy-two. He's beautiful, isn't he?'

'He is!'

'He was born in that little house you can just see in the background. It's a wonderful place, though I haven't been there for years now. The whole province was famed for its *corrida de toros*.'

Kelsey jutted her bottom lip, confused.

'Bull-fighting, dear. That's how Laureano got his first taste of applause; when he was a trainee matador. He was so handsome running with the young bulls, the women would throw their fans to him in the ring and then they'd faint with the heat watching him.' Blythe reached absentmindedly for the tissue wrapping paper that had covered her book and she folded and unfolded it now in her hands as she spoke.

'In the days before I met him, Laureano was being prepared for his first fight by the master of the bulls and he was shocked to learn he was expected to combat the most acclaimed bull in the province – a great proud beast, it was. It had gored two matadors and thrown another over its back that very season. Laureano was scared half out of his wits at the prospect. The master of the bulls was a powerful man in the town and he stood to make a lot of money from the fight. He told Laureano he was not only to defeat the bull but he was to wipe its nose with the blood of its own severed tail. The greedy old fool wanted to make his bullring – and his beautiful new bullfighter – the talk of Spain. The man could smell the money to be made from a debut toreador with a pretty face and a cruel heart.

'But Laureano refused to fight, horrified by the very suggestion. Who would do such a thing? But the master threatened him. He knew a secret about Laureano's father, you see? A business matter had gone awry some years before and his father had skipped town and was hiding out in the mountains. Laureano was protecting him, taking him food every Sunday evening. To stop his father being arrested he agreed to the fight. He prepared himself to throw down his sword and dagger and let the bull gore him to death, but on the day of the *corrida* when the creature was released into the ring, Laureano's heart broke in his chest. The poor thing hadn't been fed or watered for days. It had been freshly branded on its back and the blood was still running. Its eyes were dull. The beast barely had any fight in it. Laureano took one look at the poor bull and fell to his knees. The crowd turned upon him, hungry to see him defeat the animal. So he ran for it, gathered together everything he owned – which wasn't much, he was so poor – and he dashed for the coast with his father on one of the bullring's horses. He sold that horse at the port in exchange for passage and he brought his father here to England that very day. They had nothing except Laureano's matador costume and his beauty to live off.'

'*Wow*!' Kelsey couldn't help but smile in awe.

'He was a bit wow, yes!' Blythe smiled too, still folding and twisting the tissue paper in her hands.

'They made do, scrounging odd jobs, living hand to mouth, but that summer the RSC were auditioning in London for a Cervantes play. It was the sixties, the dawn of the package holiday; England was Spain-mad. Laureano auditioned for a background part in a fiesta scene, all clichéd castanets and swishing capes. Well, the director took one look at him and snapped him up as his protégé. He had the looks and the physique and he could project his voice across a bullring; all he had to do was learn better English.

'I was already a star by then, always hanging about at the theatre during the day, so I helped him a little with his vocabulary and soon we were in love.' Blythe's eyes glinted as she chuckled at the memory.

'We were cast together as leads soon after. People liked the look of us side by side, we were both so dainty and so powerful... and you know the rest.'

'He loved you.'

'Oh yes, very much. Laureano's father was very old by then, he passed away before the baby was born, never met little Lorcan, our boy. Then when it became clear the bosses were determined to starve me out of work, Laureano suggested we go back to Spain, live a simple life, and so we did. We spent a few happy years together, although I missed the life of the stage terribly. I couldn't do much at Valladolid with this hip, but I could shake an olive tree and work the presses and we made a very small living.' A shadow fell over Blythe's face. 'But my Laureano was far too beautiful for this world and he passed shortly after Lorcan's seventh birthday. Misfortune often brings yet more sadness in its wake, and my father passed soon after that as well. Daddy's will left me everything – I was an only child after all – but the stipulation was that I return to England and raise my son a little English boy. I had no money and I had no choice, so I came back.'

'You raised Lorcan here?'

'Yes, but he had his papa's Spanish heart in him. He missed the heat, dreamt of the sun and the dust and the sea. School holidays back at the old house weren't enough for him and he moved back there as soon as he could. He was eighteen when he left for good. He's still there now, with his new English wife. He works in Granada for an animal charity, got a little flat near the Alhambra, and they spend the weekends at Valladolid in the olive garden. They're happy.'

'I thought your lover abandoned you.' Kelsey squinted, trying to make sense of the conclusions she'd jumped to.

'No. Laureano just couldn't stay. Aging together wasn't to be part of our story. I have lived far, far longer without him in my life than the brief time I spent with him.'

'And you never married, or met anyone else?'

'Oh no, as Shakespeare said, love is an ever fixed mark that looks on tempests and is never shaken. I love him still to this day.' Blythe lifted the tissue paper to show Kelsey a perfect white paper rose which she twirled between her fingertips. 'Don't worry, Kelsey dear. You and Jonathan are facing your first tempest. He'll be back when the storm's blown over, and you mustn't wither away in the meantime, you hear me? We women must continue to bloom, even in the wintertime. You've got work to do here. Don't make the mistake I did of walking away from my occupation. I was the Duchess of Malfi once! And I let them push me out when I should have stayed and fought. Yes, I was in agony with my hip, but Laureano and I should have stayed here. He could have wowed the crowds for years and I could have fought for parts, even if I was only playing to a handful of people in the smallest of places.' Blythe smiled away the regret. 'This is *your* chance.' She slipped the paper rose behind Kelsey's ear. 'Beautiful. Now finish your tea. You've got a lot to do.'

'But what about Jonathan? How do you know he'll come round?' said Kelsey.

Blythe smiled, lifting the old photograph of Laureano to gaze at it once more. 'Love works both ways; otherwise it isn't love.'

Chapter Thirty-Five

'Our wooing doth not end like an old play
Jack hath not Jill'
(*Love's Labour's Lost*)

The winter dawn hadn't yet broken as Kelsey tramped over the frosted grass, the silvered blades giving way beneath her boots like crunching glass. Over her shoulders she hauled tote bags stuffed with provisions – bacon rolls and jam donuts – and she had two piping hot takeaway coffees in her hands.

The red curtains on the barge were still drawn when Kelsey reached Mirren's bedroom window and tapped at the glass. 'Wakey wakey, Mirren!'

Once Kelsey had roused her friend and got her to open the hatch for her to climb inside they stood looking at each other in the brash light from the sconces.

'I brought you some breakfast,' Kelsey said, handing a coffee to Mirren who was shivering in a baggy t-shirt.

'We're talking?' she replied, sheepishly.

'Of course we are. I'm sorry I was short with you on Boxing Day. I shouldn't have told you to leave like that, but once I found the ring and everything... I just needed a bit of space.'

'It's me that's sorry.' Mirren looked dejected and as though she'd barely slept. 'I didn't mean for it to go like that. I swear me and Adrian had already decided to stop looking for information about Jonathan before we'd even found any but it was too late;

Mr Ferdinand was suddenly there spilling the news and we couldn't pretend we hadn't heard it.'

Kelsey threw an arm around her. 'It's all right, honestly. It's done, isn't it? I shouldn't have set you on looking for clues, I got carried away dreaming about reuniting Jonathan with his dad. I should have gone with my gut and told Jonathan our hunch right at the start instead of carrying on like a shit Nancy Drew.'

Mirren laughed with relief, grateful for the attempt at humour.

'Have you heard anything from Jonathan yet? He must have landed by now.'

'Hours ago. I tracked his flight online, but no, nothing yet.'

'I returned Adrian's phone, he must have found it by now, and I've left him messages. I told him how upset Jonathan is, how he ran off like that. I've no idea what Adrian's planning to do. I don't know how else to find him. I don't even know where he lives!'

'It's OK. I don't think there's anything else we can do right now. Listen, you've got the day off, right?' Kelsey wanted to change the mood before Mirren could start up with the apologies again.

'I do.'

'We've got work to do then.' Kelsey unloaded the bags onto the little table in the gallery space, then rubbed her hands to warm them, scanning the empty walls. 'Let's get this exhibition sorted. It could take a few days. Reckon that'll keep us out of trouble for a bit.'

Mirren grasped the hammer and the spirit level from Kelsey's materials. 'All right, you can be the gaffer. Just tell me what to do.' She inhaled a breath, preparing to work. Kelsey only looked her over and laughed.

'You can put some bottoms on for a start and then there's bacon rolls to eat; can't work on an empty stomach.'

Mirren gripped the hem of her t-shirt and they both smiled with the relief and the affection that stretched back to their girlhoods.

'Oh, and have I got a tale to tell you,' Kelsey called through the boat as Mirren went to get changed. 'And it all begins with a beautiful Spanish matador!'

The two friends ate and talked and worked on all through the short winter's day and into the night, music playing, voices chiming with different strategies to display the photographs to their best advantage, both trying to avoid giving way to the anxiety in their hearts and marvelling yet again at the strength of their friendship, their very own fixed mark that looks on tempests and is never shaken.

After Kelsey left later that evening with the entire exhibition plotted out and the first of the pictures already displayed on the barge's low walls, Mirren laid her tired body on her bed and for the first time that day reached for her phone. She'd have sat and stared at it all day long if Kelsey hadn't turned up and she wouldn't have missed the calls from Adrian. As she was deciding what to do with his voicemails – did she really need to hear any more lies? – the phone rang in her hands.

'*Jesus Christ*!' she flinched. She hadn't realised how tense she still was from the revelations of the day before, even though she'd spent the night cursing herself for letting her resolve slip while nursing a growing anger for Adrian, the man who knew she had sworn off men but still pursued her, acting kind and considerate when really he was only after one thing, and he'd got a newspaper scoop into the bargain.

It didn't matter how many times she flicked the phone to 'busy' he rang again and again until at eleven o'clock she gave in to her rage and answered, ready to unleash her worst words upon him.

'Thank God! Mirren. It's me, Adrian.'

'You've got a lot of nerve ringing me all day. Where have you been since the twenty-sixth? I was trying to reach you? Do you know the trouble we've caused?'

'I'm sorry, I've been working a lot of lates.'

'At the paper?' she interrupted.

'Yes, but—'

'Mr Ferdinand said he'd see you on the twenty-eighth, that's tomorrow. What did you have to do at work that was so urgent yesterday?'

'On Boxing Day I went back to the offices. I wanted to look into Wagstaff and Olivia a little more.'

'So you *are* going to publish the story! No doubt you've told the whole thing to Mr Ferdinand too.' Mirren's nerves rattled and she found herself pacing through the barge. Thank goodness she'd kept Kelsey's – mistaken, as it turned out – hunch about Blythe and Wagstaff to herself, or else Adrian would now be dead set on exposing her secrets too.

'No, that's not it at all,' he was protesting. 'I only wanted to put together some pictures and some information to help this poor Jonathan guy out, help fill in some gaps for him. I've been working flat out, I guess I got absorbed in it, but I found loads of good stuff. It's all saved on a memory stick. If you meet me for a drink I can give it to you…'

'"*Poor Jonathan*"? Do you expect me to believe you feel sorry for him, after what you did to him in the summer?' The salacious front page gossip about Peony and Jonathan danced before her eyes again, with Adrian's name printed above all the lies.

'In the summer? Mirren, please, I—'

'I might be weak-willed, but I'm not stupid. You're just another sleazy journalist out for themselves. I'm only sorry it took me so long to figure you out. Just make sure you destroy that memory stick because if this gets into the paper then so help me—'

'It won't, I promise. Look, I've left the memory stick at work. I'll go get it tomorrow and drop it off at your boat, OK? Then you can do what you like with it, but honestly, I think Jonathan should see it. There are pictures of his mum, and interviews; there's even coverage of a summer gala when Olivia and Wagstaff both dressed as masquers and were photographed together. He should have those…'

'You can bring it by first thing tomorrow, but just post it through the hatch. I don't want to see you.'

Mirren hung up the phone and stalked off to brush her teeth, wondering why she didn't feel triumphantly self-righteous and relieved, only sad and sorry and disappointed with herself once more.

Chapter Thirty-Six

'I am to wait, though waiting so be hell'
(*Sonnet 58*)

The next day there was no memory stick delivered to the barge, nor the next, or the next. With each day that passed Mirren's anxiety grew and she had to ring Kelsey from the laundry room at the Yorick and tell her all about it – that in Adrian's possession there were carefully collated stories and images featuring Jonathan's mum and his biological father. He'd broken his promise to return them and Mirren wasn't even surprised. He'd probably already sent the story to Mr Ferdinand by now. She warned Kelsey to prepare for the worst when the paper went to print on Friday.

Kelsey had listened and inhaled through gritted teeth, clasping her hair between the raked fingers of her free hand. 'OK. OK. Right then.' She calmed herself. 'It's good to be forearmed. I'll let Jonathan know.'

'You've spoken to him?' Mirren's voice was full of hope.

'Not yet, no. But I'll keep on leaving messages.'

Kelsey had to believe Jonathan would come round eventually, otherwise how could theirs be true, fixed love? He'd wanted to propose only a few short days ago, hadn't he?

After hanging up the call, she rang Jonathan again, not even considering the time difference with LA where he was taking up his drama teaching residency for the rest of the winter; if he was working or sleeping his phone would be switched off anyway, or maybe he was just filtering calls and ignoring hers. Either way, the news about the memory stick full of evidence was a new, worrying development and he had a right to know about it. So she spoke down the crackling line, telling the man who'd once loved her enough to buy her a sapphire ring that, come New Year, the whole world would know about his mum's long-held secret, and it was all Kelsey's fault.

Both women spent Hogmanay alone chatting on their phones with their mums back in Scotland. Neither of them felt like raising a toast to ring out the old year, but both steadfastly made resolutions to try to be wiser in the months to come and to be more considerate of others, and Mirren renewed her vows of living a single life from now on.

Early on New Year's Day as Kelsey hung the last of the pictures at the barge, Mirren ran out to buy the newspaper whose publication they'd been dreading.

They'd agreed in advance that no matter how bad it was, how salacious and invasive, they'd stay calm and not let Adrian's bad behaviour make them behave badly in turn. They'd brought all this on themselves and they'd have to do the best damage limitation they could and that would include phoning Jonathan's mum at home and apologising to her and asking Mirren's friend in the legal department back at the *Broadsheet* if she could do anything about suppressing the story online.

Mirren almost leapt down the hatch into the barge just as Kelsey was hanging the portrait of Jonathan in the only space left on the walls and trying hard not to give in to the tears welling.

'It's not there!' Mirren called out. 'Look!' She turned the pages roughly. 'Nothing, see? There's only this.' She turned to the theatre pages and showed Kelsey.

> The Oklahoma Renaissance Players are set to make a triumphant return to Stratford with Shakespeare's *Love's Labour's Lost* following their

sell-out run of *A Midsummer Night's Dream* in town last summer and a reportedly triumphant *Hamlet* in Ontario over the autumn. Jonathan Hathaway, the company's male lead will take the role of Berowne starring alongside Peony Brown as Rosaline. This run will be Hathaway's last with the company as he steps down to pursue roles in English theatre. He'll be replaced in June by his current understudy, local boy William Greville. The Examiner will be at the play's opening performance in April which coincides with The Players' Pageant: a one-hundred actor-strong procession through town from the train station to the main theatres on riverside in a spectacle of costume and song not seen in town since the heyday of acting companies arriving by steam train for the spring season to great fanfare and crowds. The Players' Pageant is the vision of main theatre artistic director...

Kelsey let the paper fold, her eyes wide with astonishment. 'And so it goes on. No mention of Wagstaff and Olivia at all.'

The pair thought this called for a modest celebration and Kelsey had just made the tea and was talking about how maybe it was actually all over and Adrian had done the right thing, saving Olivia Hathaway from a news scandal, when the pinging notification sounded on Mirren's phone.

'It's Adrian,' Mirren shrugged. She read the message aloud:

I've been trying to call but you won't answer your phone. I hardly know how to say this. The memory stick wasn't there when I returned to the office after we spoke the other day. I've been searching everywhere for it. I've turned the Examiner building over and trawled the streets in case I somehow dropped it. I even asked Ferdinand if he's seen it, but no luck. I'll keep looking. I'm sorry. I wish you'd talk to me. A.

Kelsey sighed loudly and slumped with her mug on the gallery room floor, looking up at Jonathan's picture in its frame. 'I'll have to let Jonathan know about this too. I thought if I kept being honest with him about what was happening here and gave him time to think, he'd eventually call, but this... this'll be the end as far as he's concerned. That information's still out there, anyone could have it and we're at their mercy. We just have to wait and see where it turns up. How is Jonathan supposed to endure that?'

'Or,' Mirren chipped in, 'Adrian's refusing to give the story up just yet and he's come up with this cock and bull tale while he gathers more information – or maybe he's trying to pitch it to the tabloids, get himself a nice deal? He did say the *Examiner* was likely to fold this year and he'd be reassigned to some other provincial paper. He won't want that. This is his chance to make it big with a gossip rag.'

Kelsey reached for her phone and dialled Jonathan's number ready to break the news. On the other side of the world his phone rang, sending Kelsey straight to voicemail, just as she'd predicted.

Chapter Thirty-Seven

'Winter's not gone yet, if the wild geese fly that way'
(*King Lear*)

January got off to a busy start in Stratford. Kelsey staved off the ache in her heart, reminding herself of Blythe's words of encouragement about not give up hope that Jonathan would come round.

In her determination not to mope, she had thrown herself into getting the exhibition invitations printed and sent out. She'd invited all the local papers to the grand opening too – except the *Examiner*, of course. She'd even invited the Mayor and a few other important local dignitaries. With Valentine's Day falling on a Sunday this year, she couldn't be sure any of them would want to commit to trudging through wintry weather to look at an exhibition on an old boat, but she tried to think positively.

The cava was already on order from the Yorick, as was the loan of fifty champagne flutes thanks to Kenneth – an ambitious number since only her family and friends had actually RSVP'd so far.

She hadn't heard if Jonathan's invite made it safely to LA and she fought hard to stifle the sickening fear that kept threatening to overwhelm her; the fear that Jonathan wouldn't be coming back to Stratford for Valentine's Day at all. After all, the only reason he'd planned his flying visit was to see her. Kelsey didn't even know if he'd booked his flights before Christmas, back when all their plans for their shared future seemed so simple and certain.

One consolation was that Blythe hadn't flatly refused to attend the gallery opening. Kelsey had asked if she'd be the guest of honour and cut the great big cake which she'd ordered in a fit of what-the-hell-you-only-launch-a-business-venture-once recklessness and Blythe had looked sorely tempted, even if she did rub her hip and grit her teeth at the thought of leaving the house.

'I'll think about it, dear, I really will,' she'd said with a glint in her eye that made Kelsey buzz with excitement, even though her heart still hung heavy in her chest for Jonathan. Blythe had read her mind and told her never to give up. She may even have quoted Winston Churchill, actually. Kelsey couldn't quite remember now as they were steadily nearing the bottom of one of Blythe's homemade gin bottles at the time and what had started as a New Year snifter had ended in Kelsey ordering them both a Deliveroo of fish and chips which they devoured while watching re-runs of *Murder, She Wrote* – Blythe telling her dated gossip about the actors on screen who she used to rub shoulders with.

With Blythe's friendship and the hard work of bringing the exhibition to fruition Kelsey somehow made it through those first long days of the New Year where the lustre of Christmas has already faded, the decorations are being packed away and everyone's tired, broke and overfed.

Just as she was thinking her fortitude was stretched to its very limits, her mobile rang one day while she was at the outdoor market paying for a long roll of red ribbon for the Mayor to cut – if she showed up at the launch. She lifted the phone to her ear without even checking the caller ID, sure it would be Mirren or Mari asking her if she'd remembered to eat that morning and fussing again about her being pale and tired looking. 'Hello?'

'Kelsey?' a tentative, deep voice asked, and her heart leapt at the sound.

'Jonathan!'

'Listen… I… I'm sorry I didn't return your calls for so long.'

'That's OK, I'm just glad you're doing it now.' Kelsey was already prepared to make any concession, grovel any apology, make every promise that she'd shape up in the future, just so long as he gave her another chance, but Jonathan cut her off.

'I was a mess for a while. I couldn't take it all in, and I felt betrayed and lost and…'

'I know and I'm sorry,' she said with a plea in her voice.

'Don't say sorry. *I'm* sorry. You were trying to help me, I know that. I just wasn't ready for it, at least I didn't think I was, and all I could think about was Mom and what she would think.'

He paused at the sound of Kelsey weeping, as she made her way from the busy marketplace and tried to hide behind the clock tower – the one everybody calls the American fountain – where the shoppers couldn't see her tears.

'Mom was horrified the media might rake up her private life, in fact, I'd say she still is, but I think it turned out to be a blessing in disguise, in a way,' he said softly.

'How could it be?'

'Well, knowing that there might be an article coming out in the press I *had* to talk with Mom and Art, and actually… it was OK. We spoke about all the stuff I shoulda let Mom say years ago. I think it really helped us. It certainly helped me. Mom was upset, real upset, talking about it after all this time, and she's still nervous about what the press will say, if it ever comes out, but maybe I should be thanking you and Mirren for helping us talk as a family, getting it all out in the open.'

'Jonathan, I'm so glad for you all.'

'It was Peony that put me up to it at first. She was kinda pissed at me for taking so long to wake up to the fact I needed to just talk with Mom about it. She gave me one of her famous lectures. It was fearsome! And she kept threatening to call you on my behalf to tell you I was being a… how did she put it? Oh, yeah, "a complete tool".'

They both laughed at this and a pigeon on the fountain took flight in surprise.

Kelsey took the opportunity to ask the question she was dying to know the answer to. 'So what about Wagstaff?'

'Nothing.' The word was hard and blunt.

'Nothing?'

'He doesn't interest me right now. I have a long way to go before I know what to feel about him, OK? And seeing Mom so cut up about him all over again, it was tough.'

'OK. I won't say anything else about it.'

'I shouldn't have said what I did about your dad either, that wasn't fair. I'm sorry for that too. I know you wanted me to meet with that old actor, but that's a step too far.'

'I get it.'

'You know, it looks like that Adrian guy's telling the truth? He'd have run the story by now if he didn't want anyone to beat him to it, don't you think?'

Kelsey didn't like to say she wasn't at all sure so she tried to agree and sound as positive as she could for Jonathan's sake.

'So... if you can, I just wanna forget all about it?' he said, a note of entreaty in his voice. 'Can you forgive me for flying off the handle like that and then taking so long hurting over it all?'

'Of course I can. I already did.'

'No more secrets?' he said.

'No more secrets, I promise.' She rummaged for a tissue in her pocket. 'Are you... I mean, will you *please* come to the exhibition launch next month?'

'I wouldn't miss it for the world.'

Just like that, Kelsey could exhale the breath she'd held since Christmas and she danced in the frosty market place in the shadow of the fountain for all of Stratford to see.

Chapter Thirty-Eight

'Forgive me, Valentine. If hearty sorrow
Be a sufficient ransom for offence,
I tender't here. I do as truly suffer
As e'er I did commit'
(*The Two Gentlemen of Verona*)

All across the broad expanse of the theatre gardens leading to the marina the grass was muddy after weeks of frosty nights and rainy afternoons. In the flowerbeds the first snowdrops and narcissi drooped their heads, mirroring the white winter sky over Kelsey's barge. Valentine's Day had come at last.

Mirren had been sure to lock the doors leading to her little living area at the back of the boat and Kelsey had given the exhibition one last assessing look-over. She checked one last time that her phone was charged up and the credit card processing app was installed on it correctly – on the off chance of any launch-day buyers.

All the framed photographs were marked with price stickers, and Mirren had been given a sheet of little red dot stickers to place in the top corner of anything that sold. Kelsey had proudly put out the A-frame – once a sign advertising the Norma Arden Guided Tours Agency and now freshly painted and bearing Kelsey's business details.

Gallery: OPEN
Tuesday to Sunday 10am–5pm
Photo portrait commissions available at the town centre studio.

The job advert for a part-time gallery assistant was already in the *Stratford Observer* and Kelsey was to interview applicants next week. In the meantime, Mirren – when she wasn't pulling pints at the Yorick – and Kelsey would somehow have to manage staffing the gallery between them. The studio had certainly been quieter for most of January but Kelsey was looking forward to the school photography sessions she had booked for the spring and word had slowly made its way around town about the increasingly popular new-born photo shoots in her cosy studio.

'Are you ready?' Mirren asked.

'We should have got some nibbles or canapes or something, shouldn't we? Too late now, I suppose. Is this dress all right? Not too arty, is it?' Kelsey thrust her hands into the big grey pockets of her new linen pinafore dress which tied in front of her shoulders in two tight knots. 'This collar is choking me.' She pushed a nervous finger into the high, delicately frilled neck of her white blouse and gulped.

'You look perfect. You're Kelsey Anderson, photographer and gallery owner.'

'We're doing this then?'

'Well, we could haul anchor and putter away up the river Avon but then you'd never see Jonathan, would you?'

'You're right, you're right.' Kelsey flustered over the business cards she'd arranged and rearranged in a fan on the barge's open side-hatch umpteen times that morning. 'It's cold in here with the hatch and the door open. Is that little heater working?'

'It's fine, and everyone will be wearing their coats anyway. Kelsey, get outside on that red carpet, grab a glass of bubbly, down it, and greet your guests. They'll be here any minute.' Mirren's expression was firm. She'd put on her best black work suit and red lipstick to support her friend. Kelsey had told her she looked like a sexy bodyguard and Mirren had grinned and said, 'Accurate.'

After an entirely unnecessary tidy of her new range of birthday cards – printed with her pretty local landscapes and all priced up in their cellophane wrappers – Kelsey wobbled down the gangplank and onto the red carpet over the pavement. She'd wangled the carpet from Myrtle and Valeria's hire shop and she'd already booked it again, ten months in advance, for this December's costumed photo booth, which she'd been sure to firm up again with the Osprey Hotel since the corporate Christmas party shoots had turned out to be so lucrative this winter.

There were taxis already pulling up on the roadside and she strained her eyes across the broad marina to make out who was arriving first. Following Mirren's orders, she snatched a glass of bubbly from the silver tray which Blythe had let her borrow for the occasion. The cold cava made her shiver all the more, and she hoped it would stop her hands shaking.

Jonathan was on his way direct from the airport. Any minute now, traffic permitting, he'd be here. Could they recapture the happiness they'd felt at Christmas, she worried? Their video chats and phone calls had told her that, yes, it might be possible. They'd relaxed into their easy way of talking almost instantly after Jonathan made the first step of reconciliation in the New Year and they hadn't fought again, but still she wanted to be completely sure. She couldn't truly assess any damage she'd done until she could look him in the eyes, hold him properly and kiss him. Only then would she know if they'd get through this.

There was a new worry troubling her, something still unspoken between the two of them and she had no idea if Jonathan was thinking about it too. The ring.

She'd hidden it away back at the bedsit and despite brainstorming with Mirren about what to do for the best, they'd drawn a blank. Jonathan hadn't mentioned it at all so she could only assume he thought he'd lost it somewhere in the hire car or on the airplane when he was beating a hasty retreat from her on Boxing Day. Keeping the ring safe was all she could do, for now. The proposal was supposed to have been Jonathan's surprise. She wasn't supposed to know anything about it. Only he could bring up the topic, and so far, he'd not uttered a word. No doubt he'd changed his mind since she shook his trust in her and Kelsey was learning to accept the fact he may never fully recover it enough to think of asking her again.

Her thoughts were cut off by the realisation that: one, her glass was empty, and two, there was a tall, grinning American in baseball boots, black jeans and a big black coat running across the marina towards her and he was brandishing a bunch of Valentine's roses.

Jonathan had laid the flowers aside and scooped her up in his arms in a second, spinning her round and pressing a kiss to her lips that stole her breath away. All her nerves dissolved against the warmth of his solid body.

'Ahem! Hate to interrupt you two but there's the Mayor's car,' Mirren hissed, taking up her position by the bubbling glasses.

Jonathan lowered Kelsey to the ground and she was struck yet again by their height difference. He reached for the roses, long-stemmed and velvety red, pushing them into her hand.

'It's you, then?' Kelsey grinned daftly.

'I hope it's me,' he said, before screwing up his face. 'That didn't make any sense.'

They laughed and everything made sense in that moment. His eyes were wide, his cheeks glowing, and his grin just as appealing as she remembered. The reassuring press of his hand on hers felt like she'd been floating in space for months without him and now gravity was restored and her feet were back on solid ground again. She pressed her face into his chest and wrapped him in a hug.

'Kelsey?' She felt his deep voice rattle in his chest.

'Yes?' Her voice was small. Was this it? Was he going to ask her right here in front of Mirren and the Mayor – who was walking down the path in her glittering gold chains and an enormous feathered tricorn hat?

'I need to tell you something.' He cleared his throat as Kelsey gulped. 'My mom and Art are on their way here from Tulsa.

286

When I told them about your gallery launch they were adamant they'd come see it. I hope that's OK?'

Kelsey adjusted her line of thinking immediately. 'Oh! Yes, that's lovely! I can't wait to meet them.'

Jonathan turned, spotting the Mayor in her regalia. 'Woah, looks like the Queen's arrived. Go do your thing, we'll catch up later. Good luck.' He grabbed her hand again before she left and kissed it. 'I love you, Kelsey Anderson.'

The Mayor, her lord lieutenant by her side, was smiling and gracious, shaking her hand warmly and chatting about her new venture, and Kelsey had tried to concentrate in spite of her increasing awareness that there was a very loud rabble of Scots stepping off a minibus and tramping across the marina under a cloud of champagne bottle-shaped helium balloons and curled ribbons.

Jonathan was smiling proudly, watching the whole scene beside the red ribbon he'd just helped Mirren fix across the gangplank rails, before he walked out to greet Mari, Rory, Calum, Grandad, Ted, Alex, and even George and Mildred, who were turning in circles on their leads, yapping in excitement and getting hopelessly tangled.

'Hello, son,' Grandad said, over the noise of the Scots discussing the motorway and their long journey. He patted Jonathan's back. 'Guid to see you, again.'

Mr and Mrs Flowers from the next mooring came out with a chair for Grandad before joining the crowd themselves. Kelsey excused herself from her conversation with the Mayor and kissed her family. Rory handed over a big bunch of cornflowers, telling her he knew they were her favourite – Mari had told him so – and that he'd asked his local florist to get them in specially, and Kelsey hugged him again, realising in that moment that he was already a member of her family and that maybe she could come to think of him as a step-father as well as a friend. The reporters were arriving now too.

'Where's Blythe?' Kelsey said to herself, standing on tiptoe scanning the riverside.

'Are you going to make a speech, love?' Mari asked.

'Should I start? I hoped my neighbour was coming... maybe it's too cold for her. Maybe that grandson of hers never showed up with his car like she said he'd promised...'

'*Kelsey*!' Mirren called, pointing in the direction of the theatre and all the gathered crowd turned to look too.

Blythe, wrapped from neck to toe in a hot pink evening gown with a moulting feather boa, what looked like the entire contents of her jewellery box, and a smear of shocking pink lipstick, was sailing grandly across the gardens in her wheelchair, pushed from behind by Adrian Armadale.

'You're here!' Kelsey crossed the crowd to greet her with a kiss before straightening up in front of Adrian. 'And *you're* here?'

Mirren was by her side in an instant, followed by Jonathan who made sure to kiss Blythe's cheek before joining Mirren in staring blankly at Adrian.

'This is my grandson, Adrian. Do you know each other? You never said so, Adrian, dear.' Blythe rapped Adrian on the hand.

Adrian nodded but didn't speak.

'He's a good boy, bringing me to your launch, isn't he, Kelsey?'

'I'm so glad you're out and about,' Kelsey said, her astonishment at the sight of Blythe in daylight outweighing her shock at Adrian accompanying her.

'Tell me about it,' Adrian added, a little coyly. 'I've been trying to get her to come out with me for months, but there's always some excuse or other.'

'I'm sitting right here, you know, Adrian.'

'*You're* the grandson who brought her the flowers and the newspapers?' Kelsey said. 'But I've never seen you use the side door at St. Ninians? I live right upstairs.'

Adrian raised his shoulders. 'Really? I have a key for the front door. I let myself in. I know I could visit more often...'

'Not at all,' Blythe interrupted. 'You're there every week, and young people *must* live their lives.'

'You're Lorcan's son?' Kelsey said, still thinking hard.

'Uh-huh.' Adrian was looking at Mirren now. 'Sorry to surprise you. I didn't realise you knew gran until a few weeks ago when she showed me the invitation to the launch, and I figured if you won't speak to me and won't see me, I could… turn up as Gran's plus one and maybe you'd not hit me over the head with a champagne glass.'

'What's all this?' Blythe asked, growing impatient with her failure to understand, until Jonathan put a glass of cava in her hand.

'Do you remember I told you about Jonathan and Wagstaff?' Kelsey said to Blythe and the actress nodded. 'Well, we've been worried sick the *Examiner* was going to run a story on them… that *Adrian* was going to run the story.'

Blythe chuckled. 'Adrian? My boy wouldn't hurt a fly; he's no tattle-tale reporter.'

'Oh yeah?' Mirren was finding her voice and staring straight at Adrian. 'What about the piece you wrote about Jonathan and Peony back in the summer? The thing was full of lies!'

Just as he was about to respond Blythe chimed in and they both uttered the same word at once, 'Ferdinand!' Then Blythe said some other words that turned the cold air blue and Kelsey winced, hoping the Mayor wasn't listening.

'That man is a thief, you know!' Blythe was getting exercised now. 'My Adrian writes lovely articles like the one about me, the one that accompanied your photos, Kelsey dear, and then Ferdinand sticks his own blasted name on them…'

Adrian took over the story at that point. 'And he'll run his sloppy, ill-researched, gossip pieces under *my* name. He's been doing it a lot recently.'

'So Ferdinand wrote that awful rubbish about Jonathan and Peony?' Mirren was incensed. 'How can you let him get away with that?' She thought of her own misattributed article in the *Broadsheet*, all of her hard work and care signed off as Jamesey Wallace's. The injustice still rankled now.

'I don't know, I feel sorry for the old buzzard, I suppose.' Adrian shrugged. 'He gave me a job straight out of school and he's kept me on all these years.'

'That's no excuse for letting him spread lies about innocent people,' Jonathan waded in.

'You're right, I know. I thought if I kept my head down and tolerated him, he'd retire and I'd be left in peace. I mean, he must be in his sixties and he doesn't exactly love his job anymore. I thought if I stuck it out I might end up with the editorship. You know, in this industry it doesn't do to rock the boat, and jobs are hard to come by, especially when you don't have a degree from a journalism school.' His eyes fell back to Mirren's. 'I'm sorry, I should have stopped him running gossip pieces and claiming my work as his own, but...'

'I get it,' Mirren conceded, and all eyes turned on her. 'It's not an easy industry to work in.'

'I promise you all, I had no intention of running a story about Wagstaff. I'd never do that. Even if he *was* responsible for ending Gran's career.' His jaw flexed with anger.

'Dear boy, is that what you think?' Blythe turned to peer up at her grandson in amazement. '*I* brought my career to an end. *I* chose Laureano and my baby. *I* chose to go to Spain. *Me*.'

Adrian crouched by her side. 'But Wagstaff was blind drunk that night he fell from the stage. He spoiled the run. He ended your career.'

Blythe patted her grandson's hand. 'That season was ill-fated. The understudy did his best with me, but I was ill, darling. Very ill.' Blythe's eyes sparkled with welling tears she had no intention of letting fall. 'My hips... I couldn't go on any longer. Even if the managers hadn't pushed me out because of my stubbornness and my refusal to be ashamed, there was still no pain relief good enough to get me up on stage twice a day, not back then. The warm weather in Spain and Laureano, and seeing your dad growing up, playing in the olive garden... they all helped my recovery and it was a wonderful time in my life, truly, and that daft old bugger Wagstaff had nothing to do with my absence from the stage.'

Adrian stood again, facing Mirren, shaking his head as he tried to process all this.

'So that's why you hated Wagstaff?' said Mirren.

'Your name though?' Kelsey blurted, not letting Adrian reply. 'You're called Armadale, not Goode?'

'Stage name, darling,' Blythe chirruped. '"Goode" felt more… Elizabethan somehow, back in the day. Armadale's my given name, and I never married, so it's *still* my name. Daddy insisted Lorcan go by the family name when we came back to England and I had no objections; he was still Laureano's son. No name would change that.'

'We've all got in a bit of a mess,' Adrian said, patting Blythe's arm and keeping hopeful eyes fixed on Mirren.

'OK, this is all getting crazy,' Jonathan interrupted. 'We can talk about it back at the pub for the after-party. Kelsey, you've got a business to launch and a speech to make. Come on.'

Jonathan and Kelsey led the way back to the boat where the crowd were chatting and drinking happily. Half their glasses were empty already.

'Sorry about that,' Kelsey called out, her eyes a little dazed. 'Are we ready to cut the ribbon?'

Everyone cried out that they were and whooped and whistled. Just as Kelsey was inviting the Mayor to take the scissors, a voice behind the crowd rang out, drawing attention away from Kelsey again.

'Chop chop, Gianfranco, *dulzura de mi vida*, we're late, running at the cow's tail as my mother would say, God rest her soul.'

Advancing across the gardens in a purple jumpsuit, her severe red bob flapping, was Norma Arden, followed closely by her Italian beefcake husband carrying her coat. 'We're here Kelsey, we're here!' she announced pointlessly; half of Stratford knew she was here by now. She continued exclaiming in her familiar ten-to-the-dozen way, 'Did I miss anything? Oh look at the barge, isn't it wonderful, well done, darling!'

Kelsey quickly stepped through the crowd to hug her and, taking her hand, pulled her up front to stand beside the Mayor by the gangplank. 'Sorry about that. Everyone, this is Norma Arden... and this is her barge. Her business idea, actually.'

'No, no, no, the gallery concept was all your own. I only gave you a little nudge with the photography studio, and with your young man... where is he?' Norma scanned the crowd until she saw him. 'Yoo hoo! Hello Jonathan.'

The Mayor was beginning to look impatient with all the interruptions. She'd already told Kelsey there was a church meeting she had to get to.

Kelsey clapped her hands. 'Without further ado, I want to welcome you all here today to my gallery launch.' The words caught a little as she spoke. 'In some ways it's been a long, long road to get to this point.' She was looking at her mum and grandad now, both of whom were dabbing tissues at their eyes. 'I wasn't really going anywhere for a long time, then Norma picked me up and brought me here. She gave me a job. I found a place of my own for the first time, and I made so many friends.' Valeria and Myrtle waved from the back of the crowd where they'd been hugging Gianfranco. 'And I fell in love too. Now I've got a career ahead of me, and a happy life, I hope.'

'Hear hear,' Blythe called out.

'Thank you all for coming with me on this journey. I've loved *almost* every second of it, and if I haven't loved some bits, at least I learned from them.' Kelsey's voice was giving way to emotion and she stepped aside.

The Mayor smiled and the newspaper photographers raised their cameras to capture the moment. The Mayor pronounced: 'It gives me great pride and pleasure to be here at the beginning of another exciting new business in Stratford-upon-Avon. I declare the Kelsey Anderson Photography Gallery... open.' The scissors sliced the ribbon in two and the whole riverside resounded with the great cheer that went up.

Everyone processed through the exhibition, Blythe cut the cake, and Adrian passed out the slices wrapped in napkins. Calum fed his to the ducks who to this day still refused to leave their cosy home on top of the barge, and everyone talked and hugged and said how well Kelsey had done. Holiday-makers and locals alike joined the queues and sampled the last of the cava and squeezed themselves into the gallery space to look around. Just as the day was growing dark again, and Mirren was trying to tell Kelsey from over the crowd in a kind of made-up sign language that she'd sold twelve of the framed prints, Kelsey's mobile rang. Since everyone she knew in the entire world was here, she guessed it was a junk call.

'Whatever it is, I'm not interested,' she said into the phone, realising she might be a little tipsy.

'You haven't heard what it is yet,' whined an indignant, nasal voice.

'Mr Ferdinand? Is that you?'

'I've got a photography job for you…'

Kelsey laughed bitterly. 'You're joking? You realise you haven't paid me for the last one?'

'Haven't I? Well this one's cash in hand, I'll give it to you tonight, provided you can be discreet about it. I'll text you the time and place. Just be ready. This job's a little… sensitive…'

Kelsey interrupted him long before he'd finished speaking. 'No thank you, Mr Ferdinand, I'm not in the least bit interested.' She hung up and re-joined the party. The Mayor and the reporters had long since gone, leaving all of her friends and family, who were getting ready to head over to the Yorick for a hot meal round the inglenook. Kelsey, still in triumphant and celebratory mood, thought no more of the phone call.

Chapter Thirty-Nine

'I know thee not, old man'
(*Henry IV, Part 2*)

'May I join you?' Adrian asked, standing over her table where she nursed a glass of bubbly, and Mirren found she had no objection at all.

The Yorick bar room was packed. Kenneth had done the pub proud and set up a hot buffet of sausage casserole and a mountain of mash and everyone had tucked in greedily. Kenneth even brought out a little dish of sausages for Alex and Ted's dogs.

Kelsey and Jonathan were sitting thigh to thigh in the inglenook. Jonathan's parents had only just arrived and were smiling proudly at their son and snapping pictures of them together on Art's phone.

Jonathan's mum was as dainty and sweet-looking as Jonathan was tall and broad-shouldered, and Art – dressed in his best suit for the occasion – kept his arm slung lovingly around his wife's shoulders.

Gianfranco, Myrtle and Valeria were catching up about life after tour guiding and Blythe was sipping champagne next to Norma. The pair were absorbed in conversation. Seeing them across the room, Kelsey found herself wishing she'd brought her camera to capture them together, their outfits a kaleidoscope of pinks and purples all set off with Norma's shocking red hair, but this was her party and she was here to enjoy it, not to work, though she did snap a quick picture with her phone.

The Scottish contingent were scattered around the bar, all comfortable and relaxed, and Rory and Mari were inconspicuously clasping each other's hands behind their backs and looking even more besotted than they had at Christmas.

Mirren had felt strangely like an outsider when she sat down alone in the corner by the window, which was decked out in the strands of red loveheart lights she'd hung there herself the day before. She was thinking over the morning's revelations and reassessing her opinion of Adrian, and now here he was, with her permission, pulling up a chair beside her.

'So…' he said, running his hands nervously over his thighs. 'You look good.' His eyes swam over her face.

'Thank you.' Mirren's voice began to falter as she spoke. 'It seems I was wrong about… quite a few things.'

'You and me both. Will you hear me out if I explain my side of things?'

Mirren nodded, anxious to hear more.

'All these years I thought Wagstaff was to blame for hurting Gran's career. That old guy's dogged me for so long.' Adrian shook his head, wondering at himself. 'I think my anger made me curious about him, made me keep researching him when I should have listened to you and stopped. I was consumed with wanting to know who else he'd hurt and I spent Christmas obsessed with it, chasing him through the archives. I wanted to find out the truth for Jonathan and his mum, but a big part of me wanted to uncover all the other awful, selfish things he'd done. I think I wanted to confront him with all the evidence, but I didn't really find anything. Before I knew it, I'd been at it for hours, I don't know how long I spent scrolling through the microfilms. Eventually I realised you'd returned my phone and you'd been looking for me and left me all those messages. I was horrified to hear you say that Jonathan had run off, and that you suspected I was looking for a scoop. I abandoned the search and went home, trying to call you, but you wouldn't answer.'

'I remember. I was helping Kelsey hang her pictures,' said Mirren.

'After we spoke that night I knew I could only get you to trust me by giving you that memory stick, but the next morning I couldn't find it anywhere, and I searched for days, honestly I did, and by then I'd started to realise how much I'd hurt you when I promised you I wouldn't, and I knew you'd be beating yourself up all over again about what happened on Christmas Eve on your boat.'

'Only a little. I managed to make it up with Mum a bit, and I had some new perspective on what happened at work, thanks to you, and I managed to put my guilt about Preston to bed – well, a bit – but I wasn't eaten up with guilt like I was before. I was standing on my own two feet and taking better care of myself. I missed you, though, even when I was angry with you.'

'I missed you too.'

'Have you been overworking to compensate?'

'I've been trying not to. I've been going to the theatre a lot with Mum, spending time with my brothers. Missing you. Kicking myself for hurting you.'

Mirren smiled. 'Somebody very clever and kind – and handsome – told me that punishing yourself for making mistakes is kind of pointless.'

'He *does* sound smart.' Adrian tried to smile back.

'Well then, you need to take that handsome devil's advice, I think, and let go of all that.' She reached her fingertips to his wrist and the touch of her skin seemed to ignite a fire behind his dark eyes.

'But Mirren, that memory stick of pictures and stories that I was so obsessed with compiling? It never did turn up, and I swear I've no idea where it could be now.' He cast his eyes down guiltily.

Mirren nodded. 'Well, it would have turned up by now if someone had found it. I think we can forget about it.' Seeing the weight of the world still on his shoulders, Mirren shifted closer. 'Come here.' She reached her arms around him in a hug.

'I've missed you,' he breathed out, gently holding her, not wanting to assume too much. 'I wanted to call you every day, and every day I made myself *not* call. That was the hardest thing I've ever done, but you told me once before not to chase after you and I didn't listen then, so I was determined to respect your wishes and I just kept hoping you'd come back to me somehow.'

Mirren pulled away again, smiling. 'Do you remember that night when we were out walking and you said you'd wait for me?'

'I do.'

'I don't want you to wait for me.'

Adrian's eyes rounded with sadness but she kept talking.

'I'm done with waiting. What's the point in waiting when you've met someone you really, *really* like?' Mirren leaned in again, this time to kiss his cheek, and Adrian closed his eyes, sighing with relief.

Over in the inglenook Kelsey watched them and nudged Jonathan with a grin. 'Those two are sorting things out then.'

'Looks that way. I still owe them both an apology for getting mad. I'll head over there once Mirren puts Adrian down.' Jonathan laughed heartily, holding Kelsey's hand and rubbing his thumb over hers.

'Are we good?' he said quietly.

'Of course we are,' Kelsey replied and for a moment they were all alone in the bubble again.

'I'm so proud of you launching the gallery, and how you did it all on your own.'

'I had your encouragement, and Mirren's help, and my family were always there cheering me on, and of course, Norma started this whole thing.'

As though she knew she was being talked about, Norma caught Kelsey's eye across the room and sent her a smiling wink with the knowing air of a fairy godmother.

Kelsey was still smiling when the bar door swung open and someone stepped inside loudly proclaiming about the chilly weather.

'Who can that be? We're all here, aren't we?' she said. 'Did the "private party" sign fall off the door, or something?'

Kelsey quailed at the sight of Jonathan's smile fading.

'It's him,' he stammered weakly.

John Wagstaff had bumbled unaware into the party and was making his way towards Kenneth and his usual spot at the bar, taking off his feathered hat and clapping his gloved hands together for warmth.

'Sack and ale please, Kenneth,' he called over the noisy chatter.

Over in the corner, Mirren's head snapped up at this, and she and Adrian threw dazed glances between the old actor and Jonathan, whose only thought was for his mum.

Olivia Hathaway was tightly clasping Art's arm. She'd recognised her old lover too.

'Mom, are you OK?' Jonathan was saying, but she couldn't reply.

'Blythe Goode?' Wagstaff boomed in surprise when he noticed his old co-star. 'I count myself in nothing else so happy as in a soul remembering my good friends.' He was already quoting Shakespeare, as was his way, and towering over her.

Blythe was as smart and quick as she always was and hastened him down to her eye level.

Kelsey watched him bend to her and she already knew what Blythe was whispering in his ear.

'*Leave*?' he boomed with a jocular theatricality. 'I've only just arrived! And what a sight for sore eyes you are. Come now, let's sit, drink and be merry!'

If anything, Blythe's words had made him even louder and more exaggerated than usual. Everyone at Kelsey's party was looking at him now. Blythe was shaking her head and muttering about him being an old fool.

Suddenly Jonathan was on his feet, his face a picture of pain and regret. Olivia Hathaway was gripping his wrist and telling him to sit down.

'It's OK. I'll take him outside, talk to him there, tell him a few home truths while I'm at it,' he said to his mum.

Art, Olivia and Kelsey got to their feet too, just as Jonathan slipped out between the chairs and tapped Wagstaff on the back.

Kenneth, sensing trouble, narrowed his eyes at them from behind the bar, and George and Mildred started up their yapping at the sudden change of atmosphere.

'Yes, dear boy?' Wagstaff said, having turned to look at the tall stranger with ice-blue eyes just like his.

Kelsey watched the emotions in Jonathan's heart play out on his face, his jaw muscles tensing and his eyes pooling with tears even though he was fighting them away.

Mirren and Adrian were now on their feet too and making their way into the scene, casting wary glances at one another.

Jonathan opened his mouth and the old man looked on, his face a picture of innocence and incomprehension. Something moved Wagstaff to look past Jonathan and there he spotted Olivia Hathaway standing by the inglenook, her face frozen in alarm.

'*Good grief!*' he exclaimed. His eyes flicking back to Jonathan's, the slightest hint of realisation dawning.

That was the moment it happened. Just as Olivia burst into tears and Art shielded her from Wagstaff's gaze and Jonathan nodded gravely at the old man to confirm that what he was thinking was correct, a bright flash of light from the pub doorway lit up the bar room for a millisecond before the door swung closed again.

Everyone froze and shared looks that asked what the hell was going on. Only Mirren and Adrian moved.

'It's all right, we'll sort it out,' Mirren mouthed towards Kelsey. The two reporters dashed out the door in pursuit of the paparazzo who had caught the first meeting of the famous father and son actors on camera.

Chapter Forty

'Defer no time, delays have dangerous ends'
(*Henry VI, Part 1*)

Their boots beat down upon the wet pavements as they ran, leaping up the kerbs, dodging the couples out on Valentine's dates.

'There he is,' Mirren shouted at the sight of the figure all in black running towards the dark shadows of the churchyard.

Her heart pounded as she ran, gasping great gulps of air to power her along. Adrian kept up with her, never taking his eyes off the man. After only a few moment's pursuit they realised his pace was slowing and he was struggling to run, holding his side and staggering to a stop against the high theatre gardens wall where the trees blocked the light from the few streetlamps in this part of Stratford's old town.

Adrian grabbed his collar, forcing him flat against the bricks. 'Who are you?' he demanded.

'Nobody,' the man gasped, keeping his head down. Adrian knocked the black baseball cap from his head and squinted at the pale, wheezing man.

'Boz, it's you!' Adrian said, his tone disgusted. He looked to Mirren. 'He's the old photographer from the paper. I thought Ferdinand got rid of you?'

'He rang out of the blue, an hour or two ago. A "sensitive job", he called it. I didn't ask questions. I need the money, Adrian.'

'Do you know who you were photographing?'

'Old Wagstaff and his lad, Jonathan something,' Ferdinand said.'

'What did he want with the pictures?' Mirren asked, wrestling the camera from his hands.

'Careful with that; that's my livelihood there,' he said, a note of terror in his voice.

Adrian forced him harder against the wall, gritting his teeth as he spoke. 'What did he want with the pictures?'

'He's running a story on Friday about the pair of 'em.'

'I've got it. Look.' Mirren had the picture on the screen; Jonathan and Wagstaff face to face and Olivia weeping behind her son. 'I'm deleting it.'

'Please don't. I need that money. Ferdinand got rid of me in September without a penny of my wages from the summer months, saying he had cash flow problems. But he promised me he has a bundle of cash in an envelope ready for me to collect at the office. I'm to get it tomorrow. I need it or I'll be homeless by spring. Ferdinand's no friend of mine, but I need that money. I'm desperate.'

'Too late, it's deleted,' Mirren told him, and he winced.

'But he still knows about Jonathan and his mum,' Adrian said to her as though Boz was no longer there. 'We can stop Ferdinand running the story, but how do we stop Boz's mouth? He'll go to the tabloids and break it before Ferdinand can.'

Mirren huffed a deep breath and eyed the photographer. He certainly looked down on his luck. She peered into his face. 'He's not bad; just desperate,' she said. 'I know what to do. Come with me.'

It took five minutes to march him to the cash machine where Mirren withdrew all of her money in spite of Adrian's protesting.

'Three hundred and seventy quid?' Boz said, taking the bundle of notes, warm from the machine. 'That won't cover my mortgage for three weeks, let alone the three months I owe.'

Adrian rolled his eyes and punched his own card into the machine, clearing out his account. As he was about to hand Boz the money, he hesitated. 'Give us your mobile first.'

Mirren caught Adrian's drift and snatched the phone from Boz's hand. She scrolled for Mr Ferdinand's number and typed:

> **Job's done. You'll get your pictures first thing tomorrow.**

'That'll buy us some time to search the *Examiner* office,' said Mirren, before leaning close to Boz's face. 'Now, if you don't want us calling the police and telling them you robbed us both at knifepoint by the cash machine, you'd better disappear. You don't want to add a criminal record to your misfortunes.'

Adrian's eyes widened as Mirren spoke in the most threateningly Scottish accent she could muster.

'You won't hear any more from me, I promise,' Boz whimpered. Adrian loosened his grip and Boz scuttled off into the dark shouting his apologies over his shoulder as he went. 'I wouldn't hurt a fly, but when a man's desperate he takes what's offered.'

They watched him retreat.

'Do you think that's enough to keep him quiet?' Mirren asked.

'Should be, that was nearly four grand he got away with.'

'Four grand! *Jesus!*'

They started walking instinctively towards the *Examiner* offices.

'I was saving up to take Gran to Spain on holiday to see Dad. Might have been their last chance to spend a summer together,' he said, sadly.

Mirren circled a hand over his shoulders. 'Oh, Adrian...'

'Come on,' he said. 'Let's worry about that later. We've got a press to stop.'

The *Examiner* offices were locked up, dark and quiet. Adrian made sure to slide the bolt on the door once they were inside. 'That'll stop Ferdinand sneaking up on us this time,' he said.

They held hands climbing the stairs in the dark, Mirren lighting the way with her phone.

'Boz said there was an envelope of cash waiting for him at the office. Do you reckon that was true?' she asked.

'I wouldn't stake my life on it. Boz is a pretty simple guy. He fell for Ferdinand's lies time and again, always believing he'd get paid in the next quarter, no matter how many times I warned him to cut his losses and leave the old stick insect in the lurch. My guess is Ferdinand was desperate for the picture and cooked up a story about an envelope of cash for poor old Boz, knowing that he was skint.'

They reached Ferdinand's office door.

'It's kind of creepy in here in the dark,' Adrian said, but Mirren breezed in and flicked the light on.

'I'll search his computer, you look for that envelope. You never know, maybe there *was* cash for Boz. It might repay you some of the holiday money you lost. *Uh...* Adrian, look at this.' There on Mr Ferdinand's desk was his computer and in it's hard drive was a memory stick. 'Yours, by any chance?'

'That's the one!'

Mirren sat at the computer while Adrian began a search along Ferdinand's cluttered shelves and inside the cupboard, shoving aside empty crisp packets and piles of yellowing papers as he went. A few moths flitted up from the mess and circled the bare light bulb.

'*Bingo!*' Mirren called after only a moment's searching through Mr Ferdinand's computer files. 'That was easy. He's even called the file "The Wagstaff Exposé". What a plum.'

'He never was the sharpest tool in the box. Should we read it?'

'*Nope.*' Mirren clicked delete.

Adrian was smiling, still rummaging through the cupboard. 'Mirren, is there a key on that desk?'

She searched for a moment around the furry coffee mugs before bringing up a whole bundle of keys. 'I'd say every key Ferdinand ever owned was here.'

'Find the smallest one.'

Mirren rifled through them before singling out a squat silver key and handing it to Adrian who was crouching in front of a small safe.

'We make a good team,' he said, as he took it from her.

'Like Cagney and Lacey?'

'Or Mulder and Scully,' he corrected her with a smile.

'That works too, I guess,' she shrugged. Adrian worked the key in the safe but when the door sprang open it was empty.

'*Hmm*, that's weird,' said Mirren. 'It wasn't empty when I came for my interview. In fact, Ferdinand was stuffing that thing full of banknotes. He got quite a fright when I disturbed him with it, actually.'

'*Hmm.*' Adrian closed the safe and stood up. 'No cash for us then, never mind. Grab that memory stick and we'll go.'

'Hold on a second,' said Mirren. 'While we're here we should get Kelsey's money for her. I did promise her ages ago that I'd try.'

'Well, let's see. He transfers freelancer payments on that computer. I used to know the log-ins because it was me who paid out the staff expenses, taxis, working lunches, that sort of thing, back in the days when we actually *got* expenses. But that was ten years ago now.'

'Worth a shot? I've got Kelsey's bank details here on my phone. It's how I transfer the rent on my room at the barge to her, but do you think Ferdinand's changed the log-in details?'

Adrian gave a wry laugh and sat down at the computer, clicking the keys. 'Do you reckon an old relic like him would *still* use Ferdinand1 as his banking password after all these years? Oh... we're in!'

'You're kidding!' Mirren clapped her hands. 'It's like we're in a heist movie!'

They scrolled through the payments onscreen. 'Look, there's the last time he paid Boz, the poor bastard, back in March! He worked here for six months after that.' Adrian shook his head in disgust.

A car rolled by outside, its headlights making the blinds glow yellow. Mirren froze as it passed. 'OK, add Kelsey's payment and let's get out of here. I'm getting nervous now.'

'*Uh*...' Adrian gaped at the screen. 'Look at this... a series of payments made by Ferdinand to his own personal bank account. A hundred pounds... seven hundred. Christ, there's one for six grand! There's even more here, look!'

'That doesn't look like petty cash or expenses payments to me,' said Mirren.

'No. No it does not. Look, there's payments coming in from Eagle Media, our parent company. They're marked, "Staff bonuses".'

'And?'

'They go back seven, no eight, years. I haven't *once* had a bonus in all that time. Crafty sod's been keeping quiet and transferring them to himself.'

'He's stealing money from the paper?'

Adrian reached for the phone and dialled. 'And he's got away with it by cutting staff down to the bare minimum recently so no one would cotton on to him, by keeping the last of our freelancers hanging on and hungry, and by generally looking as incompetent and disorganised as possible. No wonder we're going under. And if that empty safe means what I think it means, Mr Ferdinand's already done a disappearing act with some other source of the paper's money.' He snapped his attention to the phone. 'Stratford police station? It's Adrian Armadale at the *Examiner*. I'm reporting the long-term embezzlement of funds by my editor, Clive Ferdinand.'

Epilogue

'The wheel is come full circle'
(*King Lear*)

'I'm not brilliant with heights.' Kelsey clambered slowly up the ladder, her cameras hanging on their straps around her neck.

'Get up there, the parade will be starting in a minute,' Mirren said, slapping her bottom.

Adrian joined Mirren on the street. 'Good view from up there, Kelse?'

'S'good thanks,' she shouted down nervously as she turned and sat on the little platform on top. 'Bit wobbly. I thought you were supposed to be holding the ladder steady, Mirr?'

'I can hardly take notes if I'm holding a ladder,' Mirren called back, but Adrian was already supporting the legs and making a thumbs-up at Kelsey and squinting against the April sunshine.

The day of the grand theatrical procession had arrived. The theatre companies had been preparing their costumes and floats for weeks. In less than twenty minutes every theatre company in town was going to set off from the station where a grand old steam train was busy whistling and puffing, recreating the old days between the wars when acting companies arrived by steam and the leading ladies and men in their furs and elegant outfits would be whisked through town in carriages, waving to the people who would make up their audiences that season.

This, however, was to be a walking parade through the centre of town, where the streets were criss-crossed with coloured bunting and theatre flags. The procession would stop when the players reached the theatres on riverside and the actors would walk in through their stage doors to await their last calls as the spectators poured into the auditoria to take their seats, ready for the very first performances of Stratford's high season.

The streets were already thronging with visitors and locals. Some of the smaller shops had closed so staff could watch the never-before-seen spectacle. Even the gallery barge was closed up so Miranda, Kelsey's smart and efficient new gallery assistant – and a budding young photographer herself – could join the crowds.

Kelsey had pitched her wooden scaffold at the corner of the High Street where the parade would turn down to the riverside and she had a two hundred yard view of the open street, long since cleared of parked cars and cordoned off to traffic by the police.

On their way here, Adrian and Mirren had recognised the two arresting officers who had come to meet them at the *Examiner* offices on Valentine's night before heading to Mr Ferdinand's house in the old town where they had found him frantically trying to hide the fifty-three thousand pounds in cash he'd embezzled over the years from the paper. It had been the talk of the town at the time, especially since Adrian and Mirren had thwarted Ferdinand's Wagstaff exposé, replacing his salacious front page story with the tale of Ferdinand's arrest for misappropriation of newspaper funds.

The court case found he'd been siphoning money away from the paper's parent company for years, paying himself an inflated salary and yearly bonus as well as stealing his staff's bonuses too, but things had settled down again now that the paper was under the careful steerage of its new editor.

'How are you pitching this story, Adrian?' Kelsey shouted down.

'You'll need to ask the *Examiner*'s new senior staff reporter that,' he called back.

Mirren delightedly tapped her pencil on the notepad. 'I'm thinking a simple who's who of the acting companies taking part, illustrated beautifully with your photographs, of course.'

'Don't forget all the special guests and acting alumni in the procession as well.' Adrian nudged her arm.

'I hadn't forgotten, boss.' She smiled at him before kissing him softly on the lips.

Kelsey grinned down at them from her perch. Her friend had grown in confidence and happiness these last few months, especially now she'd had her mum come to stay and Jeanie's first meeting with Adrian had gone well. They'd even gone to the theatre together. Things were far from perfect and Jeanie Imrie had a long road of her own to walk, living with her addiction and her new sobriety, but they spoke on the phone every few days and she was going to join Mirren, Adrian and Blythe on their Spanish holiday at Valladolid this August.

Mirren had blossomed under these new conditions, helped all the more by her new job writing features pages and special reports at the *Examiner* as well as freelancing too. Her last article had gone viral in a matter of hours: a scathing examination of institutional sexism and a culture of plagiarism in the newspaper industry in general and at the *Edinburgh Broadsheet* in particular.

Mr Angus and Jamesey Wallace were currently enjoying gardening leave while the independent investigators considered the plentiful and damning evidence supplied by a surprisingly large number of the paper's staff.

In the coming weeks, now that Jonathan had made his move to England, Mirren was engaged to help him edit his *Actors' Manual of Shakespearean Stagecraft* ready for its publication with Kelsey's beautiful headshot of Jonathan on its jacket. Yes, Mirren and Kelsey weren't the only ones using their talents to branch out.

'I heard from Jonathan this morning,' Kelsey called down to Mirren. 'He's nervous. Always is on opening night.'

'You haven't seen him in his costume yet?' Adrian asked.

'He flew in from LA late last night, went straight into a technical rehearsal and grabbed a couple of hours' sleep at the theatre. This will be the first I've seen of him since Valentine's weekend.'

Kelsey sighed at the memory of that day and that tense first meeting between Jonathan and Wagstaff. It hurt to think of it now.

After Adrian and Mirren had dashed out into the night in pursuit of Mr Ferdinand's sneak paparazzo, father and son had been left, astounded and wordless, looking at one another. When Wagstaff had tried to shake Jonathan's hand, he had shrugged him away. Matters only got worse when Wagstaff whispered the words, 'my son,' in a quiet voice so no one in the bar could hear but Jonathan.

Jonathan, close to tears, had turned his back on the old man, helped his mother to gather her belongings and they had walked out of the pub, rapidly followed by the rest of Kelsey's little party.

Kelsey had kissed her own family and friends goodbye, thanking them all for coming, and they'd made their way to their homes and hotels for the night. It had been quite a day, and Kelsey had pushed Blythe in her wheelchair all the way back to St. Ninian's Close, listening to Blythe's long testimony about what a lovely grandson Adrian was and how she hoped Mirren would give him another chance.

Jonathan had only stayed in town for two more nights after that and even though it was lovely to spend time with his parents and they'd managed to steal a few romantic moments alone together while Art and Olivia toured the sights, the events at the Yorick had put a dampener on their Valentine's reunion. Added to that, Jonathan hadn't mentioned the ring at all, not that weekend, and not any day since then, and Kelsey had made her peace with the fact he'd been spooked out of proposing.

As long as they were together, with no apprehensions and no secrets, that was all that mattered, she told herself, and most of the time she believed it, but she had often found herself snapping open the little ring box over the long weeks while Jonathan was teaching his drama students in LA, and dreaming about what it would be like if he'd held the ring out to her and said the words he'd so carefully planned to say.

She sighed again and scanned the crowds. Somewhere in town – Kelsey hadn't been able to locate them yet – Jonathan's parents and his four younger sisters were waiting to watch him go by in the parade.

Olivia had cried with gratitude and relief when she heard about Ferdinand's exposé being thwarted. Mirren had handed over the memory stick with the pictures and stories Adrian had gathered for her and Jonathan. Kelsey wondered if she'd looked through its contents yet. It hardly mattered though; the memories were there if they ever wanted them.

Kelsey knew that Jonathan had only taken a mild interest in Wagstaff after that day, but he had mentioned receiving a long letter from the old actor, sent via Jonathan's theatre company, and whatever the letter contained it had certainly lifted Jonathan's spirits after weeks in the doldrums. Perhaps there was hope for a better reunion yet.

In the distance, across town, Kelsey heard the sound of bugles and drums and the combined company musicians starting up with a jaunty Renaissance song. She stood up on the platform and lifted her camera to her eye, her heart pounding hard. The actors were on their way, with Jonathan among their number.

–

First, Kelsey's camera captured a celebrity actor dressed as William Shakespeare. Kelsey recognised him from *Casualty* as well as his lead roles at the Stratford theatres over the years. He was wielding a white quill pen like a baton and leading the whole parade.

Following behind him were the main company players dressed in their *Wars of the Roses* and *The Winter's Tale* costumes.

Their musicians marched alongside them and the medieval melodies and the cheers from the crowds filled the air.

At every leaded casement of every five-hundred-year-old building lining the route happy spectators threw handfuls of black and yellow confetti – the colours of the Shakespeare crest – into the air and they fluttered up in the spring breeze before floating down onto the people walking below.

Kelsey captured every actor as they passed, glancing quickly at Mirren who was furiously scribbling names, aided by Adrian who had his hands clasped around her waist and his head nestled softly over her shoulder.

'You getting all this?' Kelsey called, and Mirren shouted back that she thought she was.

The first of the floats went by and on its flatbed a pale Ophelia lay upon blue satin in place of the brook where in *Hamlet* she drowns offstage. The crowds cooed at the sight of her fantastic garlands of crow-flowers, nettles, daisies, and long purple dead man's fingers. The sight was eerie and beautiful.

The next floats passed by with scenes of King Lear raging against the storm, and *Othello*'s Desdemona sewing strawberries upon a linen handkerchief.

Kelsey captured them all on film and SD card, switching between her two cameras. The *Examiner* would run her digital shots and the gallery would sell her analogue ones, and she already knew which she'd prefer.

She wound her vintage camera on, pushing her thumb against the little lever, listening to the satisfying clunk of the film moving while the sun beamed down on the crowds at her feet. She spared the ghost of a thought for her dad as she always did when she worked his camera, and she smiled to herself.

Bringing the viewfinder to her eye once more, she scanned the street behind the floats. The next band of musicians passed, playing flutes and mandolins. *Click*, fired the shutter button. *Click, click, click.*

'Can you see who's next?' Mirren shouted up at her.

'Not yet, it's another float I think,' Kelsey called back.

This time the figure on the float was shrouded in a high black gauze that was suspended on posts like the curtains of a four-poster bed and sitting beneath it there was a great golden throne. Kelsey could see that the figure all in black on the throne was waving to the crowds and they were cheering back, throwing their confetti and waving their flags. It wasn't until the float was passing right in front of her that Kelsey made out the wording on the banner, painted in intricate red script against black board and suspended over the waving figure's head. It was a line from a play by John Webster. It read, '*I am Duchess of Malfi still,*' and beneath it sat Blythe Goode, reprising her greatest role just for today in an antique black lace headdress, smiling bold and bright with all eyes upon her.

She met Kelsey's astonished gaze and blew her a kiss as she passed and Kelsey documented the moment on film forever.

'Gran wanted to surprise you, made me promise not to say anything,' Adrian was shouting up at Kelsey who had by now dissolved into happy tears for her friend and her neighbour, the woman who had brought her so much happiness and given her so much good advice but who in the end had learned a lesson herself from her young photographer friend about seizing life in the here and now.

Kelsey barely had time to compose herself before she saw him at the back of the crowd, walking in costume with the rest of the cast of *Love's Labour's Lost* with his co-star Peony on his arm, and the devoted Will Greville close by Peony's side. The Oklahoma Renaissance Players were looking out at the crowds and smiling and waving but Jonathan had his eyes trained on Kelsey.

'Make sure you get some digital images of Jonathan and the cast, Kelse,' shouted Mirren, rousing Kelsey from what felt like a lovely waking dream. 'Knowing you, you'll want to snap nothing but dreamy shots on film for your gallery but we need digital images if he's going to make the front page.'

Kelsey set to work photographing his approach, her heart jumping in time with the drumbeat. The closer he got, the more handsome he appeared, dressed all in blue velvet, with a lace ruff in the Spanish Renaissance style and a pleated jerkin falling in tight lines down to his slim waist, accentuating his broad shoulders. Kelsey had never seen him in Elizabethan breeches before and she found they rather suited him – even the white hose looked good on his muscled calves which he was flashing cheekily at her with a broad grin on his face as he drew close.

She lowered the camera to laugh and to take him in. He was really here in the flesh once more, and this time there wasn't a flight waiting to take him away to America and there was a visa promising that he was staying for good.

She blew him a kiss as he passed her little platform and she watched his willpower give way. He jumped up to catch the kiss in his hand, making her laugh once more, before he broke free from the company and raced towards her, his blue cape flapping and his silver stage sword jutting out behind him. He had scaled her ladder and they were face to face and breathless in an instant. There was time for only one kiss – which made the assembled crowds '*aww*' in unison – before he lowered himself to the street again and walked out of her sight.

After that Kelsey wasn't sure what she was photographing but she kept clicking shot after shot of the passing blur until the crowds had dispersed, all following the actors down to the theatres. When they were gone, she bolted down the ladder.

'You going to be OK with this?' She pointed to the scaffold.

'No worries, I'll carry it back to the offices,' Adrian assured her. 'See you at the Willow Studio Theatre in five minutes.'

Mirren was watching Adrian collapsing the ladders with a look that told Kelsey she wouldn't be seeing either of them for quite a lot longer than that, and sure enough, Mirren followed Adrian, helping to hold one end of the ladder and saying something to him that Kelsey didn't catch but which made Adrian turn to his girlfriend and smile wolfishly.

Kelsey ran through the busy streets, searching in her camera bag for the ticket she'd stuffed in there; a front row seat for Jonathan's premiere performance of *Love's Labour's Lost*.

–

As she settled herself in the busy auditorium, now so familiar to her after her eleven months in town, she grinned to see Art and Olivia sitting a few rows behind her, ready to watch their son on stage, and there, beside Art, another face Kelsey recognised.

John Wagstaff was there, by Jonathan's invitation, to watch his boy tread the boards. The look on the old man's face told of his bewilderment and pride, and his sadness too. Kelsey watched as Olivia Hathaway leaned closer to him, offering him one of her tissues which he accepted with a modest laugh and nod of the head. Yes, he was going to weep too tonight. He would need it.

Kelsey found herself wishing her mum was there too, but Mari and Rory were somewhere in the middle of the Mediterranean on a romantic couples' cruise, leaving Grandad and Calum at home where, her little brother assured her, Grandad was really getting into mastering retro console games with his grandson.

A commotion at the back of the auditorium drew Kelsey's attention away from Jonathan's family towards a handsome, tanned man and his wife helping Blythe take her seat, still in her full Duchess of Malfi costume, headdress and all. Blythe spotted Kelsey turning round in the front row and called out across the stalls, 'It's my boy, my Lorcan, look!'

Kelsey stood up and waved to the handsome stranger who looked so like Adrian she couldn't quite stop herself from laughing while big, ridiculous, happy tears streamed down her face in full view of the swelling audience.

The house lights dimming told her it was time for the performance to begin and she took her seat again, sniffing and smiling.

The music filtered through the hushed crowd and everyone sat in rapt anticipation as the unique magic that only theatre holds spread over them.

The play was a triumph. Jonathan and Peony were wonderful in their roles, so witty and bright, their voices so clear as they spoke their lines as though they were coming to them naturally as the action unfolded, and not as though they'd spent weeks in intense rehearsals the previous autumn in Canada.

Kelsey laughed as the silly scholars made their vow of chastity and sighed as they each broke their word because love, when it came, was undeniable in its force.

Soon the audience were on their feet clapping heartily and the cast took their bows. Jonathan bit his wavering bottom lip at the sight of his two fathers standing before him weeping and clapping for him. He made a low bow just for them.

When the curtains swished closed and the house lights went up, Kelsey noticed Jonathan was still standing centre stage. For a moment she thought he'd made a blunder and somehow become trapped in front of the curtain, until she saw the faces of the rest of the cast peeking out at him, grinning and waiting for something to happen.

Jonathan wasted no time in walking to the front of the stage and kneeling before Kelsey. The spotlight followed him and the microphone in his hairline caught the sound of him nervously clearing his throat.

'Kelsey, I wanted to do this a long time ago but I blew it, I'm sorry. Would you believe I even lost the ring I had made for you? But I figured we don't need snow, or roses, or golden bands, or anything else. All I need is to ask the question.' His voice shook and Kelsey found she was on her feet and stepping towards him as everyone in the auditorium held their breath at once.

'Kelsey Anderson, will you marry me?' Jonathan's face was so sincere and his eyes so wet with tears Kelsey knew his whole heart was in his asking.

'Of course I will, yes.' She laughed and wept at the same time and Jonathan leapt from the stage to kiss her while the crowd applauded and whooped in standing ovation once more.

Mirren rushed through the auditorium doors with Adrian following behind her just in time to see their friends' lips meeting. 'Hold the front page, Adrian,' she said with a grin. 'We've got a new headline.'

Acknowledgements

It takes a lot of encouragement and understanding to get a book written; fortunately, I had my darling Nic, Iris, Robin, Mouse, Liz, the Dream Team, and Amos to will me on. Victoria and Lisa were a constant source of support and friendship too. Thank you all *so* much, I really needed it.

I take lots of inspiration and encouragement from you, my fabulous readers, and I'm so grateful to everyone who contacted me to say nice things about my writing, chatted with me on Twitter, entered my reader giveaways, subscribed to my author newsletter, and generally cheered me on. Thank you all so, so much!

If any of you would like to talk books, I'm (far too) often to be found @KileyDunbar on Twitter or at the 'Kiley Dunbar Author Book Page' on Facebook, so pop over and say hello. And don't forget to check out my lovely new website (www.kileydunbar.co.uk) where you can find all my latest offers and giveaways as well as news about forthcoming books.

Lots of wonderful book bloggers helped me spread the word about my writing this year too, and I'm hugely appreciative of all your efforts in spreading the book love. I'd be nowhere without you. Thank you especially to Rachel Gilbey (blog tour organiser extraordinaire) and everyone who took part in the *Summer at the Highland Coral Beach* blog tour in March 2020 or who signed up for the *One Winter's Night* tour this September. Thank you all times one million!

If you're holding this book in your hands, I'm thanking you too. Have a big hug from me! I'm thrilled you want to read my sequel to *One Summer's Night*. It's been wonderful revisiting Kelsey Anderson's Stratford and I am so sad to have to leave these characters who I've grown to know very well and love so much, but I'm glad they all found their Happy Ever Afters – or their just deserts – in the end.

I hope my book helps you escape the world for a wee while, and if you enjoy it, I'd be extremely grateful if you could take a moment to post a review about it on your favourite reviewing platform, or simply tell your pals you liked it! That would mean the world to me and will help other readers find their way to my books.

As always, I'm especially grateful to Keshini Naidoo, Lindsey Mooney, and all the Hera Books family who helped make this sequel happen. Thank you for giving me the chance to write it. Thank you, Keshini, for another lovely collaboration over the edits. It's always so much fun working with you and learning how to make my stories better and better. Thanks also to Jennie for your careful, thoughtful copy edits.

Thank you Diane Meacham for another stunning book cover. I was just thrilled when I first saw it and I still adore it now. I just know our readers will love it too! Thank you!

Thanks also to Mum and Dad, Mr and Mrs McGill, the Campbells, Donalds, and Buntings, Sara and Rhian, my friends and family who I've missed during lockdown, and my colleagues and students at the Writing School for your support.

2020 has been a real trial for everyone. Thank you for letting me weave my tale and escape into Kelsey's world again this year. I look forward to you joining me there. I hope your trip brings you a bit of happiness and comfort,

Happy reading,

Love, Kiley, x